THE NINJANS TRILOGY

Dave Kwan

THE NINJANS TRILOGY

Copyright © 2020 Dave Kwan

ISBN:
ISBN-13:9781777310899

KAISHI THE BEGINNING NINJANS 1

Copyright © 2020 Dave Kwan

ISBN:
ISBN-13:9781777310837

BLACK FEATHER NINJANS 2

Copyright © 2020 Dave Kwan

ISBN:
ISBN-13:9781777310851

THE GOLDEN SEAL NINJANS 3

Copyright © 2020 Dave Kwan

ISBN:
ISBN-13:9781777310875

Book Cover Credit: Artwork by Vit Kovalcik- Adobe Stock

File#: 336701841 JPEG 5634 x 3756px

DISCLAIMER

This book is a work of Fiction.
Names, characters, businesses, places,
events, locales, and incidents are either
the products of the author's imagination
or used in a fictitious manner.
Any resemblance to actual persons,
living or dead, or actual events
is purely coincidental.

This Trilogy
contains three novels.
Each book contains
a special Dedication.

KAISHI

THE BEGINNING

NINJANS 1

This book is dedicated
to my lovely wife, Merle,
who encouraged me to write.

CHAPTER ONE
The Ninja of Iga Mountain

The early mountain mist lifts as the sun rises on the horizon. The rays of light fall across the lone shadowy figure to reveal a seasoned Ninja Master, his long whispy white beard in contrast to his black outfit. The aged Ninja Master looks out over the line of young lads dressed in Ninja white, each with a bow and quiver of black arrows. The man raises his arm in the air. The young men quickly fix arrow to bow and pull back the bowstring - and hold. Most keep a steady hand, while only a few shake and wobble as they aim. One hundred feet in front of them are weathered chipped wooden posts. The old Ninja Master watches keenly how the lads stand and position their arrows — The old man drops his arm and all the young men shoot their arrows - WHOOSH! A stream of black arrows fly through the air to strike each post, each arrow tip sinks in, adding yet another hole in the perforated surface. Each and every lad hit their target. All the lads with smiles of accomplishment look over at their Teacher. The old man with twinkling eyes, nods his approval. Further away on an upper elevation, the Ninja Clan Leaders watch the training exercise with contented smiles.

The high elevation and rugged terrain of the Iga Mountains is where the Ninja Clans have built their villages. Each Clan has its own village of wooden houses, neatly and efficiently laid out to optimize any available land for their vegetables, chickens and goats. The family dwellings are constructed entirely of wood precisely cut, trimmed and fitted together like a giant jigsaw. The Japanese carpenters do not use metal nails like their counterparts in Europe and America, the Japanese carpenters cut, shape and join the wooden parts to fit and lock together. The construction of a traditional Japanese wood house is both ingenious and practical.

The Ninja Clan villagers are busy with daily life. The women prepare the food, cook meals and wash clothes; while the men care for livestock, mend fences, till the soil, and make wood items. Both young and old, both men and women, help plant and harvest rice from the water paddies. The older children tend the goats, feed the chickens, and do necessary errands. The younger children run, play and laugh, as children do everywhere. The mountain villagers are cheerful and cordial, and greet each other with traditional bows of respect.

Young lads, trainees all dressed in white, stand in the centre of a large semi-circle. Around them various Ninja Instructors display their weapon specialty. The young men are fascinated. At one end, an Instructor twirls a metal chain dart and flings it to impale a small target. Nearby, a Ninja Master deftly handles and spins two razor sharp Kusarigama - Sickles. To the left, another Instructor throws Shuriken with deadly accuracy - the pointed metal stars sink deep into targets. To the right at the opposite end, a Ninja Master swiftly runs, jumps and summersaults to land on top a large wooden post. The faces of the trainees are full of awe and wonder at seeing such skills.

A middle-aged man, Katsu, the Sword Master, approaches the group of young men. Katsu is lean and muscular and holds a Katana sword. All the trainees stand attentive and silent. Katsu looks intently at the young men to make eye contact and remarks, "Each of you will learn the Ninja weapons and fighting techniques. When you have mastered them and proved your skill - you will join our Ninja ranks." The Sword Master lifts his hand and points, "For now, you begin with the humble staff." The group of trainees walk over and stand before the Staff Master, an elderly man holding a long smooth staff. The old man gestures to a pile of poles on the ground. All the young trainees grab a pole and reassemble ready for instruction. The aged Staff Master strides over to three trainees at the front and gives each a knife. The man walks 20 yards away, then turns and motions, "You three - attack me with your knives." The three trainees look at each other, then quickly move out. One lad lunges with his blade, the other slashes wildly with his knife, and the third lad throws his weapon. The trainees watch as the old Instructor spins the staff to block the thrown knife, shoot out the pole to buckle the lunging attacker, and twirls the staff to knock the blade out of the slasher's hand. The trainees are in awe! One excited young recruit pipes up, "Master, when will you teach us to fight like this?" The Staff Master looks at the trainees, grips the staff with both hands and replies, "You must first learn how to hold the staff, then after much practice, when you are ready, I will teach you such techniques, (He pauses), for now, spread out and find a space to swing your staff without hitting others." The eager recruits find positions, and the Staff Master begins instruction on proper stance, balance, arm position and hand grip. The elderly Instructor leads the recruits through the basics - how to hold, raise, block, lower, extend and swing the staff. Each trainee is diligent and pays close attention.

Off to the side, high up in the thick brush, two Imperial Japanese soldiers hide as they spy out the Ninja villages. One soldier uses a charcoal pencil to sketch out the Ninja villages, the buildings and layout. When finished, the soldier rolls up the parchment and slides the drawing into a leather cylinder case. The two Imperial soldiers quietly sneak away undetected by the Ninja below.

Nestled among the neat rows of homes lays the Sword Master's family dwelling. Aiko is his kind and gentle wife, who kneels in the kitchen beside a low table and uses a ladle to scoop vegetable soup from a pot to pour into ceramic bowls on the table. Aiko's Japanese kimono is simple yet elegant. An intricate ivory comb decorates her pinned up hair. Her make up is modest since her features are refined and beautiful, her smile is pleasant and sweet. Katsu's two young children, his son Takeshi (10) and daughter Rei (8), sit still and respectful on cushions beside the table.

Footsteps sound on the lacquered wood floor announce the Sword Master has entered his home. Katsu stands in the home's open area, his bearing exudes noble character. Aiko, Takeshi and Rei turn and give the traditional bow of respect to their father, who is head of the household and also a Ninja Leader. Katsu nods to his wife and children, then enters a side room only to emerge moments later dressed in his comfortable home attire. He comes and sits cross-legged on a cushion beside the table. Katsu gives a warm smile to Aiko, Takeshi and Rei - then he reaches out to clasp and bring close the inviting bowl of soup. Now that the husband and father has begun to eat, Aiko and the children take their soup bowls to enjoy the savoury meal. The family members pick greens, bean sprouts and shredded cabbage from small bowls on the table to add to their soup. The family of four eat in quiet contentment.

It is late afternoon when young Takeshi makes his way to the Swordsmith Shed where his father, Katsu, is working on a new sword. As the young lad approaches and peers into the shadowy interior, he sees his dad illuminated in a golden light from the glowing coals of the forge. Takeshi enters the structure and comes beside his dad, who is intently focused on working the bellows which makes the liquid metal bubble in the cauldron. Satisfied, Katsu uses long metal tongs to grab the vessel of molten metal and carry it over to a mould nearby. Takeshi's young eyes watch as his dad tilts the tongs to pour the molten metal into the empty mould. The golden liquid metal cascades from the cauldron and runs throughout the mould to cover and slowly fill the cavity. Soon, the liquid metal rises and reaches the brim of the mould. Katsu stops pouring and sets the tongs and cauldron aside. Katsu notices Takeshi's fascination. The father looks at his son and remarks, "You are old enough now to learn the art of Japanese sword making. I will teach you the materials to use and the proper mixture, how to heat the metal and work the steel. You will learn to grind, hone and polish the blade to become a Ninja sword." Takeshi eyes light up and he smiles at his father and bows, "Father, I will study hard and be your best pupil!" Katsu grins at Takeshi's childlike enthusiasm and demeanour, "My son, knowing how to use a sword is good. But knowing how to make your own sword is even better!" The father reaches out to playfully mess Takeshi's hair, "From this day, you will be my assistant in making the swords!" Takeshi with excited eyes and fetching smile, bows low, "Thank you father! I am greatly honoured." Katsu turns his attention to the hardened newly-shaped form, and grabs the red hot steel with tongs and carries it over to the blacksmith anvil. There, Katsu repeatedly pounds the red hot steel with a metal hammer, and sparks fly at each strike of the mallet. The man hits the metal, then dunks it into a vat of water; this is repeated many times. Takeshi watches as his dad bends and shapes the metal into a thick curved flat bar - the noticeable rough outline of a curved Katana sword. Katsu lifts up the metal form to examine if it's straight, properly curved, and of the correct thickness. Next, he places the flat bar into the burning coals of the forge - the metal bar changes from black to red hot steel - then Katsu swiftly moves it to the anvil where he pounds and strikes the glowing hot metal to form the blade and point of the sword. Takeshi observes his father perspire greatly as he quickly works between the glowing coals of the forge and the hard labour of striking and shaping the blade. Finally, Katsu holds aloft the fashioned metal that now clearly represents a Katana blade. Takeshi has been quiet throughout his father's intense labour. The father glances at his boy and comments, "The blade has the proper shape, now I will grind and sharpen the steel into a proper sword." Takeshi nods his young head and smiles wide. The lad looks up at the ceiling at the far side of the Swordsmith Shed. Beautiful finished swords hang from the rafters, each sword depicts skilled craftsmanship and wonderful design in its handle and scabbard. As Katsu continues to grind and perfect the newly formed blade, Takeshi's face is full of awe and excitement.

CHAPTER TWO
The Warlord Attacks

The Warlord sits as a Monarch on his gold throne. Court Officials, Dignitaries, Military Commanders, Castle Guards, and household servants are before him. The Warlord's Concubines sit off to a distance at the side. The Castle interior is richly decorated with lavish tapestries, carved stone statues, exquisite jade art, guilded furniture, and large paintings depicting Japanese life. At the opposite end of the Throne Chamber are two massive iron doors embellished with motifs and engravings of the Warlord's symbol, a roaring tiger with claws extended. Four Guards stand sentry at the large metal doors.

Clang! Clang! The heads and eyes of everyone within the Castle Chamber turn toward the two doors. The Sentries look at the Warlord for his instruction. With a flick of his hand, the ruler motions the Guards to open the doors to grant admission. As the giant doors swing open, the two Imperial soldiers that spied on the Ninja villages stand alert and at attention - waiting to be be summoned forward. These two soldiers had learned that in the past, when someone entered the Warlord's Chamber without his approval - it cost them their lives. The duo look expectantly at the Warlord, who rises from his Throne Chair to stand and wave them forward. The assembled Courtiers, Commanders, Nobility and servants quickly part to make way. The two spies hasten to the steps of the Throne and swiftly bow - one soldier holds out his hand with the leather cylinder. A nearby Military Commander clasps the cylinder, ascends up the steps, bows and extends the cylinder to the Ruler. Upon the Warlord taking the object, the Commander backs down the steps with his eyes lowered. He immediately positions himself with the other Generals. The Warlord opens the cylinder and takes out the scroll which he unrolls to his delight: SKETCH OF THE NINJA VILLAGES. The Warlord's eyes run across the drawing showing the terrain, layout and buildings. The Warlord holds the scroll high in the air, and he looks at his Military Leaders, "Commanders, ready your troops! We march to the Iga Mountains to ATTACK!" The Commanders immediately acknowledge with a bow, abruptly pivot and quickly hasten away. The entire assembly becomes abuzz as people disperse. Officials, Regional Dignitaries and attendants scurry off in all directions. A squad of Castle Guards assemble at the base of the Throne. The Warlord stands tall and proud as he holds the scroll with a firm grip - he stares ahead with fiery eyes.

Thousands of Imperial soldiers dressed for battle, stand alert and ready with their shields, spears, bows and swords. The foot soldiers amassed in columns hold position. Battalion Banners fly in the wind. Military Commanders sit mounted on horses. The adrenaline flows through both man and animal. Suddenly, the big iron gates of the Castle creak open - and out rides the Warlord on his white stallion, dressed in his gold battle armour. Royal Guards ride behind and carry the Ruler's Ensign of a Gold Tiger against an indigo background. The Commanders and troops snap to attention. The Warlord rides up to his top Commander, who swiftly remarks, "Your troops are ready my Lord!" The Ruler looks into his eyes and orders, "March until we reach the mountains. Our surprise attack will wipe out the Ninja Clans. They have become too strong and must be destroyed!" The Commander assures his Monarch, "Your army will overpower them. Victory will be yours!" Immediately, the top Commander rides to the other Generals. He signals and the Commanders move out their troops. The long column of soldiers stretch from the Warlord's Castle far into the distance.

The Warlord on his white horse, rides with his Generals to lead the Army. The Ruler's Gold Tiger Ensign flaps majestic in the breeze. The long column of soldiers march their way past farms, fields, villages, and roadside Inns. The Japanese peasants and villagers bow low as the Warlord and his army pass by. A middle-aged farmer and his teenage son stop their labour as the Military mass approach their crop field. The father and son bow low, the son lifts his eyes ever-so-slightly to watch the soldiers and Banners go by. The farmer whispers a rebuke to his son, "Lower your gaze before they notice and gouge out your eyes!" The boy becomes alarmed and swiftly lowers his gaze to the ground. His father's face shows great relief. Time grows as the thousands of troops march past their field. The son whispers, "Father, my back hurts!" The farmer warns, "Stay bowed or we loose our lives! The soldiers will put us to their sword for dishonouring the Warlord and his Banner." The son gently nods his head, clenches his fists and holds steady. Soon, the soldiers of the Rearguard march by and move further down the road. The father and son raise themselves up. The farmer gives his son an intense look and remarks, "The army march in the direction of the Iga Mountains. We must secretly run ahead and warm the Ninja that live there!" The father puts his arm on the lad's shoulder. The son looks into his father's face and nods. The two quickly sprint across their crop field to the trees beyond.

Some time later…

The father and son run through the forest, across grassy meadows, over tilled fields, and along rural pathways used by peasants. The man and boy hasten with all their might, at one point, the lad grabs his stomach - cramps! The father looks back to see his son bent over with grimaced face, he runs to the lad's side. The boy looks up at his father, "I have to stop. My stomach hurts." The farmer coaxes the lad to lay flat on his back on the ground. With the son stretched out, the father kneads and massages the lad's stomach and lower sides. The lad's face shows relief, "The cramps are gone, I feel better." His father smiles, "Your stomach muscles are loosened up, we can move now." The man helps his son off the ground and turns to the tree grove, he puts his hand on the boy's shoulder, and speaks encouragement, "The mountains are not far. The Warlord's army is large and marches slow. We must hurry!" The son nods and both dash off to the grove of trees in the distance.

The Ninja Clan leaders are in the large wood building in the village centre. Katsu and the other Ninja Clan leaders are gathered around the farmer and his teenage son. Both stand sweaty and tired from the exhausting run, they breathe heavy to catch their breath. Hotaka, the top Ninja leader, a robust man with thick black hair and sideburns, offers them both a cup of water and points to a long wooden bench, "Sit, rest, drink some water." The farmer and lad take the wooden cups and gulp the water to quench their thirst. Hotaka looks at the farmer and enquires, "How many were they?" The farmer's eyes get wide and he waves his hand excitedly, "We saw thousands! A large army of Imperial soldiers marching toward the mountains." Kenta, a Ninja Clan leader with salt and pepper hair tied in a ponytail, positions beside Hotaka to advise, "We must prepare our people! Anyone that can fight." Hotaka looks at the farmer and son, then glances at the other Ninja Clan leaders. He directs his gaze to Masa, an older man with a face full of wisdom and understanding, "How many Ninja do we have?" Masa ponders a second then replies, "Four thousand strong!" The Ninja Clan leaders look at each other. Katsu breaks the silence, "So few against so many! We need to assemble our warriors - and send our women and children away." His words strike home in the hearts of the other leaders and they nod agreement. Hotaka paces a bit then turns toward his fellow Ninja and instructs, "The four thousand will defend our villages - our best scouts will lead the women and children to safety through the secret tunnel." All the Clan leaders nod with determined expressions. Hotaka walks over to a table and motions the other leaders to gather around. He opens a long leather cylinder case and pulls out a large rolled up parchment. Hotaka sets the case aside and unrolls the big map and lays it on the table. All the Ninja Clan leaders huddle and begin to plan their defence.

A day has passed…

Regiments of Imperial soldiers hide in strategic positions across the mountain terrain. The Warlord's troops surround the three Ninja villages. The settlements look sleepy and peaceful. A Commander waves his arm and an archer pulls back a large bow and shoots a Whistle Arrow high into the sky. A loud shrill fills the air - the signal to ATTACK! Thousands of soldiers pour down upon the Ninja villages, the Warlord's troops attack from the North, South, East and West. As the Imperial troops get near - suddenly, hundreds of black clad Ninja appear for battle. Volleys of black arrows and explosive projectiles strike and kill the Warlord's troops. The Ninja warriors with gleaming steel swords run directly at the advancing army. The small force and large army collide. Arrows fly, swords slice, axes chop, Shuriken stars strike deep - it's a brutal bloody battle! The Ninja fight off the first wave, but being vastly outnumbered, the battle cost the Ninja a great number of warriors. The Ninja look around to see thousands of Imperial soldiers still coming. Hotaka, Masa, Kenta and Katsu signal their warriors to fall back. The Ninja fight valiantly to defend their people and homes. As the fighting becomes more intense, Hotaka waves Katsu over, "Go with our Scouts and lead our women and children to safety!" Katsu lifts his sword, "I will fight beside you as the Ninja brothers we are." Hotaka smiles at his old friend, "No one knows our Ninja sword making like you. I want you to escape and keep our Ninja ways alive." Katsu looks about at the onslaught of soldiers racing toward them, he looks his dear friend in the eye.

Hotaka pushes Katsu in the direction of the mountainside behind them, "Go old friend! Lead our people to safety and take our Ninja secrets with you." Katsu watches as his friend Hotaka turns and runs toward the hordes of armed soldiers. Soon, Hotaka is in the thick of battle surrounded by Imperial troops. Katsu waves to a couple of Ninja close by, and together they race up the mountainside. A Commander and garrison of soldiers chase after Katsu and his Ninja companions. Fleeing up the winding pathway that rises higher and higher, Katsu and the Ninja see the women and children huddled in seclusion. A few Ninja have accompanied them for safety. The group get up from their concealment - relieved to see Katsu and his fellow Ninja. Katsu looks at the group, "We must quickly flee. The Warlord's soldiers are closing in." Just as he finishes his words, down the mountainside, the Commander and his troops climb toward them. The Ninja that followed Katsu look at him, then raise their Katana swords and race to intercept the attackers - sacrificing their lives to buy time for the others. Katsu and the few remaining Ninja quickly guide the women and children up the mountain path to the secret tunnel that's camouflaged by bushes. Katsu stands at the tunnel entrance and oversees as the people hasten into the dark. A couple Ninja light torches to illuminate the tunnel for the people to move forward. Soon, all the women and children are inside the tunnel moving deeper and deeper to safety. Katsu runs to the mouth of the tunnel and peers down. He watches in sadness as the last of his Ninja companions are killed by multiple blades. The Commander looks up the elevation and orders, "Forward. Catch them!" Katsu takes one of the lit torches planted in a nook in the tunnel wall. He goes to a cord that is suspended from the ceiling and puts the flame to it - it sparks and becomes a burning fuse. Katsu with torch in hand turns and runs full speed into the depths of the tunnel, the glow of his torch disappears into the darkness. As the Commander and his troops reach the mouth of the tunnel - EXPLOSIONS! The Commander and soldiers watch as the tunnel becomes filled with massive boulders, stones and debris. The large rocks too heavy and too numerous to remove. The Imperial Commander and troops cannot pursue. The Commander yells and throws his helmet on the ground in a rage!

CHAPTER THREE
Capture and Destroy

The Imperial soldiers comb the villages and scour the mountain terrain looking for Ninja survivors. The soldiers find wounded Ninja and immediately kill them. With all Ninja survivors put to death, the villages are now under control of the Warlord's army. The Warlord and Castle Guards ride into the middle of the central village. The Ruler scans the ground littered with the dead bodies of soldiers and Ninja. A Commander runs over to the Warlord and presents him with a captured Ninja Banner. The Warlord grabs the pole and lifts the SHINOBI STANDARD high in the air for all his troops to see. His army repeatedly cheer! The Ruler beckons, and a nearby Commander rides to his side. The Warlord extends his arm in a sweeping motion, "Send troops to hunt down any Ninja survivors. Put posters across the land to say the Ninja are Outlaws. A reward for anyone that helps to capture them." The seasoned Commander nods and rides away. The Warlord and his Castle Guards ride off toward a large tent that's been erected on level ground. The Ruler stops at the tent entrance and attendants scurry out to assist the Ruler to dismount and tend to his horse. The Monarch enters the shaded confines of the ornate tent. Personal servants remove his gold armour and battle gear. A servant brings a gold silk robe and the warlord puts it on. Inside the tent, servants have laid out drinks, fruits, meats and pastries on a table. A servant pours a cup of refreshment and extends the goblet to the Warlord. He takes the cup and drinks back the liquid, wipes his lips with his sleeve - then flings the goblet away.

Across the land, Imperial soldiers put up posters in villages, markets, towns and fishing ports. The Japanese gather to read the Warlord's Edict. Many are shocked at the news while others relish the reward being offered. The soldiers search the towns and countryside.

Troops stop carts and wagons to examine contents and passengers. Armed Officials enter homes and farms looking for any Ninja. In one town, the soldiers stop a group of travellers and discover they are Ninja. A fight breaks out as the Ninja defend themselves against the Imperial soldiers. The small band are fierce and deadly with their Ninja skills. An alarm is sounded and scores of troops rally to overpower and kill the Ninja men, women and children.

Twenty years pass.

Deep in the woods, the Sword Master now an old man, watches the grown man Takeshi at a homemade forge with glowing coals. Takeshi hammers the red hot metal into the shape of a curved Katana blade. The man grinds the metal blade and hones the edge to create a Ninja sword. The Sword Master inspects the blade's straightness, balance and sharp edge. The old man smiles and gives the sword back to his son. Takeshi is proud of his accomplishment and basks in the glow of his father's expert approval.

A modest thatch hut sits secluded in the forest. The peasant family go about their chores. This is the Sword Master's family living in disguise. Katsu is a fit wiry old man who chops wood logs into kindling to sell in town. Aiko, is no longer the young mother of yesteryear; now, she is a serene old lady content to weave baskets for market. She finishes a basket and hands it to Takeshi. He slips it onto the long pole from which other baskets hang. Takeshi lifts the pole to balance on his shoulder - baskets are in the front, baskets hang in the back. He looks at his mother, "I'll take the baskets to market now. Hopefully, we can sell them all." Aiko brushes straw debris from her skirt, stands up and looks at Takeshi, "Be careful in town! Remember - we are just simple peasants. No one must know who we are. Especially, watch out for robbers!" Takeshi adjusts the pole to a better position on his shoulder, "Don't worry mother. I know how to act (smiles) I will be back soon. If I meet robbers, my Ninja skills will destroy them - Father taught me well." Aiko manages a faint smile. She watches her son leave and walk the dirt path. Takeshi waves to his father who waves in return. Rei walks in from their large garden carrying eggplants, cucumbers, and green beans, and sets them into baskets for cleaning. She looks at her mom and remarks with a slight pout, "I want to go to market too. Why can't I go?" Aiko moves to stand beside her and lovingly strokes the daughter's long hair and pretty face, "Some soldier or Official may decide you should be his bride and take you away. - You don't want that do you?" Rei replies,

"No mother. Never! Someday, I will marry a Ninja warrior and have my own family." Aiko's eyes linger on her daughter, "I wish that for you with all my heart, my daughter. (Pause) The Ninja are so few and so scattered, we are still hunted as Outlaws and must hide." The mother and daughter sit down to clean the vegetables. Katsu stops chopping wood, sets the axe aside and walks in to join them. He's hot and sweaty and dips a ladle into a barrel of water and brings it to his mouth and drinks slow and deliberate to quench his parched throat. The old man glances at Rei and Aiko to comment, "The wood kindling will sell well in market. Wood for fires and fires to cook food (he smiles) everyone needs to eat!" Katsu walks back to the wood pile and begins to sort and tie the kindling into bundles.

Takeshi walks along the countryside road to market. The long pole fitted with woven baskets bounces with his every step. Far up the road Takeshi spots a large mounted unit of Imperial soldiers riding toward him. Takeshi stops and moves off the road to the side and bows respect. The long column of soldiers get close, the hooves of the galloping steads dig into the dirt roadway. The soldiers glance at Takeshi as they ride past him. When the armed force have gone by, Takeshi stands upright. Others are also on their way to market - an ox cart filled with crates of chickens, some men lead a herd of sheep, women carry bolts of fabric, and teenagers walk with baskets of fruit.

Later on that day…

Imperial soldiers hide in foliage and observe the thatched hut with bundles of kindling stacked at the dwelling's side. Puffs of smoke drift from the roof's centre opening. No one is visible, there's no activity. Suddenly, Katsu, Aiko and Rei emerge from the hut. The Imperial Captain turns to a nervous fidgety man in tattered clothes and hands him a bag of coins. The man snatches the pouch of money - bows low - and quickly runs off into the woods. The Officer raises his arm and the soldiers attack! Aiko and Rei are alarmed and afraid. The Sword Master runs to a wooden trough and pulls out two Katana swords. He runs directly at the soldiers. The aged Ninja warrior swiftly cuts down the attackers - Katsu powerfully swings his Ninja swords and delivers deep cuts, and terrible slashes that sever limbs and leave mortal wounds. The blood flies! Soldiers topple like dominoes - dead or gravely injured. The old Ninja stands battle weary, dead bodies and bloody soldiers lay around him. The Captain barks an order and soldiers with bows form a line. The archers pull back their bows and shoot a barrage of arrows at the old man — six arrows strike him in the chest and torso. With gasping breath, Katsu looks over at Aiko and Rei. Mother and daughter freeze in horror as they watch the old Ninja Master drop dead to the ground. They scream! The soldiers swiftly seize and tie them up. The Imperial Captain strides over and stands next to Rei who looks to the ground, her hair covers her face. The Officer lifts his hand to part Rei's hair and behold her beauty. He pivots about and motions the soldiers to take away the female prisoners.

Takeshi walks the well trod earthen path through the forest towards home. He notices many broken branches and large patches of trampled grass. Takeshi gets alarmed and races toward the thatched hut. As he breaks through the woods, the bodies of dead soldiers litter the homestead clearing. He quickly looks around, and to his horror, he sees his dead father in the middle of a pile of slain soldiers. Takeshi runs and kneels over his father's body and stares at the six arrows sunk deep into the chest and torso. Tears run down his cheek and drop onto the Ninja Master's face. Takeshi gently lifts and carries his dead father into the thatched hut. Moments later, Takeshi emerges with a flaming torch in hand. He turns to look at their homestead and lifts his arm to throw the firebrand, and memories of happier days with father, mother and sister cross his mind - he hesitates; then he throws the flaming torch high onto the dry grass roof. Within seconds, flames swiftly spread across the roof to engulf the entire wood and hay structure. The flames shoot high in the air and smoke rises in the sky. Takeshi stands stoic and silent as he watches their family home burn. He turns and walks to the area of trampled grass and broken branches. Takeshi spots fresh tracks of flatten grass that lead away from the clearing. He sets out in that direction.

Aiko and Rei sit bound together in the back of an Imperial Prisoner Wagon. A squad of soldiers guard them. The town's market is full of people buying goods from merchants and suppliers. Drivers steer animals pulling laden carts, venders hawk their wares to those walking by, street artists perform for the crowd, and beautiful maidens stroll together. Takeshi moves in and out amid the crowd until he's next to the Prisoner Wagon. The soldiers guarding the wagon become distracted by some passing maidens. He sees Aiko and Rei leaning against the metal bars - their eyes meet. Takeshi opens his tunic to reveal a knife handle - he nods. His mother's face shows worry and she shakes her head - No! One of the soldiers pushes Takeshi to move along and Takeshi's tunic opens and the knife handle is exposed. ALARM! The soldiers try to stop him and he uses the blade with Ninja skill - and kills them all. Takeshi quickly uses the big knife to snap off the back lock. He enters and cuts the ropes off his mother and sister. Takeshi and Rei jump out and turn to help their weaken mother get down. - Suddenly, two garrisons of soldiers race toward them. Armed reinforcements. The townsfolk scatter. Aiko is exhausted and looks into Takeshi's eyes, "I have no energy to run!" Takeshi pleads, "Mother, we must quickly flee! If they catch us - we die!" The mother reaches her hand to touch her son's cheek, "You are the last of our Clan. Go! Find someone to teach our Ninja ways.(Aiko cries) Hurry! Before it is too late - and our Ninja ways perish with us. Go!" The troops are close now. A group of soldiers stop and raise their bows to shoot arrows. Takeshi, Aiko and Rei, are crouched together beside the wagon. WHOOSH! Arrows fly around them, some strike the wagon. Aiko clasps Rei's hand and looks into her daughter's eyes - Suddenly, Aiko and Rei stand up to block and protect Takeshi. Arrows hit Aiko and Rei and kill them. Takeshi is SHOCKED! He looks at his dead mother and sister, then he sees the soldiers racing forward, he quickly runs to escape over a wall. The soldiers reach the Prisoner Wagon where Aiko and Rei lay dead, and keep running to go over the wall in hot pursuit. On the other side of the brick wall, the Garrison Captain and his men face a number of narrow streets and laneways. A soldier asks the Captain, "Which way did he escape?" The Captain scans the numerous passageways and orders, "Search them all - we must capture him!" The soldiers disperse in various groups and scour the buildings, streets and laneways.

CHAPTER FOUR

Ship to America

The wharf is packed with cranes and crews as cargo is loaded and unloaded onto ocean going ships. The big boats are berthed alongside the wide wharf, sailors scamper up and down rigging, some ships have sails unfurled while others have their vast canvass sheets lashed secure. Sailors and passengers walk up and down gangways. Piles of stacked crates cover the long dock. In this busy crowd, Takeshi stands opposite a Japanese Sea Captain. Takeshi glances over his shoulder to see if things are still safe, "I need a ship that will leave Japan." The Sea Captain, a portly man in his 50's looks at Takeshi and draws a puff of tobacco from his long narrow pipe, "Where do you want to go? Hong Kong? England? - Australia?" Takeshi glances around the crowd and replies, "I want to go far from Japan. Somewhere different!" Takeshi reaches into his tunic and brings out an exquisite piece of jade and hands it to the man, "I will trade this jade heirloom for passage." The Sea Captain's eyebrows raise, his eyes light up. He examines the fine quality of the jade, then he smiles at Takeshi and points, "That boat sails for America - a new country very different from Japan. The Captain is my friend, I will tell him you'll be a passenger. The Sea Captain takes Takeshi through the people and over to an old veteran Sea Captain. The man whispers into the old sailor's ear and shows him the jade. The old man looks at the jade and his friend, then he looks at Takeshi, smiles and nods - Yes! The old Sea Captain takes a few steps forward, turns to Takeshi and beckons to follow. Takeshi walks with the Captain along the wharf until they reach a large ship moored by the dock. The old sailor ascends the planks of the gangway and motions for Takeshi to join him. Takeshi grabs the safety ropes and walks up the gangway onto the ships's deck. The old man smiles and points to a set of stairs that lead below. Takeshi stands at the top of the stairs to survey what's beneath, he glances around and descends below deck.

Days and nights pass. The ocean changes from high winds and crashing waves, to calm waters and gentle breeze. Takeshi stands at the ship's bow as it cuts through the water, it's large sails catch the wind propelling the vessel at a good clip. Takeshi smiles as he sees dolphins racing alongside, leaping in and out of the ocean keeping pace with the ship's speed. He looks ahead at the far horizon and squints his eyes - the line between the ocean and the blue sky almost become unrecognizable, as if merging into one. He turns to observe the seamen busy at their post - swabbing the deck, rigging the jib and manning the lines. Takeshi looks at the ship's helm where the old Sea Captain stands next to a sailer steering the ship. He turns toward the distant horizon and closes his eyes and feels the warm ocean breeze on his face - and smiles.

It is morning and Takeshi ascends above deck just as the ship enters San Francisco harbour. Vessels from different countries flying their nation's flag line the long wharf. Excited immigrants disembark with suitcases, sacks, and possessions in hand. Takeshi's ship comes into position alongside the large wharf, and the sailors throw thick ropes to dock workers who tie and moor the ship in place. As people disembark the boat, Takeshi looks at the old Sea Captain, who gestures his arm toward the wharf, nods his head and smiles. Takeshi bows to the Sea Captain, then turns and walks down the gangway onto the wharf teeming with workers, sailors, passengers and immigrants. Takeshi moves with the crowd as people mill and jostle about, each making their way to destinations known and unknown. As Takeshi walks the wooden planks of the wharf, a mother carrying her baby suddenly drops a package on the boards, and she bends down to pick up her goods. To avoid stepping on the lady, Takeshi quickly sidesteps - and accidentally bumps into Cutter, a tall grizzled man in cowboy hat that holds a saddle in one hand and a Winchester rifle in the other. Cutter scowls with a mean stare, pushes the saddle hard to shove Takeshi aside, then continues his stride through the crowd. Takeshi regains his composure and makes his way off the wharf onto a busy city street. San Francisco is a bustling port city. Ships load and unload cargo, vendors hawk their wares, streets are clogged with horses, buggies and wagons, people mill about buildings, shops and saloons. Takeshi walks the city streets observing the sights and sounds. It's early evening and dusk has arrived, Takeshi walks down a street lined with saloons on both sides of the road. He happens to stop at the entrance of an alley between two buildings and hears a commotion down the pathway. Takeshi turns to see a middle-aged man on his knees begging for his life as Cutter holds a pistol against the man's forehead. The desperate man pleads, "Mister, I'm sorry! Powerful sorry for anything that offended you. Please don't shoot me!" The man on his knees turns his eyes toward Takeshi standing at the edge of the alley. Cutter notices the man's diverted gaze and turns to see Takeshi, then refocuses his anger at the man kneeling, "It's not what you did that offends me, it's what you are - a nobody! A pitiful excuse for a man." Cutter cocks back the gun's hammer. The man pleads with all his might, "Mister, please don't kill me - I have a wife and children. We're just homesteaders looking for land." Cutter grins, eases back the revolver's hammer and takes the gun barrel off the man's forehead, "Don't worry partner. You're not going to die on your knees today." Cutter steps back and holsters his gun and the man gets up and stands to his feet. Cutter turns and gives Takeshi a cold stare - then Cutter draws his pistol and shoots the man dead, his body falls to the ground with a thud. Cutter pivots and stares at Takeshi - Takeshi turns away and walks on down the street disappearing from the alley entrance. Cutter smirks and holsters his pistol, steps up to the dead man's corpse and kicks it, "Said you wouldn't die on your knees!" Cutter walks out of the alley and enters a nearby noisy crowded Saloon. The Saloon is a wild and boisterous place full of drunken patrons - rowdy sailors, dapper gamblers, ragtag miners, wild cowboys and flirtatious dance girls. Cutter pushes his way up to the bar and stands beside a rough gruff hombre. Cutter slaps the countertop to get the barkeep's attention, "Give me a Whiskey!" The barkeep brings over a short stout glass and pours a shot. Cutter grabs the barkeep's arm, "Leave the bottle." The barkeep sets the bottle down and goes to serve others at the bar. Cutter grabs the shot glass and belts back the amber liquid and slams the empty glass on the counter. The man next to him extends his glass and Cutter fills both glasses. Cutter holds up his shot of Whiskey and looks at the man beside him, "I'm heading inland - gonna start me a gang! Gonna rob, pillage and get rich." He belts back the liquor. His companion pipes up, "Easterners. Settlers. Farmers. All easy targets." Cutter reaches down and pulls out his pistol and spins the chamber, "This is the only Law out West! I aim to do as I please - Plenty of shootin' and killin' - and no one's gonna stop me!" The man beside him nods and grins. Cutter pours them both another shot and they belt back their drinks. Cutter slams the empty glass on the countertop. The barkeep comes over and remarks, "That'll be two bits for the bottle." The Cutter pulls out his pistol and lays it on the counter with the barrel pointed at the barkeep's belly. Cutter gives a mean look and sneers, "What did you say?" The barkeep stares at the gun barrel and replies timidly, "The Whiskey's free - on the house." Cutter nods and smiles. The barkeep quickly leaves for the far end of the long bar. Cutter looks at his tough friend and lifts his gun off the counter, and boasts, "This is what people understand - what people fear!" Cutter slaps the man's back and motions to leave. The two ruffians shove and jostle their way through the drunken crowd and out the Saloon's swinging front doors.

CHAPTER FIVE
San Francisco Chinatown

Takeshi works his way through the backstreets until he comes across wooden signs with Chinese Characters - He has discovered San Francisco's Chinatown. Asian immigrants have journeyed to America in search of a new life. Takeshi sees Chinese men and women, but most are transient men from China, South East Asia, Indonesia, Thailand and Singapore; husbands, fathers, brothers, sons - they have left their country with dreams of finding gold, work, or a piece of land to call their own. The Orientals mingle together in the fledgling shanty town at the outskirts of San Francisco proper. The Chinese immigrants have created their own community complete with stores, restaurants, laundry, hostels; and a gold exchange for the scores of Chinese miners that return from the mines with gold nuggets in their possession. Takeshi slowly meanders along the wooden boardwalk and peers in the open doorways that reveal Asian life that he's seen before - families at tables with bowls of rice, vegetables and soup, mothers with babies bundled to their back, groups of young men talking and drinking, young women washing clothes and folding laundry, and old men read newspapers and smoke tobacco from bamboo water pipes. Takeshi stops an approaching man, "Room? Rent?" The middle-aged man shakes his head, No, and keeps on walking. Further up the street, Takeshi stops beside three young men who are standing there smoking and talking, "Pay room?" The young men look at him, shake their heads and point down the street. Takeshi nods, and goes in that direction. As he moves a distance down the road, he nears a wooden two storey building and makes eye contact with an old man sitting quietly on the porch bench. He approaches the old timer, "Room. Pay!" The old man points to the building's wall behind him, "This is a Boarding House. Rooms to rent." Takeshi comes up onto the porch and sits beside the elderly man, "How?" The old man's face gets a wide grin and he chuckles, "My sister owns this building - I'll take you inside and you can ask yourself?" Takeshi nods and points to his chest, "Takeshi. Takeshi Shinobi." The aged fellow stops for a second, "Takeshi is a Japanese name." The old man pauses then smiles, "My name is Chow Zu Fu. I come from Guangdong, China." Takeshi replies, "Iga, Japan." Chow Zu Fu eyes Takeshi, "Everyone in America has left their homeland. Everyone is the same." The old man and Takeshi get to their feet and the man shuffles to the building entrance, stops and gives Takeshi a glance, "I moved quick like a fox when I was young, but now I move like a turtle." Takeshi replies, "You wise!" The old man's eye's brighten, "You're pretty wise yourself for a young man." Takeshi smiles, "Father. Mother." The old man taps his finger on Takeshi's heart, "You carry a treasure that's better than gold." The old man opens the door handle and they both step inside the building and walk to the side where an elderly lady sits behind a modest counter. The lady is wearing a ruby red silk dress and her silver hair is pinned up with a lacquered comb that features painted song birds. She looks up at Takeshi, while her brother leans in over the counter, "This man wants a room." The lady peers at Takeshi, "The rooms are five bits a week - if you like - two bits a night." Takeshi nods and holds up one finger. The old lady remarks, "One night?" Takeshi shakes his head. She utters, "One week?" Takeshi nods his head and smiles. The old lady nods agreement and extends her hand with open palm, "Pay before getting the room." Takeshi smiles and slips his hand into his trousers and brings out five coins in his hand. Old lady Lee takes the money, opens a carved ivory box and puts in the coins and closes the lid. She reaches her arm under the backside of the counter and produces a key on a leather cord, "Room 15. Upstairs in the back hallway." Takeshi takes the key, turns to the old man and smiles, "Talk. Good." Takeshi climbs the stairs to the second floor landing. He looks down at the old man and his aged sister at the counter, then he turns and walks the hallway to the back corridor and looks at the room numbers. His room is located on the right and he goes down the back hallway and stands before his new temporary home - Room 15. Takeshi inserts and turns the key - Click! He opens the door and gazes about the dark quarters lit only by shafts of moonlight coming through the window. Takeshi sees a kerosene lamp on a small nearby table, and picks up the matches and lights the lamp's wick - immediately light floods the room. Takeshi replaces the glass cover and sets the lamp on the table. He looks about the modest room - it has a single bed with a simple cabinet with washbasin on top and a little table with a kerosene lamp. The accommodation is small, simple, and spartan.

Early next morning, Takeshi is at the docks watching gangs of men load and unload cargo. He approaches a rotund man in his 60's sitting on a crate puffing a big cigar. He ambles over and stands close by. The portly boss barks to his crew, "Be careful with those crates! That's glass!" The workers handle the cases with more care after receiving his rebuff. The man glances over at Takeshi, "What do you want?" Takeshi looks into the man's eyes and points to the workers. The man gives a quick look, then turns back, "You want work?" Takeshi smiles and nods firmly. The stout man gets off the empty crate and comes up to Takeshi to grab and squeeze his forearms and biceps, "You're strong enough - you'll do." He looks into Takeshi's eyes, then points to the closest crew that's busy carrying cases up the gangway to the ship, "You can work with them." The man waves to a large black man walking down the gangway and he comes over. The black man asks, "What do you want boss?" The boss flips his thumb at Takeshi, "He's on your crew so give him some work - report back how he does." The black man wipes sweat from his brow, eyes Takeshi and motions to come along. Takeshi follows and the crew chief shows a large pile of wood boxes and points to the ship, "Move these boxes onto the boat." Takeshi nods and quickly picks up a box and goes up the gangway to deposit the box on deck. He hastens down the gangway and continues to move the crates. The black man rejoins his crew and keeps his eye on Takeshi's progress. Later around noon, the black man notices the pile of wood cases have dwindled, and looks over to see Takeshi busy moving another box onto the ship. The black crew chief smiles as he continues to supervise his workers.

Through the years that he lives and works in Chinatown, Takeshi becomes involved in various jobs to earn the means to survive. He sells vegetables at the local market, and works at a Chinese Laundry shop washing, scrubbing and ironing customers' clothes; and he labours in a leather factory cutting, dying and sewing leather goods. As much as possible, Takeshi learns English from his co-workers and Chinese from the people of Chinatown. At the Chinatown Festivals, he watches the colourful celebrations complete with Dragon Dances and noisy fire crackers. One of Takeshi's favourite pastimes is to visit the local Kung Fu Schools and watch the teachers and students train to fight in Tournaments. Takeshi becomes familiar with the various Kung Fu fighting styles. Throughout it all, he still maintains his room at Grandma Lee's Boarding House, however his kind friend Chow Zu Fu passed away a few years ago, but his sister, the old lady, still runs the place from behind the lobby desk. Who would have known on the evening Takeshi wanted a room, he would eventually become the longest tenant at the Boarding House. Over the years, Takeshi works hard and saves his earnings and often trades money with miners in exchange for gold nuggets. No one knows except he and the old lady, but Takeshi stores small pouches of gold nuggets in a leather duffle bag that is locked away safe in a private room in the basement of the Boarding House.

Five years pass…

The wood steps creak as Takeshi walks up from the basement of the Boarding House, the large black leather duffle bag is slung over his shoulder. He walks over to Grandma Lee, napping with her eyes closed. Takeshi clears his throat to announce his presence. The old lady's eyelids flutter and she looks up to see Takeshi standing before her, "Are you off to work?" Takeshi gazes fondly at her, "Grandma Lee, I travel to the Great Plains." The old lady ponders a couple seconds for his words to sink in, "You are leaving us - leaving your home?" Takeshi nods and reaches into his bag and brings out a small pouch and places it before her wrinkled face, "You and your brother made me feel at home while I stayed here. Thank you Grandma Lee - this pouch is for you." The old lady clasps the pouch and brings it close. She opens the drawstring and sees the gold nuggets and looks up. Takeshi smiles, then he turns and walks across the lobby and out the Boarding House front door. Grandma Lee gets off her perch and goes to the window and peers out and watches as Takeshi disappears through the people and the busy street of Chinatown.

CHAPTER SIX

The High Sierras

From an elevation, Takeshi looks back at the port city of San Francisco spread out before him, the settlement buildings, stores and homes, the Bay and its water that leads the ocean, and the many ships anchored in the harbour. Takeshi turns around and moves to rejoin the long line of travellers making the hard climb over the Sierra Mountains. The terrain changes from the farmable soil in the lowlands, to the pebbles, stones and rocks of the highlands, then it becomes the huge boulders, cliffs and outcrops of the high elevations where the nights are bitter cold and the air gets difficult to breathe. Slowly, carefully, the line of pilgrims climb up the high Sierras; men, women and children, young and old, people of various nations, all in the quest for opportunity and a fresh start. On route, various groups of travellers cross paths, groups seeking San Francisco and the California coast, and those trekking across the mountains toward the Great Plains of the American West. On the journey, Takeshi encounters mountain men with furs, miners and prospectors with shovels and pick axe, families of homesteaders in wagons laden with possessions, Cowboys packing six guns, traders and vendors hawking wares, weary looking railroad workers, and lone drifters. As the columns meet each other on the Trail, there's no time to exchange conversation or have friendly banter. Whenever people made eye contact, nothing had to be said because everyone understood - all were simply moving on, searching, inwardly yearning, looking for that special place where they could build a better life.

One cold morning on the back side of the Sierras, there's a buzz among the people, voices of excitement, whispers of relief and outbursts of happiness. Takeshi strides toward the large group assembled on a wide rock ledge overlooking the horizon. As he works his way to the front of the people - his eyes widen and his heart races -

there before him is land as far as the eye can see, - vast sections, an ocean of land, with enough space for families to build homes, good ground for farms and ranches, enough territory for entire towns. This is the Great Basin of the American West. A succession of hills and watersheds that lead to a territory with wide open plains and seas of rolling grass, a place known as the Great Plains - home to Native American Indians.

Having made the descent from the Sierras, the group that Takeshi travels with disperse, some are part of homestead groups, while others simply go their own way. Takeshi sets out across the Plains with duffle bag slung firmly over his shoulder, his stride deliberate and with purpose, his steps sure and steady. He notices the landscape, vegetation and creatures are different that his native Japan - the sage brush, the cactus, the Juniper tree, desert rattlesnakes and vultures. What intrigues Takeshi greatly are the wild mustangs he observes from time to time as he hikes across the land. He watches the herd with fascination and takes delight in the spirited nature of the horses - so wild and free. Takeshi camps out under the stars, the glow of his campfire keeps the animals at bay, the only sound are crickets and the lonesome cry of a coyote.

As Takeshi moves on, the ground ahead becomes rugged and rocky and he enters an area with pine trees, thick brush and hard rock terrain. Suddenly - DYNAMITE BLASTS. Takeshi turns to where the sound came from, and with curiosity Takeshi heads in that direction. He navigates between the pines and rugged gullies - only to emerge on the top of a rocky escarpment. Takeshi stops to behold the spectacle - hundreds of men labour under the hot sun to build new railway tracks through rock cuts. He looks at workers who are sweaty, dirty and tired. The work pace steady, the scattered groups resemble busy ants. From his high vantage point, Takeshi watches as teams of men clear ground, shovel gravel, carry heavy iron rails, lay thick timber beams, and hammer spikes to secure rails. Up ahead at the front of the work, are Chinese workers who place and light the dynamite - they also have the precarious job of carrying the volatile nitroglycerin. However, at this moment, no work is being done at the front section of the track. The Chinese and their Foreman have stopped and all stand idle. Off on a hill at the opposite end of Takeshi's position, is the Operation Tent and inside is Buford Pick, a mean gruff Railroad Boss whose background is ex-military. Pick's tall stature intimidates others as he leans over them barking orders that make subordinates cringe. Buford stands with his hand on the mounted brass telescope, as he scans across the railroad operation. He looks closely at everyone - Foremen and workers alike - no one can escape his steely gaze, he scrutinizes every person's effort. Buford Pick is someone greatly feared - his word is Law! Buford pans the telescope across the work and abruptly stops. He steps back and flips the telescope down in anger, "What are those Orientals doing down there? I told Jackson to keep up the pace. Now, they've fallen behind." Fuming mad, Buford turns to a man that stands to his side, Pick yells, "Boys! Ride down there and put those Chinamen back to work. I'm not paying them to stand around." The man gives a quick nod and exits the tent and immediately goes over to a bunch of rough mean-looking cowboys. This group is the Barlow Gang, a bunch of ruffians that stand ready to do Pick's bidding. They're uncouth, ill-tempered brannigans, always eager to dispense the Boss's justice. The leader injects, "Bout time we get to knock some heads together - can't stand this waiting around." One man remarks, "Never beat one of those pigtails before. YEHAW! Let's have some fun!" The Barlow Gang mount up and swiftly ride down the hill to the tracks below and race their horses to the front section where the Chinese workers are. As the Chinese workers are gathered together, the ruffians ride in and quickly dismount and begin to rip into the group - shoving, punching and kicking. The Chinese workers scatter to safe positions yards away. The Gang leader yells out, "Bossman doesn't like the hold up! What in tarnation is going on?" A fellow ruffian bellows, "Get back to work pigtails!" Out from the ranks steps Guan Yet Dee, an elderly Chinese man with braided white hair and a long white beard, "Velly Solly. No work. Velly Solly!" A gang member raises his boot and shoves the old man aside. The elderly man steps back and looks at Jackson. The Foreman steps out to stand beside Guan Yet Dee, and looks at the Gang leader and remarks, "The Chinese workers are scared of the nitro! They won't carry the nitro jars." The Barlow Gang look around menacingly at the workers clustered in separate groups. The cowboy leans forward, "Well, what happens when they carry the nitro?" Jackson glances about his workers and looks at the Cowboy leader, "They blow up! The Chinese get blow to smithereens!" His remark makes the Barlow Gang break out laughing! The Chinese workers become agitated and start to speak loudly in their vernacular language, their arms wave in animated gestures of concern and anger. The ruffian leader quips, "You mean to tell me these pigtails can't carry a wooden box?" Foreman Jackson replies, "It's not just carrying the box -

it's carrying the nitro in the hot sun. Nitro explodes when it's gets hot!" The Gang leader grabs the reins and spins his horse around to gaze fiercely at the Chinese, then spits out chewing tobacco, "What's all the fuss! We gots lots of Chinamen - so what if they gets blown up, we gots lots more!" The rest of the Barlow Gang mount their horses - pull out their pistols and rifles and cock back the hammers. Their leader threatens Jackson, "You get them back to work! If they won't work - we'll put a bullet in any pigtail that refuses. Let's ride boys!" The gang turn their horses around and ride out kicking up a dust. With the ruffians gone, Jackson looks around at his work crew, then he motions Guan Yet Dee over to him, "You tell them to work. No work - you die! (He points with his finger) Bang! Bang!" Guan Yet Dee waves his arm at the Chinese workers to gather around and he explains to them that they must go back to work - or be shot dead!

Through all this, Takeshi stands atop the wilderness ridge, his dark black garb in contrast to the clear blue sky. He unslings the black duffle bag and sets it by his feet, and continues to observe the entire railroad operation, and notes the track crews, supply carts, construction materials, and the area for the workers' tents. Takeshi looks toward the track's front portion and fixes his eyes on where the Chinese are busy toiling away.

CHAPTER SEVEN
The Chinese Workers' Camp

At night when the day's tough work is over, the Chinese Workers' Camp is a welcome refuge from the harsh labour. The weary men relax in tents, while others sit in small groups to talk and smoke pipes or cigarettes. In the centre of Camp, Chinese cooks prepare the evening meal of rice, meat and vegetables. The head cook steps away from the kettles and lifts his voice, "Everyone - Come on! The food is ready." The Camp responds with men coming out of their tents and others get up from their groups. They collect the tin plates and utensils, but many still prefer to use chopsticks to eat their meal. The men stand eager to receive their grub. As the men gather, one worker notices a lone dark figure at the far edge of Camp. The worker cries an alarm, "Intruder! Intruder!" All the Chinese workers stop eating and getting their food, and just stare at the solitary figure. No one moves. No one does anything. Out from the ranks steps the elderly Guan Yet Dee accompanied by several muscular men. The aged leader approaches within a few yards and stops and gently studies the newcomer. The strong men with him stand ready for any trouble. The old man speaks, "Greetings stranger! What brings you to our camp?" Takeshi scans the old man and those along to protect, then he raises his arm up and jingles a small pouch of coins, "I'm hungry and will pay for food." The elderly leader moves closer, but one of the strong men named Lion puts out his arm to block him, "Grandfather, how can we trust him? He's a stranger. We know nothing of him." Guan Yet Dee looks at him, "Lion, who are we to refuse a hungry man food. Do not Generals feed their captured enemies. This man needs to eat!" The old man moves aside Lion's arm and walks to within a couple feet and bows, "My name is Guan Yet Dee. You are welcome to join us for food." Takeshi replies, "Thank you for your hospitality! My name is Takeshi." The elderly leader's eye brows raise and he stares more intently, "Takeshi - that is a Japanese name." Takeshi replies again, "Yes Grandfather, it is a Japanese name - for I am Japanese." The elderly leader steps closer and extends his arms with open palms, "Japanese. Chinese. Out here everyone is the same. We all are far from home! Please - eat." Takeshi nods and bows respect and carries his gear as he follows the old man through the throng of onlookers toward the kettles of food. The leader motions and a cook dishes out a heaping plate of rice, meat and vegetables. As Takeshi reaches to receive the plate, Guan Yet Dee notices the newcomer looks physically tired and weary from trekking the wilderness. Takeshi turns and extends his free arm and offers the small pouch of coins, "I will pay as promised." Guan Yet Dee gently moves the arm with coins to Takeshi's chest, "The Railroad gives us more than enough food. They like their workers healthy and strong. What we have we share - no need to pay. Eat." Takeshi spots a log to sit on and starts to dig into the rice, meat and vegetables - savouring the food with every bite.

Lion, some strong men and others, are at the far side of the Chinese Camp. They are suspicious of the stranger they've just encountered. One man remarks, "I heard the stranger tell Grandfather - he is Japanese!" The others are shocked at the news and begin to murmur. Another man speaks up, "He's not Chinese - he should not be in the Chinese Camp." Members of the group nod their agreement. One nervous fellow remarks, "What if he's with bandits, and others are waiting for his signal to rob us." A fellow quickly blurts, "No one is getting my money. I'm sending it back home to my family in China." By now, the group is worked up and scared, they look at each other, then turn their attention to Lion. Lion stands up, squares his shoulders and sticks out his chest, "No one will steal our money. We are strong enough to stop any bandits (he scolds) remember your Kung Fu!" The men look with expectation at him, one asks, "What will you do?" Lion puts his arm on the man's shoulder, "I will force this Japanese intruder to leave our camp." A man quips, "What about Grandfather? He gave the stranger permission to stay." Lion gazes about the group with a determined look and remarks, "Grandfather is old and soft. He should have stayed in the quiet courtyards of China. This rough wilderness needs strong men like us!" With that statement, Lion sets off toward the other side of the Chinese Camp. The rest of the group follow him.

Guan Yet Dee and Takeshi are in conversation when Lion strides up with his group of followers. The entire Chinese Camp stop what they're doing and watch intently. The elderly leader stands and politely bows, "Lion, you looked unsettled. Is something wrong?" Lion in anger points his finger at Takeshi, "He is Japanese! He should not be here - he must leave!" By this time, all the Chinese workers have gathered around to see what will unfold. Guan Yet Dee cups his hands together to plead with Lion, "Lion, this man is our guest, a fellow traveller, someone far from home like us all." Lion huffs and kicks dirt to reinforce his point, "Grandfather, you are old and lack the strength to make him leave. But I am big and strong - my Kung Fu will make him run away." With those words, Lion steps back and assumes a Kung Fu fighting stance circling his arms in a menacing manner, taunting Takeshi to fight him. Takeshi turns and bows to the old man, "Grandfather, thank you for the kindness you've shown me! I'm sorry to have caused a problem in the Camp. I will take my things and go." Guan Yet Dee replies with a sad expression, "I too am sorry, Takeshi! Not all Chinese men value the honour and respect of ancient times." As Takeshi turns and makes his way through the Chinese workers, one of Lion's group shouts, "He has fellow bandits waiting to rob us! How else could he survive this wilderness unless he's part of a gang." With such words, the whole Camp becomes upset, workers start to voice their fear and worry. Takeshi continues to walk through the men when one of Lion's group throws a punch at him. Takeshi's reflexes are lightning fast, he dodges the punch and grabs the man's arm and flips him into the dirt. The attacker gets up embarrassed and angry. Suddenly, Lion and his four Martial Arts companions surround Takeshi, each takes a classic Kung Fu fighting stance. The rest of the Chinese workers back up and fan out to give lots of room to fight. Takeshi watches Lion and the other opponents circle him. He recognizes the different Kung Fu fighting styles he saw and studied when he lived and worked in San Francisco Chinatown. Takeshi knows that he's being confronted by the Kung Fu fight styles of - the Tiger, the Leopard, the Crane, the Snake and the Dragon. With attackers moving around him, Takeshi stands relaxed, he closes his eyes and concentrates, then Takeshi quickly assumes a Ninja fighting stance. Lion forms a Tiger claw with his fingers and forcefully swings and rips open Takeshi's garment at the shoulder. Lion strikes again but Takeshi jumps and spins to kick away Lion's hand. Takeshi pummels the big man with a flurry of blows that drop him to the ground moaning and groaning. The man with the Leopard style attacks with a series of swift strikes and Takeshi deftly blocks the strikes and kicks the attacker unconscious. Suddenly, the Crane, lunges in with a torrent of fluid jabs, strikes and punches. But Takeshi is quicker and he dodges the jabs, deflects strikes and blocks punches. Takeshi flips backward and kicks the Crane under the chin to knock him out. Takeshi lands on his feet - poised and ready. Only the Snake and the Dragon remain. Both men look at each other and attack in unison. Takeshi blocks the pointed spear hand of the Snake, but the Dragon's fist hits full force and Dragon powerfully kicks Takeshi in the groin. Severely struck, Takeshi is momentarily off balance and out of breath. He teeters briefly but quickly regains his footing. The Snake on his left, the Dragon on his right, both close in - however, Takeshi counterattacks. He runs and jumps high to deliver a powerful kick to the back that pushes the Snake forward into Dragon's mighty fist. Dragon's punch knocks out the Snake. Takeshi lands and turns about - Dragon is momentarily distracted. Takeshi hits hard with a flurry of blows that strike his opponent's vulnerable areas. Dragon collapses to the ground in heap. Takeshi stands alone - and victorious! The Chinese workers are amazed and have never witnessed this kind of fighting style. They question and murmur among themselves. The elderly leader approaches, "Takeshi, I saw the tattoo on your shoulder. I know what you are!" Takeshi pleads, "Grandfather, please do not tell anyone, it must remain a secret." The aged man reassures, "Your secret is safe with me. - Have a good journey wherever you travel." Takeshi bows, "Thank you Grandfather! I will not forget your kindness." Takeshi turns and walks to the edge of the encampment and disappears into the woods. The elderly leader looks over at Lion and the other Kung Fu fighters who are recovering from their beating and nursing their injuries. Guan Yet Dee turns and retires to his tent.

CHAPTER EIGHT
Frontier Town of Emerson

Takeshi walks over vast rolling grasslands and climbs to the top of a big hill and stops to rest. He looks out to see a frontier town, the wood frames of new buildings and the numerous wagons and horses speak of a growing community. As he approaches the town limits he sees a sun bleached chipped sign with the words - The Town of Emerson. Takeshi enters the settlement and walks down the dusty busy main street and notices the townsfolk, settlers and Cowboys. He sees railroad workers, soldiers and drifters, those getting supplies at the Mercantile and loading up their wagons, while others drink at the Saloon, eat meals at the Cafe, or get shaves and haircuts at the Barbershop.

Emerson is a major Station on the Stage Coach route. The Station is a complex of wood structures in the middle of town. A large building for passengers and travellers, a Blacksmith and Livery Stable for the horses and wagons, and a bunkhouse for the drivers and workers. Takeshi watches a Stage Coach race into town, the driver snapping the whip and the horses kicking up a trail of dust. The team of horses and the Stage Coach come down the dirt road and pull into the Station. The horses are tired, sweaty and breathing heavy. Station workers quickly come out and open the Stage Coach doors to assist the passengers stepping down. Takeshi resumes his exploration of the town and strolls the wooden sidewalk taking him past buildings and stores. He stops in front of a wood building with large glass windows and notices the sign above the front entrance - LAND REGISTRY OFFICE. Takeshi looks through the front window at the Land Registry Agent seated behind a large desk tending papers. He opens the front door and steps inside and moves to stand before the Agent. Takeshi voices his purpose, "I want to buy farm. You have farm?" A skinny man with wire frame spectacles peers up at Takeshi and adjusts his glasses. The Agent clears his throat, "Do you have money to buy a farm? We have farms for sale - Easterners tried homesteading but gave up." Takeshi pulls out a tan leather pouch full of dollar coins and jingles it, "I have money. Enough money for land!" The Agent takes the pouch, opens the drawstring and shifts coins with his fingers, "Appears you got more than enough for a farm!" The Agent takes out the correct amount and hands the pouch back to Takeshi, "Well, come over here and look at the map." The man pushes his chair back and walks over to a large territory map on the wall. Takeshi follows him, his eyes scan across the map. The Agent points with his finger, "This is the town of Emerson (Points to other spots) and these are the farms for sale." Takeshi studies the map and notices a farm located alongside a river. He taps the map at that spot, "I take. This farm good. - Water!" The Agent tilts his head and grins, "You picked a good one alright! Only a two hour ride from town and right beside a river." The Agent and Takeshi return to the desk, and the Agent opens a drawer and pulls out a Land Registry Document. The man writes in the purchase details - then stops at NAME and looks up with an inquisitive expression. Takeshi speaks up, "Takeshi. Takeshi Shinobi." The Agent replies, "Can you write that down, please?" Takeshi leans forward, takes a pencil and writes his name in English. The Agent writes TAKESHI SHINOBI as the registered property owner - stamps the Land Registry Seal - and hands the Document to Takeshi. Takeshi inspects the paper, folds and puts the Deed inside his tunic. He smiles and nods his heads, "Thank you Agent San!" The man remarks, "If there's anything else you need, I'd be glad to help." Takeshi goes over to the big glass window and points to a buckboard in the street, "I need wagon. Wagon and horses." The Agent grins, "That you do. You can get a wagon and horses at the Livery Stable. Ask for the Station Master." Takeshi bows, then opens the door and leaves. The Agent gets up and goes over to the Office window and watches Takeshi go up the street. The man returns behind the desk and flips open a Ledger and mumbles, "I wonder how long he's gonna last?"

CHAPTER NINE
The Stage Coach Station

Takeshi approaches the Station and climbs the wooden steps of the large veranda. He stands on the porch in the shade and hangs his head - he's tired. The Station door opens and out steps Blake "Boots" Connors, the Station Master. He's a tall rugged man in a well-worn Stetson that wears Cowboy boots with silver toe caps. Only his friends can call him "Boots", all the others respectfully call him, Mr. Connors. The man greets Takeshi, "Where you off to Mister?" Takeshi lifts his head to make eye contact. The Station Master stops speaking - momentarily taken back at seeing an Asian man before him. Takeshi replies, "I want wagon - horses for farm." Blake Connors lifts his hat and sets it back again, "We usually don't get your kind." Takeshi reaches into his tunic and pulls out a gold nugget, "I pay for wagon, horses. You take gold." The Station Master's eyes grow big and he takes the nugget and rolls it in his fingers. The man looks at Takeshi and smiles, "For you, Partner, we can find a wagon and a team of horses!" Takeshi slightly bows, "Thank you Connors San!" The Station Master turns and opens the door and yells inside, "Get out here! You got work to do. This man needs a wagon and horses." Quick as can be, Boy, a twelve year old Indian lad appears in the doorway. His clothes are tattered, his hair wild and messy, and he looks a bit undernourished. The lad chimes, "Yes Sir!" The young lad looks over at Takeshi, then waves his arm to follow. The lad takes Takeshi across the street to the large Livery Stable and leads him inside to stand before three empty wagons. The lad points to the last wagon near the wall, "That's the best one Mister! The wheels and springs are good and strong." Takeshi slides off the duffle bag and walks over to inspect and check the wagon's wheels, buckboard, seat and hitch. He nods and smiles at the lad, "Good! Very good." Next, the lad guides Takeshi to where the horses are kept and goes beside a tan Mare and pats her side, the horse neighs, "This Mare is nice and gentle. Easy to handle." Then the lad walks between some horses to a chestnut Morgan. Takeshi asks, "This one okay?" The lad looks at Takeshi, "This horse is strong and steady - real good for pulling a wagon." Takeshi smiles at the lad and comments, "Horses like you. Very good!" The lad tenderly brushes the coat of the Morgan, "I've been living in this stable since bossman Connors found me. Been around horses ever since." Takeshi looks at the young lad with compassion.

Outside the Livery Stable, the lad harnesses and hitches the horses to the wagon as Takeshi stands beside the front wheel. Blake Connors strides over and tips his hat, "Fine wagon and team of horses." Takeshi looks up at him, then reaches into his tunic and pulls out a pouch and gives it to the Station Master. Blake Connors opens the pouch and pours gold nuggets into his calloused palm, "This will do fine. Yes Siree!" Takeshi turns and lifts his arm to point at the lad, "I want boy! Help on farm." Blake Connors gives Takeshi one long stare, glances over to the lad by the two horses, then eyes Takeshi and exclaims, "That lad tends my horses and wagons and helps clean up the Stable. He's important to me!" Takeshi grabs the duffle bag and reaches inside and brings out a black leather pouch and tosses it to Connors, "For boy - much gold!" Blake Connors feels the weight of the pouch in his hand, then he opens the draw string to look inside - and takes out a big gold nugget. He sifts his fingers through the nuggets, grins and looks at Takeshi, "You want to pay this much gold for the boy! He's just some Indian kid I found wandering the brush." Takeshi turns to watch the lad gently stroke the Mare's forehead. He looks at Connors with determination, "You take gold! I take boy. Good!" The Station Master tips back his Stetson and bounces the pouch of gold up and down in his hand, he looks at the lad, then he looks at Takeshi with a big smile, "Mister, you got yourself a deal. Mind you - I'm getting the better part!" Takeshi throws the duffle bag into the cargo box, then he climbs up and takes a seat on the wagon. Blake Connors waves the lad to come over. Connors puts a hand on the lad's shoulder, "Boy, go get your clothes and things. You're going with this man here - You work for him now!" The Station Master turns and walks away. The lad looks up at Takeshi and stands there silent for a bit, then he turns and goes into the Livery Stable. Moments later, the lad returns carrying a few clothes, a rucksack, and a horse bridle. He climbs up into the wagon and sits beside his new boss. Takeshi grabs the reins to move out the horses, the wagon rolls away from the Livery Stable and Station. With the lad quietly beside him, Takeshi steers the wagon down Emerson's main street heading out of town. Blake Connors stands on the shaded porch and watches the wagon disappear out of sight. He holds the pouch firmly in his hand, "With this much gold, I could hire a bunch of Indian boys to work horses." He adjusts his Stetson, opens the front door and steps inside.

CHAPTER TEN

The Abandoned Farm

Takeshi and the young lad ride the wagon over the packed earthen road. The team of horses draw the wagon at a good clip. The lad watches a rabbit dart across the grass, he looks up at birds flying overhead, and notices a patch of wild flowers alongside the road. Takeshi glances at the lad then passes the reins over to him and smiles, "You drive now." The lad breaks into a big grin and takes the reins with gladness. As the lad coaxes the horses along Takeshi observes how the boy steers and handles the wagon. Takeshi sits back and pulls out the Property Document and studies it. The paper shows the road they're on, the river and the farm boundary. He returns the paper inside his tunic. The wagon passes through tree groves, across grassy meadows and along the slow moving river. As the lad steers the wagon and horses around a bend - the lad pulls the reins to stop. Takeshi and the boy sit transfixed beholding the farm property. It's located right near the river and the farm house looks decent and in good repair. A small veranda marks the front door. There's a modest barn with a corral that lays a hundred yards from the house. To the right near the river, are some oak and ash trees that stand as a windbreak and provide patches of cool shade from the hot sun.

The lad pulls the horses and wagon up near the house, jumps out and lashes the reins to the corral post. Takeshi gets down and walks over to inspect the farmhouse, the lad follows him. Takeshi and the lad walk to the front entrance and Takeshi opens the door and they both enter the clapboard structure. Takeshi and the lad gaze around at the interior - the Easterners abandoned in a haste and left their furniture and household goods behind. Whether it was the trouble of packing and trekking everything across the wilderness all the way back to the East Coast, or whether it was sheer discouragement and frustration that made them leave their possessions; whatever the reason, there in the farmhouse stood their homestead furniture and provisions. Takeshi steps over to a wood chair and draws his finger across the seat to make a line in the dust. He glances at the lad, "We clean. Very dirty - we make good. (Pauses) We put horses and wagon in barn." The lad nods and both exit the front door. The boy walks to untie the reins from the corral post and they walk the horses and wagon across the farmyard to the barn. The lad grabs the barn door and swings it open to reveal a mess of boxes, wood crates, junk and debris. Takeshi and the boy are taken back some, Takeshi remarks, "We clean barn too!" The lad leads the team into the barn and unbridles and unhitches the horses. He finds two feed bags that still have oats and sets it before the Mare and Morgan. Takeshi and the boy move the wagon into a better position. Takeshi looks about and spots two tin buckets near the inside wall. He goes over and picks up the buckets, motions to the lad, then they exit and close the barn door. The two walk toward the house when Takeshi stops a few feet before the veranda and turns to the lad and hands him the tin buckets, "Go to river. Fill with water." The lad runs with the buckets to the river, kneels down beside the riverbank and dips in one bucket at a time to fill with water. When both are full, he scoots back to Takeshi at the front door. Takeshi grabs a pail - opens the door and they both go inside. The lad watches as Takeshi rolls up his tunic sleeves and gets two clothes from the duffle bag - he tosses one cloth to the boy. They both begin to use the dry cloths to remove the layer of dust on the furniture and house interior.

Later on in the evening, one very tired young lad rests on his cot beside the far wall. The boy opens his eyes to see Takeshi at the fireplace with a good fire, he's bent over a kettle adding ingredients. Takeshi reaches into a bag and brings out more items to drop into the kettle, next he grabs a wood ladle and begins to stir the simmering water. He lifts up the ladle to taste the broth - Ahhhh! Takeshi looks over at the lad who now sits up alert and awake. Takeshi announces, "Soup ready. We eat." The lad gets off the cot and comes over to the wood table and sits down. Takeshi fills two bowls with soup and brings them over to the table and sets one in front of the boy, he hands the lad a spoon. Takeshi places his bowl on the table at the other end, sits down and starts to spoon the soup into his mouth. He lifts his eyes to observe the boy heartily devouring the soup - when finished the lad picks up the bowl and licks the inside. The boy looks at Takeshi and shows the empty bowl. Takeshi grins and motions to the kettle. He watches as the lad eagerly get up, goes to the kettle to refill his soup bowl, and returns to his chair and makes short work of his second helping. The young lad scoops out the last of the soup and tilts the bowl to lick it clean. The lad sets the bowl down and uses his sleeve to wipe his mouth. Takeshi smiles, gets up and walks to his cot against the opposite wall, sits down and stretches out to relax. The lad still tired, Yawns, then ambles over to his cot and lays down. The burning wood in the small fireplace dies down and becomes radiant embers that cast a warm glow across the farmhouse interior, the golden light falls on the faces of Takeshi and the lad, both fast asleep from a very busy day.

Early next morning, the lad and Takeshi walk to the barn and commence to clean and tidy the structure. They lift and carry the boxes and crates and stack them orderly against an interior wall, then they shuffle sacks of grain to create more room in the middle. Afterwards, they gather all the discarded tools and assemble them in a spot near the Barn door. Takeshi grabs two shovels and places his hand on the lad's shoulder motioning that they leave. Walking out of the Barn, Takeshi leads the lad to an wide patch of open ground. The boy watches as Takeshi takes his shovel to dig and til the ground into clumps of overturned earth. He glances over to the lad and motions to do likewise. Under the early morning sun, Takeshi and the lad dig up the ground to create a big section of freshly tilled dirt. Takeshi hands the lad his shovel and leaves to go inside the house and quickly returns with a sack and one of the tin buckets. He takes out a sharp metal awl and pokes holes in the bottom of the bucket. Next, as the lad keenly watches, Takeshi puts his hand into the sack tied to his waist and brings it out full of seeds which he scatters across the tilled earth. Takeshi gives the bucket to the lad, "Get water." The boy scampers to the river, dunks in the bucket and brings the leaky pail back and hands it to Takeshi. The man begins to walk over the area with the leaky bucket and water drips onto the scattered seeds. He hands the bucket to the boy and motions to continue what was demonstrated. As the lad waters the dirt, Takeshi continues to scatter seeds across the patch of fresh turned earth. During their work, the lad makes several trips to the river to fill his pail and water the large patch of ground. At noon, the sun is high in the sky and very hot. Takeshi and the lad walk over to the leafy trees to rest in the cool refreshing shade.

It's evening and dark outside, there's a roaring fire and Takeshi has another soup in the kettle. He stands beside the kettle and adds greens, dried mushrooms and sprinkles of seasoning. He looks over at the lad sitting patiently at the table eager to eat. When the soup is ready, Takeshi brings over two full bowls and sets one in front of the lad. The boy grabs his spoon and digs in with a hungry youthful appetite. Takeshi sits down and takes a spoonful and slowly sips the broth as he watches the boy eat. As before, the lad quickly finishes his bowl and looks expectantly at Takeshi, who smiles and nods. The lad gets up and goes to the kettle to fill up another helping, then returns to the table and begins to eat. Takeshi observes the boy with a fatherly gaze. When the lad finishes his soup, he pushes the bowl aside and looks at Takeshi. Now that the lad has eaten, Takeshi arises and goes over to the big leather duffle bag, reaches inside and brings out a red pouch tied with a gold cord. He walks back to the table, sits down and opens the drawstring and removes an ink bottle, brush and a roll of parchment paper. Takeshi unrolls a section of paper, opens the small ink bottle and dips in the brush. He writes a Japanese Kanji on the parchment and blows on the ink. Satisfied the ink is dry, Takeshi holds up the paper and shows it to the boy who's been keenly watching. Takeshi points to the Japanese Kanji then points to the lad, "You - Minarai. New name for you. - Minarai." The boy's eyes lock onto the paper and he attempts to repeat the word, "Min-ar-ai. Minar-a. Minarai!" Takeshi nods and smiles approval, "Hai! Minarai. - I call you Minarai." Takeshi puts his hand into his tunic and brings out a small knife and cuts off the piece of paper and hands it to the boy. The young lad reaches for the paper and holds it up as his eyes trace the ink details of the brushwork. The lad smiles deeply, "Minarai. Minarai. Minarai." The boy gets off his chair and goes over to sit on his cot and stares at the paper. The flickering flames of the fire make shadows dance across the room. Even as Takeshi has gone to sleep, Minarai stares at the paper in the fading light.

It's morning and Minarai rolls out of bed and pulls his suspenders over his shoulders, he walks over and opens the front door. Takeshi is sitting on the veranda step whittling a piece of wood with his pocket knife. The lad looks intently at Takeshi who keeps shaving curls of wood off the stick. Minarai bends down to sit beside Takeshi and watches the man shape the wood stick into a handle. The man is aware of the young lad's curiosity so Takeshi looks at him, "Minarai. You hear story? My story? I tell." With Takeshi's broken English he rehearses his story for the lad. He talks about his family living in the Iga Mountains of Japan, and how a Warlord attacked his people killing many and sending the rest into hiding. Takeshi tells of crossing the ocean on a ship to America, and how he lived and worked in Chinatown where he traded money for gold nuggets. He spoke of the Railroad tracks and walking the wilderness to reach Emerson where he bought the farm, wagon and horses - and how he wanted to free Minarai and help care for him. Afterwards, Minarai sits fascinated hearing Takeshi's story. This was the most words and longest time that anyone ever spoke to Minarai before. Takeshi finishes speaking and glances at Minarai, "Enough talk - we fix barn." The two rise to their feet and walk past the corral toward the barn.

CHAPTER ELEVEN

Fight at the Mercantile

Two Months later…

Minarai drives the wagon and team of horses as Takeshi sits quietly on the bench beside him - they're going into town for supplies. The lad aptly handles the wagon as the horses trot along the dirt road past the grove of trees, through the meadow and over rolling hills - right into the town of Emerson. The wagon rolls past the Hotel, Barbershop, Saloon, Cafe, Land Office and Bank, until Minarai pulls the reins to stop the horses in front of the Mercantile. The lad pulls the brake handle and lets go of the reins. Takeshi gets out and stands on the boardwalk, he looks at his young friend, "Minarai, you stay wagon. I go see store." The lad nods, "Yes Sir!" Takeshi turns and enters the big general store, and scans around at the interior packed with various dry goods, hardware items and homestead supplies. He walks the thick wood planks and moves through the aisles of stacked merchandise. Takeshi sees - sacks of grain, barrels of straw brooms, crates of fragrant soap, bags of baking flour, boxes of nails, coils of rope, and bolts of fabric. The Mercantile stocks lots of items, almost anything you'd need to live in town, or on a ranch or farm. Takeshi collects 3 bags of seed, a bucket, an axe, 2 kerosene lamps, a coil of rope, and 2 candy sticks. He takes the items over to the long wood counter and lays them before the storekeeper. The man looks the items over and slides them to the side, "Will that be all? Takeshi smiles and gives a polite nod, "2 months - buy again." The storekeeper scribbles down numbers on a long list beside him and gives Takeshi his attention, "Well - everything comes up to three bits." Takeshi hands the man the money and he gathers the items up in his hands.

Minarai sits quiet and peaceful on the wagon bench waiting for Takeshi to return. A few buildings away, a rowdy bunch of Cowboys come out of the Saloon and start to proceed down the boardwalk. They are loud, noisy and really drunk. As the Cowboys approach the Mercantile, they see Minarai sitting in the buckboard. The Cowboys stop beside the wagon and begin to threaten and menace the young lad. Minarai has experienced drunks before and swiftly diverts his gaze to the ground. One drunk Cowboy bellows, "Look here boys - we have us an Indian!" A couple of the Cowboys move into the street to confront Minarai's attempt to look away. A couple fellas put their boots onto the wagon to intimidate. A Cowboy pipes up, "Where'd you get this wagon redskin? - Steal it?" Minarai is a skinny twelve year old kid while these Cowboys are big strong young men wearing holsters with guns. Minarai raises his eyes to glimpse around, then quickly lowers them. A Cowboy yells, "Maybe this Indian brat needs a whoop-in' to learn respect." One Cowboy climbs into the buckboard and roughly grabs the back of Minarai's collar. At that moment, Takeshi comes out of the Mercantile carrying the supplies. He sees what's happening and quickly lets go - the items fall onto the planks of the boardwalk. CLUNK! The Cowboys turn their attention to Takeshi who stands at the ready. A Cowboy snickers, "Well - wouldn't ya know it - a Chinaman!" The Cowboys break out laughing! One of their group remarks, "A mangy Indian kid and an ole Chinaman." The guy beside him barks, "Maybe we should whoop them both. Let's start with the old man - then the kid." All the Cowboys sneer and nod. They begin to move toward Takeshi. Great concern comes over Minarai's face, he's frozen in fear. Townspeople have stopped to see the fuss and commotion. Down the street a man runs into the Saloon and let's loose, "Hey everybody! The Cowboys are gonna lay a beating on someone." Everyone gets up and the Saloon crowd spills out into the street. The people scurry to the Mercantile. By now, quite a number of townsfolk are gathered in front of shops and buildings opposite the Mercantile. The Mercantile Storekeeper comes outside to try and stop the Cowboys, "Now see here - you bunch stop this! Clear out of here." One of the older bigger Cowboys shoves the Storekeeper back inside, "Not your fight old timer - stay outta this if you know what's good!" The overpowered Storekeeper sheepishly steps back into the safety of the store. The Cowboy leader strides over and throws a punch. Takeshi blocks the swing and thrusts his fingers into the nape of the neck, the ruffian crumples to the planks - Gasping! Two Cowboys attack, one kicks with his boot while the other throws a mean punch. As the young man kicks his leg, Takeshi grabs the boot heel and flips him backwards into the street below, then he turns to catch and powerfully torque the Cowboy's fist and flips him onto the wood planks. Thud! The three remaining Cowboys start to lunge - Takeshi jumps high and kicks one unconscious, then he lands with a roundhouse to blast the other down the boardwalk. Just one Cowboy left - he looks at his fallen amigos, he won't fight and raises his hands in surrender. Takeshi looks over at Minarai - the lad is stunned! Takeshi glances around at the large crowd of onlookers, many totally astonished at such a display. Takeshi goes near Minarai, "You okay? No hurt?" The lad replies, "I'm okay - didn't get hurt." Takeshi is relieved, "You safe. Good!" Takeshi gathers and loads the supplies. He climbs into the wagon, grabs the reins and lets loose a whistle and snaps the leather reins. The horses pull away from the Mercantile, the crowd of townsfolk watch as Takeshi and Minarai go down the street heading out of town. Many of the townsfolk still amazed at what they witnessed. As the Cowboys collect themselves and regroup, two of them full of anger, pull out their pistols and aim at Takeshi and Minarai. The two cock back the gun hammers ready to fire. BOOM! BOOM! Emerson's Sheriff, Marshall Miller and Deputies stand nearby with rifles raised. The Sheriff steps up and looks at the Cowboys, "Put away your guns! There's no shootin' around here." The Cowboys look hesitantly at each other, then the two Cowboys holster their pistols. The Cowboy leader approaches the Lawman, "Sorry Marshall! We were just having some fun - right boys?" All the Cowboys nod and feign innocence. The Lawman replies, "Alright then! Just remember you're in my town and I don't cotton to gunplay. Understand?" The Cowboys nod compliance, "Yes Siree, Marshall - we understand." Marshall Miller eyes the group, "Good! (Turns to crowd) Now everybody…" A loud gruff voice breaks through the air, "What's all the ruckus?!" Cutter and his gang stand on the boardwalk, each man tough and gritty with a rough mean appearance. The drunk Cowboy leader squints his eyes at Cutter then gives a surprised yell, "Uncle Cutter! - Is that you?" Cutter steps off the boardwalk and strides over to his nephew and slaps his back, "Last time - you were just a scrawny kid. Look at you now, all grown up." The nephew remarks, "I'm riding the cattle drive from Arizona (points about) We're together, just in town to let off some steam." Cutter grins at his nephew and looks at Marshall Miller. The Sheriff injects, "Those boys were about to shoot some fellas. Not in my town!" Cutter eyes the Cowboys then addresses the Sheriff, "Well, nobody got shot! - like the boy said - just letting off some steam. Don't fret Marshall, I'll take the lads with me (Cutter puts an arm around his nephew) We gots catching up to do!" Cutter and his gang and the Cowboys head toward the Saloon. Marshall Miller turns to the crowd of onlookers, "Okay everybody! Go back about your business - nothing to see here." The townsfolk, shopkeepers, farmers and drifters disperse and go back to their activities. Out on the road back to the farmhouse, Takeshi steers the wagon as Minarai sits quietly staring ahead, occasionally, Minarai looks at Takeshi with a pensive glance.

CHAPTER TWELVE
Minarai's Ninja Training

Minarai and Takeshi are sitting relaxed on the step of the veranda when the lad turns and asks, "You fought so many at the same time. How did you do it?" Takeshi stares out at the tree grove then looks intently at the boy, "You want fight like me?" Minarai stands up excited, "Yes! I want to protect myself…and help others too!" Takeshi fastens his eyes on Minarai who stands with nervous energy waiting a reply. Takeshi picks up a twig, bends his head down as he draws in the dirt, "What I teach very old - from Japan - Ninja very hard!" Minarai stiffens himself with determination, "Teach me, please! I'll work real hard!" Takeshi studies the young lad and sees the resolve in his eyes, "You good worker, I know, I watch (Pause) Ninja very hard - maybe you stop?" Minarai makes direct eye contact, "I can do it, and train hard too!" Takeshi ponders the boy's words and attitude, then stands up and puts his hand on the lad's shoulder and smiles, "Okay! You train Ninja!"

The next morning, Takeshi sits bareback on the Morgan as the horse trots along the road with Minarai running to keep up. Takeshi coaxes the horse into a slow gallop to pick up the pace and looks around at Minarai who's starting to strain and breathe heavy. Three miles further up the road, Takeshi stops the Morgan and waits - he dismounts and stands on the road looking for a sign of Minarai. Takeshi squints and sees Minarai as a tiny figure coming toward him. After many minutes, Minarai appears with a slow jog, the lad meanders to and fro on the road. Finally, when Minarai reaches Takeshi's spot, the lad wobbles over and collapses on the grass by the roadside gasping for breath. Takeshi walks over to where Minarai lays and watches the boy's lungs heave to get air. Minarai glances up and blurts out, "How did I do?" Takeshi grins, "Okay start. Now run back!" Minarai eyes bug out as he fights for air, "Run back - now?!" The man bends down for eye contact, "Yes! Run to fight - fight to run. You run now!" Takeshi flicks Minarai's shoe and waves come on. Breathing heavy, Minarai stands to his feet and watches Takeshi climb onto the Morgan and turn the horse toward the farmhouse going slow. Minarai launches out and jogs beside Takeshi and glances up, "Glad I can rest tomorrow." Takeshi eyes Minarai with a stern look, "No rest - tomorrow you run - every day run - get strong!" Minarai can hardly believe his ears and has a bewildered expression, "Run again tomorrow! What about breaks - rest?" Takeshi smiles coy, "Train Ninja - run each day - train each day - get strong!" As the Morgan's gait increases, Minarai starts to fall further back with Takeshi going farther down the road, the lad mutters, "Run, get strong…get strong, run. (Pause) He doesn't want a Ninja - he wants a horse!" Minarai maintains a steady pace as he jogs alone on the road back to the farm. When he reaches the farmhouse, Minarai is hot, sweaty and tired. He slowly jogs past Takeshi at the veranda, past the farmhouse, and keeps jogging up to the riverbank and jumps into the cool water. Splash! As Minarai stands up waist deep in the river, he looks over to see Takeshi having a good laugh. The lad flops backwards in the water and just floats to let the refreshing river water cool him down. Later at the evening meal of rice, vegetables and rabbit, Takeshi hands Minarai a pair of short wood sticks. The lad holds the sticks in his fingers and watches Takeshi use his pair of wood sticks to pick up and place vegetables on top of his rice. Minarai asks, "What are these?" Takeshi scoops in a mouthful of rice and extends his hand and demonstrates opening and closing the sticks, "Chopsticks. Chopsticks to eat." Minarai positions his fingers like he sees Takeshi and attempts to pick up a piece of celery - it falls onto the table. The lad tries again - and again - and again - until finally, he can hold a piece of vegetable without dropping it. Takeshi smiles as Minarai pops the celery chunk into his mouth, "Good. Very good!" Minarai smiles at Takeshi's comment and the lad commences to slowly and carefully eat his bowl of rice by adding other ingredients. Both enjoy their meal of steamed rice, savoury vegetables and cooked rabbit.

Minarai's regime for Ninja training not only has long distance running, but also includes learning to balance - on a tree branch, atop the corral fence, then with one leg on a wagon wheel. Minarai climbs overhand on ropes suspended from the barn to strengthen his arms. He stands motionless for long periods of time - in the hot sun and through the cold night. Month by month, the physical exercises help the lad to grow strong, tough and agile. As the seasons pass, and through the hard training and healthy eating, Minarai becomes taller and more powerful, no longer the skinny under-nourished kid that he was when Takeshi found him.

Seeing that Minarai is now fit and muscle-toned, Takeshi begins to instruct on how to hold and handle the wooden practice sword to attack and to defend. Being capable with the wood sword, Takeshi moves Minarai to train with the Katana - the steel sword. Minarai's aptitude and attitude impress Takeshi as the boy handles the steel sword with improved speed and skill. Next, Takeshi introduces his young apprentice to the other Ninja weapons - and in quick time, Minarai aptly proves himself with all the Ninja weapons - the staff, the sword, bow and arrow, chain dart, blowpipe, and the Shuriken - the sharp metal throwing stars. Takeshi teaches Minarai how to create poisons and explosions, and in the evening after their mealtime, the lad learns to read Japanese and the ancient Ninja scrolls.

One morning as Minarai walks out of the farmhouse ready for another day of Ninja training, Takeshi motions to accompany him. The both walk to a prepared area behind the barn where Takeshi has constructed a homemade forge complete with anvil, tongs, hammers, water trough, straight irons and waterstones. Minarai looks at the set up and asks Takeshi, "Master, what is all this?" Takeshi picks up a set of tongs and turns to the youth, "To handle the Katana sword is very good! - To know how to make a Katana sword is better! Minarai, you will learn how to make a Ninja sword." The lad's eyebrows lift and excitement fills his eyes. He stands and keenly observes as Takeshi begins the sword making process. Over the succeeding days, Minarai watches and studies how Takeshi works the bellows to heat the fire to melt the iron sand and coal, then pour the molten metal into a blade shaped cavity in an earthen cast. He notices how Takeshi hammers the red hot steel bar into a sword blade. The youth focuses on the way Takeshi grinds and hones the steel blade into a sharp shiny sword with a razor edge. When it's all finished, and the sword handle and scabbard are carved, painted and lacquered - Minarai is thrilled when Takeshi presents the completed Katana sword for him to examine. Minarai's hand respectfully holds the sword and brings in for a close inspection. The lad runs his fingers over the high gloss finish of the lacquered wood. He pulls the sword partly out and fixes his gaze on the polished steel blade and sharp edge - then Minarai extends his arm to fully draw the sword out of the scabbard and lifts the gleaming blade up in the air. Takeshi watches as Minarai swings and maneuvers the Katana with skill and quiet grace. As he returns the sword into the scabbard, the young man looks at Takeshi with a smile, "The Katana is beautiful! So well balanced in the hand." Takeshi looks at Minarai with a twinkle in his eye, "The Katana is yours! (Pause) You've trained hard - earned it!" Minarai breaks into a big happy grin and clutches the Katana with childlike delight as on Christmas morning, "The Katana is mine! - My own sword?" Takeshi nods. Minarai's eyes are lost on the Katana, then the young man turns to Takeshi and bows very low, "Arigato Sensi! Thank you Master!" Takeshi replies, "Time for supper. We rest in our home." The two make their way to the farmhouse, Minarai carries his new sword with deep pride.

CHAPTER THIRTEEN
Yuji - The Ninja Master

Ten years later…

Takeshi is dressed in an ornate Japanese kimono with embroidered trim and details. A long white banner with a large Japanese Kanji - SHINOBI, flows in the breeze. Bouquets of bright flowers decorate around a rectangular straw mat where Takeshi kneels. In front of him an exquisite crafted Katana sword sits in a wood cradle. Minarai kneels opposite Takeshi and wears a black Ninja outfit. Takeshi lights incense sticks and begins to chant Japanese words. When finished, Takeshi picks up the sword with both hands and offers it to the graduate. Minarai receives the sword and bows in respect. As Minarai is bowed low, Takeshi chants Japanese as he passes the burning incense sticks over the young man. The moment the chanting stops, Minarai raises upright and looks straight ahead. Takeshi takes a white paper with Minarai's name and burns it in a bronze bowl. Next, Takeshi takes a calligraphy brush and writes a Japanese Kanji - YUJI - on a piece of white paper in red ink. He holds up the paper and hands it to the graduated apprentice and remarks, "Your new name is Yuji - Good Son! From this day on you will carry the name Yuji." The young man bows and holds the sword extended with both hands, "Hai! Yuji. My name is Yuji!" Takeshi smiles fondly, then passes over all his Ninja weapons, possessions and the ancient scrolls to Yuji. The young man shows deep humility at such a great honour. Both arise to their feet and look at each other. Yuji bows to Takeshi who bows in return, they both stand peaceful and silent. After a moment that seemed to last forever, Takeshi gives Yuji a smile, then walks to the farmhouse, enters and closes the door. He leaves Yuji to stand as his own man - as a Ninja Master!

The following morning Takeshi sits at the wood table and looks at the tea cup, tea pot, small bamboo ladle, clean linen cloth, and the flower arrangement on the table. This morning is unlike all other mornings because Yuji is performing the ancient Japanese Tea Ceremony to honour his Teacher and Master. The older man watches carefully as Yuji masterfully executes each step of the Tea Ceremony with the utmost care. Takeshi and Yuji take up their tea cup and drink in respectful silence. After the Tea Ceremony is finished - and a quiet pause - both men stand up. Yuji crosses the floor and picks up the black leather duffle bag and slings it over his shoulder. He walks to the door, opens it and turns to Takeshi and bows low, "Arigato Sensi! Thank you Master for helping to raise and care for me! Thank you for teaching me to be a Ninja!" The old man and father-figure with quivering voice replies, "I have loved you as a son. I have taught you everything I know. Now you are ready to make your own way." Yuji answers with watery eyes, "I will never forget you Sensi!" Yuji bows to Takeshi one last time, then the young man exits and quietly closes the door. Takeshi sits down and claps the tea cup with a smile of deep contentment and happiness!

CHAPTER FOURTEEN

Yuji Walks Shoshone Lands

Yuji walks across plains and grasslands and through wilderness forests. He sees farms and homesteads and gives them a wide berth. The young man traverses streams and fords swift flowing rivers. He climbs over rock formations and hikes rough escarpments. As the late afternoon sun begins to set on the horizon, Yuji camps on a mountain peak and views the pristine wilderness, he lays out his equipment and picks up a honing stone to sharpen his sword.

The next day, Yuji treks over the rough terrain and stops to adjust the duffle bag. He looks down and notices he's standing in the middle of a blueberry patch. Feeling a bit hungry, Yuji bends down to pick handfuls of berries to eat. To the far side, figures hidden by the forest carefully watch Yuji. A hunting party of Shoshone warriors observe the lone traveller from their wooded seclusion. Bear Claw, the leader of the group, stands with Eagle Feather, Two Knives, Thunder Cloud, Otter and other braves. Otter raises his bow to shoot an arrow at the unsuspecting traveller, but Bear Claw quickly stops him, "Hold! Do not shoot. He walks our land only seeking a path. We will not harm without cause." Otter gives a brash reply, "He walks our Tribe's land and takes our food. He has no right." Bear Claw gazes fatherly at the impetuous young warrior, "Our forests and rivers have many animals, birds, fish and berries. One man passing through will not remove our plenty." The others in the hunting party agree and support Bear Claw. Eagle Feather speaks up, "Bear Claw has spoken wise. Let the stranger pass untouched." Two Knives steps up, "Last night, I dreamed an eagle flying above a small fox. The eagle did not attack the little creature." The fellow hunters nod upon hearing such words. Eagle Feather turns to the others, "The sky bird is Bear Claw and the little fox is the stranger. If we attack - the Great Spirit will be angry with us.

Bear Claw is right!" The hunting party heartily accept such insight and prepare to continue their expedition. The braves follow single file along the forest path. Bear Claw pauses momentarily to look back at the traveller, then he resumes his pace with the group. Otter also looks back at the stranger, his fingers brush the arrow feathers; suddenly, Otter turns and runs to catch up with the hunting party.

Yuji treks through a hollow in the woods with embankments on both sides. Up ahead, he notices flat rocks that jut out of the ground to create a dead end. As he walks, Yuji feels one of the leg straps is loose and he bends down to tie it secure. When he lifts his head - Yuji looks directly into the eyes of a large black timber wolf. The wolf snarls and bares its sharp fangs, the animal's saliva drips from its teeth, the hairs on its body becomes bristled. Yuji hears other sounds and turns around to see a pack of wolves surrounding him on all sides. The animals growl and snarl exposing their vicious teeth. In an instant, Yuji pulls his two sharp swords from the duffle bag - the polished steel blades gleam in the sunlight. In his right hand, he grips the long Katana and in his left hand is the short Ninjato sword. Yuji takes a fighting stance - swords ready for battle. The wolf pack leader, the Alpha male, confronts Yuji, snarling and snapping its jaws as it inches closer and closer. Around him the other wolves move in. With a loud snarl, the big wolf leaps to attack. Yuji steps forward and swings the long blade hard slicing open the Alpha wolf's neck. It falls yelping and dies. Then a timber wolf on his left attacks and Yuji stabs it with the Ninjato sword. A wolf behind him lunges and sinks its fangs into his Achilles tendon. Yuji twists his torso and kills it with the long sword. Suddenly, a wolf from the right runs and leaps toward Yuji's head. He blocks with his right arm, the wolf buries its fangs into his forearm. Instinctively, Ninja training kicks in and Yuji uses his left arm to plunge the short sword deep into the wolf's chest. It drops dead. Yuji does a quick turnabout to size up the situation - he sees four dead animals on the ground and eight more wolves circle to get closer. Yuji looks at his right arm which is loosing blood and he can only hobble because of the torn Achilles tendon on his left leg. The frenzied wolves snarl, growl and howl - thirsty for blood! Yuji looks at the stone outcrop yards away. The rock offers some form of defence - there he can protect his back from attack. The wolves creep in to lunge and bite at his feet and legs. Yuji frantically swings the two swords to fend off the animals. He hobbles and drags his left leg to get closer to the rocks. The wolves repeatedly snap their jaws at him - he fights them on all sides. Finally, Yuji reaches the stone outcrop and plants his back firmly against the flat granite. The stone is both a defence and a support for his body. Yuji leans back to catch his breath. He reaches into the duffle bag and brings out a bracket with sharp metal spikes and slips it over his right foot to create another weapon. He looks out to see the wolves run back and forth in front and to the sides. His eyes track the eight wolves - the two swords and the foot spike will only kill three - five more wolves can still attack. Yuji begins to feel weak from the loose of blood, his strength wanes, he's tired and breathes heavy. An outburst of snarls alert Yuji the wolves are closing in for the kill. The pack lunge in again and again to bite and grab his feet, arms and legs. Yuji bravely flails and kicks at the wolves. As he stabs a wolf on his left, the wolf on his right bites into Yuji's calf, its fangs sink deep into Yuji's flesh. He raises the long sword and drives the blade into the back of the wolf and kills it! Yuji lifts his head just as another wolf leaps and knocks him to the ground. In the tumble, the duffle bag slips off. The wolves converge and begin to bite and tear at his legs, torso, arms and head. Yuji rolls and uses his hands and arms to protect his face; but now his torso and legs are vulnerable. The wolves ferociously bite his body all over - Yuji fights for his life! Suddenly, GUN SHOTS! Bullets strike and kill four wolves, the other two remaining wolves yelp loud and run off. Yuji lays on his back with his clothes bloody and ripped - his legs, arms and body riddled with bites and torn flesh. With fading strength he looks up to see blurry figures loom over him. Yuji passes out!

Bear Claw, Eagle Feather, Two Knives, Thunder Cloud, Otter and the others stand over Yuji. Eagle Feather bends down to examine the damage - he looks at the wounds and cuts, bites are everywhere. He stands up and points to Yuji, "We must bring him to our camp or he will die." Otter bends over to peer at the stranger's face and motionless body. The young brave turns to Bear Claw and asks, "What Tribe does he belong to? He is not a white man." Two Knives speaks up, "His clothing is strange. He is not Pawnee, Sioux or Cheyenne." Thunder Cloud studies the stranger before them, "He is not Crow, Arapaho or Blackfoot." Otter looks at Bear Claw, "If he is not from the tribes we know - what tribe is he?" Bear Claw looks at Otter in silence, then gazes down at Yuji and turns his gaze to the hunting party, "The Healers in camp will help him. We must care for him until his strength returns." The leader motions to some braves and they find long branches to construct a litter to carry Yuji back to their camp. Bear Claw picks up the two swords, metal bracket and duffle bag. He gives the bag to Otter to carry and hands the two swords and bracket to Thunder Cloud. The braves carefully lift Yuji and place him into the sling. When Bear Claw sees Yuji is secure, he motions for the group to head back to camp. The Shoshone hunting party trek the path home - through soaring trees, past waterfalls, over lush meadows, and across rolling grassland. This time, instead of carrying an elk - they carry a human being.

CHAPTER FIFTEEN

The Shoshone Village

The Shoshone camp is picturesque and serene, nestled on the large bend of a wide gentle river. Eighty-nine tepees are spread out to form the Tribal village. Ample space lays between each dwelling for people and horses to manoeuvre. Smoke rises from many tepees as the women cook for the evening meal. The Chief's tepee stands in the centre, taller and much larger than the other dwellings. This is the place where the Indian leaders meet for Tribal Council. Bear Claw and the hunters stand on the crest of a grassy hill, the Shoshone village spread out before them. Thunder Cloud fires his rifle and waves his arm and shouts the customary signal. People at the edge of camp turn their heads in the direction of the gunshot. They hear the signal and see the braves on the hill. The excited villagers announce the news, "Bear Claw and the others are here." Another man shouts out, "The hunting party have returned." Word quickly travels through camp and everyone stirs to move and greet the hunting party. Men, women and children scurry past the Chief's tepee to welcome the returning braves. Out from the large tepee steps the Shoshone Chief Buffalo Sky, dressed in his buckskin outfit embroidered with beadwork and decorative metal. A feathered headdress adorns his braided snow white hair. Buffalo Sky stands noble and regal as he waits.

Bear Claw, Eagle Feather, Thunder Cloud, Two Knives, Otter and the other braves are greeted by the delighted villagers. Suddenly, their excitement turns to quiet wonder as they see the braves carry a strange person in the sling. The villagers walk with the hunting party, the people talking among themselves. Some inquisitive ones get close enough to peer in at the badly wounded stranger. By now, the hunting party are surrounded by the entire camp, everyone buzzing with curiosity about the man in the sling. Bear Claw and the returning warriors approach Chief Buffalo Sky's tepee. He awaits them with the Tribal Elders.

Buffalo Sky welcomes Bear Claw and the hunting party, "Your moccasins have carried you home. My heart is warm to see you and the braves again!" Bear Claw and the hunters stand respectful before their revered Chief. The seasoned hunter remarks, "There were no elk, sheep or bear on our hunt. We did find a strange man walking our lands!" Buffalo Sky looks at Bear Claw, "We will see this stranger." Bear Claw motions to the braves to bring the litter up for Buffalo Sky to see. The Chief and Tribal Elders come close for a better glimpse. Bear Claw points at Yuji, "This one showed great courage! He fought a pack of wolves by himself - killing many." Bear Claw's words catch Buffalo Sky's attention and the Chief lowers down to examine Yuji and notices the many injuries, "The wolf bites are deep and many!" Bear Claw speaks out, "He needs our Healers or he will die! This one is brave and has strong medicine." As Bear Claw and the hunting party stand before the Chief, many of the tribe's onlookers converse loudly among themselves about the stranger. Buffalo Sky looks around at his people and raises his hand high in the air, and the camp becomes quiet to hear his words, "Take him to the Healers' tepee. They will help him live. When he walks again, we will talk with him." Eagle Feather and Bear Claw smile at the Chief's decision. The hunting party turn and carry the litter past many dwellings before coming to the Healers' tepee. The villagers follow at a respectful distance. By this time, word of the events have reached the Healers. They emerge from their decorated tepee.

The hunting party bring the litter before the Healers as they stand at the entrance of their dwelling. Their Shoshone garb and markings identify them as Great Spirit Walkers. These are the ones to whom the Shoshone people bring their sick to be healed and restored. The Healers mix special plants, roots, herbs and flowers to make ointments, salves and compresses. Then the Shoshone Healers sing and chant to call on the Great Spirit. Bear Claw instructs the braves to gently set the litter down, and he speaks with the oldest Healer, Grey Bird. Next to the elderly man is a young Shoshone maiden called Bright Star, and beside her is a Shoshone woman known as Hair That Dances and a middle-aged brave called Burns With Smoke. Bear Claw points to Yuji, "Your medicine can help this man to recover from his wounds." Grey Bird steps closer, bends down and stretches out his weathered hand to move aside Yuji's clothing to see the injuries. His eyebrows raise, "He is greatly wounded! We must get him inside. He will need our special medicine if he is to live." Grey Bird stands up and motions with his hand for the braves to bring Yuji into the Healers' tepee. As the braves carry the litter through the opening, Hair That Dances guides where to lay the wounded stranger. The braves gently lay him down on a knee-high platform covered with Buffalo hides. Burns With Smoke carefully cuts away and removes the bloodied clothing to reveal terrible bites, gashes and torn flesh. Grey Bird looks at Bear Claw, "We will care for him until his strength returns. If the Great Spirit calls for him - we have no medicine for that." Bear Claw nods as he glances over at Yuji's body with it's life-threatening injuries - the hunter understands. He turns and leaves through the tepee entrance, the other braves follow.

Grey Bird begins to amass various roots, herbs and plants. Hair That Dances pours water into a blacken kettle and sets it over the coals of a fire pit. Burns With Smoke starts to grind seeds, flower petals and coloured powders together in a gourd bowl. As the three Healers are busy, Bright Star stares at Yuji. The fire and the hot coals cast a glow upon Yuji's face. Bright Star has never seen someone like him before. Burns With Smoke finishes grinding and holds out the gourd bowl, Hair That Dances takes it and dumps the mixture into the kettle of water. Grey Bird brings over a thick bundle of herbs, roots and plants, and drops in the items. He takes a wooden ladle and stirs the kettle to mix everything together. Burns with Smoke gets up and comes over to stand beside the old man, "I will make the stranger ready and smear Buffalo grease over the cuts and wolf bites." Grey Bird turns to him, "Hair That Dances will place the poultice on his wounds and torn flesh. When he is covered with our tribe's medicine, we must ask the Great Spirit to walk with us. Only then can he be strong again." The elderly man watches as Burns With Smoke applies the Buffalo grease, and Hair That Dances covers Yuji's injuries and wounds with the healing poultice, then she lays some fur blankets over Yuji. Next, all four Healers sit on the tepee floor and begin to sing and chant tribal songs to call on the Great Spirit. Outside the Healers' tepee, a full moon bathes the village in luminous light, their singing carries across the grassy plains.

Night has settled over the Shoshone camp and the Chief and Elders have gathered for Tribal Council. The leaders sit cross-legged to form a large inner circle. The other warriors stand around the tepee's interior wall. Bear Claw, Eagle Feather, Thunder Cloud and Two Knives stand before Buffalo Sky and the Elders. Bear Claw tosses the black leather duffle bag into the centre of the circle. Buffalo Sky opens the bag and takes out the long and short sword and the metal bracket to examine them, then he passes the items around to the Elders. Next, the Chief lifts up the duffle bag and empties the contents onto the tepee floor. Out fall assorted leather pouches, different bundled clothes, tied scrolls, cloth bags, a knotted black rope, a black metal hook, black metal stars, a hollow reed, and a pouch of coins. The Chief passes these items to the Elders for their inspection. Buffalo Sky looks up at Bear Claw, "This stranger is unlike any we have ever met. When my eyes fell on him - I did not see a white man." An Elder remarks, "He must be an Indian from beyond our lands." Eagle Feather picks up the Katana sword and raises it high, "We saw him fight the wolves with his long knives. In his tribe, he must be a mighty warrior." Buffalo Sky rolls the pointed metal star with his fingertips, then he picks up the hollow reed and looks through it, "These are strange things before us. Things we have never seen - things our hands do not know." Bear Claw lowers down eye-level to the Chief, "When the stranger becomes strong, we will bring him to speak with our Chief and Elders. He will tell us about his tribe and lands." Buffalo Sky ponders a minute then stands to his feet and lifts his arms and looks around the tepee, "Until Bear Claw brings the stranger to us - we will hunt, fish and ride our horses after Buffalo." The Elders and the assembled warriors nod approval. The Chief signals and the hunting party and all the warriors leave the tepee. Only Buffalo Sky and the Elders remain.

CHAPTER SIXTEEN

Cutter and the Outlaws

The American Wild West attracts all kinds of people seeking its wide open spaces, fresh water, farmland and beautiful wilderness. Young and old venture forth to etch out a place for themselves. From railroad settlements, mining camps and frontier towns, to big ranches and small humble farms, the people work hard to make a new and better life.

Somewhere in the wilderness...

Cutter and his gang of outlaws sit around a roaring campfire. Cutter leans back against his saddle on the ground. The men smoke cigarettes and pass around a bottle of booze, some play cards within the flicker of the firelight, while others clean and polish their pistols and rifles. A rough-looking cowboy turns to Cutter, "Who we robbing next? That bank was a tough one!" The gang leader stares at the flames of the fire, "Farms! We gonna rob farmers. Take things easy for a while - til the next gold shipment by stage coach." Gang members close to him look at each other, sneer and grin. As the night presses on, some of the bandits try to get some shuteye. A few keep at their card game. Cutter stretches out his long legs, closes his eyes and repositions his cowboy hat to cover his face.

In the flats of a gentle valley, a farmer, his pretty young wife and their three youngsters are busy with chores. The oldest son chops wood and the two younger ones help carry the kindling to the house. The wife hangs up freshly washed clothes on the laundry line. Their playful spotted Collie suddenly turns and starts to bark at the far grove of trees. The farmer and his wife turn to see a group of men ride out from the cover of the woods. The young mom waves the children to her side. The farmer takes the wood axe and sets it on the ground against his leg. The nine outlaws gallop toward the huddled family. A number of yards away, the group splits up, three ride to the left, three riders go to the right, while Cutter and two men stop in front. The young family are trapped in the middle. The farmer and his wife glance around at the riders - the men are dusty and dirty with the look of meanness etched into their scruffy unshaved faces. Cutter looks around at the farmhouse, barn and water well. The farmer takes a step forward, "You men can water your horses and you're welcome to any food we have." The farmer looks about and notices the men leer at his attractive young wife. Cutter stiffens his legs in the stirrups and stands tall and gives the farmer a mean stare, "Who are you to tell us what we can and cannot do? We aim to do as we please." The farmer makes eye contact with his frightened wife and scared children, then he looks up at the gang leader, "I meant no disrespect. I was just being hospitable." The man on the horse beside Cutter speaks out, "You're trying to be (strutters) hos-pit - hosp-it." The gang leader frowns and gives the man a glaring stare. Cutter speaks out, "Hospitable." The farmer smiles, "Yes Sir, that's right! Just wantin' to be neighbourly." Some of the riders snicker loud as they look at the young lady. One outlaw remarks, "We like neighbourly...neighbourly means sharing (he eyes the wife) and we like sharing." The farmer instinctively moves to stand in front of his pretty wife and raises the axe from his side, "You men are more than welcome to food and water. After that, I'll be seeing you leave." The riders chuckle and snicker. A man yells, "What if we don't want to leave. Who's gonna stop us all - you?" The farmer stands straight and tall, "I will if I have to!" The exchange makes all the bandits break out laughing, some mock, some jest, and some have icy stares. The gang leader moves his horse out from the others and brings his mount a couple feet in front of the farmer and stares at him, "Sod buster, I like your grit. Yes Sir, I truly do." Cutter spins his pistol chamber, "But this here tells me we can do whatever we want!" The riders let out loud yahoos and shoot their guns in the air. The farmer with a sad face, turns to his trembling wife with tears running down her face - and urgently pleads, "Run! Run!" The farmer turns back to the gang leader, and Cutter points his gun and shoots the farmer square in the chest. The farmer drops dead to the ground. The wife and frightened children watch in horror - instinctively they flee to the farmhouse. The young mother reaches the porch and frantically waves to her children, "Run!Hurry - Run!" The riders open fire and shoot the children in the back. The terrified mother watches in horror as her three children tumble to the ground like discarded rag dolls, their lifeless bodies lay in the dirt. The family dog barks angrily at the intruders, and an outlaw aims his pistol and shoots the dog dead. The young woman lifts her eyes off her dead children and sees the men dismount and slowly walk toward her. Terror comes over her, she instantly knows her fate at the hands of these ruthless men. She races inside and bolts the heavy door and lays a thick wood beam across its back. Then she quickly goes to the two windows and locks the strong wood shutters. The badmen are now on the porch, some try to force open the door but no success, others try the windows but they're are sealed shut. The young lady can hear the sound of boots and spurs going across the wood porch. She turns her head to the glass frame that holds their family portrait. It's more precious than ever and she reaches out and brings it to her bosom. Outside on the porch, the bandits are frustrated and angry at being thwarted by a young woman. Cutter strides up with the axe in hand and tosses it to a man in front of the door, "You boys really need to think more!" Cutter motions for the man to begin chopping. The others start to holler and yell with excitement! Inside the house, the young lady shutters as she hears the axe chip away at the thick wood door. She holds the cherished photo and collects all the kerosene lamps in the house. The young wife goes into her bedroom and takes a lingering look at her husband's clothes, her dresses, her fancy collectables, her daughter's dolly, and her youngest son's teddy bear. She opens the lamps and throws kerosene on the bedroom door, the wood floorboards, the walls, the furniture, and the mattress. She garbs a box of matches, her fingers tremble as she tries to strike a flame - it goes out - she lights another and it goes out. She strikes the third match and it burns bright. The young woman lifts her head as she hears the axe break through the door. The bandits kick-in and bust down the big door and barge into the interior. She puts the lit match against the kerosene on the door, then she drops the burning match on the floor. Then she goes and lays down on her bed and presses the family photo against her heart. In seconds, flames engulf the bedroom, everything becomes ablaze - the bedroom door, the walls, the floor and the furniture on fire. The badmen reach the burning bedroom door but a wall of flames bar their access. The heat is intense and the men back off. Cutter pushes his way through to the front and peers through the flames and meets the haunting eyes of the young woman. She lays serene as she holds the family picture. Suddenly, the fire reaches her bed and she disappears in a shroud of flames. Now, the entire bedroom is an inferno and fire quickly spreads throughout the farmhouse. The nine riders hack and cough as they flee the burning smoke-filled building. They race to their horses and mount up. Cutter looks at his men, "Let's go boys! Nothing here for us. Let's ride!" The group of heartless outlaws gallop away, riding past the dead bodies of the farmer and his three young children laying in the dirt - the wood farmhouse burning in the background.

CHAPTER SEVENTEEN
The Jacobs Farm

Abner Josiah Jacobs and his wife Mary Jacobs sit at a large kitchen table for a late afternoon meal with their two sons, Edison (22), and the youngest, Henry (19). Mrs Jacobs has prepared a hearty supper. The oldest sons, Levi (26) and Daniel (23), are tending livestock in the barn. The father looks over to his youngest, "Henry, go call your brothers for supper! (Smiles to his wife) We sure don't want your mother's fine cooking to get cold." Henry promptly gets up, "Yes Sir Pa! Right away." Henry scurries across the wide front porch and jumps off into the dirt yard. He high-tails it to the big wood structure and stands outside the barn doors and calls to his brothers, "Levi. Daniel. Come on for supper! Pa says right away too." Henry happily nods, pleased that he delivered the message, turns and heads back to the large farmhouse. He runs and takes a flying leap onto the porch and quickly enters the house. Inside the barn, Levi holds a baby calf that has lost its mother and needs to be nursed. He has a glass bottle of milk in his hand. Daniel stands next to him and reaches out to brush the calf's forehead, "Will the calf manage until we're back from supper?" His older brother looks at him, "You go on ahead - tell mom I'm sorry for missing her nice supper, but this little calf needs help." Daniel lifts his arm, smiles and messes Levi's hair, "Okay, I'll tell her, and just so you know, I'm eating yours too!" Levi grins and raises his boot to give a playful kick, but Daniel is too fast and he's out of the barn for the house. Levi glances down at the little calf in his arms and whispers, "We didn't need him anyways." Levi finds a wood bench and sits down and cuddles the calf and feeds it the bottle.

On a hilltop overlooking the Jacobs farm, Cutter and his gang sit on their horses. The men survey the large farmhouse, big barn, the stone wall, and the corral of horses. Cutter stands tall in his stirrups and leans out so him men can see him, "Boys, looks like easy pickings' - and all ours for the takin'." The riders sneer - their faces have gloating smiles.

Abner and Mary Jacobs and their sons, Edison, Henry and Daniel, finish up their family meal. Mrs. Jacobs rises and prepares a plate of food and covers it with a checkered cloth and hands it to Daniel, "Daniel, you take this plate of supper to Levi. He needs food just as much as that little calf." Her son promptly stands and takes the plate from his mom, "Yes Ma'am! I'll be as fast as a Jackrabbit." Daniel carefully carries the plate, opens and closes the front door on his way. Outside, he steps off the porch and begins to walk to the barn. Halfway between the house and the barn, he hears the neigh of horses and looks around. Daniel sees nine riders coming down the grassy slope toward the farm. He yells loudly, "Pa! Pa! Riders are coming. Riders are coming." He turns and dashes to the barn, quickly enters and shuts the doors behind him. Abner swiftly goes to the front door to look outside - he sees nine cowboys riding hard toward the house. The father closes and bolts the door secure. Abner dashes to the wall cabinet and swings open the double doors - inside the cabinet are Winchester rifles, shotguns, pistols, boxes of ammo, and sticks of dynamite. He turns around and yells, "Ma. Edison. Henry - grab a gun and ammo - get ready for shooting!" Mrs. Jacobs and her sons come over and each grab a gun and a box of ammo. Henry and his mom go to the kitchen window, and Edison stations himself at the parlour window. Abner with Winchester in hand, unbolts and opens the front door just enough to stick his head out. He sees the riders stop some distance out from the house. The gang of bandits aim their rifles and pistols at the farmhouse. Cutter stretches up in the saddle, "You folks in there better come out if you know what's good! No sense hiding and making it difficult and all." Mr Jacobs cracks the door open and shouts a warning, "You men are trespassing. You best leave while you can!" Abner's remark angers Cutter and he fires a bullet that hits the door - Abner quickly shuts the door and locks it. Cutter reins his horse in a tight circle and faces the farmhouse, "We're here to take your farm - and we'll kill anyone who tries to stop us!" Hearing those words, Abner, Mary, Edison and Henry, break window glass and aim the rifles at the riders. The outlaws see four rifles pointed at them. The gang becomes uneasy. An outlaw speaks up, "Boss, I think this farm isn't worth the trouble." Cutter leans over and swats the man across the face, "The problem is you try to think. Don't! Leave the thinkin' to me -

that's my job. We're taking this farm, there's lots here for us. Come on boys!" The riders start to fire their guns at the farmhouse, bullets hit the walls, door and windows. They turn their horses toward the stone fence and ditch for cover. Abner and his family open fire blasting away - bullets hit three of the gang knocking them off their horses. One is shot in the chest, another struck in the back, and one wounded in the shoulder. From inside the barn, Levi and Daniel watch the commotion from between the barn doors. Levi motions to Daniel, "The tool box has a rifle and ammo!" Daniel hustles to the tool box and gets the rifle and ammo. Returning back, he tosses the gun and box of bullets to Levi, "You use it - you're a better shot." Daniel grabs a nearby pitchfork and shakes it, "If they get close, I'll use this." A round of gunfire alert their attention and they peek out the doors to see what's happening.

The gang of outlaws are hunkered down behind the stone fence and their horses are tied at the ditch. Cutter lifts his head and looks at the two bandits laying dead in the dust, then he glances at the man with the wounded shoulder who can't shot no more. Cutter looks over at a couple men close by and orders, "You two sneak over to the barn, try to get behind the house." The two men nod and the gang commence to shoot guns at the farmhouse while the two bandits duck low along the wood fence to the barn. The duo manage to get a hundred feet from the barn. Levi and Daniel spot the two outlaws sneaking to the barn and the two brothers hurry to the barn side door. Levi cocks the Winchester to chamber a round and looks at Daniel, "When I tell you - open the side door so I can get a shot off. We'll surprise them good!" Daniel nods and puts his hand on the door latch and waits for the signal. Levi takes a deep breath and nods, "Okay - Now!" Daniel pulls the side door open and Levi leans out to aim. The two bandits slinking along the fence are surprised and caught off guard. The two men aim their guns but Levi fires the rifle and kills the man in front. His partner unloads his pistol as he scoots back along the fence. Levi ducks inside as slugs take out chunks of the door and barn siding. The survivor works his way back to the gang. When Cutter sees the man return he gets mad, "What went wrong over there?" The man is shaken and angry, "Someone in the barn had a gun. Morgan's dead!" Cutter swats the fence with his hat in seething anger, "Two killed. Riley can't shoot. Now Morgan's dead!"

At the house, Edison and Henry guard the parlour window, Abner and Mary are at the kitchen window. Edison strains to look outside and remarks, "Pa! Pa! What's going on? What are they doing?" Mr. Jacobs peers out the kitchen window and looks at his two sons, "They're hold up at the fence - likely figuring a way to get in here." In the momentary lull, the family check their rifles and reload ammunition. Henry pipes up, "We got three of them didn't we Pa? I saw three go down." The father replies, "Two are dead. We just wounded the other." Edison steps away from the window and looks at his parents, "I heard gunfire at the barn." Mrs. Jacobs gives Abner a worried look and reaches out to clasp her husband's arm, "What about Levi and Daniel?" Abner places his hand on her shoulder with firm assurance, "The lads will be fine. Levi knows about the rifle I keep in the tool box. They're both great shots." Mary relaxes a bit, "You're right! Our lads are good with a gun." Abner gives his wife a smile and a gentle squeeze. Mary nods her head and manages a smile. Abner chambers another round and looks out the window.

The gang is spread out along the stone wall with guns in hand - unsettled and antsy. One bandit asks the leader, "What are we gonna do boss?" Cutter makes a contorted face and replies, "Just let me think! - they got four rifles in the house and a gun in the barn. Five of them against five of us. (Laughs) We can storm the barn - only one gun there." The gang members agree and someone remarks, "Just give the word boss." The leader nods and all the outlaws get ready to rush the barn. Cutter signals and the gang members hunch their way toward the structure. Abner becomes alarmed as he spots the bandits heading toward the barn and notifies his family, "We got to help Levi and Daniel - they're going for the barn!" Edison and Henry rush over to their father, "Henry and I can run to the barn. Our extra guns will help!" Mary Jacobs puts a hand on each son's shoulder, "No! That's too dangerous. You both stay put." Mr. Jacobs looks at Mary and the two lads, "Edison, You and Henry and your mom pin them down. I'll take another rifle to the barn." They all exchanges glances and nod agreement. Mary puts her hand against her husband's face, "Abner, be careful!" He gives a firm smile and rushes to the cabinet to get another rifle. He goes by the front door and unlocks it, "Lay down lots of fire! Keep 'em busy so I can reach the barn (Abner cracks the front door open), "Okay. Now!" Edison, Henry and mom open rapid fire at the gang of robbers. Abner dashes out the door and heads full speed for the barn. The riders see Abner run for the barn and begin to open fire on him. Bullets whiz all around him - slugs hit the house, porch and posts. The gunfire from the farmhouse is fast and relentless. Edison hits one of the bandits in the arm. The hot lead makes the men duck for cover. As Abner gets inside the barn, Levi and Daniel are surprised and relieved to see their father. Abner tosses the spare rifle to Daniel, who catches it and checks the weapon and cocks the lever for action. Levi eyes his father, "Sure good to see you Pa!" The father looks at the two, "They were fixing to rush the barn. Too many for you (lifts his rifle) We just evened the odds." Then, Abner, Levi and Daniel go to the side of the barn and point their gun barrels out through the opening in the boards.

Cutter raises up his head to take stock of the situation. He sees three rifles sticking out from windows at the farmhouse, then he looks over to see three gun barrels pointing out from the barn. The outlaw flops back down and grumbles, "I don't like being pinned down like this!" One man exclaims, "Look! Now they got guns at the barn just like the house." Cutter jabs his finger in the man's face, "Shut up! Just shut up!" Cutter looks at his gang, lifts his head to take another look at the house and the barn, and barks, "Make a run for the horses, boys! We'll go some place else." The outlaws skedaddle for their horses and quickly mount up and ride off.

Mr. Jacobs sees the gang take off and turns to his lads, "They're leaving. High-tailing it out of here!" Daniel exclaims in excitement, "We beat them Pa! We scared them off." Levi swings open the barn doors, and all three step out into the barnyard. The front door of the farmhouse opens and Edison, Henry and Mrs. Jacobs walk out onto the porch. They all watch the riders disappear out of sight. Both groups meet and hug each other with big smiles and cheers! Edison chimes, "We sure showed them - didn't we!" The mother wraps her arm around Edison, "We sure did son! We sure did." As the four lads look in the direction the outlaws rode off in, Mr. and Mrs. Jacobs hug and kiss each other. Young Henry looks at his big brother, "What happens if they come back?" His three brothers look at him and Levi slaps Henry's back, "We'll take care of them. We'll shoot them all!" The mother comes over to her sons, "Evil men like that get what's coming to them." Levi tilts his head and gives his mom an inquisitive expression, "All this shooting has made me hungry - is there any more supper?" Mary Jacobs grins, shakes her head and waves Levi to go inside. Abner, Edison and Henry all burst out laughing. They all turn and ascend the steps of the wide porch, go inside and close the door. A couple minutes pass and the front door opens and Abner sticks his head for one last look around. He scans the horizon. Nothing. Abner with a confident smile, closes and bolts the door.

CHAPTER EIGHTEEN

The Healers' Tepee

Bright Star sits beside Yuji as her eyes trace the features of his face. Hair That Dances comes up to stand on the other side. The women exchange glances. The older woman comments, "He's not like Indians we know. That is what the camp is saying." Bright Star tilts her head as she continues to study Yuji and replies with a curious tone, "Does he have family? Brothers? Sisters? Where does he come from?" Hair that Dances lifts the fur blanket to inspect his wounds. She looks at the young maiden, "Grey Bird says he will be strong in three moons. We must wait until his tongue knows to speak again." Bright Star gets up from her position and firmly remarks, "I will guard and watch over him with my eyes." Hair That Dances teases, "It is good for young eyes to watch over such a young warrior." Bright Star blushes. Hair That Dances walks to a ledge and grabs a small medicine pouch, "I must take some healing roots to Foxtail - their little girl is not well." The woman opens the tepee flap and leaves as Bright Star resumes her vigil over Yuji. Over the next three moons, the Healers keep giving their Tribe's special medicine to Yuji. Grey Bird and Burns With Smoke prepare soothing healing ointments, and Hair That Dances applies fresh dressing to the many wounds. During the evenings, the Healers sing and chant calling upon the Great Spirit. They take note of the young stranger's progress. At night during sleep, Grey Bird closely observes as Yuji tosses and turns as he sweats and repeatedly mumbles. One morning, the fever breaks and Yuji opens his eyes. Gradually, he becomes better and his health and strength return. The young man can sit up on his own, and over the succeeding days he begins to stand - and days later, Yuji walks. At night when Yuji peacefully sleeps, Bright Star tenderly watches him.

It is a warm day with a gentle breeze when Yuji comes out of the

Healers' tepee to set foot outside. He stands and takes a deep breath to fill his lungs, beside him stand Grey Bird, Smoke That Burns, Hair That Dances and Bright Star. High above in the sky, a magnificent eagle soars overhead and cries out! Yuji and the Healers look up and Grey Bird comments, "The sky bird is a good sign!" Yuji lowers his eyes and looks around the Shoshone camp that's busy with the routines of daily life. Indian women carry firewood, children run and play, braves lead horses around, old men sit outside their tepees, and young maidens work and prepare leather skins. Five tepees away, Bear Claw and a group of braves turn their attention to Yuji and the Healers, and begin to walk toward them. The group walk up and Bear Claw scans Yuji from head to toe, then he looks at the Healers, "The Great Spirit has returned his strength. The stranger looks better!" Grey Bird muses, "After much medicine, chanting and singing - he will walk in moccasins again." Bear Claw turns and waves to a brave in the back of the group. The young brave brings up the black leather duffle bag and hands it to Bear Claw. The veteran warrior lifts the bag and holds it out. Yuji with an expression of appreciation, nods and takes the duffle bag and sets it down beside him. Yuji looks at Bear Claw and the group of braves - then he bows low before them. Bear Claw watches Yuji with curiosity and puzzlement as he's never encountered such a new and strange gesture. Bear Claw turns to Grey Bird, "In three fires, Buffalo Sky and the Elders will speak with the stranger." Grey Bird glances over at Yuji and replies, "He is strong now. His moccasins will carry him to the Council Fire." Bear Claw nods and he and the braves leave. Grey Bird, the Healers and Yuji go inside the decorated tepee.

CHAPTER NINETEEN

Yuji At The Tribal Council

The evening of the Tribal Council, Yuji is dressed in Shoshone garb and stands still. As the Healers chant, Grey Bird uses an eagle feather to wave smoke over him. Bear Claw and Thunder Cloud step into the tepee and Grey Bird remarks, "He is ready!" Bear Claw approaches Yuji to check his Indian clothing - everything is in order and he's pleased. Grey Bird takes Bear Claw aside and whispers into the warrior's ear - Bear Claw turns and gives Yuji a probing gaze. The warrior leader exclaims, "This evening, our people will hear his tongue and learn of him." Bear Claw gestures for Yuji to follow him and the three men step outside. They walk past many tepees and the villagers watch as they arrive at the Chief's dwelling. Inside the large central tepee, Buffalo Sky, the Elders and the warriors have gathered for the Tribal Council. The men talk with keen anticipation! Bear Claw, Thunder Cloud and Yuji step through the door flap and remain standing. All conversations stop, everyone looks at them. Buffalo Sky raises his hand high and gazes around to address the assembled warriors, "Tonight, the stranger will speak at our Council Fire. We will learn of him and his people." Bear Claw leads Yuji to stand before the Chief and Elders. He sits down cross-legged and motions Yuji to sit down also. Bear Claw eyes the Chief and the Elders, and remarks, "I have Big Medicine to tell - Grey Bird said the stranger spoke Shoshone words during the fever!" Buffalo Sky, the Elders and all the warriors are shocked and surprised. Everyone turns their gaze to Yuji. The Chief watches Yuji for a couple of moments then speaks, "The stranger speaks the white man's tongue. Jumping Horse will talk with him so we can learn." The Chief waves his arm to beckon Jumping Horse who comes and sits down beside Yuji. Buffalo Sky leans toward Jumping Horse, "Ask who he is? - And where is his tribe?" Jumping Horse turns to face Yuji and opens his mouth in English, "Tell us about yourself? Where do you come from? Who are your people?" Yuji's eyes light up at hearing English. He looks at Jumping Horse, "I was five years old when a white man, Blake Connors, found me wandering alone in the brush. I lived at the Stage Coach Station in Emerson, and looked after the horses." Jumping Horse translates what Yuji said and The Chief, Elders and all the braves listen intently. Then Jumping Horse asks Yuji, "Where is your family? Where are your people?" Yuji replies, "All I remember is getting separated from my mother and big sister. I remember some Indian words they spoke." Jumping Horse translates again and Buffalo Sky asks, "What Indian words can he speak?" Jumping Horse turns to question Yuji, "Speak the Indian words you know." Yuji opens his mouth slightly and pauses - he glances around at all the warriors - then he blurts out, "Bia'- Ape'- Sadee'- Bambi - Baa'." Buffalo Sky, the Elders and everyone are totally stunned. The men turn to each other in shock, an Elder comments, "He speaks our tongue - Shoshone!" All the men in the tepee are spell-bound, their eyes riveted on Yuji. The Chief motions to Jumping Horse, "Ask how he became lost?" The brave relays the question, "How did you get lost? Do you remember?" Yuji lowers his eyes and stares at the flickering flames of the fire and begins to speak, Jumping Horse translates each line Yuji utters, "Bad men attacked our village. My mother, sister and I ran to hide in the tall grass. Mother told me don't make a sound. The bad men found us - so we ran as fast as we could through the tall grass. They were ahead but I could not keep up. Suddenly, they were gone! I could not see them anymore, so I hid in the grass a long time and stayed quiet. Then, I wandered for a long time. - Blake Connors found me by a river bank, picked me up and carried me to town. There, I lived in the big horse barn." The entire tepee is hushed and silent - everyone transfixed by Yuji's story. Jumping Horse makes eye contact with Buffalo Sky, then asks, "How did you come to us from the white man?" Yuji turns toward Jumping Horse and replies, "When I was twelve years old, a Japanese man named Takeshi hired me as farm help. But he became as a father to me. Over the years, I learned his Japanese ways and language. Later, Takeshi taught me his ancient Ninja skills." As Jumping horse translates - everyone is fascinated. The Chief motions to Jumping Horse, "What is Ninja?" The Shoshone interpreter asks Yuji, "The Chief and Elders want to know - what is Ninja?" Yuji scans the tepee. All eyes are on him, Yuji replies, "Ninja is from a land very far away called Japan. You travel many days on a large boat over a great water called the ocean. Ninja skills were born in the Iga Mountains. Ninja is called the Secret Way!" Jumping Horse translates Yuji's account and all the men are enthralled. Buffalo Sky requests Jumping Horse enquire of the stranger, "Tell us of Ninja?" As he speaks and Jumping Horse translates into Shoshone, Yuji tells the history of the Ninja Clans that lived in the Iga Mountains of Japan. The Ninja developed their fighting skills and guarded their Ninja knowledge and secrets for generations. A mighty Warlord made a surprise attack on their villages. Four thousand Ninja fought against forty thousand soldiers. Overpowered and greatly outnumbered, the remaining Ninja escaped and scattered across the country taking their special knowledge with them to keep it secret. The Japanese man, Takeshi, was the last of his Ninja Clan. He searched for someone to pass on his Ninja skills. Takeshi found me and trained me to become a Ninja! Yuji turns to look at the Chief and Elders, then looks at Jumping Horse, "When I learned all he taught - Takeshi made me a Ninja Master, and gave me all his Ninja possessions, weapons and ancient scrolls." The entire tepee sits in a long hushed silence, then, an Elder stands up and comes over to Yuji and closely examines his facial features and appearance. The Elder turns about for all in the tepee to see and hear, "His Shoshone tongue has been buried living in the white man's town. My heart tells me he is Shoshone. His moccasins have found their way home to his people." Buffalo Sky stands up, smiles broadly and lifts his arms and proclaims, "We must celebrate and dance - a lost Shoshone boy has returned to us - a strong young man!" Everyone stands. The Chief, Elders and assembled warriors yell Shoshone victory cries of celebration! Yuji looks about as he stands still and silent.

CHAPTER TWENTY
Shoshone Camp Celebration

A huge bonfire lights up the night sky. All the Shoshone, both young and old, gather to celebrate Yuji's return. The drums beat, the singers chant, and the people dance - there is food, fun and festivity all about. The children play games and enjoy treats. Young warriors dance with young maidens, and Buffalo Sky and the Elders watch the special event with gladness. Yuji stands next to Jumping Horse, Bear Claw and Eagle Feather; the young man looks out at the celebration and remarks, "I have never been treated like this by so many!" Jumping Horse smiles and replies, "You were lost little brother, now, you are among your people." As the night goes on, many villagers come up to Yuji to welcome him - old folks, children, warriors, maidens, young braves, and Elders. Yuji politely smiles and nods as the people show their support and acceptance.

The following day, Yuji sits with Bear Claw, Thunder Cloud and Jumping Horse as they begin to teach him Shoshone words and customs. Bear Claw would point to an object and speak the Shoshone word and Yuji would attempt the pronunciation. Yuji would repeat each word until Bear Claw would grin satisfaction. Thunder Cloud would take Yuji around the village to identify things and Yuji would try to sound out the word as Bear Claw and Jumping Horse encouraged him.

Early one morning, Bear Claw rises and exits the tepee and walks through the village until he abruptly stops and watches transfixed. In the rays of the morning sun - Yuji practices his swordsmanship handling the Katana blade with amazing moves of speed, agility and skill. The expression on Bear Claw's face shows that he's greatly impressed and he quietly moves on not to disturb Yuji's Ninja discipline.

Life in the Shoshone camp is pleasant and peaceful, and Yuji becomes well-adjusted to the daily routines. It is on his walks about the village that Yuji begins to notice Bright Star. One afternoon, they happen to be near one another as people watch the children play a game. It is on that occasion that Yuji and Bright Star exchange interested glances and shy smiles. One morning, Bright Star strolls along the riverbank and stops to admire some water Lillies - Yuji notices and wades into the river and reaches his hand into the water to pick out a beautiful flower from the surface. He climbs out of the river and comes up to Bright Star and offers her the lovely flower. Bright Star takes the Lilly and gives Yuji a sweet smile. From that day onward, the villagers would often see the young man and the young maiden walking together. One day, Eagle Feather and Gold Flower stand outside their tepee and see Bright Star and Yuji together. Eagle Feather has a proud smile.

CHAPTER TWENTY-ONE
Chief And Elders Want To See Ninja

Yuji sits with Chief Buffalo Sky and the Elders; Bear Claw, Thunder Cloud, Eagle Feather, Two Knives, and Jumping Horse are also present. Jumping Horse turns to Yuji to ask, "The Chief and Elders want to see Ninja" Yuji replies, "I can show them and the whole camp tomorrow." Jumping Horse relays the message and Buffalo Sky and the others briefly talk; when they finish - The Chief looks at Jumping Horse and nods approval. Jumping Horse informs Yuji, "The whole village will be there." Yuji glances around at the Chief and others and politely smiles and nods to them, "Ask the Chief to pick out your ten best warriors to fight me." Jumping Horse speaks Yuji's request and Buffalo Sky and the other men look oddly at Yuji. The Chief turns to Jumping Horse, "Tell him there is great danger in what he asks! Does he know this?" Jumping Horse translates the Chief's question and Yuji replies, "Make sure you select your strongest fighters. Tomorrow, you will see what my Master, Takeshi, taught me." Hearing from Jumping Horse, all eyes fix on Yuji - Buffalo Sky glances around the gathered men - then nods agreement. Yuji stands to his feet and bows respectfully to the Chief and the Elders, then exits the tepee. After Yuji has gone - Buffalo Sky turns to Bear Claw with an inquisitive look and asks in all seriousness, "What he asks is very strange. Did he hit his head fighting the wolves?" Bear Claw responds with a puzzled grin, "No. He did not injure his head - I also do not understand what he asks?!" Chief Buffalo Sky dismisses the assembly and everyone leaves. Alone in the large tepee, Buffalo Sky stares quietly at the fire.

The next day, the entire camp is assembled, all the villagers from the youngest to the oldest watch with interest and excitement. Ten of the best and most capable Shoshone warriors stand ready; armed with knives, tomahawks, war clubs and spears. Buffalo Sky and the Tribe's

Elders watch from their vantage point. Yuji emerges from his tepee dressed in his Ninja outfit and walks to the large clear area and stands in the middle. He looks at Jumping Horse, "Tell them to attack me with their weapons." Jumping Horse shouts out the instructions. The villagers are a buzz at hearing such words. Yuji nods to Jumping Horse and the brave shouts aloud, "Attack!" The warriors yell war cries and each with weapon in hand, begin to move and circle the lone defender. Yuji looks around and assesses each attacker's weapon and position. He takes a Ninja battle stance. All eyes are glued to the impending action. Suddenly, one of the bigger braves runs at him and lunges with a knife. Yuji grabs the brave's arm and throws him high in the air to land head first in the dirt. Another warrior attacks with a raised tomahawk. Yuji blocks the tomahawk swing, grabs the man's arms, rolls backward and catapults him through the air to land hard yards away. Thud! Buffalo Sky, the Elders and Bear Claw and warriors are amazed at Yuji's speed and agility. Yuji pivots and scans about just as two braves attack at the same time, one from the front, the other from the back. Yuji quickly spins and kicks one attacker to knock him out; then Yuji turns and pummels the other attacker with a barrage of rapid blows that immobilize him - Yuji takes the knife from his hand and tosses it away. By now, the entire camp are wide-eyed and totally captivated. The six remaining warriors glance at each other and attack in a rage with loud shouts and war cries. Bright Star is worried that Yuji may become harmed. Eagle Feather and Gold Flower see her concern. As the six braves launch their attack, one brave throws a spear at Yuji who catches the spear by the shaft, twirls it to strike another brave unconscious. One brave wildly swings his war clubs and Yuji ducks and dodges the assault. Yuji moves in to block and deliver punches to drop the brave to the ground. The last three warriors lunge toward the lone fighter. Yuji jumps high to kick and knock out two braves! He lands and puts the last brave in a sleeper hold until the warrior stops struggling and passes out. Yuji lets him fall to the ground. Yuji stands alone and victorious in the middle of the battle area; the ten braves are beaten, bruised and defeated, their weapons lay in the dirt. Buffalo Sky, the Elders, Bear Claw, Thunder Cloud, Two Knives and Jumping Horse are all stunned and excited after witnessing such an incredible fight. The Chief looks at Jumping Horse, "Bring him before us." The brave fetches Yuji and brings him in front of Buffalo Sky. The Chief motions to Jumping Horse, "Ask if he will teach our warriors to fight his way?" Jumping Horse conveys the Chief's request and Yuji bows low before the Chief and Tribe's leaders, "Shoshone warriors saved my life! Tell the Chief and Elders that I will pick Shoshone braves to train as Ninja." Jumping Horse smiles and gladly translates Yuji reply. Hearing Yuji's answer, Buffalo Sky steps forward and looks into the young man's eyes, the Chief slowly speaks, "N - in - ja! Nin - ja! Ninja!" Yuji bows, smiles and replies. "Aho! Ninja." At that moment, Bear Claw reaches into his beaded buckskin tunic and brings out a large black eagle feather and offers it to Yuji. Yuji takes the black feather and admires its beauty and quality. Jumping Horse leans near Yuji and comments, "Bear Claw has greatly honoured you! The Black Feather is only given to our very best warrior." Yuji exchanges eye contact with Bear Claw and Yuji bows very low before him. Yuji remarks, "Osereirimasu! My highest thanks to you." Yuji turns and walks away and returns to his tepee. As he passes by the villagers, they stare at him in awe and wonder.

CHAPTER TWENTY-TWO
Young Romance

It's a beautiful summer day with blue skies and puffy white clouds. Bright Star and Yuji walk by the river appreciating some uninterrupted moments together. Yuji picks a pretty flower and gives it to Bright Star. She brings the flower close and smells its fragrant scent and looks at Yuji with a delighted smile. Then they continue to walk side by side along the riverbank. Later in camp as Bright Star lifts a water jug, Yuji comes up and takes the water jug and carries it for her. And during chores and activities in the village, Yuji looks over at Bright Star whenever he can. Because of Shoshone rules between young braves and young maidens, Bright Star and Yuji can only give one another shy smiles whenever they pass each other. As Bright Star sits with the other young maidens, she watches him with reserved affection. On one afternoon, Yuji approaches Bright Star and stands before her and holds out a lovely beaded necklace. Bright Star's eyes widen at seeing the fine decorative piece. He looks at her, nods and extends the necklace toward her. She clasps the pretty item and puts it over her head to wear. Bright Star's delight is very apparent and she beams with happiness. After some weeks have passed, Yuji eats the evening meal with Eagle Feather, Gold Flower and Bright Star. Gold Flower knows Yuji is hungry and gives him generous portions. As he devours his food, Eagle Feather, Gold Flower and Bright Star grin.

CHAPTER TWENTY-THREE
Shoshone Ninja Trained And Tested

Only the sound of forest birds fill the morning air, everything else in the Shoshone camp is quiet. All able Shoshone braves stand in the open ground with space between each of them, Otter is also there. Around them the entire camp have gathered to observe this new thing brought to their tribe. Yuji stands before the warriors and walks past each one to observe his physical condition, muscle tone, and the manner he presents himself. Buffalo Sky, Bear Claw, Thunder Cloud, Eagle Feather, Two Knives, and the Elders watch from the side. The Shoshone braves stand with anticipation, their physical bodies strong and muscular, their stance tall and proud, ready to be selected to honour their tribe. Some are so filled with nervous energy they can only breathe short shallow breaths, while others stand calm and still. The villagers that ring the Tribe's candidates remain quiet, no one saying anything, no one talks, everyone wants to pay close attention to which brave will be selected. Yuji moves through the braves and makes his selection by looking into the candidate's eyes and tapping their shoulder. Yuji walks back to his central spot and slowly scans the group of young men as he ponders and thinks - then Yuji steps out and comes up to stand in front of Otter. Yuji looks directly into Otter's eyes and studies the young man, then Yuji reaches out his hand and taps Otter on the shoulder. Yuji returns to his position content he has found ten suitable braves for Shoshone Ninja training. Yuji smiles and looks over to Jumping Horse and nods success. Jumping Horse lifts his voice loud and clear for all to hear, "If your shoulder was touched - stay - all others must leave." The braves who did not have their shoulder tapped, move out in all directions and join the circle of onlookers. Yuji and the entire camp look upon the ten braves that stand intersperse in the open ground. The successful braves exchange eye contact with one another, then look at Yuji who smiles at them. Jumping Horse makes the announcement, "These are the braves to be trained by Yuji to become Shoshone Ninja warriors!" The Chief, Elders, and all the Shoshone people shout out cries of Celebration!

The Shoshone novices are assembled deep in the forest miles away from the Shoshone camp. The season of Ninja training is to commence. Yuji sits mounted on a Mustang and eyes the young men - all eager and ready. He waves his hand for them to follow and then charges through the forest with the young braves in hard pursuit. Yuji keeps the horse at a pace the braves can manage as they run over the forest trails, rugged terrain and shallow river beds. Yuji looks back to keep an eye on the trainees, the young men are challenged and tested as they try to keep up with Yuji on horseback. Yuji rides out of the trees and across the rolling grassland, the young braves are sweaty and strained, and follow a distance back. Yuji enters camp and rides to the Chief's central tepee where Buffalo Sky and the Elders are standing, he dismounts and joins them in waiting. Soon, they see a weary and worn bunch of braves slowly run toward them, many barely able to move their legs, all are winded, huffing and puffing. Finally, the braves reach Yuji and the tribe leaders - and collapse on the ground gasping for air. Yuji glances over at Buffalo Sky, the Elders, Bear Claw, Jumping Horse and the others. Yuji grins and remarks, "Good! No one abandoned. Everyone finished the run (he smiles) Now, that I know what I have, we can begin the Ninja training!" Jumping Horse translates Yuji's remarks to the leaders. Buffalo Sky and the leaders watch as the young men regain their strength and stand to their feet - alert, awaiting Yuji's instructions. the Chief and the leaders look at Yuji and nod their approval.

Over the succeeding weeks, months and years, Yuji puts the Shoshone braves through gruelling training to test their metal and to instil strength, agility and skill. Yuji has the braves lash together long branches and instructs them to stand, balance and walk along them. Many fall off. He makes them stand for hours at a time exposed to the hot sun, the driving rain and the cold of night. Some collapse to the ground, their leg muscles no longer hold them up. In a dry riverbed, Yuji instructs them to grip and carry big heavy stones to build strong arms. The Ninja Master teaches the recruits to run, jump, flip, twirl and summersault. Soon, the braves become quick and agile! Yuji instructs the braves in hand-to-hand combat. The volunteers who attack get their lumps - The other trainees playfully tease each other. Over time, the braves become skilled at combat and learn to grapple and toss their opponent, throw punches, deliver kicks, block and deflect attacks, and apply chokeholds. Sometimes, a brave gets floored during training and the others laugh and poke fun. As the seasons change, Yuji teaches the braves to make and use camouflage as Ninja strategy, white outfits for the Winter, brown clothing for the Fall, green apparel for the Spring, and black outfits for concealment night and day. As the trainees get older, stronger, tougher, Yuji makes them run through knee-high snow, swim swift flowing rivers, and run hard and long in the hot sun. On many occasions, at a grassy elevation near a waterfall, Yuji and the Shoshone trainees sit in a circle - deep in peaceful meditation. With the recruits toughened and hardened through the rigorous training - Yuji now introduces weapons. He shows them the skills and techniques to use the staff, knife, tomahawk, spear, war club, bow and arrow - and lastly, the Ninja swords. The braves begin training by using wood swords. Yuji instructs on proper stance, foot placement and balance. He teaches them to use the sword for offence and defence during battle situations. Yuji observes closely as the braves wield their wood swords to block, deflect and disarm their opponent. He watches intently as the braves swing their swords to attack, overpower and defeat their enemy. The Ninja Master is very pleased with their progress.

For the final and most important phase on training, Yuji introduces the trainees to the steel swords used for battle - the short Ninjato sword and the long Katana sword. He passes the Ninjato and Katana swords around so each trainee can see and feel each sword in his hand. Yuji carefully demonstrates the Ninja techniques and tactical skill for both swords. The recruits keenly watch as Yuji holds each sword to spin, twirl, slice and chop the blade at an imaginary enemy. One day as the recruits gather at their training ground, Yuji motions for them to follow. He leads them into the forest some distance until they arrive at a large clearing. In the centre of the vacant ground Yuji has created a homemade forge complete with bellows, tongs, anvil, hammer and a large basin of water. A few yards from the forge sits large sacks, one with iron sand and the other with chunks of coal. Near the sacks are three blocks of wood, each contains a different waterstone used to grind and polish the steel blade. Yuji steps into the middle beside the forge and he motions the trainees to fan out and sit down. As the braves sit down on the ground, Yuji lights the coals of the forge to start a fire, then he puts portions of iron sand and coal together in a metal cauldron and sets it in the flames. All the trainees carefully watch as Yuji carries out the forging operation, working the bellows to increase the heat to melt the mixture into molten metal. When ready, Yuji grabs the tongs and moves the cauldron of red hot liquid metal over to a mould set in the earth, then he pours out the molten steel into the blade-shaped cavity. Yuji repeats this process until molten metal rises to the top of the blade shaped form. The heat of the forge and the hard work makes Yuji perspire. He wipes sweat from his brow and continues. He checks the mould to inspect if the metal is ready. With tongs, he extracts the crude red hot steel from the mould and brings it to the anvil. He picks up the hammer and hits the hot metal repeatedly, hammering, striking, bending and shaping the glowing metal bar into the recognizable shape of a Katana sword. Each trainee is mesmerized to witness the sword making process. Yuji hammers the steel, returns the blade to the hot coals, removes it again and hammers it more. At times Yuji dunks the hot steel into the basin of water and steam gushes out, then he brings out the smouldering metal. After Yuji has hammered and bent the steel into the shape of a Katana sword, he stops and looks at his trainees - then he holds up the katana blade for all to see. The recruits shout cries of victory and celebration as Yuji displays the newly created sword. Over the week, Yuji and the trainees gather at the forge and the braves watch as Yuji uses the waterstones to grind and further prepare the blade. He slides and presses the blade against the waterstones to remove layers of metal to produce the edge needed for a Japanese Katana sword. Yuji closely inspects the improved finish of the steel blade, when he started out it was rough cold black metal, but after skillful use of the waterstones, Yuji now holds a gleaming highly polished Katana steel blade. He presents it for the Ninja trainees to examine - everyone is in awe.

Finally, the day arrives for the Shoshone Ninja trainees to face their ultimate test - trial by combat! The Chief and the Elders have agreed that Yuji will choose one trainee to fight and defeat five Shoshone braves. Once again, excited villagers gather to watch a special event - how a Shoshone Ninja trainee will perform in actual combat with proven warriors. There is so much anticipation in the air, it's almost palatable. The people stand in a large circle with the fighters in the middle of a wide open area. The Ninja Master walks to the group of trainees, all are poised and ready. Yuji looks into their eyes as he scans each one, with his decision made, Yuji picks Otter to do battle. At one side, Bear Claw stands with five braves selected for their prowess and fighting ability. Yuji sends in Otter. As Otter stands and faces the five braves, Yuji looks at Jumping Horse and nods. Jumping Horse cries out, "Let the contest begin!" The five braves move toward Otter and spread out. Otter takes a fighting stance and waits. As one brave runs at him with a knife, Otter sidesteps and trips the attacker sending him into the dirt. The brave jumps to his feet and violently swipes the knife blade. Otter dodges and strikes the assailant with a flurry of blows to knock him out. Then, two braves lunge in at the same time, Otter quickly spins to kick one unconscious and strikes the other with disabling blows. Otter looks at the two remaining braves, one rushes at him with a tomahawk and swings it back and forth. Otter blocks the tomahawk and wrenches the braves arm, then leans backward to catapult the attacker to hit the ground hard yards away. Otter turns toward the last attacker, a big brave with a spear. The huge brave swipes the spear tip at Otter's face to force him further and further back. Otter watches his opponent carefully. As the brave repeatedly thrusts the sharp spear, Otter quickly ducks and moves with powerful strikes to greatly stun the big brave. As the brute teeters back and forth, Otter steps up and takes the spear from his opponent's hand as the brave falls over into the dirt. Thud! Otter stands alone as the contest champion! All the people break out with Shoshone cries of victory, celebration and honour. Yuji approaches Buffalo Sky, the Elders, Bear Claw, Thunder Cloud, Two Knives, and the other leaders - they beam with pride. Yuji comes up to the Chief and leaders, bows low and lifts up with a big smile. Buffalo Sky calls Jumping Horse to tell Yuji, "Our braves can fight like you - like Ninja!" As Jumping Horse translates, Yuji remarks to Buffalo Sky, "This is **KAISHI** - **The Beginning!** Now, these new warriors can teach others." When the Chief hears Yuji's reply, he carefully attempts the pronunciation, "Kai-shi". Yuji responds, "Aho! Yes! Kaishi." Buffalo Sky smiles and remarks, "This is good! Our people can remain strong and well protected!" Yuji bows, leaves the Tribe leaders and walks over to Otter and the other trainees to congratulate and dismisses them. Each young brave is jubilant and relieved that they have passed the Final Test!

CHAPTER TWENTY-FOUR
Shoshone Ninja Graduation

The Graduation Day has arrived!

The trainees are arranged in a straight line, each kneels on a woven mat. Each dressed in a black Ninja outfit with their own Ninja sword at the side. The entire village surrounds them in silence - respectful of this solemn and special occasion. Chief Buffalo Sky, the Elders and the lead warriors observe with a deep sense of pride and satisfaction. In the open area, Yuji kneels dressed in a ceremonial kimono with a glossy lacquered red Katana sword in a wood cradle before him. Bouquets of flowers decorate the perimeter of his large mat. Yuji begins to chant and sing Japanese words as he lights incense sticks and makes five circular motions, and then bows. The Ninja Master returns upright and fastens his gaze on the row of black clad graduates before him. Yuji loudly speaks the Japanese word for trainees, "Kenshusei!" All the trainees bow and reply in unison with the Japanese word for Teacher, "Sensei!" The graduates raise themselves up. Yuji runs his eyes along the line of Shoshone young men, then he cries out the Japanese word for warrior, "Bushi." All the trainees bow a second time and together reply, "Hai!" Next, Yuji reaches out and lifts the red Katana sword from the cradle and holds it out with both arms. Each trainee grabs his sword and holds it out in front like the Sensei. Yuji loudly cries - "Ninja!" All the trainees reply in unison with the Japanese word for I pledge, "Chigiri!" Yuji makes a second declaration, "Ninja! - Ninja!" The young men reply loudly as a united group, "Chigiri! - Chigiri! Yuji holds the red Katana in both hands and bows low and remains. All the graduates with swords in both hands bow low and remain. After a moment of silence, save only the sound of the wind and forest birds chirping, Yuji raises up and rings a bronze bell to signal the young men can return upright. Yuji looks out at the graduates with a big smile, each one returns his gaze with deep respect. Yuji bows one last time and the graduates bow in return, then Yuji looks over at Jumping Horse and nods. Jumping Horse steps out from the ranks, points to the row of young men and lifts up his voice, "Today, we celebrate - we eat, sing and dance - our tribe now have Shoshone Ninja warriors!" All the camp erupts with loud cries of victory, joy and jubilation! The people and family members move out to congratulate their new warriors. This is a very special day in the history of the tribe.

CHAPTER TWENTY-FIVE
Buffalo Hunt

The villagers are busy with morning routines when Two Knives and another brave ride into Camp from the eastern grasslands. The two men ride their mounts past the tepees and head directly to the Chief's dwelling; they quickly dismount and go inside. The commotion peeks the interest and curiosity of many and soon a number of people congregate near the Chief's tepee. Within a few moments; Buffalo Sky, the Elders, Two Knives and Bear Claw emerge to face the growing crowd of men, women and warriors. Hushed comments and chatter ripple through the crowd. The Chief holds high his arm and the people become quiet. Buffalo Sky raises his voice for all to hear, "Our scouts have found the Buffalo herd - three days ride from camp." The villagers become stirred at the news. Shoshone warriors yell out hunting cries with excitement! Bear Claw exclaims, "We will kill many Buffalo. This winter, our tepees will have meat and fur." Braves from across the village gather on horseback and raise their rifles, bows and spears in the air with cheers. A warrior brings over the Chief's horse and Buffalo Sky mounts up and looks around at his people, "The Shoshone ride to hunt Buffalo!" The warriors on horses are eager and ready with their weapons. The Chief glances at his mounted braves, then he waves his arm and they all charge forward and ride out of camp. The men, women and children watch as the Hunting Party head toward the eastern grasslands.

The Shoshone braves ride across an ocean of rolling grassland stretching out as far as the eye can see. On the horizon, Buffalo Sky and the warriors see a lone figure riding toward them, soon the silhouette of horse and rider becomes more clear, everyone can recognize it is Two Knives. The veteran scout rides up to the Chief and Bear Claw, he's breathing rapidly and his eyes are energized, "The Buffalo herd is large. They graze not far away." Bear Claw turns to everyone, "We will approach quietly not to stampede the herd." Two Knives points in the direction and the Shoshone ride off. They follow Two Knives as he leads them down into a deep grassy gully where they keep moving until he lifts his arm to stop. Two Knives points to the hilltop. All the Shoshone dismount and quietly lead and walk their horses to just below the grassy ridge. As a brave holds their horse reins, Buffalo Sky and Bear Claw crawl up to peer over the crest of the gully. Before their eyes are thousands of Buffalo - enormous Bull Buffalos, female Buffalos and their small calves. The large herd graze upon the lush grass and move at a slow pace. The Chief and Bear Claw return to their horses and stand ready. The Shoshone braves grab their horse reins and await the Chief's signal. Buffalo Sky looks at Two Knives who nods. The Chief waves his arm and all the Shoshone quickly mount up and sprint their horses over the crest of the hill and descend upon the slowly moving herd in a surprise attack! The Buffalo herd becomes alarmed and swiftly run from the oncoming danger. Shoshone warriors bravely ride beside and between the huge beasts as the animals criss-cross and jostle about. The herd thunders forward making the very ground shake and tremble. Braves ride among the animals and kill the Buffalo firing their rifles, shooting their arrows and thrusting their spears. Riding among the stampeding herd is extremely dangerous and a Shoshone brave collides with a large Bison. The brave is thrown from his horse and trampled to death. The Shoshone chase the herd until Bear Claw signals enough. The Chief and braves stop and regroup. They look across the grassland and see the many fallen Buffalo - the Shoshone braves yell loud victory cries into the air. Buffalo Sky turns his gaze to his warriors, "We took many Buffalo today, but the herd took our Shoshone brother. We will remember him in our hunting songs." The braves acknowledge with head nods. Then the Chief motions and all the braves break into groups of twos and threes. They ride to their kill and begin to skin and butcher the slain Buffalo. Bear Claw looks at the Chief, "This winter, our people will be warm and have plenty of food." The Chief gently smiles as he watches the braves collect their hunt trophies, "It has always been this way! The Shoshone and the Buffalo are joined together in life." The sounds of the rejoicing hunters carry far across the plains. The Shoshone make travos and secure the poles to the horses. They pack on the butchered meat and buffalo furs to create heavy loads. The Hunting Party will travel back home at a much slower pace, the riders on horses fitted travos must ride with extra care. Buffalo Sky and the warriors beam with great happiness as they journey back to their village.

CHAPTER TWENTY-SIX
The Chetowa Of The North

Far up in the distant north, in the lands that belong to the Tribe known as the Chetowa, a raiding party on horseback are gathered outside the tepee of Chief Kicking Horse. The Chief and his son, Spotted Bird, a strong young brave, emerge from the dwelling. The son looks at his father, "We travel to new territory - past the land of the Crow." The Chief smiles, "Good hunting my son! Bring back many horses." Spotted Bird grabs the reins and jumps onto his horse and gazes down at his father, "Catches Snake and Running Dog go with us. They know the lands and say there are many horses." Spotted Bird turns about to the warriors and waves his arm. As the raiding party race off with whoops and cries of excitement, Kicking Horse and the Chetowa Elders watch as they leave camp.

On the second day, the Chetowa enter central Wyoming and the land of the Crow. The Chetowa raiding party travel across the grassy plains until they meet a small band of Crow braves. The two groups stop a distance from each other and wait. According to an ancient custom, when braves from another Indian tribe meet, there is be an exchange of gifts to signify good will and peaceful intentions. Catches Snake glances over at Spotted Dog, then moves his horse forward at a slow careful pace. At the same time, the Crow brave moves his horse forward. The Chetowa warrior and the Crow warrior slowly ride to a few yards of one another and stop. Catches Snake holds up a tomahawk and watches as the Crow brave lifts up a tobacco pipe. With the items still held high, the two warriors steer their horses until their mounts are beside each other. Catches Snake offers the tomahawk handle first and the Crow warrior extends the tobacco pipe. They both exchange items and part, each returning to their group. When Catches Snake reaches Spotted Dog and the Chetowa, they watch as the Crow braves let out whoops and cries as they ride off in the opposite direction. Catches Snake smiles, "Soon, we will enter the far lands. Fine horse are there." Spotted Dog nods, "We will take many. Our people will sing songs about us and speak our names with pride." Spotted Dog looks about and motions forward and the Chetowa resume their trek across the plains.

Two Days pass.

The Chetowa raiding party hide in the grass as Running Dog, Catches Snake and Spotted Bird spy out the camp before them. The men see only a few braves and some old men. As they study the Indian village, Spotted Bird become wide-eyed as he sees Bright Star walk from her tepee to fetch water at the river. Spotted Bird turns his head and looks at the Chetowa braves, "The maiden with silver in her hair is mine! You can pick from the others." The raiding party acknowledge the young leader's claim. Catches Snake comments, "Running Dog and I will get the horses." Spotted Bird quickly remarks, "The other braves and I will capture the maidens." The Chetowa divide into two groups, Catches Snake leads one group off while Spotted Dog and the others descend on the unsuspecting camp. In the village, the people are about their daily routines, when suddenly - they hear loud whoops, yells and war cries. The villagers look to see strange warriors bearing down on them. The women and children flee to their dwellings. Bright Star races back to her tepee. The young braves and the few old men brace to defend their village. The fighting and tussling does not last long. In the short skirmish, a zealous young brave and a stubborn old man are killed, the rest are overpowered and unharmed. Spotted Bird rides up and dismounts outside Eagle Feather's tepee. The young brave boldly enters and is confronted by Bright Star holding a knife and standing as far away as possible. Spotted Bird suddenly stops - struck by her beauty. As he strides over, she raises the knife, screams and attacks. Spotted Bird easily overpowers her and takes the knife away. He picks her up and puts her over his shoulder and exits. Outside the tepee, Spotted Bird holds Bright Star as he ties her hands. He lays her across the pony and then binds her feet with rawhide cords. Spotted Bird jumps on his horse and looks around. The other Chetowa also have captured maidens. Catches Snake and Running Dog and their group ride up with many horses in tow. The Chief's son declares, "We found good hunting! Many will sing our names around the camp fires." The raiding party let loose loud victory cries and ride off with the maidens and horses.

CHAPTER TWENTY-SEVEN

Shoshone Warriors Persue

The next day…

Chief Buffalo Sky and the Shoshone hunting party ride over the grassy crest and come into camp with their horses pulling travos piled high with meat and Buffalo furs. The Chief and the warriors are puzzled that the villagers are not greeting them with shouts of joy; instead, the people have sad expressions indicating something is wrong. As the Chief draws close to the middle of camp near the large tepee, Elders approach him with downcast faces. Buffalo Sky asks, "Why are your hearts so heavy at our return? We have much meat and furs!" An Elder steps out and looks directly at the Chief, "When you and our braves were hunting Buffalo, a raiding party stole our maidens and horses." Buffalo Sky and the warrior's expressions turn to anger and rage. Buffalo Sky cries out, "What maidens were taken?" The Elder cast his eyes down to the ground, he can barely get the words out, "They took Foxtail's oldest daughter, Singing Rain, Two Knives' sister Willow, and many others." The Elder looks at Eagle Feather, "Bright Star was also taken!" Eagle Feather, Yuji and Bear Claw are stunned by the news and rush their mounts up beside the Chief's horse. Bear Claw strongly urges, "We must send warriors after them now, before they get too far!" Buffalo Sky looks out at the gathered villagers, the women weep for their daughters, and the fathers and old people look at him with despair. Yuji speaks up, "Let me and the Shoshone Ninja help rescue the maidens." Eagle Feather adds, "I know Yuji cares greatly for Bright Star. Let him ride with me." The Chief turns to Bear Claw, "Take our warriors, Yuji and The Shoshone Ninja, and go after them. I will remain with our people for their hearts are broken." A rescue party is quickly formed as warriors run to tepees to gather weapons, clothing and provisions of food. Yuji races to his tepee, enters and grabs the Ninjato and Katana swords, bow, quiver of arrows, and some leather pouches. He exits and runs back and mounts his horse, ready to ride. Bear Claw, Eagle Feather, Thunder Cloud, Two Knives, Yuji and the Shoshone warriors assemble on horses near the Chief's tepee. Buffalo Sky emerges and lifts his arm high, "Ride swift. Be strong. Fight well. Return our daughters to us!" The Shoshone let loose loud yelps, whoops and war cries as they ride with haste and steely resolve.

Somewhere across the vast plains and rolling hills, the Chetowa warriors ride steady, their horses show fatigue. Running Dog and Catches Snake ride up beside Spotted Bird. Running Dog relays his worry, "Our horses are tired. They need water and rest." The young Chetowa leader looks at Catches Snake for his advice, "What he says his true. Our horses will need all their strength to reach our lands." Spotted Bird glances over his shoulder at the weary group, "Find water and rest the horses. Have braves see we are not being followed." Running Dog reins his horse around and sends out a scout to help find water. Next, he dispatches four braves as a rearguard. As the Chetowa continue riding, Bright Star nonchalantly looks about, with no one watching, she chews a piece of rawhide off her binding and spits it out. No one notices the piece of leather fall to the ground. The scout that Running Dog sent out, rides over a hill and sees a small stream at the bottom of the gully. The scout races back and rides up to Spotted Bird and points, "Fresh water not far!" Spotted Bird waves his hand and the Chetowa head in that direction. They reach the gully and dismount to water their horses, themselves - and then their captives.

Following in hot pursuit, the Shoshone ride hard to catch the perpetrators, their horses are tired and sweaty. They stop near some large rocks. Two Knives dismounts and walks the terrain looking for clues, he checks the tracks and notices the deep hoof impressions in the dirt. He looks at Bear Claw and the others, "They went this way. Some tracks show horses carry two people." Bear Claw reins his horse around to look at the group, "Soon, we will catch those who stole our women and horses. He glances over at Eagle Feather and Yuji, "We will bring back Bright Star and the other maidens!" The Shoshone braves launch out with renewed determination and let out yells, whoops and war cries!

The landscape changes from grasslands and rolling hills to that of higher elevation with rugged terrain. Spotted Bird and the Chetowa are now leaving Crow territory. The north highlands lay ahead in the distance. The high country forces the horses to follow closer together and move slower over the rough ground; this allows Bright Star to make eye contact with the other maidens. She shows courage to help and assure the others. As the ponies get beside each other, Bright Star gets Willow's attention and whispers, "Our warriors are not far behind. They will rescue us. Soon, we will be free." Willow and Singing Rain both nod and manage a faint smile. The Chetowa keep winding their way up the escarpment when Catches Snake rides up to the column front, "I found a good place to make camp." Spotted Bird turns to glance back at the group, "Good! We can rest and travel at sunrise." Catches Snake then leads them to the site he selected. At the spot, the Chetowa tie their horses and Running Dog makes a small fire, the surrounding rocks hide it from view. The braves set the maidens on the ground in a group and post guards to watch them. With horses and maidens secure, the Chetowa warriors relax and rest around the fire's glowing embers.

The day draws to a close and light grows dim. Bear Claw and the Shoshone try to follow the tracks but it's dusk and daylight is fleeting. Seeing is difficult and Two Knives remarks, "It is too dark for tracking." Bear Claw relies, "We will camp here, rest our horses and start fresh in the morning." The Shoshone braves dismount, tie the horses and make a camp fire. Some of the braves stand guard while the other warriors take their rest. Yuji walks up onto a rock ledge and looks out into the night, into the direction they pursue. Eagle Feather approaches, "Two Knives is our best tracker! They will not escape us. We will get Bright Star and the others." Yuji looks at the older man, "We do not know these Indians. I worry that she might be harmed." Eagle Feather positions himself beside Yuji and the two men stare out into the dark night.

The rays of the morning sun streak across the sky as the Chetowa break camp and get their horses and captives ready. Running Dog and Catches Snakes ride up and the young man remarks. "Soon, we will reach our village. Kicking Horse will be pleased at our success!" The warriors whoop in response. The raiding party promptly launch out toward their lands.

At first light, the Shoshone braves make ready their horses and weapons. Bear Claw motions to the group, "We must ride fast to catch them!" The warriors acknowledge and release strong war cries and bolt their steads forward to give chase. As the Shoshone ride over a knoll, Two Knives is off his horse and inspects the ground. He picks something up and holds it high for the others to see. Bear Claw, Eagle Feather and Yuji ride up, "Look! I've found chewed rawhide. Someone left this." He passes it to Bear Claw and he examines the small teeth marks and replies, "One of the maidens left us a sign to follow. - Hurry!" The Shoshone rally and race ahead in the direction where Two Knives points.

CHAPTER TWENTY-EIGHT

The Chetowa Camp

Spotted Bird and the Chetowa begin to see familiar terrain and landmarks as their horses get more north. Spotted Bird glances down at Bright Star slung across his horse, "Soon, you will be my squaw, cook my meals, and bear many young braves." Bright Star clenches her teeth with defiance, "I will never be your woman! My heart belongs to another." The young leader turns and looks behind, then he returns his gaze, "We will be deep in Chetowa lands. No one is behind us. Your people are far away." With his pronouncement made, Spotted Bird nudges his horse and quickens the pace. The raiding party travel down the escarpment, along a river, through a forest, and onto a large savannah - then the raiding party stop. Before them lay the sprawling Chetowa village with a great many tepees. Scores of people mill about. Chetowa villagers at the edge of camp cry out, "Spotted Bird and the warriors return!" One man tells his young son, "Run. Tell Kicking Horse and the others that our braves have returned." The lad races through the tepees and disappears. As the raiding party steer their horses through camp, villagers come out of dwellings to welcome them back. The people see the bound maidens and the many horses in tow. Spotted Bird, Catches Snake and Running Dog smile proudly. Excitement floods the camp! Soon a swarm of people follow, young people and children playfully accompany the returning warriors. Ahead at the large central tepee, Kicking Horse and the Chetowa Elders emerge from the structure and watch the procession approach. Spotted Bird and the braves stop yards away. The Chief sees the maidens and horses, "Welcome my son! We are happy to see your hunt was a success!" Spotted Bird manoeuvres his horse to display Bright Star, "I claim this one for myself. She will become my squaw!" Bright Star become feisty at his words and struggles to get free. Kicking

Horse, the Elders and the people break out laughing. The Chief remarks in a teasing manner, "This one is a wildcat! You will have much work to do." Spotted Bird grins and slaps Bright Star's behind, "She will soon learn her place." Bright Star gets fuming mad. The Elders and Kicking Horse continue to chuckle as the braves take the maidens into the tepee next door. Some of the maidens resist with shrieks and screams, but to no avail.

Inside the tepee, Spotted Bird and the braves set the maidens down and tie them together as a group. Willow, Singing Rain and Bright Star show defiance, while some of the girls cry tears. As the warriors exit the tepee, Spotted Bird looks at Catches Snake, "Have two braves outside guarding at all times." Catches Snake nods and selects two braves as guards. The others in the raiding party go off to their own tepees. Spotted Bird walks over to his Father's dwelling and steps inside. Kicking Horse and the Elders are talking when Spotted Bird enters, the Chief looks at his son, "The maidens will make good squaws for our braves." The Elders nod agreement. The young man steps closer, "I will marry the one who fights. She will bear me strong children." Kicking Horse motions his hand, "Sit with us and tell of your journey." Spotted Bird lowers himself to take a place in the circle.

CHAPTER TWENTY-NINE
The Shoshone Rescue

The Shoshone carefully travel through the strange new territory, Two Knives informs the group they are in the land of the Chetowa. He reads the trail signs and leads them to the Chetowa village. The vast camp stretches out before them, it's much larger than their Shoshone camp back home. Bear Claw, Thunder Cloud, Eagle Feather and Yuji hide and spy to gather information. From the high elevation, they see the braves that guard the dwelling beside the large central tepee. The Shoshone rescuers decide to wait until just before sunrise to free the maidens. During the early twilight hours, the Shoshone get ready to enact their plan while it's still dark. Bear Claw looks at the others, "Thunder Cloud and I will scatter their horses." Yuji replies, "Eagle Feather, the Ninja warriors and I, will free Bright Star and the others." Bear Claw nods and the Shoshone split into two groups and strike out. Bear Claw's group sneak up near the big horse coral, and Two Knives and Thunder Cloud knock out the sentries. The Shoshone braves remove the thorn barricades to create a wide opening. Bear Claw and his group enter the horse compound to scare and stampede the horses by waving hands and bows. The large horse herd spook and race off toward camp. Bear Claw turns to the group, "We must rejoin with Eagle Feather and the others." Meanwhile, Yuji, Eagle Feather and the Shoshone Ninja sneak through the camp, quietly moving past tepee after tepee. They avoid detection and silence any encountered Chetowa. Their group reach within a few feet of the maiden's tepee. Suddenly, loud cries and yells fill the air, "Horses are loose! The horses are getting away. Everybody help!" There's mayhem and confusion as the horses stampede through the Chetowa camp. People exit tepees and try to stop the runaway horses. When the sentries at the maiden's tepee get distracted, Yuji and a Ninja warrior knock out the guards.

Bright Star and the maidens hear the commotion outside and become frightened. Suddenly, the entry flap lifts and Yuji appears. Bright Star breaks into an overjoyed smile. The other girls are happy and relieved as Yuji, Eagle Feather and a Shoshone brave untie them. The Shoshone Ninjas stand guard outside. Eagle Feather looks at the maidens, "We must hurry! Bear Claw has troubled their horses so we can escape." The group quickly exit the tepee. The entire camp is in turmoil and chaos. Chetowa braves attempt to capture their valuable loose horses. In the confusion, the rescue party sneak through the tepees in the dark. Coming around some dwellings at the edge of camp, they run into a group of Chetowa warriors who attack! Yuji and the Shoshone Ninja swiftly defeat the Chetowa with their Martial Arts skills. With the woods nearby, the Shoshone escape into the forest and rendezvous with Bear Claw, Thunder Cloud, Two Knives and the others. Together and reunited, the Shoshone steal away. The Chetowa braves are busy everywhere, cornering and collecting their all important mounts. Spotted Bird bolts into the tepee and sees it empty, the maidens are gone - he exits in a screaming rage! Kicking Horse and Chetowa warriors quickly rally around, "I will not loose my prized woman! We must ride out now." The Chief turns to Catches Snake, "Assemble our warriors. We will hunt them down and reclaim the maidens." Chetowa warriors run to tepees to collect weapons and provisions and then rally back, mounted and ready to ride. Running Dog and others yell loud yelps and war cries! The shroud of twilight gives way to the light of the early morning sun. Kicking Horse climbs up and spins his horse around and lifts the War Lance high in the air. The Chetowa war party ride off with a vengeance!

The Shoshone rescuers race through Chetowa lands, speeding through forests, crossing rivers and climbing high plains. Bear Claw and Two Knives use their wilderness skills and tricks to cover their horse tracks. Next, Two Knives and some others create a false trail to misdirect the pursuers. As the rescue party press on, they go over rolling hills, plains, rivers and flat-top buttes. Yuji and Bright Star ride beside each other. The pretty maiden speaks softly, "My heart was glad to see you!" Yuji's eyes his sweetheart, "Your freedom and safety mean everything to me." Bright Star reaches out to touch Yuji's arm.

Behind them.

Catches Snake and Running Dog examine the ground for clues. Running Dog finds a mountain shrub with a broken branch. He stands and points in that direction. Kicking Horse, Spotted Bird and the

Chetowa resume their chase. The Chetowa ford streams, ride down ravines and across grassy plains. Their pursuit stops at a stream - the trail cold. Catches Snake slowly rides his horse into the middle of the shallow stream and studies the riverbed - he suddenly stops. Mossy rocks are overturned. He looks over to Kicking Horse and points down the stream, "They went this way! Their horses turned over the rocks." Kicking Horse waves his arm and the War Party ride their horses into the water and follow the stream.

Up ahead.

The Shoshone gallop over hills and through ravines until they find a pond to water their horses and quench their thirst. Bear Claw climbs up onto the rocks to view the land ahead. The elevation descends toward the lower grasslands and wide open plains. He comments to those nearby, "We will cross the land of the Crow. They may stop us." When the horses have drank their fill and everyone has been refreshed, the Shoshone mount up and ride out. Travelling the lower grasslands, Two Knives brings his mount alongside Yuji and Eagle Feather, "That was the last water hole until we reach our border." Eagle Feather remarks, "We must not push our horses past their strength. Without water the horses will die." Yuji looks at Eagle Feather, "If what Two Knives said is true - the Chetowa will also water their horses there." Eagle Feather nods, "Yes! The other water holes are in Crow lands. Why do you speak this?" Yuji chimes, "Eagle Feather, follow me." Yuji and Eagle Feather gallop up to Bear Claw at the front of the group. Bear Claw sees Yuji's expression, "Is something wrong Yuji?" The Ninja Master replies, "I have an idea to slow down those who chase us!" Bear Claw asks, "What is it?" Yuji replies, "Let me and Eagle Feather return to the last water hole. There is something I must do." The Leader scans around at the group, "We will move at a steady pace not to strain the horses. When you finish - quickly join us." Yuji nods, and he and Eagle Feather ride off in the direction they came from, going past the group. As Yuji rides past Bright Star, they exchange glances. Eagle Feather and Yuji ride hard and retrace their trail back to the watering hole. Approaching close to the water hole, they quietly make their way to the site. They scan about and see no one is there - it's safe! Yuji swiftly dismounts and goes to the edge of the pond. He reaches into the pouch on his side and brings out a handful of black powder and scatters it across the water. The black dust sits momentarily on the surface then dissolves into the water. He turns and looks at Eagle Feather who is dismounted with his ear to the ground, "Riders are not far away. We must leave now!" Yuji and Eagle Feather jump on their horse and gallop off in haste.

In a distance behind, Spotted Bird and Kicking Horse lead the Chetowa onward. Up ahead, Catches Snake and Running Dog search for tracks. Catches Snake waves his arm to follow. Before long, the Chetowa War Party ride over the ridge and down to the pool of water. The horses are sweaty and tired, the braves are weary and worn out from the chase. The pond is not large enough for all the horses and warriors. While the first group gather around the pond, Kicking Horse, Spotted Bird and the others wait. As the horses and warriors drink long and hard to quench their thirst - suddenly, the front legs of one horse buckle - another horse lets out a loud neigh and keels over to fall on a brave. Within seconds, other horses collapse to their knees. A number of braves begin to crumple over grabbing their stomach and groaning - a few vomit! Kicking Horse runs to the pond and waves his arms, "Stop! Don't drink! The water's bad." Spotted Bird and Catches Snake examine the fallen horses and ill warriors. Catches Snake shakes his head, "These cannot ride! We must find other water before going on." Spotted Bird become frustrated and agitated, "The Shoshone are ahead - we can catch them!" Running Dog comes beside the young leader, "Without water - our horses and warriors will have no strength to fight. We must find water." Spotted Bird reluctantly agrees and mounts his horse. The Chief looks at the warriors, "Catches Snake and Running Dog will find us water. We will follow them." Kicking Horse orders the braves and horses that became ill to stay behind at the pond. Catches Snake and Running Dog start to head north, opposite the direction of the chase, the Chetowa war party wearily plod behind. After a number of hours, Catches Snake and Running Dog find a small waterfall. The Chetowa quench their parched throats and liberally water the horses. The warriors are bone tired and rest a good while. Watching the group lay about idle and still, Spotted Bird grows impatient and strides into their midst and looks about, "We must hurry to catch them!" The young man looks over at his father, "They are getting away!" Kicking Horse sees the anguish in Spotted Bird's face, the Chief grabs his horse's mane and mounts up, "Get on your horses - we ride!" The Chetowa warriors quickly rise and get on their horses and race off with Kicking Horse and Spotted Bird leading them.

CHAPTER THIRTY

The Rescue Party In Crow Lands

Bear Claw and the Shoshone cross the Great Plain grasslands - an expanse of rolling hills and vales. They are in the bottom of a vale and ride slow and steady when a group of Crow braves ride over the hill crest. The Crows stop on the grassy ridge and study the travelling Shoshone. Bear Claw spots the Crow party and turns to the others, "Stay clam and do not act hostile. They must see we only want to pass through." The Crow braves yell whoops and yelps as they ride down the slope and gallop circles around the slow moving group. The Shoshone stop and remain calm as Bear Claw instructed. The Crow regroup and approach - they halt their horses a hundred yards away. Both Indian groups study each other. Then the Crow leader rides forward and stops thirty feet away. Bear Claw raises his arm high with an open palm - and slowly rides out and stops ten feet from the Crow brave. The two warriors look at one another. Bear Claw lifts up his beaded buckskin pouch over his head and offers it to the Crow brave. The Crow warrior scrutinizes Bear Claw, then the Crow brave offers his bone handle hunting knife. Bear Claw gently nods and slowly moves his horse forward, and the Crow brave slowly moves his horse ahead. As the two reach side by side, Bear Claw extends the beaded pouch and the Crow warrior offers the bone knife at the same time. Both men exchange their traded items. The Crow brave sprints off to rejoin his friends, and they ride up over the ridge and disappear. Bear Claw returns to the Shoshone group, "It is safe now. They will not bother us." The Shoshone warriors and maidens resume their trek home.

CHAPTER THIRTY-ONE
Guns and Gold

Cutter and his gang rob an overland stage coach. The outlaws point their pistols and rifles at the driver, shotgun and five passengers; the Eastern travellers are scared out of their wits. One outlaw climbs onto the stage coach and shoves the big strongbox off the roof. Thud! He jumps down and shoots off the lock and pries open the lid and looks inside - Empty! Cutter walks over and stares at the empty hollow interior and becomes angry. He points his gun at the driver's head and pulls back the hammer, "Where's the gold, ole' timer?" The man gripped with fear can barely get the words out, "The Mine sent it by train! The owners decided last minute." One bandit can hardly believe it, "What - No Gold?!" The badmen become livid and starts to murmur and complain. Cutter turns to his gang, "Well boys, you know what to do!" Cutter pivots and shoots the driver square in the forehead. The outlaws begin to empty their guns and rifles killing all. The bodies of the shotgun, three women and two male passengers are riddled with bullets. Cutter and the gang look at the bloody mess with cold callous eyes. Cutter motions his arm and the outlaws ride off.

CHAPTER THIRTY-TWO
Shoshone Take The Long Way

The Shoshone wake up from a good night's sleep. Bear Claw and Two knives are bent down over a patch of earth as Two Knives draws in the sand, "This is the route ahead. We pass too close to the Crow village. Dangerous!" Thunder Cloud looks at the sand markings, "Is there another route away from the Crow?" Two Knives glances up at his friend and draws another line in the sand, "There is another way, but it will take longer." Bear Claw studies the two drawings with a pensive look - then stands up, "Better to avoid the Crow and take the longer route!" Two Knives adds, "The longer way will be safer for our maidens." They all agree and go to mount their horses. Atop his stead, Bear Claw looks at everyone, "We take the longer route to go around the Crow. We cannot risk any trouble in their lands." The Shoshone braves and maidens get on their horses and they head out as Bear Claw and Two Knives lead the way.

Across the plains, Kicking Horse and the Chetowa race to cover ground to make up for lost time. Ahead in the distance, Catches Snake and Running Dog find Shoshone tracks. The large Chetowa war party quicken their pursuit across the grassy plains and over wilderness streams. The Chetowa group see Catches Snake and Running Dog stop. Upon approach, Kicking Horse and the warriors find evidence of a recent camp. The Chief turns to Catches Snake, "Tell us where they went?" The brave examines the tracks - then points West, "The Shoshone circle the Crow. Their fire is not old, we are not far behind." Kicking Horse turns to his warriors, "Soon, we will catch them - slay their braves and recapture the maidens." The Chetowa War Party sound out loud yells, whoops and war cries. The group ride out with great urgency.

Up ahead.

The Shoshone trek over some rugged terrain going slow, careful not to injure their horses' ankles. When the group reach rolling grasslands, they resume their regular pace as they ride over a seemingly endless expanse of grass. Two Knives scouts ahead and rides his horse to the top of a grassy elevation.

Running Dog and Catches Snake suddenly spot Two Knives on a distant ridge and alert the Chief, "They're up ahead! Kicking Horse and the Chetowa warriors spurn their mounts on with loud war cries!

Two Knives scans the direction from which they come - he's shocked! The Chetowa War Party ride toward them. Two Knives reins his horse around sprints down the slope to the others and cries, "The Chetowa are riding toward us!" Bear Claw yells out, "Everyone! Quick, ride! We must outrun them!" The alarmed Shoshone bolt their horses forward, the Shoshone ride hard eating up the ground.

The Chetowa chase the Shoshone across the plains. Bright Star, Willow and Singing Rain are afraid. Bear Claw, Thunder Cloud, Eagle Feather and Yuji ride beside them to encourage them on. Two Knives rides ahead and sees a grove of trees and brush to the left, he turns to Bear Claw and points and goes in that direction. The Shoshone steer their horses toward the cluster of trees. Riding into the grove, Bear Claw motions the group to stop. He sizes things up, "Take the maidens to the middle of the grove for safety. We will strike as they approach." He turns to his good friend Two Knives, "Ride to our people and get our warriors!" Two Knives nods and quickly races his mount through the trees and out the other side of the grove. Yuji comes beside Bear Claw, "The Shoshone Ninja and I will ambush them." Bear Claw nods agreement and the Shoshone braves take positions in the outer trees. Eagle Feather's group reach the middle of the grove - there's a clearing with a large pond of water. They dismount and tie the horses and ready their weapons. Eagle Feather steps over to Bright Star and the other maidens, "Take this rifle, these knives and tomahawks for defence." Bright Star grabs the rifle with resolve, "They will not take us without a fight!" The maidens grab weapons and stand ready. In the perimeter trees, the Shoshone hold their positions. The air fills with loud Chetowa war cries and battle screams. Bear Claw and the other braves watch from the woods.

The Chetowa thunder toward them - suddenly, Kicking Horse lifts up his lance and the riders stop. The war party halt a good distance out from the tree grove. The Shoshone look out at their pursuers - the Chetowa warriors poised for battle, their horses snort and paw the ground. Kicking Horse and the Chetowa observe the grove for movement within - nothing but an eerie stillness. Catches Snake remarks, "The Shoshone are hiding - waiting for us." The Chief ponders his warrior's words, then turns to a seasoned brave on his left and raises his lance, "Take a small group into the trees." The brave nods and waves those around him to ride forth. As the Chetowa riders approach the trees, the braves are met with rifle fire and arrows - most are killed except a few. The surviving Chetowa scurry back to rejoin the war party. Kicking Horse orders, "We will divide our braves and attack from two sides." The Chief signals and the Chetowa divide into two groups. Catches Snake leads a group to the left and Spotted Bird takes a group to attack the right. Within the trees, Bear Claw sees what the Chetowa are planning to do, "I will take braves to the left. Yuji - take your fighters to the right." Both Shoshone groups quickly disperse and rapidly run to their section of the trees. Outside the grove, the two Chetowa forces reach their position. Bear Claw and the Shoshone braves stand ready to stop Catches Snake and his group. On the opposite side of the trees, Yuji and the Shoshone Ninja are poised against Spotted Bird's warriors. Chief Kicking Horse and the remaining Chetowa warriors observe from a distance. The Chief lifts his spear and the two groups ride full force into the trees. As Catches Snake and his warriors ride into the grove, they are met with rifle fire, arrows and spears from Bear Claw and his braves. Yuji's fighters jump from trees, rocks and bushes to attack with swords, knives, metal stars and tomahawk - their Ninja skills have deadly accuracy. The two Chetowa groups suffer heavy casualty and retreat to rejoin Kicking Horse and the warriors. Catches Snake rides his horse up and the Chief notices the arrow in the braves's right thigh. Catches Snake grimaces and breaks off the arrow shaft, "The trees give them protection!" Kicking Horse studies the grove then turns to his warriors, "We will burn them out. Make ready your fire arrows!" Spotted Bird, Running Dog and others start small fires. The Chetowa warriors wrap grass and cloth strips around arrow heads, then dips them into the fire. With arrow ablaze, the Chetowa warriors tilt back, bend their bows and shoot flaming arrows into the trees. Bear Claw, Yuji and the others watch as flaming arrows land in the branches, trees and grass around them. With too many arrows to put out, Bear Claw, Yuji and the Shoshone braves run to the middle where Eagle Feather and the maidens are. They look around in all directions. Fire rages in the trees and grass, the flames moving toward them. Bear Claw and Thunder

Cloud untie the horses to let the animals escape through the trees. Some braves show deep worry. Some maidens start to cry. Bear Claw is at his wits end as he sees walls of flame creeping toward them. Yuji looks at the pond and the reeds near the water's edge. He quickly runs over and pulls out a reed and cuts off both ends. All the Shoshone are puzzled by his action. Yuji looks at them, "Watch me and do the same!" Yuji jumps in and wades to the middle of the pond until he stands chest deep. He puts one end of the reed in his mouth and submerges and leaves the reed's open end above the water. A few seconds later he rises dripping wet. The Shoshone are stunned! Bear Claw is perceptive and yells, "Do like Yuji - cut reeds to stay under the water." Yuji lets everyone know, "Breathe through the reed. You can stay under the water and escape the fire!" As Yuji guides, the Shoshone swiftly cut reeds and enter the pond to the middle. They look around - the surrounding trees and grass are an inferno. At Yuji's signal they submerge under the water. A few braves and maidens swallow water - panic and stand. Yuji helps them to keep the reed at the right position to breathe. At last, all the Shoshone are under the water and safe! The fire burns the grove interior and everything is ablaze. Flames lick at the water's edge. The fire and smoke rise high in the air.

Kicking Horse and the Chetowa warriors watch the fire consume the grove, all the trees burning with fire, the flames shooting high in the air. When the fire dies down, all that remains are charred trees and scorched earth. Catches Snake, Running Dog and Spotted Bird ride up and are surprised to see no Shoshone - just blacken stumps and smouldering ground. The young tribe leader questions aloud, "Where did the Shoshone go" How did they escape?" The Chetowa warriors cannot believe their eyes and start to wonder aloud and murmur. Running Dog races his horse around the burnt grove and spots fresh horse tracks. He points, "Their horse tracks go this way!" Kicking Horse and the war party launch out in hot pursuit to follow Running Dog. The Chetowa war party disappear over the hill top.

A few moments pass...

Yuji lifts his head out of the water just enough to peer about. All around is burnt black with pockets of smouldering ground. Yuji taps Eagle Feather and Bear Claw to rise. The Shoshone braves and maidens stand up in the water and gaze around. The once green lush tree grove now nothing but black burnt ruins - and no Chetowa in sight. The group quickly stride out of the pond - everyone safe - everyone dripping wet. Bear Claw turns to his people, "We head for our Tribal lands on foot!" They all exchange quick glances and run out of the charred area and head south - toward home.

The Shoshone race across the grasslands. The pace is hectic, the braves assist whenever a maiden stumbles or falls down. The weary rescue party move at a steady rate going through the afternoon and into the evening. The sun sets and a full moon appears at night, its moonlight illuminates the ground. Bear Claw coaxes their travel through the night hours, and they take breaks whenever they get too tired.

As the sun rises, the braves and maidens walk in the early morning light. The group travel down the middle of a large grassy vale. All at once they hear yells, screams and war cries! The Shoshone turn about and see the Chetowa warriors off in the distance thundering toward them. The people look at Bear Claw, "We cannot outrun their horses. We make our stand here!" The Shoshone braves take forward positions to face the oncoming threat. The maidens move behind their warriors for protection. All the Shoshone stand ready with weapons in hand. Yuji glances at Bright Star, "Stay near me, I will protect you!" Bright Star grips Yuji's arm as the Chetowa warriors get closer and louder. Kicking Horse and Spotted Bird steer their horses to the side to stop and observe the battle. The encroaching first wave of Chetowa warriors let loose their arrows and spears. The Shoshone dodge and duck the barrage. Some arrows wound a couple of Shoshone braves. Oncoming Chetowa warriors ride up and leap from their horses and attack with tomahawks, knives and war clubs. The Shoshone Ninja repeal the assault - the fighting is intense. Yuji and the Shoshone Ninja use swords, tomahawks, chain darts and stars to cut down the attackers. The Chetowa are overpowered and destroyed by hand-to-hand combat. The Shoshone defeat all their attackers. They catch their breath and get ready for another assault! Kicking Horse is shocked and angry at the loss of so many of his warriors. He raises his Lance high before the large remaining group of Chetowa braves, "Kill them all - even the maidens! Avenge our fallen warriors!" The Chetowa begin to move in mass. Bear Claw, Eagle Feather, Yuji and the Shoshone brace for the impending doom. The Chetowa charge toward the small group.

Suddenly - Multiple Gun Shots!

The Shoshone and the Chetowa turn toward the gunfire. Chief Buffalo Sky, Two Knives and hundreds of Shoshone warriors ride over the hill crest. The Shoshone braves fill the air with loud war cries, yells and battle screams! The large Shoshone force descend the grassy slope toward Bear Claw and the others. Seeing the Shoshone warriors en masse, Kicking Horse, Spotted Bird and all the Chetowa braves turn around and flee. Spotted Bird insists to fight, "Father, the maidens are there. We are so close!" Kicking Horse looks at his young impetuous son, "We will not fight so many this far from home! - Quick! We return to our lands." The Chetowa war party bolt their horse and dash away putting distance between them and the big Shoshone war party. The small Shoshone rescue group break out in victory cheers! Buffalo Sky and the Shoshone braves ride up, and Bear Claw conveys his gratitude, "You brought our warriors in time!" The Chief replies, "Two Knives rode like the wind. His horse died after reaching camp. We knew you were in trouble." The Shoshone rescuers rejoice with big smiles, happy to be safe. The Shoshone braves hoist the rescuers atop their horses for the journey back to Shoshone lands. The massive Shoshone group head back home.

CHAPTER THIRTY-THREE
Yuji And Bright Star Are Married

It's a beautiful day with the sun shining in a clear blue sky. A gentle breeze flows through the trees and the meadows are filled with colourful wild flowers. Chief Buffalo Sky is in full regalia and feathered headdress. Eagle Feather wears a richly decorated tunic. The Shoshone Elders stand nearby. The entire village gather with happy faces and joyful expressions for the Wedding Ceremony. Yuji and Bright Star are getting married! Bright Star wears a soft white buckskin dress with exquisite beadwork and moccasins with fine embroidery and adorns herself with Yuji's beaded necklace. She looks like a beautiful Indian Princess! Yuji is dressed in a white kimono with detailed embroidery. He looks stately and handsome. The young couple stand before Eagle Feather and Buffalo Sky.

Eagle Feather lifts up his arm to the sky and chants a Shoshone prayer to the Great Spirit. Then he burns a bundled stalk of sweetgrass, sage and thyme - and waves the smoking bundle around the couple's heads, sides, front and back. Next, Eagle Feather joins the hands of Bright Star and Yuji together and wraps a sash of elaborate embroidery around the couple's hands, and speaks to them, "Your hands are joined together with the sacred cloth. Together in love! Together in life! - Bright Star, Yuji's tepee is now your tepee. He is your Dainah - you are his Wa'ipi! - Yuji, Bright Star is now yours to protect and care for! May your tepee be full of love, laughter, and little ones!" Eagle Feather tosses red powder in the air on all four sides of the couple. Next, he holds an eagle wing and passes it over the new husband and wife as he chants a Shoshone prayer. - Finished, Eagle Feather turns to Buffalo Sky. The Chief raises his arm and braves bring a stunning Appaloosa horse to him. The Chief passes the reins to Yuji, "We, the Shoshone people give you this handsome painted pony as a wedding gift!" Yuji bows respect. He and Bright Star stand with big smiles of joy and gratitude. The Chief lifts his hand, "Tonight, there will be a feast in honour of Yuji and Bright Star!" The villagers cheer in celebration.

As Bright Star and Yuji gaze around at the people sharing their happy occasion, Bear Claw, Thunder Cloud, Two Knives and Otter come up to the newly weds and lead the surprised couple away - the villagers follow. Bear Claw and the couple and the entourage merrily walk past many dwellings until they reach a newly constructed tepee. Bear Claw turns to Yuji and Bright Star, "The Shoshone braves and our Ninja warriors made this for your new home. Our wedding gift to you!" Yuji is humbled and bows to Bear Claw, the braves and the Ninja warriors. Bright Star's eyes sparkle as she views her new home. She's eager to enter and grabs Yuji's hand and pulls him to go inside. Bear Claw, the braves, the Shoshone Ninja, and the villagers laugh and chuckle at her excitement. Yuji looks at Bear Claw, "Bright Star wants me inside now - I must go." Bear Claw grins and jests, "The brave is the head, and the woman is the neck! Many times in life, you will find yourself being turned!" Yuji grins and waves to all as he and Bright Star enter their new home.

Two years later.

Outside his tepee, Yuji nervously paces back and forth. He stops, looks at the tepee, then begins to pace again. Eagle Feather, Bear Claw, Thunder Cloud, Two Knives and Otter grin and chuckle as they stand nearby. Yuji watches as old Shoshone women go in and out of the tepee. Yuji goes up beside the entrance to peer in and an old Shoshone woman shoes him away. He walks over to Eagle Feather, "I have faced battle - but I don't know if I'm ready for this!" Eagle Feather, his father-in-law, puts his hand on Yuji's shoulder, "You will do well." Loud cries and deep groans cause them to rivet attention at the tepee. They hear Bright Star strain - and then cry out - then silence. The men look at each other. Suddenly, the sound of a baby crying! Yuji's face lights up full of joy! He looks at the men close by and they all nod with happy smiles. The tepee flap lifts open and an old Shoshone woman waves Yuji to come inside now. Yuji enters the tepee and pauses. Bright Star is on a platform of fur robes - she's exhausted and perspiring, yet she beams with pure joy. The young mother holds her new baby! Yuji comes over and kneels beside mother and baby. Yuji is in awe! Bright Star smiles and lifts her hand to touch Yuji, "You have a son!" Yuji reaches out and tenderly lifts up his newborn and gazes at him with wonder and deep joy, "A son! I have a son!" Bright Star looks up at Yuji and baby, "What name will you give him?" Yuji softly gazes at the tiny infant in his arms, he looks at Bright Star, then looks again at the baby, "I name him - Kamatsu! It means victorious son." Bright Star replies with a sweet expression, "It is a good name!" Yuji lovingly holds the baby that's wrapped in a soft blanket and carefully exits the tepee. He carries the newborn to Eagle Feather, Bear Claw, Thunder Cloud, Two Knives and Otter to see. Yuji announces, "Bright Star and I have a son! A healthy baby boy!" The men tenderly gaze at the baby and wide smiles break out. Yuji proudly carries his newborn son back inside the tepee.

Kamatsu grows to become an adorable two year old with bright dark eyes and a cute smile to melt the heart. One afternoon, Yuji and Kamatsu are in the forest to enjoy nature. Yuji laughs as little Kamatsu chases after fluttering butterflies. In the meadow, Yuji points and shows his son a chipmunk. The little boy is so intrigued as he holds a beautiful flower in his tiny fingers. Father and son watch a bird chirp as it sits on a tree branch. Yuji shows Kamatsu some baby bunnies - it's pure fascination for the tiny tot. In the grassy meadow, Kamatsu giggles as he chases Yuji. And when Yuji chases, Kamatsu giggles some more. An afternoon of play is hard work, and the father and son take a break. Yuji lays on his back in the meadow, and the son sits on dad's tummy being playful. Suddenly, Kamatsu becomes frozen - his eyes stare ahead. Yuji notices his son's stillness and with a hand on Kamastu, he rolls over and stands to his feet. Not far away is a large black timber wolf. Instinctively, Yuji steps in front of Kamatsu to shield and protect him. He keeps one arm on the boy. Yuji reaches behind to grab his short Ninjato sword still in the scabbard. Yuji brings the sword in front to be ready. Surprised! Alarmed! Yuji scans the forest - there are no other wolves. Yuji and the big wolf lock eyes! Yuji can hear the sound of his own heartbeat quicken. Thump! Thump! Thump! Yuji and the big timber wolf lock eyes for the longest time. Then, the large animal suddenly turns and swiftly disappears into the forest. Yuji sighs relief and looks down at tiny Kamatsu who has a big smile. Yuji lifts his son onto his shoulders and heads home. As Yuji and Kamatsu enter the family tepee, Bright Star greets them with a loving smile.

CHAPTER THIRTY-FOUR

The Ninjans and Cutter's Demise

High up in the rugged mountains, Shoshone hunters and trappers trek through the forest trail, their horses laden heavy with animal furs. The quietness is shattered with gunshots from rifles and pistols. The Shoshone braves are shot off their horses and hit the ground. One brave, wounded in the shoulder, gets up and runs to escape. Bullets whiz around him but he disappears into the dense brush. Cutter and a large group of bandits emerge from hiding. The outlaws rush in to grab the horses and furs, then rob and scalp the dead Indians. The outlaws revel in the excitement. Cutter barks at his men, "Make sure those Indians are dead!" Cutter and his gang lead the fur ladened horses up the forest trail to an old abandoned mining camp. The camp has four wood buildings, Cutter and the outlaws use the large wood building as their hideout. The bandits offload the horses and store the furs inside their quarters. The afternoon sun sets and night takes over.

A day and a half pass.

Inside the large wood bunkhouse, Cutter and his men relax and gloat over their stolen bounty of horses, furs, gold and scalps. Some men drink Whiskey while other smoke cigarettes and play cards. Some are sprawled out asleep or just rest. A few clean their pistols and rifles. On the front porch outside, a bandit hangs the Shoshone scalps on a line to dry. Whoosh! Whoosh! A black arrow pierces deep into the outlaw's shoulder. In great pain, he stumbles inside shouting, "Indians! We're surrounded by Indians!" Cutter and the men grab their guns and race to the door and windows. They break the glass and aim their pistols and rifles. Whoosh! Whoosh! Black arrows rain down on the dry wood structure - hitting the door, walls and windows. Cutter and the bandits fire their guns. There's a momentary lull. Then - repeated thuds! Burning arrows strike the door, porch, roof and walls.

Flames start to spread across the dry wood building - the large cabin quickly catches fire and smoke begins to fill the room. Cutter hunkered down at a window, coughs and bellows, "Shoot your way out - Kill 'em all!"

The outlaws pour out of the hideout with guns blazing! Cutter and the outlaws try to scatter. Many are killed by sword, tomahawk, arrows and sharp metal stars. As others are being decimated, Cutter manages to reach the barn where two braves attack him. He gets sliced deep from the sword and shot with an arrow, but he manages to shoot the attackers. Greatly wounded, he stumbles out of the barn and over to a large tree where he slumps down against the trunk. He grimaces in pain! Cutter lifts up his eyes to see dark figures coming toward him. He points his gun. Click! Click! Empty! Cutter leans back against the trunk and grabs his side as blood gushes out to form a small pool. He watches the figures dressed in black get close. Their outfits - a blend of Indian and Ninja. Each warrior wears fierce war paint and bristles with deadly weapons - swords, tomahawk, knife, war club, bow and arrows. The leader comes up and stands before Cutter - It's Otter! Cutter looks at Otter from head to foot and smirks, "Indians." Otter bends down and looks Cutter straight in the eye, "Ninjans! - We are Ninjans!"

In the mountain forest, a pack of timber wolves sniff the air, the fresh scent of blood alert their appetite. Howls erupt! The wolf pack start to run. The wolf howls carry to the mining camp. Cutter turns his head to the woods, then back toward Otter and frantically pleads, "You can't leave me like this! - Not like this! Give me some bullets. Some ammo!" Otter and the other Ninjans watch stone-faced, then turn and walk away and disappear into the forest.

Cutter is gripped with raw fear! He glances about every which way. The wolf pack run past the big building littered with dead outlaws, and make straight for the wounded bleeding man. Cutter watches as the wolf pack surround him - snarling and growling. The wolves bare their sharp fangs and snap the jaws. Cutter looks in front as the big Alpha wolf creeps closer and closer, the animal's saliva drips from its open jaw and sharp teeth. Cutter grabs the pistol with his trembling hand to use it as a club. The big wolf lets out a vicious snarl - then leaps!

THE END

BLACK FEATHER

NINJANS 2

This book is dedicated
to honour my deceased parents,
Raymond and May Kwan;
who adopted me and gave their love and care.
Their example as hard working immigrants
with personal sacrifice and open generosity,
provide me with a valuable legacy
to deeply cherish and fondly remember.

Thank you Dad and Mom!

CHAPTER THIRTY-FIVE

The Ninjans Return

Otter and the fellow Ninjans stride past the perimeter trees and move deeper into the forest. After a number of paces, they stop to look back at the open clearing. Cutter, a mean wicked outlaw, sits propped up against a tree trunk - he's bleeding out, exposed and vulnerable. Blood seeps from the deep gash in his side and pools beside him. Vicious wolves surround him and creep closer and closer; growling, snarling - snapping their jaws. Saliva drips from their sharp teeth. The hair on their bodies bristled, the animals crouch low to the ground as they close in on their prey. Cutter is gripped with horror - the wolf pack can smell his fear - and the scent of fresh blood. The large black Alpha wolf edges forward and locks eyes with Cutter as he trembles and squirms. The Alpha wolf lets out a loud growl - then leaps. The wolf pack descend upon Cutter in a frenzy. He screams wildly as the wolves bite and tear into his flesh. The evil outlaw is no longer visible - covered up by the wolf pack. The Ninjans turn away and resume their direction. The warriors are muscular and agile and move swiftly over the forest terrain. Their pace is strong and steady with few breaks - all day and through the moonlit night and into the next day. It is late afternoon when Otter and the Ninjans arrive back in the Shoshone camp. The villagers throng the returning warriors as they walk to the Chief's large central tepee. The atmosphere is filled with excitement and jubilation! Chief Buffalo Sky and the Elders are standing outside. As Otter and the fellow Ninjans approach, the braves bow low to show respect to the Tribal leaders. By now, the entire Shoshone village are gathered, everyone energized and alert to the moment. Buffalo Sky sets his eyes on Otter and the Ninjans, and speaks, "How was the raid?" Otter replies. "The outlaws walk the earth no more!" All the Shoshone know full well the injustice and suffering caused by Cutter and his gang of outlaws when they killed and scalped the Shoshone hunters and fur trappers. Chief Buffalo Sky lifts his arm high in the air and the entire camp becomes still and quiet, all eyes on their Chief, everyone's ear ready to hear his words. Buffalo Sky looks out at his people and speaks with a loud clear voice, "Our fallen braves are avenged!" The Shoshone villagers erupt with cheers, cries of celebration, and loud yells of victory! The people crowd in to congratulate their Ninjan warriors. When the outpouring of gratitude subsides and the people disperse, Otter and his fellow Ninjans leave, each one going to his tepee.

On route to his place, Otter meets Yuji, Bright Star and little Kamatsu. Otter bows low as he greets his former Sensi and Ninja Master. Yuji bows in return and comments, "The Ninjans have a fine leader!" Otter smiles and replies. "That is because I had a great teacher." Bright Star grins at the friendly exchange. She reaches out and touches Yuji's arm, glances at Otter, then turns to Yuji and nods. Yuji is reminded of the couple's earlier talk, and asks the young man, "We want you to sit at our evening meal." Bright Star holding little Kamatsu on her hip, looks Otter in the eye and adds, "You would honour our tepee!" The young man is delighted at the invitation and grins, "Yes! Everyone knows your venison and bannock are the best in the village!" Bright Star's modesty makes her blush at the compliment. Yuji cheerfully remarks, "We can eat and talk as we did so many fires ago." Otter nods with a big smile, bows respect, and turns in the direction of his dwelling. Yuji and Bright Star stand and watch Otter leave, they are happy at Otter's acceptance. Around them, the camp is busy with mealtime, there's family activity at each tepee. As the afternoon sun begins to set - Yuji, Bright Star and tiny Kamatsu make their way home.

The small family walk past many dwellings to their tepee. Yuji lifts up the entry flap as Bright Star lowers slightly to carry Kamatsu inside. After his wife and son have gone within, Yuji steps inside and reaches behind to pull down the buckskin flap. Most Indian tepees, even those of other tribes, share a common design and construction. Fourteen to seventeen wooden poles from sixteen to eighteen feet long, are tightly lashed together at the top, then covered with a thick canvas that is secured to the wood frame. The top opening allows smoke to rise and escape, while inside, the people enjoy the fire for warmth, light and to cook meals. The open living space is designated - an area to prepare and cook food, a sleeping section, and a free space for family and visitors to sit, relax and talk. Any important objects or personal possessions are tied to the tepee interior that circles the family quarters. The beauty of a tepee is that it only needs wood poles and fabric, and the structure can be easily set up or taken down to relocate elsewhere. It was a simple and practical solution for nomadic Indian tribes that migrate in search of hunting and fishing grounds. Yuji and Bright Star's tepee was of this nature, it was where they showered tiny Kamatsu with love and care, and where they lived as a happy family in the Shoshone village.

Yuji takes Kamatsu from Bright Star so she can arrange the evening meal before Otter's arrival. The young wife and mother lays out the already cooked food in wooden and shallow gourd bowls. She sets out the fried bannock, an Indian staple that everyone enjoys from youngsters to older folks. Next, she places fresh hand-picked blueberries and raspberries in a gourd bowl. Bright Star picks up the cooked venison and lays the meat strips on a smooth cedar board, then she places the clay cups and clay pot of fresh water nearby. Yuji and Kamatsu keenly watch as Bright Star checks that everything is ready for their guest. Bright Star glances at her meal setting, then she looks at Yuji and nods with a smile, "The meal is ready. I hope he likes the venison?" Yuji replies, "No one cooks venison like you. Otter will eat well tonight." Tiny Kamatsu fusses a bit and puts out his little hand toward his mom, Bright Star reaches over and takes her son in her arms and cradles him and gently kisses his forehead. The tiny tot breaks into a big smile and grabs a lock of Bright Star's hair. Yuji stares at his beautiful wife and adorable son, lost in a sublime special moment. At that instant, the entry flap lifts and Otter announces his presence, "Otter is here!" Yuji replies, "Join us brother. You must be hungry!" Yuji and Bright Star welcome Otter with smiles and gesture that him sit beside them. Otter crouches as he steps into the tepee interior and walks a few paces and sits down cross-legged. The young warrior grins as his eyes fasten on the food items arranged before him. Bright Star gives Otter a shallow clay bowl and comments, "Your presence with us warms our hearts." Otter replies, "I've not eaten in two days, since we left camp to avenge our fallen braves." Yuji remarks, "Your mission was a success! You and the Ninjans rid the earth of those evil men." Yuji picks up Kamatsu as Bright Star dishes out food for their guest and old friend. Bright Star smiles as she heaps Otter's bowl with generous portions of venison, bannock and berries. She pours him a cup of water and sets the water pot aside. Once Otter has his food, Yuji and Bright Star pick up their bowls and get their meal items. The young mom takes little Kamatsu from Yuji and lays him on the blanket beside her. Otter's hunger is apparent as he ravishes and chews the venison strips enjoying every bite. He soon devours all his venison, bannock and berries. Bright Star grins at Otter's hearty appetite and takes his empty bowl and loads it with more food, and passes it to him. Otter smiles as he receives his second helping, and proceeds to feast as only a hungry young man can. They eat and relax like the good friends they are. Yuji finishes eating and sips his water as he quietly waits for Otter to complete his meal. Bright Star plays with Kamatsu to keep the tot occupied. Otter finishes eating and sets aside his clay bowl and takes a drink of water. Little Kamatsu reaches out to Otter and the young brave picks up the youngster. Kamatsu is intrigued with Otter's long hair and decorative trinkets and plays with them but soon becomes tired. Bright Star remarks, "He's sleepy. I will take him now." Otter hands Kamatsu to his mom and she carries him to the sleeping area, tucks him in for the night, and then returns. Bright Star and Yuji make eye contact, then Yuji looks at Otter and speaks, "My brother, we want you to train Kamatsu. My years and strength are fading - no one knows how long the ground will know his shadow." Otter is honoured but somewhat surprised, "Sensi. You are still strong." Yuji gazes fondly at the young warrior, "You were my best student. I must know that you, and you alone, will train Kamatsu when he is of age." Otter is quiet for a few seconds, glances over at the sleeping boy, then looks at Yuji and Bright Star and replies, "Sensi. I pledge to train Kamatsu - like you once trained me!" Yuji smiles relief, "Your words give me peace." As Otter sits quiet and reflects on what's been said, Yuji gets up and retrieves an object from under a blanket and returns and sits opposite Otter. Yuji unfolds an embroidered buckskin to reveal a large stunning Black Feather and hands it to Otter. The young warrior is wide-eyed and speechless! Otter's hand slightly trembles as he clasps the Black Feather and humbly bows. Otter remarks, "Sensi. This is too great an honour for me!" Yuji reaches out his hand to encourage his former trainee to lift upright, "You have proved yourself worthy many times. - It is my honour to give you the Black Feather!" Otter bows low and raises up, "Sensi. Arigato gozaimasu!" Yuji gazes at the young Ninjan leader and bows and replies 'go ahead' in Japanese, "Hai dozo!" Bright Star beams with happiness at Otter's pledge to train her son, and feels proud to have witnessed Otter receiving the highly regarded Black

Feather. Throughout the remainder of the evening, the three friends enjoy each other's company and conversation as they bask in the warm glow of the tepee fire.

CHAPTER THIRTY-SIX
Otter Trains Kamatsu

The seasons change as the warmth of summer gives way to the cool breeze of Fall. The colourful meadow flowers have wilted and the forest leaves turn yellow, brown and gold, and later, flutter from trees to carpet the ground during the days of Autumn. Soon, the forest has only bare trees with dead brittle leaves on the ground. A cold wind begins to blow and brings with it big snow flakes of delicate ice crystals, that dance in the air before landing on the ground to form a blanket of snow. All of Nature undergoes a transition, even the coats of wild animals change; the fox's red jacket becomes white fur, and the rabbit's brown beige appearance becomes that of fluffy white, allowing the small creature to safely hide in Winter's landscape. The black bear no longer looks for honey or forages all day long in the berry patch, the weighty bruin slumbers in deep hibernation in a secluded wilderness cave. The fast flowing rivers and the placid lakes become covered with frozen sheets of ice. At times, the frozen lakes and rivers crack and creak, making Indian hunters and trappers careful as they walk across the frozen surface, wary that the ice may break and they fall through into the frigid cold water. However, such seldom happens, because the American Indians know the forest and rivers from an early age. Indian people live in harmony with nature, respecting the animals, plants and bounty of their Tribal lands.

It is during the Springtime when Otter begins to teach Kamatsu hand-to-hand combat. The youth is quick, strong and agile, and poses a worthy adversary. Yuji and Bright Star smile as Otter and Kamatsu grapple, wrestle and jostle about, each trying to overpower and off-balance the other. Otter is breathing heavy as he battles the wiry teen. Otter grabs Kamatsu's arm to flip him, but the teen twists and turns to block Otter's attempt, then pivots to put Otter in a hold. Otter glances at Yuji and Bright Star and grins, then the Ninjan Master clutches Kamatsu's arm and swiftly spins the youth - right into a submission hold. Kamatsu groans as he struggles and strains to break free but cannot. Realizing he's defeated, Kamatsu taps surrender and Otter releases his young trainee. Once free and mobile, Kamatsu stands straight, faces his Sensi and bows low. Otter bows in return. Having concluded the training exercise, Otter puts his hand on Kamatsu's shoulder as the two walk toward Yuji and Bright Star. Otter remarks to his pupil, "You almost had me in that hold!" Kamatsu replies, "Why didn't it work? I used the right technique!" Otter responds, "Your hold was correct, but your body position was wrong - letting me to get free." A pondering expression comes over Kamatsu's face, then he remarks, "Now I see it! I should have positioned my right leg better and leaned back." Otter smiles acknowledgement, "Your arm hold and body position would have locked me good. Next time, remember!" Kamatsu nods with a grin. The two approach Yuji and Bright Star on the high ground, and bow. Yuji and Bright Star bow in return. Yuji remarks, "I see improvement since the last time." Kamatsu eyes his Teacher and replies, "Apparently not enough improvement, or my hold would have worked." Bright Star smiles and adds in a motherly way, "Next time my son." Otter looks at his old friends and comments, "Kamatsu has greatly improved from when we started. He's becoming more capable each time we train. (Otter grins) The day will arrive when I can no longer beat him.(Otter glances at the lad) I look forward to that day!" Bright Star speaks motioning with her hand, "Food in the tepee will help replenish two hungry warriors." Otter and Kamatsu nod their heads and smile. Kamatsu playfully remarks, "My Sensi may out fight me - but he can't out eat me!" The adults laugh at Kamatsu's words as they leave the training area.

The day dawns and rays of bright sunlight pierce the morning mist on the ground. Otter and Kamatsu stand in front of the wide forest tree, the trunk covered with small open dimples. Otter has a handful of Shuriken and turns to his teenage apprentice, "Arm position and finger grip determine the direction when throwing at your target. Watch me." Kamatsu's eyes lock in on how and where his Sensi holds the pointed metal star, and notes the Master's arm position and throwing technique. Otter flings his arm and releases a Shuriken at the tree. Whoosh! The metal star spins in a blur as it sails toward the trunk - Thud! The Shuriken strikes the trunk and the sharp metal point embeds deep into the wood. Otter glances at Kamatsu and remarks,

"Now, you try - remember to aim and release the Shuriken at the right moment." Kamatsu nods, adjusts his leg position for better balance, looks at the tree trunk, and flings his arm and opens his fingers - the black metal star spins and twirls toward the tree only to curve and miss the trunk completely. Kamatsu is stunned since he thought the Shuriken was going to hit the target. The young trainee looks over to his Sensi, and asked puzzled, "Master, How come I missed?" Otter copies how Kamatsu positioned his fingers and the way he flung his arm, and demonstrates the throw. As Otter throws, Kamatsu observes the star going straight at the trunk, then moves in an arc to miss the tree. Otter positions his arm and fingers in the proper technique - shows Kamatsu, then throws - the Shuriken twirls in blinding speed to sink deep into the trunk's perforated surface - Thud! Kamatsu's eyes light up as he realizes why his throw missed the tree and his Sensi's throw hit the target. Otter encourages his student, "Try again like I showed you." Kamatsu copies his Teacher's finger placement and arm position, takes a breath, then swings his arm and watches the Shuriken spin straight toward the tree and strike the trunk - sinking deep into the wood. Kamatsu smiles accomplishment and looks at his Sensi. Otter nods his head with approval and smiles, "Your throw was correct. Remember, finger grip and arm position determine the various ways to throw a Shuriken." Kamatsu nods tight lipped, he understands. For the latter portion of the training exercise, Otter instructs Kamatsu in the various ways to throw a Shuriken - depending on the target and the distance. For the rest of the morning, Kamatsu throws, retrieves, throws again, retrieves the Shuriken, and repeats this throughout the rest of the training session. Otter gazes up at the bright sun overhead and comments, "Time to stop - rest - and eat some food." Kamatsu is so focused on developing his throwing technique that he forgets how hungry he is. The lad turns to his Sensi with a grin, "Did you say food?!" Otter teases Kamatsu, "Yes! Food. I know teenagers are always hungry. (Smiles) It was like that when I was a teenager." Kamatsu teases back, "Oh! You were a teenager?" The man laughs, walks away, then turns and motions for the teen to come on along.

As the weeks, months and years pass by; Kamatsu grows taller, bigger, and more muscular. He is quick, agile, and more experienced with the Ninjan fighting techniques. Yuji and Bright Star observe as Kamatsu shows his ability with the various weapons. The young man masterfully spins and aims the chain dart to strike a small target - he capably handles and throws the tomahawk - and shoots black arrows and never misses the target - he swings and twirls the Ninjan war club with great competence - and displays his prowess in hand-to-hand combat with blocks, punches, strikes, kicks, throws and choke holds. Kamatsu has progressed mightily and has excelled in all manner of weapon and combat. Now, only the last phase of Ninjan training remains - swordsmanship. Otter begins Kamatsu by using the wooden sword and teaches the basics. Kamatsu is a fast learner and quickly shows competency with using the wood sword for defence and offence. His parents watch as Otter and Kamatsu spar against each other with their wooden sword - there is a flurry of action as both swing and block, thrust and deflect, chop and slice at their opponent. The Sensi has a tough challenge from his vigorous athletic apprentice. But as adapt as Kamatsu is, the young man is out manoeuvred by his Sensi, and Otter attacks with a flurry of swings, chops and blows that has Kamatsu backing up in defence. Finally, Otter spins his wood sword with such force that Kamatsu's sword flies out of his hand - leaving the young man weaponless and defeated. As Otter stands with the wood sword pointed at his student - Kamatsu nods and bows low to honour his Teacher, "Sensi. You have taken away my sword - I surrender!" Otter steps close to his student and comments, "You have outgrown the practice sword - Now, you will train with the steel Katana sword." Kamatsu bows and replies, "Arigato Sensi! I'm ready for your instruction!" Otter smiles at his student's improved ability and humble attitude.

It was on a breezy Autumn day when Otter walks to their training area. Otter carries two swords and wears his black Ninja outfit, Kamatsu is dressed in a white Ninja outfit. Arriving at the location, Otter hands Kamatsu a glossy white Katana sword to use for his Ninja training. The Sensi looks at his pupil, "You must learn how the steel sword feels in your hand - its weight and balance. First, we will start with a practice Kata - follow how I hold and use my sword." Kamatsu takes a quick breath and nods. Otter steps a few yards away for a safe distance, and positions himself and grips his shiny black Katana. Kamatsu copies his Sensi's body, arm and sword position, and waits. Otter looks at his student, then steps forward and slices downward at a 45 degree angle. He looks over at Kamatsu and nods. The young man copies his Teacher's move and sword slice, then glances at Otter for his response. Otter nods his head and grins, then launches out with an upward left and upward right cut. Kamatsu follows suit. All during the morning, with the crisp Fall air making their breath show, Otter leads Kamatsu through the first training exercise with the steel sword. Over the next number of weeks and months, Kamatsu matches his Sensi perfectly. The two Ninja warriors move in synchronized manner like two field birds that fly through the sky, each keeping the same distance apart, each moving and turning at the same time. Anyone observing would see that both men hold their sword at the same angle, swing their blade at the same moment, and keep together as the two steel blades - swing, twirl and slice through the air at imaginary foes.

Now the moment has arrived when Otter feels Kamatsu is ready to spar with the Katana. Basking in the bright morning sunshine, Otter and Kamatsu face each other with steel sword in hand. Otter takes a battle stance and remarks to Kamatsu, "Whenever you are ready!" Kamatsu firmly grips his Katana and assumes a fighting position and locks eyes with his Sensi - then launches out with a barrage of swings, thrusts and chops. Otter's sword is kept busy blocking and deflecting Kamatsu's attack. The two quickly move around the flat training ground, shuffling their feet from one battle stance to another. Otter eyes his pupil, then attacks with a flurry of strikes that keeps Kamatsu's sword on the defence. The sparring session is intense, both warriors seeking to conquer their opponent. There's a sudden lull as Otter and Kamatsu stop to catch their breath. Otter comments to his student, "You handle the Katana very well!" Kamatsu smiles and replies to his Sensi, "That is because I had an excellent Teacher! The older man raises up the palm of his free hand, "Let's stop for today. (Otter grins) There will be many more days to spar." Kamatsu nods and they both leave the training ground and head toward the village tepees.

CHAPTER THIRTY-SEVEN
Kamatsu The Ninja

In a lovely forest setting, Yuji and Bright Star stand side by side, they no longer have the shiny black hair of yesteryear, now their hair is fully grey - the colour of old people. Their skin no longer smooth and supple as in their youth, now their faces are wrinkled and etched from the experiences of life. On this special day, their eyes sparkle with hope, their spirits soar, their hearts are filled with joy, as they observe Otter and Kamatsu, both dressed in Ninjan black outfits. Otter is now middle-aged, and Kamatsu is a full grown man. The two warriors respectfully kneel across from each other on the large ceremonial straw mat with bouquets of flowers that decorate the edge of the woven surface. In the middle between them, a glossy black Katana sword sits nestled in its wooden cradle. A small ceramic bowl with burning incense sticks sits at one side of the Katana, and on the other side lays an embroidered buckskin pouch and a small bronze bowl and wood stick. Yuji and Bright Star watch with anticipation.

Otter looks at his graduate, bows and lifts up. Kamatsu bows and returns upright. Otter clasps the ceramic bowl and extends it toward Kamatsu, and circles the burning incense and sets the bowl aside. Otter looks at Kamatsu and chants, "Bushi - Chigiri!" Kamatsu bows low and holds steady and replies, "Chigiri Sensi!", then he lifts up. Otter looks at Kamatsu, reaches with both arms to pick up the Katana and extends it. Kamatsu reaches out to clasp the Katana and holds it. Otter release his grip and Kamatsu holds the Katana with both hands, brings the sword against his chest, then bows low and remains still. Otter keeps his eyes on the bowed graduate and speaks in an authoritative tone, "Bushi - Ninjan! Bushi - Ninjan!" Kamatsu clutching the sword and bowed, replies, "Aho! Chigiri Ninjan! Aho! Chigiri Ninjan!" Otter smiles at Kamatsu's firm response and picks up the wood stick and strikes the bronze bowl to emit a ringing sound that envelopes their forest setting. Kamatsu lifts upright with a sparkle in his eye as he holds the Katana. Otter, his lifelong Sensi, smiles and stands to his feet. Kamatsu rises and stands to his feet to face his Sensi. Otter remarks, "You are no longer a trainee - an apprentice. From this day onward - you are a Ninjan!" Otter bows respect to Kamatsu and Kamatsu bows in return. Kamatsu smiles victoriously and turns to look at his father and mother who have witnessed his Graduation Ceremony. Bright Star is happy and crying with tears flowing down her face, and Yuji stands tall and proud with a big smile.

CHAPTER THIRTY-EIGHT

Chief Buffalo Sky Dies

It is an overcast sky the day the Shoshone villagers gather at the Tribe's burial grounds, their hearts are sad because their great Chief Buffalo Sky has died. The Chief's lifeless body rests high up on the wood burial tower. His rifle, tomahawk, hunting knife, bow and quiver of arrows, lay beside him. The entire Shoshone tribe stand in a circle to surround the burial tower. The Tribal death drums pound as the people watch Eagle Feather, now an old man, chant Shoshone prayers to the Great Spirit as he casts white powder into the air. Everyone observes in silence, no one talks, not even the little children; there's only the sound of the wind, Eagle Feather's chanting, and the beating of the drums.

Five fires have now passed since Buffalo Sky has died, and the Tribal Elders meet at the large central tepee to decide who should be the next Chief. Inside the tepee, the Council Fire burns bright and makes the faces of the Elders and lead warriors glow. There is much discussion among the Elders. Outside the tepee, all the Shoshone braves stand in clusters, talking among themselves about who will become their new Chief. The entry flap of the tepee lifts up and Eagle Feather steps out. All the braves stop their conversations and everyone looks at the old warrior. Eagle Feather scans across the throng of braves and speaks, "Tomorrow we gather to honour our new Chief!" The braves realize the Tribal Council have reached a decision and they begin to disperse toward their homes. Eagle Feather lifts up the entry flap and steps back inside.

It is a sunny morning and all the camp have assembled near the central tepee. The Elders stand in the middle of an open area and the Shoshone people surround them. Eagle Feather holds the tribe's War Lance, the weapon that will belong to the new Chief. An Elder beside him holds the Chief's Feathered Bonnet, the tribe's visible symbol of honour and leadership. The mass of people are abuzz in lively chatter about who will be the new Chief. Eagle Feather lifts up the War lance and all the people stop talking and rivet their eyes on the respected warrior. He looks about and lifts his voice, "The Tribe's Elders have made their decision. Now, you, the Shoshone people, must show your acceptance. Only when the Elders and the people accept the decision, can he become the new Chief." Eagle Feather pauses and gazes around at the faces of the villagers. The grownups and young ones understand his words. Eagle Feather steps out from the Elders and stands alone, and calls out, "The Elders decide that Bear Claw will be our new Chief!" Bear Claw is standing with Gold Flower, Yuji and Bright Star. He looks at them and they smile proudly. The seasoned warrior steps out from the group of villagers and walks to stand next to Eagle Feather. As the Elders and the entire camp watch, his old friend Eagle Feather fits the Feathered Bonnet on Bear Claw's head and hands his the War Lance. As Bear Claw stands wearing the Chief's Feathered Bonnet and holding the War Lance, Eagle Feather steps aside and points to the Tribe's new Chief - and all the Shoshone people, from the old to the young, erupt with loud cheers, and cries of victory and celebration. The Elders have a contented smile that they picked well. With the entire camp visibly and vocally honouring their new Chief, Eagle Feather leans close to his lifelong friend and remarks, "I am happy for you old friend! You were the best choice as our new Chief. (Pause) The Great Spirit will help you lead our people!" Bear Claw looking majestic in the Chief's Feathered Bonnet and holding the tribe's War Lance, looks out at the happy Shoshone people, then smiles and nods to his friend, "I will need the Great Spirit very much!" An Elder holds up his arm and the boisterous people ebb to a silence. The Elder speaks out with joy, "Tonight, we will sing, dance, eat - and celebrate our new Chief Bear Claw!" The Shoshone villagers break out with cheers and cries of happiness. As the merry people disperse, The Elders, Eagle Feather and Chief Bear Claw enter the tribe's central tepee; now the new home for Bear Claw and Gold Flower.

Deep in the forest, amid the tall pines streaked with shafts of sunlight, where the ground is carpeted with soft pine needles, two figures dressed in Ninjan black, kneel opposite each other on a woven straw mat. Flower bouquets decorate the perimeter of the mat. Kamatsu, now a late middle-aged man, faces a mature Shoshone brave. Kamatsu's expression shows pride as he presents a polished black

Katana sword to the warrior. The Ninjan receives the weapon with humility and gazes at the sword with deep appreciation. He looks at Kamatsu and bows low and remarks, "Arigato Sensi! " Kamatsu bows in return and replies, "You have surpassed my expectations. You are now ready!" Kamatsu reaches into his Ninjan tunic and brings out an embroidered buckskin pouch and unfolds it to reveal a large black feather. Kamatsu's fingers clasp the quill portion and he lifts the feather up toward the sky and chants some Japanese words. The other man bows low and replies, "Chigiri Jungyo!" (Pledge Obedience). The warrior raises up and Kamatsu offers the black eagle feather to him. As the man receives the symbol, his hand slightly trembles as he holds the Ninjan black feather. He is speechless and in awe at such an honour. The warrior fastens his eyes on the glossy Katana, and stares at the black feather as it glistens in the sunlight. The Ninjan bows low to his Sensi, and Otter nods and remarks, "Aho! Hai!"

CHAPTER THIRTY-NINE

A New Century And A Whirl Through Time

TIME: 1880

Chief Bear Claw and a group of Shoshone braves ride their horses to the top of a high hill. The old Chief and the braves look out across the wilderness, then gaze down at a passenger train that rolls along the railroad tracks below. The Shoshone warriors watch puffs of black smoke pour out from the locomotive engine and drift into the sky above. Chief Bear Claw remarks, "The farther we ride, the more iron horse we see. Railroad tracks cover the land and cut across Buffalo hunting grounds." An aged brave next to the Chief comments, "The iron horse brings much people and many things. Everywhere the iron horse goes - White men build villages and towns. I have seen this." Chief Bear Claw looks at the seasoned brave and replies, "Our way of life is changing fast. I am afraid, soon, we will be no more!" Bear Claw's words echo in the hearts of the Shoshone braves around him and they nod their heads in agreement. The warriors on horseback gaze at the moving train below. Inside one of the passenger cars, a young girl in a frilly pink calico dress lifts her eyes off the book she's reading and looks out the window and sees Indians on the hill. The youngster tugs on her mom's arm with excitement, "Mommy look - Indians! - Real Indians!" The mother lifts her eyes toward the hill, stares a bit, then looks down at her daughter and brushes her child's hair, "Don't worry Emily, we're safe! It's different now, things are civilized!" The little girl smiles and goes back to her book, while the mother continues to look out the window. Perhaps she realizes the American Wild West will soon fade into history books, like the book she reopens - "King Arthur's Roundtable". Up a couple rows, a man sits dressed in a suit, tie and bowler hat, and holds up a newspaper to read. He turns the pages and his eyes fall on the various advertisements for new inventions; one promotes a sewing machine, another shows a telephone, and one advertisement displays a typewriter.

TIME: 1900s

The American West undergoes change far beyond the control of local and territorial residents. The days of the Pony Express, Telegraph Wire, Pioneer Wagon Trains, Overland Stage Coach, and Calvary soldiers at wooden Forts - start to change and fade away. The rugged wilderness and open prairies of Chief Bear Claw and the Shoshone braves, soon become populated with settlements and villages. Growing towns become fledgling cities bustling with inhabitants, commerce and industry. This is the age of the Industrial Revolution in America and Europe, where mechanized factories, plants and mills, turn out new products and processes using electricity. Henry Ford invents the Model T car and makes it available to people across the nation from his automotive factory in Michigan. Two brothers, Wilbur and Orville Wright, make the first successful flight of a powered airplane. Over time, flying would become a new form of travel for many people.

TIME: 1920s

This is the age known as the Roaring Twenties's. Americans in the thousands buy Henry Ford's Model T car and start to travel far and wide. Towns and cities continue to grow and expand, providing jobs and new business. People move from rural life to live and work in urban centres. Big bands are popular, and everyone wants to dance the Jitterbug. Fashion conscious men wear pin-striped suits and straw hats; while ladies favour the fancy hats and frilly dresses of the 'Flappers'. During this era, the Federal Government brings in Prohibition and outlaws alcohol production and consumption. Those wanting alcohol visit an underground club called a 'Speakeasy' and drink their booze in secret from the Police and general public. In homes across the nation, families and individuals purchase and enjoy modern inventions like - electric toasters, washing machines, vacuum cleaners, radios and television.

TIME: 1930s

The Crash of the New York Stock Market sent America into a great panic with millions of people losing millions of dollars, the economy was in ruins. What followed was the Great Depression that created a nation-wide scarcity of employment and food. Individuals and families lost pretty much everything they owned - personal savings, businesses, homes and farms. People took to moving across the country looking for work. These people camped out or stayed in shantytowns built near towns and cities. These crude ramshackle enclaves were commonly known as 'Hoovervilles', so named after President Hoover.

TIME: 1940s

The Great Depression gave way to the emergence of World War on the international stage. Japan attacked Pearl Harbour on Dec.7, 1941, causing the United States to enter World War II. Men across the nation enlisted and went off to fight overseas, and the women back home began to work in plants and factories to manufacture the equipment and supplies needed by troops abroad. Citizens at home listened to Jazz from Big Bands like Count Basie, and watched Fred Astaire dance in Hollywood movies; while over in Europe, Allied troops were serenaded by the sweet voice of Vera Lynn. The War in Europe came to an end when Germany surrendered to the Allied Forces on March 8, 1945, the Armistice became widely known as VE Day, Victory in Europe Day! Japan surrendered to America on September 2, 1945, but the official Armistice began on August 14, 1945.

TIME: 1950s

Thousands and thousands of the men return from WWII to find companies and factories strong and productive from the War Effort. The former soldiers enter the workforce and apply their military training and skills with a winning attitude. Most of the women return to domestic life and caring for family. Over time, a 'Baby Boom' sweeps the nation as men and women began to have children and start families. With companies in steady production, consumer goods available, and new family houses being built - the American life and dream was better than ever! Elvis Presley introduced the music of 'Rock-a-Billy' and became an instant star. Young people listened to popular singers were Buddy Holly, Chuck Berry, and Eddie Cochran, while older folks listened to Doris Day, Connie Francis and Perry Como. The 1950s were the carefree fun-loving days as portrayed in the TV shows, movies, and music. Overseas, America fights the Cold War against Communism, while stateside, people join the Civil Rights Movement.

TIME: 1960s

The major events of this era include the Vietnam War, the Hippie Movement, and the Assassination of President J. F. Kennedy and Dr. Martin Luther King. Young people drop out of Society and join the

Hippie movement to experiment with drugs and live a free lifestyle. America experiences the "British Music Invasion" from groups like - The Beatles, The Rolling Stones, The Who, Herman's Hermits, and The Byrds. While American 'Pop Music' includes the sounds of the Beach Boys, the Supremes, the Jackson Five, Paul Revere and the Raiders, the Temptations, and Johnny Cash. There's a Space Race between America and the Soviet Union, and America is first to land a man on the moon.

TIME: 1980s

Governor Ronald Regan of California became the 40th President of the United States. Young people listened to emerging music like New Wave and Punk, and Rock bands had 'Big Hair'. People used the Apple, Atari and Commodore personal computers on the Internet, and enjoy new technology like the Walkman, Cable Television, CVRs, video games, and music on CDs. Fashion ranged from the 'Preppie' style of golf shirt, knit sweater and pleated pants; to jean jackets, T-shirts, and faded jeans. This was the time of the Dot-Com Bubble with the sudden rise of internet companies and big stock investments. When the Bubble burst, which became known as the dot-com crash, trillions of dollars were lost and many businesses failed.

TIME: 2000s

The September 11 attack on the World Trade Towers and the US Pentagon by international terrorists will forever stand out in the America psyche. President George W. Bush was in Office when America was involved with the War on Terror and the Gulf War. There were oil spills in the environment and Hurricane Katrina battered the US Gulf States. People discovered the iPod, Google, YouTube, and Social Networking. And the increase of divorce brought changes to the traditional family unit. President Ronald Regan passed away June 5, 2004, and Barack Obama became the first black President of the Unites States on January 20, 2009.

TIME: PRESENT DAY

Desert region of the Northwest United States.

CHAPTER FORTY

Life in a Desert Town

A popular area Roadhouse is crowded with rowdy patrons as the band rocks out with some ole' fashion Rock 'n' Roll. The dance floor is packed and people sing along as the band plays their favourite tunes. Throughout the 'watering hole' people are drinking, feasting, flirting, and some are fighting. Outside, shiny vehicles fill the Bar's parking lot - gleaming trucks, classic muscle cars, fast Imports, and luxury Sport Utility vehicles. Most of the guys and gals are inside having fun and letting off steam. Only a few people linger about in the cool night air of the desert.

An old rusted pickup with its headlights off, creeps up to the edge of the parking lot. Spike, the gang leader gives the okay and three gang members jump out of the cargo box, their shoes hit the gravel with a crunch. Tommy, the new recruit is one of them. Before them sits a glitzy new Cadillac Escalade. One of the crew pulls out a thin metal bar known as a Slim Jim, slides the bar down between the glass and the driver's door - and gives a quick pull - CLICK! The door unlocks and the kid quickly gets in and hot-wires the car - VROOM! Tommy and the other accomplice get in. A couple of men having a smoke outside, spot them and start to yell! The kid at the steering wheel floors the engine and tears out of the parking lot onto the highway. The old pickup races from behind to catch up. The men run to the road but it's too late — the thieves are gone! The stolen Escalade and the old pickup race over the desert highway for a number of miles, then turn down a forlorn dirt road, and fly over shallow hills and dips until reaching an old abandoned gas station out in the middle of nowhere. The site reminiscent of something from a cheap horror film. The Escalade and pickup pull into the back of the weathered derelict building and the engines cut. Everyone jumps out and gathers around the Escalade to admire the stolen trophy. Spike swags up and lays his arm across Tommy's shoulder and remarks with a proud grin, "Homes! That's how we carjack!" Tommy stands a bit nervous and replies, "Man, my heart is pounding!" Spike slaps the new recruit's back, "There's still more ahead, Homes!" As a couple gang members grab a old faded tarp and cover the SUV, the other members gather around their leader. One guy pipes up, "We hitting old Joe's?" Spike looks at the guy with a smirk, "Had my eye on that place for weeks. It's 'Pay Day' bro! - Let's roll." Everyone piles into the old truck, three cram the front, and two others and Tommy jump into the back. The old rust bucket fires up and tears off down the lonely dirt road.

Old Joe's Sporting Goods store is out on Canyon Road, the route that people take to get out into the outdoors where there was hunting, fishing and camping. It was a well-known location and folks from near and far shop there to get hunting rifles, fishing equipment, camping supplies and outdoor apparel. Tonight, the only sentinels guarding the place are two lampposts that cast a sodium orange glow across the storefront and parking lot. The store's neon sign is turned off and a closed sign hangs inside the front door. The Store's big windows are full of merchandise - displays of outdoor clothing, field binoculars, camouflage outfits, compound bows and arrows, fishing rods and lures, electronic fish finders, camping equipment, sleeping bags, and assorted backpacks.

The old pickup roars into the parking lot and drives behind the large cement block building and slams to an abrupt stop - the headlights slice through the small cloud of dust that wafts in the air. Three jump out of the truck cabin, and Tommy and the other two bolt out of the cargo box to land in the dirt. Spike waves his hand and they all form a quick huddle. Spike remarks, "The front door and windows have alarms. (He chuckles) The back window has nothing! The money's inside because the deposit goes to the bank in the morning." All the gang members grin and nod their heads except Tommy. The gang leader eyes the new recruit and points, "Tommy, you'll go through the back window. Once inside, you kill the alarm and unlock the front door. - This break-in is your initiation, Homes! Do it - and you're in the gang!" Tommy looks composed on the outside, but inside he's nervous and feeling hesitant, "Okay!...Got it." A gang member hands Tommy a knife and a small flashlight. He holds the knife in one hand and the flashlight in the other. They walk from the pickup to the store's back window and two guys help boast Tommy so he can reach window level. Spike instructs, "Slide the blade to trip the widow latch." Tommy looks down, all eyes are on him. He works the knife blade along the crack in the window frame until … Click!…the metal latch pops free and Tommy pushes the window open. He tosses the knife off the side to land in the dirt and turns on the flashlight to look inside. Tommy leans in and struggles to wiggle through the open window - he falls through and Tommy hits the floor inside - Thud! - Stuff scatters around, and the flashlight rolls across the cold cement floor. Spike gets below the open window, "Hey! - You okay?" Tommy replies, "Yah! I'm fine." Spike injects, "Look for the big red button - it turns off the alarm! We'll be at the front door." Tommy feels a bit bruised from hitting the cement floor and looks around and sees the beam of the flashlight. He gets up, grabs the flashlight and scans the interior and spots the alarm's blinking red button. He walks over and pressed it off - no more blinking! Meanwhile, the gang run to the store entrance and wait. Inside, Tommy walks the store's rear corridor and enters the back of the store. The light from the lamppost casts an eerie orange glow onto the store aisles and merchandise. Tommy walks up the aisle and sees Spike and crew standing outside. He unlocks and opens the front door wide. Spike the gang spill into the store and start to grab items - watches, electronics, expensive fishing reels, hi-tech equipment, guns and boxes of ammo. They pillage through the store taking anything that's worth money, then they stash the loot in the truck cargo box. Spike uses a crowbar to bust open the cash registers. He lifts out the trays full of money and dumps the contents into a canvass sack. Suddenly, there's the rumble of a big diesel engine, and a transport rig rolls into the parking lot just off the highway - brakes and idles. The gang members freeze. The trucker exits the cab and circles the rig and makes a couple hasty inspections. Satisfied, he jumps back in, fires up the cylinders and moves out and goes down the road. Tommy is rattled and turns to Spike, "That was close!" Spike grabs the canvass sack full of bills and coins, "Let's go! We got the money." Everyone piles into the pickup. The driver floors the engine and the off-road tires spray dirt as the truck spins about and roars off into the darkness. A cloud of dust wafts in the light of the lamppost. Its orange glow reveals the front door left wide open - a baseball cap lays in the doorway.

CHAPTER FORTY-ONE

Evidence At The Crime Scene

The Store Manager and staff at Old Joe's stand near the cash registers as Police Chief Rogers jots info on a notepad, "We need serial numbers and descriptions of what's been stolen." The Store Manager hands the Police Chief a print out, "Sure thing! Got a list of everything stolen… Ole Joe gonna have a fit!" Chief Rogers motions and an Officer next to him takes the paper. Chief Rogers finishes his scribble and comments, "Tell him, we'll catch the thieves soon - that cap gave us a lead!" The Police Chief turns and exits the front door, and the Manger and his staff prepare the store to reopen for business. Officers outside remove the yellow Police tape. After a few minutes, Police Chief Rogers and the Officers get into their squad vehicles and drive off.

At the Police Station, Officers gather in a meeting room. There's lots of chatter as the men and women await the Briefing. Chief Rogers enters through a side door and positions himself at the front of the room. He holds a pile of printouts and a ball cap and scans across the interior - and waits a few seconds for everyone's attention. The Police Chief walks over to an Officer in a front chair and hands the papers and motions for him to distribute. As the papers get passed around and Officers begin to peruse the information, Chief Rogers comments, "This looks like the same gang that hit the Liquor store in Tyler two weeks ago! Forensics has traced the tire tread, and the ball cap gives us a solid lead. This new info gets us closer…(Pause)…Now let's go get 'em!" The Officers get up and disband in teams of two. Officer Stibbs stays behind and waits until all the others are gone, then he approaches Chief Rogers, "I think I know who owns that ball cap!" The Police Chief picks up the cap to show the inside. Stibbs examines the name scrawled in felt marker on the inner lining. The Chief asks, "Ring any bell?" Officer Stibbs replies, "When I worked the Rez, there was a kid that went by that name. He did Juvie stuff - skipped school, busted windows, got drunk." The Chief grabs the cap and shakes it, "Well, if it's the same kid, he's in the big leagues now! This gang is part of the Northwest Crew that controls everything from drugs, carjacking, break-ins, to Meth labs and extortion!" Officer Stibbs takes a deep breath and replies, "I'll drive out to the Rez…see what I can find out." The Officer turns and walks toward the exit door and Chief Rogers calls out, "Be careful Stibbs! You're just another paleface with a badge." Stibbs turns about, gives a quick nod and exits the room.

The sun is high overhead and it's really hot. The kind of temperature when you look down the highway, the air weaves and ripples with waves of heat that come off the sun-baked pavement. Officer Stibbs drives the Police cruiser along the State Highway, then turns onto Indian Reservation road, and keeps driving until he sees a cluster of cinder block buildings on the horizon. Stibbs knows from his days as an Officer on the Rez that lots of local kids hang out here near the Convenience store. He steers the cruiser off the dirt road and pulls up in front of the store's shaded veranda with its cement half wall and square pillars. A group of Rez teenagers are perched on the wall drinking soda pop and smoking cigarettes. As Stibbs gets out of the Police car and puts on his western style Police Stetson, the kids watch him with wary eyes. He slowly ambles over and stands before them in the sun as they sit under the veranda's shade. The teens eye the Policeman with casual indifference. Stibbs lifts and repositions his Stetson and remarks, "Sure is hot! Any cool drinks inside?" The kids look at each other and smirk. One guy quips, "Not as hot as the Slammer!" The youths grin! Another teen pipes up, "Ya! Those cement beds get crazy hot! All the teens snicker and laugh! An older teen eyes Stibbs and asks with slight bravado, "What do you want Mr. Po-leece-man?" Stibbs gives a slight grin and glances about, "Is Desert Dawg still around?" Suddenly, the teens' faces change from prankster grins to dead-serious. The older teen replies, "No one here by that name! Sure you got the right Rez?" The kid sitting on the wall next to him remarks, "Don't know what you're talking about - Fuzz!" Officer Stibbs smiles and steps back and reposition his stance, "Well, if you happen to see Desert Dawg - let him know Stibbs dropped by." Stibbs gives a quick nod and walks back and gets into his cruiser, starts the car and drives off. The group of teens cheer and celebrate his departure.

CHAPTER FORTY-TWO

The Long Grass House

Kathy Long Grass, Tommy's grandmother, prepares some food items in the kitchen. She's an attractive mature lady with lovely long hair and a radiant smile. Kathy exits the kitchen and approaches the dining table bringing a tray of snacks and beverages for her grandson and his two friends. Tommy remarks, "Thanks Grandma! We're starving!" As she begins to lower the tray to the table - Tommy's two friends snatch items and gobble down the goodies. A voice comes from the front door, Carl Long Grass, Tommy's grandfather, stands by the front door holding a bag of groceries; he chides, "Your friends need to remember their manners! Tommy looks at his grandpa, "They're just hungry… been really busy lately." Carl remarks in a fatherly tone, "I know you've been busy - out all night. Twice this week!" Kathy walks over and takes the bag of groceries from his arm and goes back into the kitchen. Carl steps over to the side and hangs his buckskin jacket, then walks over and sits down in an armchair. Kathy's voice beckons from the kitchen, "You boys want some more food?" The two friends glance at Tommy and shake their heads. Tommy replies back, "We're okay grandma! Thanks anyways!" A friend's cell phone BUZZES and he checks the screen. The kid blurts out, "We gotta bounce!" The other friend injects, "See ya later Homes!" The two guys get up and knuckle bump Tommy, and he comments, "Later bro!" The two guys leave the table and exit the side door they came in through. Tommy turns and glances at his grandfather. Carl looks at Tommy with a fatherly gaze, "I don't know where you got your friends. You've changed since being with them - you're different!" Tommy replies in a feisty tone, "Don't get on my case grandpa! They're the only friends I got. No one else cares about me!" Tommy gets up and retreats to his room and slams the bedroom door. Kathy stands in the archway of the kitchen with a sad expression, then steps back inside. Carl eyes the bedroom door of Tommy's room. He stands up and is about to go speak with the boy, then he pauses and slowly sits back down. He picks up the tv remote and turns on the Evening News.

In the morning, Tommy has the front seats of his car, a blue 1985 Ford Mustang, on the yard as he installs new carpet. This was his dad's old car and it's the one thing Tommy deeply cherishes. He's got tunes cranked up on the car radio as he works away. Kathy stands at the big picture window and watches her grandson outside. Carl comes up beside her and he looks out as Tommy positions and trims the auto carpeting. Kathy comments, "I know he still hurts bad — not every kid looses both parents in an accident. - The drunk driver should have got a tougher sentence - three years for taking two lives!" Kathy shakes her head as she looks at the nearby photo of their son, daughter-in-law, and eight year old Tommy. Carl takes a deep breath, "Tommy needs our love and support…now more than ever before!" Kathy turns and looks into her husband's eyes, "I'm happy he comes over for meals, but he keeps living in that old house - with his mom and dad gone, it's just cold and empty!" Carl reaches out a hand to gently clasp Kathy's shoulder and replies, "He's our grandson! We'll just have to be there for him." As his grandparents continue to watch and radio tunes blare, Tommy trims and positions the new carpet into place.

CHAPTER FORTY-THREE
The Northwest Gang

Spike sits across the worn tavern table from Bossman, leader of the Northwest Gang, a big scary man with a scar down the left side of his face. Some say he got the scar in a street fight when he was a young punk, others say Bossman got it in prison during a jail yard rumble with another gang. No one knows for sure but either way, Bossman is one mean scary dude with a quick fuse. Spike looks around at the musclebound gang lieutenants sitting nearby - all tough and menacing. Bossman looks at Spike and remarks, "We need more high-end cars for overseas…(he leans forward)…You can handle that right?" Spike gives a confident yet faltering reply, "Don't worry Boss! Our numbers have grown - it's as good as done!" Bossman eyes Spike and sneers, "Anyone gives you a problem - just send word (Bossman tilts his head to crack his neck) I miss killin' people!" Spike nods compliance. Bossman gets up and stands tall and imposing, "And I mean anyone… Nobody is going to stop our expansion. This territory is ours!" The big man turns and strides away and motions the gang lieutenants to follow. Alone at the back of the Bar, Spike feels nervous and takes a deep breath and chugs the rest of the beer at the bottom of the bottle.

The Northwest Gang moved into the region a number of months ago. At first it was just a few gang members - sent to scout the area and report back what they found. Then, more and more members of the gang showed up, and soon the whole territory was flooded with the Northwest Gang. The gangsters dominated the local bad boys and operated everywhere - area towns, high schools, the Indian Reservation, truck stops, ranches, and even parties. The city gang muscled out any of the local small town hoods. The Northwest Gang dealt drugs to the locals and started to rake in cash. Crew members began to boost cars, steal electronics from warehouses, set up Meth labs, and extorted businesses for protection money. The gangsters were everywhere - and everyone feared them!

At the Police Station, a Forensic Officer hands the Police Chief a file. Chief Rogers opens the folder and peruses the papers, then asks, "Prints on the ball cap match the record? You sure about it?" The Forensic Officer replies, "100 percent sure. A perfect match!" Chief Rogers taps the file folder against his right hand, looks at the man and remarks, "Time to catch a thief!" In a matter of minutes, Chief Rogers and six Officers head out the cement steps in back of the Police Station, and get into their Police cruisers. Chief Rogers is the first to pull out, then, three cruisers follow him. They drive through town and out onto the Highway toward the Indian Reservation 10 miles away. On the highway, Chief Rogers flicks on the Police Lights but doesn't put on the siren. The other Officers do the same. As people travel into town, they pass the four Police cruisers with flashing lights and wonder what's happening. Some miles later, Chief Rogers stops at the side road to the Indian Reservation, pulls over onto the shoulder of the road and he gets out. The other Officers stop their cruisers behind the Chief's car, exit and walk up to join him. Chief Rogers turns his head and gazes at the large road sign: INDIAN RESERVATION, then looks at his Officers, and addresses them, "We're after this kid. (Shows photo) We're going to be on their land - whatever you do - don't show any disrespect. We don't want any trouble!" The Officers nod, and they return to their cars and Chief Rogers pulls out and the others follow. The Police drive onto the Reservation and go past buildings, stores, trailers, and clusters of homes. Groups of people watch the four Police cars drive by - the peoples' faces clearly show a wary curiosity and concern. The Police Chief leads the others down a dusty lane to an old weathered wooden house. The Police stop and get out.

Tommy is asleep on the sofa in the living room, the commotion and the slamming of car doors wake him up. Tommy goes to look out the window and sees the flashing lights of the Police cars and quickly turns to dash through the back of the house. Tommy flings open the back door and runs right into the arms of a Policeman. The lad struggles and yells, "Let me go! - Let me go!" Chief Rogers approaches the squirming youth and remarks, "You'll have to come with us, son. There are some questions that need answering!" An Officer holds Tommy as another Policeman reads the Miranda rights and handcuffs Tommy and put him into the back of a Police cruiser. The Police leave the property and return they way they drove. As the Police drive through the Reservation, people see Tommy in the back of the cruiser. Soon, the Police vehicles pull off Reservation land onto the highway and head toward town. Later that morning, Tommy is secured in an Interrogation Room. Tommy sits in the sculpted metal chair and drums his fingers on the metal table before him. He scans around the room - just a ceiling, floor, bare walls, and a metal door with a narrow observation window. He returns to drumming his fingers and sighs. At that moment, Police Chief Rogers opens the door and enters carrying a paper bag, and sits down opposite the youth. Tommy diverts his eyes and stares at the floor. Chief Rogers pulls out the ball cap and tosses it on the table. Tommy's eyes rivet to it. The Police Chief comments, "We know this is your ball cap, Tommy. Your fingerprints are on it, and your name is in it!" Tommy swallows and gives a glance at the Chief, "I want to go home!...I don't belong here." Chief Rogers replies in a stern tone, "I'll tell you where you belong...in jail for stealing cars and robbing stores. - That's where the bad kids go!" Tommy gets nervous and blurts, "Some gangbangers forced me to join or else!" Chief Rogers studies the teen and asks, "Where was this? Tommy replies, "A month ago...I was at Eddy's Pool Hall with some friends. Gangbangers pressured me to join. I told them no way. They beat me up bad!" Chief Rogers pulls out a pen and small notepad, "You say you were with friends? Witnesses to back up your story. Who were they?" Tommy sighs and casts his eyes to the floor, "Yah! Like they'll ever talk to you. - Fat chance of that!" The door opens and in walks Officer Stibbs. Tommy is surprised! Chief Rogers gets up and remarks, "I believe you know Officer Stibbs!" The Chief exits the room and Stibbs looks at Tommy and smiles, "Hi Tommy!" The teen is elated at seeing a familiar face, "Haven't seen you in years man! (Tommy eyes Stibbs) You look bigger - working out?" Officer Stibbs walks over and partially sits on the end of the table, and grins, "You know I believe in keeping fit!... And I also believe in helping out friends!...Tommy, I'm sorry about your dad and mom." Tommy looks at Stibbs with a puzzled expression, "How did you hear about it?" Stibbs replies, "I know the Trooper that was called to the accident. He told me." Tommy gets really quiet and a sad look covers his face, "Not the same without them, Homes!...Sometimes, I expect to see my mom cooking in the kitchen - and my dad fixing his car...But they're not there - no one's there!" Stibbs gets up and moves closer, and leans against the table near Tommy and offers solace, "Hey! I'm here for you...will help out best I can! (Pause) Your cap was found at Old Joe's. Stores have been hit all around. We traced it to one crew. - What can you tell me about them?" Tommy sits with a somber stare and replies, "Real gangbangers Homes! They claim this territory...even the Rez too. They're into everything. Real hardcore stuff. Word is out - anyone talk, your family won't walk!" Suddenly, the door opens and an Intake Officer pops his head in and looks at them both, "He goes to Lockup now!" Officer Stibbs pats Tommy on the shoulder, "Hang in there Tommy!" Officer Sibbs watches as the Intake Officer escorts Tommy out the door, down the hall and around the corner out of sight.

CHAPTER FORTY-FOUR

A Juvenile in District Court

The District Courthouse is an impressive structure of Georgian architecture style with wide cement steps that lead up to four white fluted Corinthian columns that identify the building's front entrance. This structure is the judicial centre of the territory where the area's legal cases are presented before the District Judge, and at times, before a Jury. It is here that Tommy's case, as well as others, will be heard and decided upon. Within the Courtroom, the space is filled with plaintiffs, defendants, prisoners, Prosecutors, lawyers, Public Defenders, families, friends, and curious spectators.

Tommy and his Public Defender sit at a polished oak table. His case is the first of the day, and the room is filled with whispers and quiet conversations as everyone waits for the proceedings to commence. Off to the side of the Courtroom, a Court Bailiff stands alert and ready. Suddenly, the side door opens and in walks Judge Spencer, a senior man with a full head of grey hair, wearing his black judicial robe. The Bailiff calls out in a loud clear voice, "All rise! Court's in session - Judge Spencer presiding!" Everyone in the Courtroom stands to their feet as Judge Spencer ascends the wood steps to the Judge's bench and sits down and puts on his wire frame reading glasses. The Bailiff announces, "All may be seated!" Judge Spencer reaches toward the stack of case dockets and picks the top one. He lays the folder before him and opens the flap and scans through the papers, then peers over his glasses at Tommy and his College-aged lawyer. Judge Spencer clears his throat - "Ahem!", then motions for the Bailiff to approach the Bench and hands him a piece of paper. The Bailiff looks at the note and stiffens up to formally remark, "The State vs Tommy Long Grass!" The Public Defender stands to his feet and tugs on Tommy's sleeve to stand up. Tommy gets off the chair and stands like a-deer-caught-in-the-headlights, he's never been inside a Courtroom and never faced a real Judge before. As the young lawyer stands attentive and professional, Tommy shifts his weight and fidgets a bit. Tommy looks at his lawyer and he gives Tommy an encouraging smile and turns his attention back to the Bench. Judge Spencer peruses over the papers, stops to glance at Tommy, then scans the file. The Magistrate adjusts his spectacles and gives a direct look at Tommy and his lawyer, flips through the docket and remarks, "Young man, you are facing some serious charges!...Grand Theft Auto, Break and Enter, Accessory to Commit a Crime, and member of a Criminal Gang." The Public Defender looks at the Judge as he extends his arm toward Tommy, "Your Honour, this teenager is genuinely remorseful and sorry for his actions and involvement. He was a naive participant, pressured to take part under the threat of bodily harm." Judge Spencer looks at the papers before him - then looks at Tommy and responds, "I will consider the fact he's a teenager of impressionable age. My concern is - will he re-offend?" The young lawyer replies, "If it please the Court, Your Honour, I'd like to have a Police Officer familiar with the boy to speak on his behalf. (Lawyer turns) We call Officer Stibbs to the stand." The Policeman gets to his feet, exits the gallery seating and makes his way to the Witness Stand and sits down. A Court Clerk approaches with a Bible and extends it level toward Stibbs. The Court Clerk comments, "Please place your right hand on the Bible and repeat after me...I promise to tell the whole truth, and nothing but the truth, so help me God!" Stibbs places his right hand on the Bible and repeats the Oath. The Clerk returns to the side area and the Judge looks directly at Stibbs and asks, "What can you tell the Court about this young lad?" Officer Stibbs turns to look at Tommy, then turns to face Judge Spencer and remarks, "Tommy lost both parents three years ago in a terrible car accident. He was thirteen at the time. Since then, Tommy has been staying in the family home - alone and unguided. He has an older brother, but he works construction and travels a lot and is seldom home. - For the most part, Tommy lives by himself!" Judge Spencer lifts his eyes off Stibbs and looks at Tommy, then the Judge scans the people in the Courtroom, the faces of many have an expression of sympathy and compassion. The Judge looks at the Policeman and asks, "Does he have any other relatives?" Stibbs replies, "He has a grandfather and grandmother - Carl and Kathy Long Grass. They live on the Indian Reservation." Judge Spencer scans the gallery, "Are the grandparents present in the Courtroom?" The Public defender quickly replies, "Yes, your Honour! The grandparents are present." Judge Spencer asks in a loud voice, "Would Tommy's grandparents please stand." Halfway in the middle on the left side, Carl and Kathy stand to their feet. The Judge looks at them and asks, "Are you Tommy's grandparents - Carl and Kathy Long Grass?" Both Carl and Kathy firmly nod in compliance, "Yes, we are!" The Judge glances at Tommy, then addresses the Courtroom, "To show the Court's mercy and compassion in providing a second chance to a young offender; Tommy will be released into your care and responsibility. Tommy would have to live at your home according to Court guidelines and restrictions… Do you accept the conditions of this arrangement?" Carl and Kathy eagerly reply, "Yes Your Honour! We accept! Tommy would be welcome to live with us." Judge Spencer removes his glasses and remarks, "Under these special circumstances, and to avoid the incarceration of a juvenile in a Federal Correctional Facility - I release Tommy Long Grass into your custody as his legal guardians, from this day forth until his twenty-first birthday when he will be of legal age." Judge Spencer pounds the gavel, Stibbs returns to his seat in the gallery. Tommy stands transfixed and his lawyer turns and puts his hand on Tommy's shoulder, "You're free to go now - under Court orders. You've got to live at your grandparents' house and be under their care and authority." Kathy and Carl rush up to hug and hold Tommy. Kathy with tears exclaims, "Let's go home!" Tommy's face shows relief. As Tommy and his grandparents make their way toward the Courtroom's exit doors, Tommy stops when he gets near Stibbs. The youth looks at the Policeman and smiles, "Thanks Homes! I owe you!" Stibbs smiles and replies, "You don't owe me anything Tommy! Just glad I was able to help.(Pause) Tommy, always remember - I'm your friend!" Tommy nods his appreciation and the trio resume their exit of the Courtroom. Tommy, Carl and Kathy go through the thick polished oak doors and enter the busy hallway and walk toward the front entrance. When they emerge onto the wide front steps of the Courthouse, Tommy, Carl and Kathy share a quick hug of celebration as they bask in the warm sunshine.

The trio descend the Courthouse steps and walk the parking lot to Carl's Chevy Malibu. Carl and Kathy get into the front seats and Tommy climbs in the back seat. The grandpa starts the engine and pulls out of the parking spot and exits the lot. At the stop sign, he signals left and steers the Malibu down Main Street that leads out of town. They pass buildings, stores and homes along the way. Tommy looks out his door window and notices town kids sprinkled here and there, hanging out in front yards and chilling at street corners. The middle class kids wear nice designer outfits. Tommy looks down at his cheap worn out clothes. Carl drives the car toward the traffic light that connects Main Street to the local Highway. He gets the red light and stops, and signals right. At the green light, the man turns the vehicle right and presses the gas pedal to reach Highway speed and heads in the direction of the Reservation. Kathy turns her head toward Tommy and remarks, "We can have bannock, fried fish and corn for supper - would you like that?" Tommy politely nods, "Sounds good grandma!" Kathy turns back toward the windshield and looks at Carl with a smile of accomplishment. Carl smiles. The Malibu goes down the Highway around curves, over hills and dips, and the long straight stretch before reaching the turnoff. Carl signals and turns right onto Reservation Road and proceeds through the Indian Reservation.

CHAPTER FORTY-FIVE
A New Home - A New Start

Heading home, Carl and Kathy wave to folks they know. Some time later, the Malibu turns onto Plains Road and soon Carl slows down and steers into the driveway of their ranch style bungalow. At the end of the driveway beside the road is a mailbox with large letters - LONG GRASS. Arriving home, everyone exits. They leave the car and approach the cement stoop and front door. Carl uses his key to open the front door and merrily comments, "Your new home Tommy!" Tommy tilts his head and replies, "Grandpa…you know I've been here before." Standing behind, Kathy beams a big smile and places her hands on Tommy's shoulder and remarks, "You just visited before. From now on you're going to live with us!" They enter the house and Kathy goes directly to the kitchen to prepare the meal. Carl and Tommy walk over to the side hallway and Carl opens the door that Tommy sometime uses as his bedroom. Tommy stands quiet as his grandpa inspects the room, furniture, walls and ceiling. He comments, "We're gonna get you some new furniture and paint your bedroom. (He looks at Tommy) What paint colour do you want?" Tommy scans the room's interior and replies, "Something blue like the sky." Carl smiles and nods, "We can do that." Carl turns and leaves the room and Tommy sprawls out on the bed and looks up at the ceiling. The lad takes a deep breath and lays relaxed and still - the sounds of dishes being set on the table carry into the room. Kathy has set out the flatware and cutlery and laid out the bannock, fried fish and cobs of corn. The food looks appetizing. Kathy cheerfully chimes, "Supper's ready! Come and get it!" Carl gets off his favourite armchair and Tommy exits the bedroom. Everyone gets seated at the table and Kathy begins to pass around the food. Tommy scoops healthy portions onto his plate - he's really hungry. Carl and Kathy look at each other and grin. As the small family eat the meal, Carl asks Tommy, "There's something I want to talk with you about later?" Tommy is devouring his food and pauses, "What about grandpa?" The man gazes at the young lad, "Special training that would be good for you." Tommy stops chewing and takes a sip of fruit juice, he looks at his grandpa and comments, "You know I'm not good at school stuff." Carl smiles and remarks, "This type of training is not school stuff - it's different - special! It will help you in every area of your life." Tommy's interest is peeked and he stops eating and looks at his grandfather and remarks, "So grandpa, what is it?" Carl makes direct eye contact with his grandson and replies in a pleasant tone, "Martial Arts!" Tommy gives a slight chuckle as pushes his empty plate aside and comments, "You mean the Kung Fu stuff I see in movies!" Carl shakes his head, grins and replies, "No Hong Kong movie stunts - just a local Martial Arts program with a good instructor! - Interested?" Tommy sits and reflects upon what Carl just said, and he shrugs, "Hey, why not! - I'm gonna be bored living out here all the time!" Kathy and Carl smile at Tommy's reply. Kathy gets up and collects the dishes and takes them to the kitchen sink. Carl looks at Tommy, "Fine! I'll speak with my friend and mention that you'll be joining his class." Tommy gives a quick nod and gets up and goes to his room. Kathy starts to wash the plates and cutlery. Carl stands up and goes beside his wife to help dry the plates, glasses and utensils. After he's finished, he walks into the living room and over to sit down in his armchair and flips open a newspaper.

CHAPTER FORTY-SIX

Gold Eagle Martial Arts

The Chevy Malibu drives into the one story strip plaza and stops in front of a brick building with a large glass window. Carl and Tommy exit the car and Tommy looks up at the building's overhead sign: GOLD EAGLE MARTIAL ARTS. Tommy looks through the window and sees teenagers dressed in white Martial Arts uniforms practicing moves. A man dressed in a white and black outfit stands to the side of the mat area and observes the students go through their routines. Carl puts a hand on Tommy's shoulder, "Let's go meet your Instructor." Carl pushes the front door open and he and Tommy enter inside. The Instructor looks at them, smiles and walks over. The man glances at Carl and Tommy and remarks, "Hi Carl! (Turns to Tommy) and who is this young man?" Carl puts a hand on Tommy's shoulder and gives a little squeeze and replies, "This is my grandson, Tommy. (Looks at Tommy) This is Morgan Jeffrey your Teacher - Your Sensi!" Morgan puts out his hand to welcome the young lad, "Hi Tommy! I'm glad you decided to visit us. We've just finished class - right now, the students are practicing today's lesson." Carl remarks, "Sensi, we'll keep out of the way and watch from the side." The Instructor leaves and Carl and Tommy position themselves off to the side. The Sensi maneuvers around his pupils - he corrects body position and approves proper form. After a few minutes, Morgan walks to the front of the large exercise mat and faces the class. The students stop their routines and quickly assemble in neat rows. Morgan lowers down onto both knees and the entire class does the same. Some kids are still catching their breath from the workout, while others knee quiet and composed. The Sensi looks at his students and comments, "Next month, there'll be testing for belts. I want you to practice and work hard toward your goal." The class reply in unison, "Yes Sensi!" Morgan gives an encouraging smile and remarks, "Remember - when leaving the Dojo, how we're to be at home and school - obey your parents and do your chores - and listen to your teachers and do your homework." The students heartily reply, "Yes Sensi!" The Instructor gazes across the youthful faces, "You're dismissed!" Morgan bows to the class and the students bow in return. With class over, the kids fetch gym bags, collect belongings, and get ready to leave - some walk home while some others wait for their ride. Morgan walks over to Carl and Tommy still at their spot at the side of the floor mat. Carl comments, "You got a fine group of students!" Morgan replies, "They really got heart! I train them and they work hard. (To Tommy) So Tommy, what do you think? Are you ready to join us?" Tommy shuffles his stance and answers, "Never done this stuff before." Carl leans in a bit and comments, "You'll be fine! You're a quick learner - and you're strong and healthy." Morgan adds in, "When you start - if it's difficult, I can give you extra instruction." The grandfather asks, "What do you say, Tommy? - in?" Tommy stands quiet for a few seconds as he looks around the Dojo, then nods, "Okay! I'll try it - see what happens." The Sensi responds to Tommy words, "Great! Your first class is next Wednesday. See you then!" With Tommy's decision made, Morgan leaves the two and walks to the Dojo office. Carl and Tommy exit through the front door and get into the Chevy Malibu. Carl starts the engine, reverses the car, shifts the stick and drives off. Tommy lifts his eyes to the sign overhead - GOLD EAGLE MARTIAL ARTS - He eyes the Club's Logo of an impressive flying eagle with talons extended for battle.

Somewhere in town, Spike and Crew hang out at the popular Fast Food outlets located at the outskirts of town near the highway. The outlets are busy with lots of cars and customers. Spike and gang members are hungry and grab a bite to eat. Around them are big shiny trucks, tricked out imports, expensive SUVs, rocket bikes, and family vans. As the gang chill leaning against their rides, a gangster comments, "Tommy hasn't returned my text! - Maybe he's scared." Spike sneers in reply, "He's not scared - he's a traitor, Homes! Plain avoiding us! My gut tells me he turned on us." The Homie beside Spike asks, "What are you gonna do about it?" Spike pulls out of his lean and stands up straight with a determined expression and replies, "Gonna find out where that traitor stays - gonna pay him a little visit. (punches fist into his palm) No one leaves the Northwest Crew. No one Homes!" The gang members eye each other and nod their heads in agreement.

CHAPTER FORTY-SEVEN
Attending District High School

Carl stands outside beside Tommy's car, lays his hand on the car roof and leans down near the driver's window, "You got to be in High School - regular attendance. Court Order!" Tommy stares ahead and replies, "I'll be there!" Carl senses something is bothering his grandson and asks, "What's wrong?" Tommy raises his gaze to Carl and replies, "School and me don't work out. Hate being there!" Carls bends down to be eye level with Tommy and speaks in a fatherly tone, "Promise me that you'll be at school.(Pause) Your got your grandma and me - we'll do this together." Tommy smiles as he replies, "Okay grandpa. - I promise!" Tommy fires up the engine and drives onto the paved road toward town. Kathy watches from the home's living room window.

The District High School is an 60's construction two storey brick complex with a sizeable parking lot, and a small landscaped circle with a flag pole that flies the beloved American flag - the Stars and Stripes. The morning rush for class brings in busy school traffic - buses, parents in cars with kids, pick up trucks, family vans, and motor bikes. There's a mix of teens from around the surrounding towns, farms, and the Indian Reservation. It's a typical High School like so many across the nation - with jocks, nerds, cool kids, rich kids, techies, hipsters, outcasts, and Rez kids. As students rush to class, two teachers monitor the activity from the school's elevated front steps. The majority of kids hustle to class, and some just mosey along. A few sneak off to skip school. With the last student through the door, the teachers shut the door and lock it.

Inside Tommy's new classroom, students jostle and grab desks - some are victorious and others have to settle for the desk they get. Tommy enters the classroom and spots an empty desk halfway down the left side of the room, he grabs it and sits down. In front of him sits a big jock wearing a Varsity Football jacket. Behind him is a nerd with thick glasses, and to his right sits a posh girl in designer clothes. Tommy gives a slight sigh - he's feels totally out of place. As the kids are busy chatting or on their phones, a teacher walks into the room carrying a brown leather satchel and a stack of papers. She closes the door and goes to the teacher's desk, sets down the papers and satchel, turns to grab a dry marker and begins to write her name on the whiteboard - Ms. Meagan Mills. The thirty-something lady pivots about and looks at the students and remarks, "Welcome class! My name is Ms. Mills and I'm your homeroom teacher. (Passes out papers) You gather here each morning before going off to your other classes. I'm handing out your schedule - follow it and you'll be fine! (Pause) There'll be Attendance in the morning so make sure you sign your name - otherwise, the school Office sees you as truant - missing school - then the Office will call home (looks at class) And we don't want that - right?" A couple guys poke their buddies and snicker. A prime and proper young lady at a front desk puts up her hand, "Ms. Mills?" The lady turns and looks at the student, "Yes!" The girl asks, "Do we come back here after our last class?" Megan Mills replies, "Good question! - the answer is no! Teachers take attendance at the beginning of their class. No signature means no attendance! - Makes sure you put your name down." She walks to the whiteboard that covers the room's wall behind her desk - picks up a big marker and writes in large cursive letters - American Geography - and turns to face the class. She walks over to a side rack and pulls down a large map of the American Northwest States - Washington, Oregon, Idaho, Utah, Colorado, Montana, Wyoming, and North and South Dakota. Ms. Mills announces to her students, "In class, we'll be studying these States - learning about topography, surface terrain, river systems, climate, agriculture, industry and population." A guy near the front asks, "Will we do reports?" The kids buzz at his suggestion. Meagan Mills replies, "There will be two kinds of reports: one you do on your own - and the other as part of a team." Many students begin to murmur - and a few mildly cheer. A guy on the right side of the room quips, "Do we get to pick our teams?" Ms Mills scans the group and remarks, "No! Each student will be assigned a team. - I'll pick names from a box." Now, the kids murmur and groan! A kid on the left pipes up, "What about marks?" Megan Mills pivots around to look at the entire class and replies, "50% of your mark will from class - 15% from your individual work - and 35% will be from your team report." The students take a few seconds to digest what she just mentioned - some kids sit stoic and tight-lipped, and others sit with pouty unhappy faces. SCHOOL BELL RINGS. Ms. Mills quickly injects, "See you all tomorrow!" The kids get up out of their seats and the classroom quickly empties as kids rush off to another class. There's some chatter as a few kids check their Schedule for room numbers and classroom location. The school halls get crowded.

The school day comes to a close and everybody leaves in assorted vehicles - buses, cars, bikes and vans. Tommy hustles to his blue Mustang and cranks the engine - VROOM! He pulls out of the parking lot and heads toward the highway. Tommy motors past gas stations, strip plazas, stores and bars. People are out and about - workers getting off shift, parents picking up kids at school, families buying groceries and running errands. The lad takes it all in. Tommy cruises along until he approaches the Reservation Road exit. He turns and heads along the main artery. The buildings on the Rez are hit and miss - some businesses are well-to-do, while others are in need of maintenance and repair. Tommy watches as his Native American people do the same as the townies - get off work, buy supplies, taxi kids from school, and get groceries. He signals and turns the wheel onto Plains Road that will take him home. He navigates the bends, dips, curves and straight stretch before reaching the house. He steers into the driveway and parks the car beside the large tree on the property. Tommy cuts the engine. Kathy stands in the doorway with the front door open and calls out. "Tommy! Can you please help?" Tommy replies, "Ok grandma! Be right there." Tommy exits and shuts the car door and hurries up the front steps and into the house. Inside the living room, Kathy is standing next to a large mirror with ornate antique trim. His grandmother beams and mentions, "I picked it up at a garage sale. Beautiful - isn't it?" Tommy walks over and checks out the mirror, "Looks pretty cool! (Inspects details) How's you get it here?" Kathy proudly grins, "The lady and her brother drove it out here. He carried it in but didn't have time to help hang it." Tommy bends and picks up the mirror with a hand grip on each side, "I'll lift this and you can show me where you want to hang it." With Tommy lugging the mirror, Kathy steps back to stand in the centre of the room and scans around the living space, looking here and there. The mirror is getting heavy, even for a strapping young teen, and Tommy remarks, "Grandma, you find a spot yet? This mirror is getting heavy!" Kathy's eyes light up as she points to her designated place and chimes, "There

- Perfect!" Tommy carries the mirror over to the wall and Kathy gets a measuring tape and locates the correct spot and height. She pencils a mark and pounds in the anchor hook - then steps back. Tommy lifts the mirror to the proper level and attempts to latch the back wire onto the hook. After three attempts, the wire finally catches and the mirror hangs secure. He steps back and joins Kathy. They both eye-ball the new piece of home decor. Kathy steps forward and grabs the frame to correct the tilt until the mirror sits level and true. Tommy remarks, "Looks good grandma!" Kathy beams a contented smile and replies, "Yes it does! (To Tommy) Thanks Tommy, couldn't have done this without you!" Tommy steps closer and preens himself, "Glad to help grandma!" Kathy looks at her grandson, "Supper soon! Fried chicken and macaroni salad." Tommy grins and remarks, "Great! - I'm staving!" Kathy walks into the kitchen and Tommy goes into his room, tosses his backpack in the corner and flakes out on the bed - and stares at a Martial Arts poster.

CHAPTER FORTY-EIGHT
Making New Friends

Officer Stibbs and Tommy are spending some catch-up time at a local Ice Cream Parlour, each enjoying a double scoop cone. This is a 'buddy time' for the two friends as they reconnect after not seeing each other for a while. Officer Stibbs and Tommy joke, laugh, and carry on with fun silly antics. Tommy takes a bite of his Chocolate Blast and comments, "It's sure good to see you, Homes!" The Policeman looks at the teenager, "I wanted to know if things are working out?" Tommy smiles and replies, "Grandpa and grandma treat me real good - I even joined a Martial Arts class - gonna start soon!" Stibbs takes care of some dripping ice cream on his cone and remarks, "That's good, Tommy! What about school? You doing okay?" Tommy adjusts his stance on the sidewalk and leans against the street light and replies, "School is school - but this time it seems different." Stibbs perks up, "Different - How?" The teenager licks his ice cream and gives his reply, "This time, I find the stuff interesting - not bored like before." His Policeman friend puts out his hand and messes up Tommy's hair, "Sounds to me like you got the attitude of a winner!" Tommy laughs and remarks, "At least I ate my cone first!" Tommy reaches out and tries to grab his friend's Police hat. Stibbs laughs as he fends off the playful attack.

Later on, Wednesday evening, Tommy wears his white Martial Arts uniform and stands in a row with other students - attentive and ready for instruction. Sensi Jeffrey assumes a fight position before the class of eager teens, and announces, "Today, we will learn the Dragon Fist technique to disable an attacker. Pair up and take positions." The students quickly pick partners and find floor space. First timer Tommy doesn't know anyone much less what to do. He stands between two students, a tall kid named Connor to his left, and a girl named Sarah who is shorter than him that stands to his right. Sarah turns to Tommy with a smile, "You're new here, so I'll be your partner - if that's okay with you?" Tommy glances around at the matched up pairs and replies, "That's okay! I don't know what to do anyways." Connor pipes up, "She's tough dude!(Chuckles) You'll be sorry." Sarah gives a rebuttal, "Never mind Connor! He razes all the newbies (to Tommy) The Sensi demonstrates the new technique. We form pairs and practice our moves." Tommy looks at her and quips, "Does it matter if I'm bigger than you?" Connor overhears and snickers! Sarah smiles and remarks, "Don't worry about that!" With the class teamed up, all eyes focus on Sensi Jeffrey. He moves and fixes his body to illustrate correct position for the legs and arms, then he strikes forward with the Dragon Fist. The Sensi comments, "The Dragon Fist increases your force upon an opponent. - Hit the centre of the stomach at the diaphragm, it delivers a powerful punch and knocks the wind out of your attacker! Watch me again (Demonstrates) Now, practice with your partner. One will deliver the punch - the other will block. Later, you can switch." Sensi Jeffrey rehearses the maneuver more slowly and all the students keenly watch his arm position and fist formation. When he finishes, he motions for the class to begin their practice. Tommy observes Sarah and notes her stance and limb position. Tommy checks his foot placement - then looks at Sarah. She asks, "You feel ready? Tommy nods and replies, "Think so!" Tommy no sooner got his words out when Sarah strikes with blistering speed - and stops. Tommy never even got to move. He looks down at her fist a quarter inch from his stomach midsection. Sarah comments, "You didn't protect yourself." Tommy replies, "How could I , you were so fast!" Sensi Jeffrey walks up, smiles at the two and comments, "Tommy, I see you got yourself a good partner. Sarah is one of our top students. She wins Competitions every year!" He points his arm and Tommy glances over at the Trophy wall lined with Awards. Tommy grins and replies, "Guess size doesn't matter." Sensi Morgan puts his gaze on the young lad and comments, "Size is just one factor. Martial Arts teaches you Offence and Defence - how to use your opponent's size and strength to your advantage. We teach you ways to protect yourself, and how to stop an attacker." Tommy glances over to Sarah, "Well - all I know is Sarah's fast and got the drop on me." The young lady encourages, "You'll be able to do what I can once you learn." Morgan Jeffrey remarks, "Look around Tommy (sweeps arm across the room) Every student started where you are today - and in time, you'll be able to do martial Arts like them." The Instructor gives Tommy an encouraging pat on the shoulder and resumes his tour of the other students. Sarah gets Tommy's attention, "See my fighting stance. Notice how I form my fist. Look at my strike position." Tommy observes all that Sarah mentioned. He copies her exactly and responds, "I think I got it now!" Sarah remarks, "Good! Now, attack me!" Tommy lunges forward and Sarah blocks. Tommy repeats again and again, each time Sarah deflects his punch. Tommy pauses - refocuses. Sarah holds position. Suddenly, Tommy strikes with speed and force - and hits Sarah in the stomach - Sarah buckles. Tommy stops and blurts, "I'm sorry Sarah! I didn't mean to hit you." Sarah straightens up and grins, It's okay Tommy! You got past my block - you did good. Real good!" Tommy's face lights up at Sarah's comment. As they continue in the practice, Tommy's expression begins to show more confidence as he and Sarah spar. Toward the end of class, Sensi Jeffrey takes his place at the front of the mat. All the students stop working out and assemble in rows. Tommy stands beside Sarah, he's breathing heavy from the workout. He proudly smiles. The Instructor and the students all lower to their knees. Sensi Jeffrey remarks, "Please remember our Dojo Motto - At home, at school, anywhere - Be your best! Do your best!" All the students in unison reply, "Yes Sensi!" Sensi Jeffrey glances over at Tommy and gives an encouraging smile, then he looks across the neatly formed rows of students and bows to them. The entire class bow in return. With instruction over, the kids get their backpacks, duffle bags and belongings, and head off. Some get on their bicycles and motor bikes, while others wait for rides from parents. Tommy heads toward the exit. As he walks past Sarah, she comments, "I was happy to be your partner today! You did really well for your first time!" Tommy looks at the gal, "Thanks Sarah! I learned a lot from you - You're good!" She replies, "So maybe next time we can buddy up again?" Tommy ponders a few seconds and remarks, "Yah! I'd like that. - See you." Tommy goes out the front entrance toward his Mustang, and Sarah stands with a gleam in her eye.

Next week at suppertime, Carl and Kathy treat Tommy to dining out at a popular local eatery. They enter the establishment's front doors and see the restaurant is busy with patrons having meals. Waitresses carry plates of food and line cooks put up orders ready to be served. Carl, Kathy and Tommy look over the crowd and spot an empty table midway in the restaurant. Carl leads the way through the tables - then he abruptly stops. There at a table before him sit Morgan Jeffrey, Steve

Armstrong, Barry Osprey and Eli Waters having their meal. The men stop eating and look up at Carl - who is quickly joined by Kathy and Tommy. Carl remarks, "Hi guys! How's it going?" Morgan replies with a grin, "The roast beef is excellent!" Carl puts a hand on Tommy's shoulder and comments, "Tommy, you know your Sensi, Morgan Jeffrey (Tommy nods). Let me introduce these other men to you. (He points) Steve Armstrong is a welder, Barry Osprey is an Auto Mechanic, and Eli Waters runs a horse ranch." Tommy speaks out, "Pleased to meet you!" The three men smile and give the lad a friendly nod. Carl injects, "Well, better let you guys get back to your food. (Grins) I know you all got big appetites." Morgan playfully waves Carl to move along. Kathy, Tommy and Carl reach their table and get seated. A cheerful waitress comes up and gives each a menu - then pulls out her pen and order pad.

A few days pass and Tommy is about to enter his High School Homeroom. Megan Mills sits at her desk as the students pour into class. It's a moment of organized confusion as kids bump into each other to grab their seats. Tommy is the last one through the door, and Ms. Mills asks, "Tommy, please close the door." Tommy turns and shuts the door and walks to his desk. One of the big jocks sticks out his foot and trips Tommy. His books and notebook go flying as Tommy stumbles. The class breaks out laughing! Ms. Mills scolds, "Students - that's not funny!" A kid in the back snickers and mumbles, "Oh yes it is!" Tommy regains his poise and picks up his books and notebook - gives a cut-eye to the culprit, moves to his desk and sits down. A student on the far right of the room remarks, "Miss Mills. I lost my homework - almost finished the assignment too!" Some of the guys make sad faces and wipe their eyes with boo-hoo tears. Megan Mills asks, "Where did you put it last?" The youth replies, I put it on the kitchen counter but it disappeared!" Ms. Mills looks at her class and suggests, "Will someone in class be willing to share their assignment notes?" The teacher looks around - no student seems interested - then Tommy puts up his hand, and comments, "My notes aren't the best, but he's welcome to them!" Megan Mills nods her head with a smile, "Good! Now that that's settled - let's open our textbooks to Topography and Physical Features."

As the students are in class, outside the school at the back of the football bleachers, a gangster called Griffin holds a clear plastic bag with coloured pills. The tough guy chides, "If you want the full dose - then pay the full price!" The four students rummage through their pockets and count out their money. One kid collects the bills and hands the cash to Griffin and comments, "There! Should be enough bro." The student standing next him is edgy, "Hurry up! - Before a teacher sees us." Griffin grabs and counts the bills, then offers the bag of contraband. One kid takes it and nervously stuffs the plastic bag into his pants. Griffin steps forward and puts his face inches from one student, and threatens, "Get this! - I'm not your bro!" The students sheepishly slink back, turn and race toward the school building. Griffin smirks and pulls out a big wad of bills and adds in the new money. He strides over to his muscle car, cranks the engine and presses the gas pedal - DEEP ROAR - then peels away.

CHAPTER FORTY-NINE

Spike and Crew Come Calling

Carl, Kathy and Tommy are in the living room when they hear - VROOM! VROOM! VROOM! They quickly go to the big picture window, move the curtains aside and see three cars with tinted glass pull into the driveway and stop. The cars shimmer and shake as the powerful engines idle and rumble. Next, the car horns blare loud and hold......H-O-N-K!! The first car's driver window rolls down and Spike sticks his head out and yells, "Tommy! Tommy! Come out Homes - your old crew is here!" Tommy stands with Kathy and Carl at the picture window and looks out at his former gang. Suddenly, Carl disappears from view. Spike and the gang laugh as they repeatedly honk their car horns. Carl opens the front door and steps out onto the cement stoop. The horns abruptly stop. Carl raises his voice in a firm tone, "Tommy's not coming out! He won't be running around with you anymore!" Spike looks at his gang members and gets mad and steps out of the car. The other car doors open and the entire gang get out of their cars. Carl looks and sizes up things - eleven young toughs standing macho! Carl steps off the stoop and moves to the middle of the large front lawn. With his crew in tow, Spike swags over and confronts the older man. The gangsters spread out to surround Carl. They hold knives, crowbars and lead pipes, and move their weapons in a threatening manner. Carl turns to look at the living room window, Kathy is on her cell phone and Tommy is frozen just starring. Spike barks at Carl, "Look old man! Tommy is one of us - once you're in - you don't get out!" (Spike Yells) NO ONE GETS OUT!" Carl gives the young punk a steely stare and replies, "I'm telling you and your gang to get off my property - NOW!" Spike turns to his crew, smirks, then suddenly lunges at the grandfather - Carl grabs Spike's arm and flips him hard face-first into the ground. Spike scrambles back up - with bruises and a bloody nose. The young thug embarrassed and hurt, cries out, "Get the old man! Beat him up!" The angry gang members around Carl begin to swing and move their knives, pipes and crowbars to and fro - then rush in. Carl lets loose knockout kicks, powerful punches, disabling blocks and lightning strikes. The old man decimates the young toughs and renders them knocked unconscious, doubled-over, and reeling in pain with broken noses, broken bones - and broken pride! The gangsters limp and carry themselves back to their cars. Spike stands livid and scowls holding his twisted arm, and yells out a threat, "Nobody does that to us and lives! Hear me old man - you're a dead man! A dead man - you got that!" The defeated gang leader gets into his vehicle and all three cars fire up their engines and tear off the property. They floor it down the road and outta sight. The front door opens and Kathy and Tommy race to Carl's side. He has a cut on his arm and shoulder, and a scrap across his forehead. Kathy looks at Carl's wounds and remarks, "I called the Police! They should be here any minute." Just as she finishes speaking, SIRENS approach. Three squad cars and a Paramedic van pull onto the grounds. Officers quickly exit and the Reservation Police Chief comes over to them. He scans the trio and comments, "We radioed to set up road blocks - they won't get far! (Checks Carl) Better get you looked at!" The Police Chief motions a Paramedic over and he starts to check things out. Carl shows his arm and comments, "Just a small cut - a few stitches." The Paramedic ushers Carl to the back of the ambulance and Carl parks himself on the edge of the interior. The Paramedic cleans and dresses the wound, and remarks, "Good thing the cut wasn't deeper - otherwise a severed artery!" Kathy and Tommy walk up to Carl, he looks at them, raises his arm to show the stitches and remarks, "Hey look - a battle scar!" Kathy rolls her eyes and Tommy is partially still in shock, then he asks excitedly, "Grandpa - how'd you do it? - I mean - take on all those guys at once?" The grandfather gazes at his grandson and replies, "When I was your age, someone taught me Martial Arts. This time, I used it for Self Defence!" Tommy is pumped, "Wow grandpa! I had no idea!(Pause) Will I be able to fight like that?" Carl remarks, "First things first! - Stick with your Martial Arts training!" Tommy gives some quick Karate chops, "I'm ready man!" Carl smiles and he reaches out and messes Tommy's hair, "All in good time!" Carl gets off the back of the ambulance, and the three walk past Officers collecting discarded weapons and other evidence. They go up the front steps and into the house.

CHAPTER FIFTY
The Northwest Gang Intimidate

Out in the rugged desert region, inside an old industrial auto yard warehouse, boisterous gangsters gather in a big circle. It's sparring time! In the middle, Bossman faces five enormous thugs. Bossman has jeans and no shirt - his body ripped with muscle and covered with tattoos. The five opponents are wielding chains, clubs and knives. Bossman assumes a Martial Art fighting stance as he eyes the five attackers. Suddenly one thug swings a metal club while another swipes his knife blade. Bossman kicks the knife away then pivots with a roundhouse to KO the guy, then he blocks and grabs the club and repeatedly smashes the club against the attacker's head putting him down. The other three close in to attack - Bossman spins about with his heavy boot and kicks two unconscious - they drop to the cement floor. Bossman grabs the last thug and pummels him in a flurry of blows - then tosses his motionless body aside. Bossman looks at his defeated attackers unconscious and withering on the floor and he lifts both arms high in victory. The gangsters around him CHEER! They break out chanting the name of their leader, "Bossman! Bossman! Bossman!" Bossman smiles wide and thoroughly revels in the adulation and attention.

CAR HORNS SOUND!

Spike and his crew roll into the large auto yard littered with assorted stolen vehicles. Armed Northwest Gang members and Lieutenants give cold stares. Spike exits the car nursing his sprained arm and calls out to a nearby Lieutenant, "I need to see Bossman!" The gangster leader waves to a thug by a door and he runs inside. Soon word spreads.

LOUD MECHANICAL NOISE.

Two large industrial steel doors split apart - and out strides Bossman and a group of musclebound thugs. Spike and his crew stand tense and nervous. The gruff gang leader swags up to Spike and gets in his face, "What you doin' Homes? Don't you have cars to jack!" Spike is tiffed about their recent defeat and belly-aches, "We got trouble! - Big trouble!" Bossman steps back, tilts his head and eyes Spike and the gang, "What kind of trouble?" Spike remarks in a shaky voice, "A home boy cut out on us - stays with his grandparents. We went to get our soldier - but his grandfather stopped us!" Bossman is stunned and gets wide-eyed, he can hardly believe his ears, "Stopped you!?...... Stopped your whole crew!" Spike is totally embarrassed and replies, "He's a tough old man! - Knows that Karate stuff!" Bossman scans the local crew and bellows, "Karate! Tough guy! - Where's this guy live?" Spike remarks, "Some old Indian on the Reservation! He lives on Plains Road - the mailbox says Long Grass!" Bossman motions to a lieutenant and whispers in the thug's ear. The gangster nods and quickly rounds up some other thugs and they depart with haste. Bossman turns to Spike and crew, then orders, "You and your crew get back to business - we need those cars! - I'm gonna send this tough guy a message!" Bossman pivots about and heads back into the big warehouse with his posse following. Spike and his crew climb into their cars and tear out of the auto yard toward town.

The next day, Carl comes out of the hardware store carrying a gallon of paint and some brushes and rollers. As he walks to the Malibu he notices a black sedan with darken windows parked to the far side. The sedan looks out of place in the store's parking lot. Carl loads the supplies into the car trunk and gets behind the wheel and starts the Malibu. The black sedan's big engine also fires up! DEEP RUMBLE! As Carl pulls away, he notices the black sedan starts to follow him. He drives out of the parking lot, down the street and around town a bit - the black sedan follows at a distance. Carl takes the street out of town and turns onto the Highway and speeds up on a straight stretch, the black sedan also speeds up to follow and keep pace. Carl glances in the review mirror, the sedan's opaque windows limit him from knowing who's inside that car. He looks down the road and floors the Malibu and races down the straight stretch and the other car does the same. Carl suddenly brakes and stops on the Highway and he glances in the side mirror, the black sedan is also stopped and hangs back at a distance with its powerful engine rumbling. Out in the middle of nowhere, the two cars just stop and idle, surrounded by desert sand and cactus. It all seems odd and somewhat threatening. Carl is just about to exit his car when he hears the black sedan's tires squeal, and looks in the rearview mirror to see the sedan turn around and race off toward town. Carl takes a sigh of relief - then a pondering expression comes over his face. He shifts into drive and goes toward the Reservation.

Kathy just got her hair done at her favourite Salon. She stands at the cash register and pays the stylist and leaves her a generous tip. Kathy exits the front door and stands on the sidewalk. She watches a black sedan with dark windows pass by her ever-so-slowly. It gives her the creeps and she shutters. Kathy turns and walks down the sidewalk and gets into her car parked by the curb. She starts the engine and signals to merge with the traffic. An off-road pickup stops to let her into traffic, Kathy waves thanks to the young couple in the truck's front seat as she leaves the curb. As she drives down the street and goes through an intersection, Kathy notices the black sedan pull out from a side street and get behind her a few cars back. She changes lane and the black sedan changes lane. Kathy turns left onto another street and the black sedan turns and keeps tailing her. Now, Kathy begins to feel stressed and afraid. Her forehead begins to get moist from some slight perspiration, her heart beats faster. As Kathy drives along the street she sees a plaza up ahead on her right and notices a Police cruiser in the parking lot. She cranks the wheel and zooms into the parking lot and pulls into a spot near the Police cruiser and cuts the engine. Kathy looks out at the street to watch the creepy black sedan drive by and keep going. Kathy takes a deep breath and glances down - her hands are trembling!

Later that evening at their house on Plains Road; Carl, Kathy and Tommy are dining on baked salmon, home fries, green peas, corn, and garden salad. Carl and Kathy are both more quiet than usual. Kathy looks at her husband, "Honey, you seem lost in thought - anything wrong?" Carl comes to life and shifts his gaze to Kathy and replies, "No Dear - I'm good! Just thinking how to fix Tommy's room. (Smiles) Want to make it A-Class!" Tommy shovels more fries onto his plate and remarks, "Grandpa, I'm okay with it now! You don't have to do anything special for me." The grandfather looks at his grandson with fondness, "To your grandma and me - you are special! That's why we want to give you the best room we can." Kathy leans over and gives Carl a kiss on the cheek, smiles and comments, "Who's ready for some Blueberry pie with French Vanilla ice cream?" Tommy and Carl's eyes light up. Kathy gets up from the table and goes into the kitchen and returns with a flaky golden crust delicious Blueberry pie and a quart of vanilla ice cream. She cuts and dishes out the dessert and tops each serving with generous vanilla scoops. Tommy and Carl take the helping with eager delight. Kathy serves herself a modest portion. All three savour their yummy dessert! As they eat, Carl clears the throat, and pauses to comment, "It seemed some car was following me today!" Tommy stops his spoon halfway and looks at his grandpa. Kathy puts down her fork, looks directly at Carl and remarks in an alarmed tone, "There was a car that followed me today too! A creepy black car with dark windows. It kept following me everywhere I went - ever since I left the Beauty Salon." Carl quickly injects, "That's the car that followed me! A black sedan with tinted windows!" Kathy and Carl look at each other. Tommy remarks, "In the gang, I remember hearing about a black car with really dark windows - it belonged to a gang leader." Kathy with a worried expression reaches out to clutch Carl's hand, "Honey, what are we going to do?" Carl cups her hand with his and replies, "Darling, things will be okay! I'll let the Police know what happened. Officers will keep a close watch on the car. If anything - the Police will nab them in a heartbeat!" Kathy feels more relaxed after Carl's assurance and she smiles relief. Tommy looks at his grandparents, then turns away and stares in silence.

CHAPTER FIFTY-ONE
Tommy At Martial Arts

Sensi Jeffrey observes how Tommy has developed his ability and skill in the Martial Arts class. The Instructor closely watches as Tommy correctly performs the Katas and fight techniques. During the session, Tommy spars with a fellow student - and wins! Sensi Jeffrey walks over to Tommy and comments, "You're showing real improvement! Keep up the good work." The teenager replies with a determined nod, "Thank you Sensi! I try to practice every moment I get." The Instructor moves to the front of the exercise mats and addresses all the students, "Regionals are in two months. We are allowed five entries. If you want to compete - please let em know!" The class get excited at the news and chatter fills the room. Sarah looks at Tommy and asks, "Tommy, why don't you enter?" Tommy waves his hand and shakes his head, "Sheesh - No way! I'm just a beginner." Sarah encourages her buddy, "It's an open Competition for all Dojos - even new students can enter." Tommy glances around the room to point and remark, "There're guys better than me. I wouldn't stand a chance!" Sarah steps closer and looks Tommy in the eye, "Remember, it's not about size or strength, it's about how good you are - and Tommy, you're good!" Tommy stands quiet and reflects on what Sarah said. Just at that moment, Sensi Jeffrey comes over to them both and gives his insight, "Tommy - I think you should enter Regionals. It would be a great experience and I believe you'd win!" The young man is gobsmacked at his Teacher's comment. He glances at Sarah and Sensi Jeffrey and replies, "Ok! I will do it! Go to Regionals." The Instructor and Sarah smile their approval at Tommy's decision.

TWO MONTHS LATER...

Martial Arts competitors, family, friends and spectators, fill the well-lit modern auditorium. Various Martial Arts Clubs and Sensis wear their coloured Dojo outfits. Tournament Judges are seated behind a long table situated on an elevated platform, enabling the Judges to see the Contestants and the entire Tournament floor. Sensi Jeffrey and the Gold Eagle Dojo members are gathered in the assigned zone at the mat's side. All the Dojos line the mat's perimeter. Everyone is excited! There's a CLICK and an electric HUM fills the auditorium - then an announcer's voice comes over the PA system, "Welcome everyone to our Regional Martial Arts Tournament! Our Competition will commence at 9:00 am. (All eyes on the wall clock) Sensis, please have your students ready for their scheduled bouts. - Thank You!" The microphone clicks off. Tommy, Sarah and the others look at Sensi Jeffrey as he peruses the Tournament Schedule printout. Morgan Jeffrey announces to the kids, "Sarah, you compete at 9:15 and Connor is at 9:30 am (Scans sheet) and Tommy, you go on the mat at 10 am. The others are in the afternoon." The kids buzz among themselves. Tommy stares out at the large open mat area and comments, "Such a big space - so wide and open!" Sarah leans in and remarks, "Has to be big so we can fight and move. It also let's the Judges clearly see what we do." Tommy turns his gaze toward Sarah, "Sparring in our Dojo is one thing - fighting a stranger in front of everybody is something else!" Sarah gives Tommy's arm a friendly squeeze and she tries lift his confidence, "You'll do fine! Just remember what you've been practicing." Tommy grins sheepishly. Sensi Jeffrey comes over, "Tommy, remember your routines! Watch your opponent's hands, feet and eyes, - especially the eyes! They tell you when a move is coming." Tommy repeats, "Watch the eyes!" Sarah smiles and remarks, "Yes! Watch the eyes."

AUDITORIUM BUZZER!

The first two contestants, one in a blue outfit, the other wearing a red outfit, walk out onto the centre of the mat and stop. They both turn to face the Judge's table and bow respect. Next, they turn and bow to each other, then step back and stand alert. RINGSIDE BELL! Quickly, both contestants take a fighting stance and eye each other. The red contender unleashes a roundhouse kick and the blue contestant swiftly ducks and backs up. The red fighter attacks with punches - the blue fighter blocks and strikes the red opponent with a solid blow. A voice over the PA announces, "2 points. Blue." The two fighters back off to regain position. The blue opponent quickly drops to sweep his leg and knocks the red fighter off balance. The blue fighter grabs his opponent in a chokehold - the red contender breaks the grip and powerfully flips the blue fighter onto the mat. THUD! The voice on the PA speaks, "2 points. Red" 1 MINUTE WARNING BELL. With just one minute remaining to defeat your opponent, both fighters blitz. The red guy throws a punch and the blue guy blocks. The blue fighter kicks and it's blocked by his red opponent. There's a flurry of strikes and blocks. Both fighters keep up the intense battle. TOURNAMENT BUZZER. The audience cheer and applaud the competitors. A Referee steps between the two contestants, both are sweating and breathing heavy and stand with anticipation. The Referee and the two fighters watch the Judges' table and await the outcome. Tommy turns to his Sensi, "Who won?" Morgan Jeffrey comments, "It's a close one! Let's see what the Judges decide." There's a momentary lull across the crowded auditorium. Everyone watches as the Judges confer in whispered conversation. The blue contestant and the red contestant eye each other as perspiration runs down their face. A slim older man with grey hair and beard steps up to the microphone at the Judges' table, he looks at the two fighters and remarks, "The Tournament winner is Blue!" Loud applause fills the interior. Both fighters shake hands and exit the mat to their Dojo section. The blue contender walks with his arms raised in victory. Sensi Jeffrey looks at the Schedule and remarks, "Sarah, you're up next!" Sarah checks her Gold Eagle outfit and replies, "Ready Sensi!"

AUDITORIUM BUZZER

Sarah ascends the mat and moves to the centre. Her gold outfit gleams under the Tournament lights. From the opposite side strides a large teenage guy in green attire. The two combatants face the Judges and bow, then face each other and bow. RINGSIDE BELL. The green opponent unleashes a front kick and Sarah steps aside - grabs his ankle and flips the guy backwards onto the mat. THUD! The PA system announces, "2 points. Gold" The green fighter springs to his feet and sends out a barrage of punches which Sarah deftly blocks and deflects. She quickly spins with a roundhouse that blasts her opponent off his feet and onto the floor. In his excitement Tommy yells, "Way to go Sarah!" The Announcer's voice fills the interior, "3 points. Gold." The green opponent spins and twirls to his feet and runs at Sarah - jumps to flip and kick Sarah in her back shoulder area to knock her off-balance. The fellow's Sensi pumps his fist and yells, "Yes!" The PA system carries the score, "3 Points. Green." ! MINUTE WARNING BELL. The green contender forcefully grabs Sarah to execute a chokehold - but Sarah squirms free. He reaches out and grabs her collar and she ducks her head, spins her body around and kicks him hard in the stomach. The guy crumples to the mat with a contorted face. AUDITORIUM BUZZER. The Referee walks to the mat's centre stage. Sarah is on his left and the green opponent in on the Referee's right. Sarah stands calm while the big guy grimaces in pain. All eyes are on the Judges as they compare scores and talk in muffled tones. One Official leans into the mic to announce, "Tournament Winner is Gold!" Sensi Jeffrey, Tommy and the Gold Eagle members erupt with cheers and high fives! Sarah turns to shake her opponent's hand - and he slights her and walks away unhappy. She looks over to Sensi Jeffrey and he tilts his head and shrugs his shoulders. Sarah walks off the mat and Sensi Jeffrey, Tommy and the teammates congratulate her. Tommy looks at Sarah and with a big grin, "Awesome! You were totally awesome!" Sarah takes a breath and replies, "Thanks Tommy! The two place themselves at the mat's edge and watch Connor get into position on the Tournament floor. Before Connor, stands a girl with a ponytail wearing a purple outfit. They bow to the Judges's table, then bow to each other and step back into a fight position. RINGSIDE BELL. Connor and the girl circle around to size each other up. Connor moves in to strike but the girl ducks the punch. She swiftly spins around to hit Connor's chin with her elbow - it knocks Connor backwards. The PA announcer informs the score, "2 points. Purple." Connor recovers and grabs the girl's sleeve and throws her hard to the floor. THUD! She's nearly knocked out and slowly gets to her feet. The announcer voices, "3 points. Gold." Connor eyes his opponent and quietly remarks, "That'll teach you!" The female fighter gives a hard look and with lightning speed unleashes a flurry of kicks and punches that Connor cannot block - she strikes Connor repeatedly! The Announcer exclaims, " 3 Points. Purple." AUDITORIUM BUZZER. Both fighters lock eyes in a fierce gaze. The Referee comes into the centre of the two contestants and all three face the Judges. The Officials huddle and speak with muffled voices - then a lady Judge speaks into the microphone, "Tournament Winner is Purple!" Connor and the girl face each other and shake hands in sportsmanship spirit, as they shake hands the girl gives Connor a haughty smirk. They both walk off to their Dojo areas. Connor exits the mat and looks at Morgan Jeffrey. The Sensi comments, "Don't worry losing Connor! There's another Competition in the Fall." Connor is upset, "I could have beat her! Next time, I'll be prepared." Sarah, Tommy and others gather around Connor to lift his spirit. Sarah comments, That was a good throw! Textbook move." Connor looks at

Sarah and replies, "I learned that from you. Remember, you gave me pointers last year?" Sarah nods. Tommy watches their exchange and gets worried. Sensi Jeffrey puts his arm on Tommy's shoulder and encourages, "You're ready for this - just watch their hands, feet and eyes." The first-timer mutters, "Especially the eyes!" Tommy manages a faint smile and turns toward the Tournament mat. Pumped and nervous, Tommy repeatedly clenches his fists. The Gold Eagle teammates stand near him.

AUDITORIUM BUZZER

Tommy ascends the mat and walks toward the middle - there's a thick spongy feel to his feet, the mat surface is tactile yet cushioned. He reaches the centre. From the other side walks a young man dressed in a black outfit with an embroidered dragon crest on the front. The opponent approaches with confidence and stops a few feet away. On cue, both young men turn and bow to the Judges and then bow to each other. They both step back and assume a fighting stance. RINGSIDE BELL. Suddenly, Tommy's opponent sends out a straight arm punch. Tommy turns his torso and deflects with a block. The opponent swings his other arm and Tommy stops the strike. Both contenders back up and reposition. The PA system informs, "2 points. Gold." The opponent quickly pivots and kicks Tommy's side. Sensi Jeffrey yells out, "Watch his feet Tommy!" The Announcer speaks into the mic, "3 points. Black." Tommy and his opponent circle each other eager for battle. Tommy notices his opponent's eyes blink before he goes to punch or kick. Tommy braces himself. Sure enough, the other contender's eyes blink as he lunges in to strike. Tommy spins and delivers a powerful kick that knocks the attacker to the floor. The fellow's Sensi yells a warning, "Curtis, watch your guard!" The PA system carries across the auditorium, "3 points. Gold." 1 MINUTE WARNING BELL. Pressure shows on both fighter's faces. The black dragon opponent reaches to put Tommy into a chokehold - Tommy grabs and locks his opponent's arms - leans forward and flips the contender to the mat. THUD! Morgan Jeffrey and the entire Gold Eagle team shout out cheers! AUDITORIUM BUZZER. The Referee walks to the centre of the mat and Tommy and his opponent stand in flank position. They watch with anticipation as the Judges compare notes and converse quietly. The auditorium waits in excited silence. An elderly man edges to the microphone and speaks out clearly, "Tournament Winner is - Gold!" Tommy and his opponent shake hands and exit in opposite directions. Tommy walks back to his area with a new found confidence. He looks - and Sensi Jeffrey, Sarah and all his teammates have big smiles. Tommy descends off the mat and everyone gathers around to congratulate his victory. Morgan Jeffrey remarks, "Congratulations Tommy! You were excellent!" Sarah leans in with a happy smile, "Yay Tommy! - You won!" Tommy looks at his Teacher, "Sensi, I did what you said. He blinked before each attack. I was ready!" The rest of the Gold Eagle team crowd around Tommy bombarding him with High-Fives and pats on the back. Some mess up his hair. Tommy thoroughly enjoys it - he's all smiles.

TOURNAMENT AWARD CEREMONY

As the family, friends and spectators watch, all the various Dojos with their Sensis and teams stand before the Judges in neatly arranged groups. The Competition Officials award the respective Dojos their Tournament Trophies and the crowded auditorium loudly cheer and applaud. Sarah and Tommy stand in front of the Officials. Two Judges approach, each holding a tall shiny Trophy. Tommy glances over at Sarah - she smiles and gives Tommy a happy wink. One Judge presents Sarah with her award, and the other Judge hands Tommy his Tournament Trophy - Tommy stares at the shiny details. They both turn and rejoin their Gold Eagle Dojo group. Sensi Jeffrey and the fellow teammates greet the duo with cheers and celebration. The auditorium spectators clap their support.

Back at Gold Eagle Martial Arts Dojo, all the students are assembled in neat rows. Sensi Jeffrey places Sarah's and Tommy's trophies high up on the wall of awards. Tommy watches in awe. Sensi Jeffrey turns to address the class, "Congratulations again to Sarah and Tommy! Our trophy collection continues to grow. Remember class, you too can have a trophy up there! - Now, let's get back to training." The students pair up and practice their routines. Tommy and Sarah work as partners. Tommy moves with skill and confidence. Sensi Jeffrey observes and nods with approval.

Carl and Kathy peer out the kitchen window - Tommy is in the backyard practicing his Martial Arts routines. The teenager executes the moves with noticeable skill and speed. Tommy unleashes a barrage of punches, kicks and leg sweeps. To Carl and Kathy's shock and surprise - Tommy even does a backflip to land in a fight position. Carl turns to Kathy and exclaims, "He's coming along real fine!" Kathy replies, "Whenever I see him - he's always practicing, every chance he gets." Carl closes the kitchen curtain and looks at Kathy with gleeful expectation, "Any more of that pumpkin pie?" Kathy gives Carl a playful shove and quips, "I'll see what I can find." Carl smiles wide.

CHAPTER FIFTY-TWO

Trouble At School

Ms. Mills hands out test scores to the class. Students' expressions range from frowns to broad grins. Ms. Mills stops beside Tommy's desk and hands him the paper face down and comments, "Keep up the good work Tommy!" Tommy turns over the paper and sees 82% at the top. He takes a deep breath - and stares at the mark. A big smile breaks across his face.

THE SCHOOL BUZZER

Students in class grab their books and backpacks and begin to exit the door. Outside the classroom, it's a high school traffic jam - the halls are clogged with throngs of kids moving to class. Tommy walks past some lockers and some brash townies block his path. He steps aside to go around, but two guys cut him off. Tommy finds himself corralled in the middle of the townies. One townie barks, "What's the big hurry - Rezskin?" Tommy scans the group and keeps his cool and replies, "Come on - I need to get to class!" The townies make fun of him with OOOO! And AWWWW! One guy knocks Tommy's books to the floor, and another townie kicks them away. Tommy eyes the culprits. The one kid challenges, "You have to go through us first!" Tommy replies, "I don't want any trouble - just want to get to class." One big guy leans in with a threat, "Guess what Rez - you got trouble!" By now, other students in both directions of the hall stop and watch the commotion. Some hold up their cell phone to video. The townies notice the crowd and get bolder. A townie speaks loudly, "You Rez kids are all the same - come to this school - but you don't belong! This is our school!" The group of townies start to push Tommy about. Tommy tries to stay upright. One townie throws a punch but the Martial Arts training kicks in and Tommy catches his fist and puts him in a wrist hold. The kid buckles to the floor. Another townie throws a punch - Tommy ducks and the fist strikes another townie in the face resulting in a bloody nose. At this point the kids jamming the hall begin to chant, "Fight! Fight! Fight!" Suddenly, there's an AIRHORN! Several teachers and the Vice Principal steer through the crowd of students. The teachers and Vice Principal exert their presence and authority. The Vice Principal looks at the townies and Tommy and orders, "I want to see all of you in my office - right now!" The other students quickly disperse to class and the hall soon empties. The teachers escort Tommy and the group of townies down the hall to the school office. Entering the office waiting area, the two male teachers point to the chairs and give the townies and Tommy that look - Sit Down! The townies sit on one side and Tommy finds a chair against the opposite wall. The townies try to stare down Tommy to intimidate him. Tommy simply keeps his cool. The Vice Principal calls in the students one by one. Tommy finally gets his turn to sit in front of the big desk. The Vice Principal looks at Tommy and asks, "How did this fight start?" Tommy gives him respectful eye contact, "I was just going to class - those guys jumped me!" The man with glasses, white short sleeve dress shirt and blue striped tie, opens Tommy's folder and looks through it. He peers over his eye glasses at Tommy and remarks, "It says here you were once arrested - in Court for a serious crime!" Tommy feels embarrassed by his past involvements and replies in a quiet voice, "Yes, that's true! - But that was before - in the past! I've changed!" The Vice Principal takes off his glasses and gives a stern look, "Well, fighting's not much of a change, son!" Knock! Knock! Knock! The Vice Principal remarks, "Come in." The School Secretary opens the door and steps inside holding a cell phone, and comments, "A student brought in their cell phone. You need to see this!" The lady hands the cell phone to the man and his eyes study the video taken during the hallway altercation. He pauses - hands the phone back to the Secretary and she exits and closes the door. The Vice Principal leans back and looks at Tommy sitting before him, and remarks, "It appears you didn't start the fight - just on your way to class." Tommy replies, "That's right Sir!" The Vice Principal closes the file and slides it to the side of the desk and remarks, "You can go now. This school incident has been sorted out. My apology for any misunderstanding!" Tommy stands to his feet, turns to exit the room, then pivots to address the administrator, "I know what I was like before - It's different now! I really want to learn!" The man smiles and responds, "Glad to hear that Tommy!" Tommy exits and closes the office door, walks past the Secretary and leaves the

School Office area - and steps out into the empty hall.

234

CHAPTER FIFTY-THREE

The Practice Session

Carl steers the Chevy Malibu out of the driveway onto Plains Road, and drives through the Reservation past homes, stores and buildings until he reaches the Highway. He turns right and takes the Highway route for several miles then turns onto a Concession Road that leads to Canyon Run - Eli Water's horse ranch. Carl steers off the Concession onto the property's lane and drives toward the ranch house. As he gets closer he sees other vehicles parked near the long barn and large corral - Morgan's gold Dodge Mini Van, Barry's slate grey Chevy Silverado truck, and Steve's dark blue Ford F 150 pickup. Carl glances over and notices Eli's red Jeep Wrangler parked beside the house. He steers in and parks beside the other vehicles and exits his car. Carl walks over and slides open one of the large barn doors, enters inside and shuts the door. He scans the barn interior and spots his friends gathered in the wide sandy area in the structure's middle. Carl grins and starts to amble toward the group. As the guys stand in a casual huddle, Eli spots Carl approaching, smiles and calls out, "Glad you could join us today, brother!" Morgan, Barry and Steve turn around and wave a greeting to Carl, and he waves in return. As Carl joins them in the centre of the open arena, Barry asks, "How's Tommy doing?" Carl looks at the guys and replies, "He sure is coming along - trying his best at school (eyes Morgan) and doing really good in Martial Arts!" Morgan nods and remarks, "Tommy has caught on quick - he's a natural (grins) a bit like his grandpa! All the guys chuckle and Eli remarks, "Well guys, speaking of Martial Arts - we better get started with our monthly practice!" The men nod agreement and all begin to step back to form a large loose circle. Eli scans about and remarks, "Hand-to-Hand! Who's going first?" Barry replies, "Guess I will" and steps into the middle of the open space. Then, Steve steps into the middle opposite Barry, grins and remarks, "Brother, I hope you brought your 'A' game?" Barry laughs and quickly assumes a Martial Arts fighting stance and chides, "Bring it brother (chuckles) if you got it?" Steve grins as he shakes his head side to side - suddenly, Steve springs into a fighting stance and descends on Barry with a flurry of punches. Barry blocks Steve's series of punches, quickly pivots and counters with a roundhouse kick that Steve capably ducks. Steve jumps with a flying kick and Barry tilts his head to avoid impact. Steve lands in a fighting stance in the dirt behind Barry, who spins around to release swings and strikes and Steve deflects and blocks Barry's attack. Both men stop, move apart and step back. Steve grins and remarks, "I see you haven't lost your skills, brother!" Barry catches his breath and replies, "And you too brother - still quick and nimble." Steve and Barry exchange looks, bow respect and then rejoin the circle. Barry eyes his friends and asks, "Ok! Who's next?" Eli steps into the middle, looks around and remarks, "Sticky hands!" Carl walks into the middle opposite Eli. Both men raise and extend their arms out until the back of each man's hand is pressed against the other's. Eli grins with a friendly ribbing, "Hope you remember how to do this?" Carl smiles and replies, "Just try and keep up old friend!" Both men laugh as they begin to circle and rotate their hands together in unison. The purpose of 'Sticky Hands' is for both participants to keep their hands in continuous contact without breaking apart - the exercise is to test your opponent's skill and reflexes in Martial Arts hand-to-hand fighting technique. Steve, Morgan and Barry watch intently to see who will break first - Eli or Carl. The two friends lock eyes and concentrate as they move in synchronized harmony - their hands quickly turn, spin, rotate, push and pull in circular motions. Suddenly, Eli's hand slips and breaks away. The others yell, "Whoa!" Morgan cries out, "Carl's the winner!" Eli pats Carl's shoulder and grins, "Next time! I'll beat you next time, brother!" Carl smiles and the two step back into the circle. Eli remarks, "Morgan, you're the only one left." Morgan steps out and replies, "Time to perform the Dragon Kata!" The others smile and Barry pipes up, "I haven't seen that in a while." The Martial Arts instructor steps into the middle and quickly assumes a fighting stance - Morgan swiftly delivers a flurry of strikes at an imaginary attacker, spins with a roundhouse kick, then flip backwards three times into a fighting stance. He runs and summersaults to land on his feet to deliver fierce blows and punches to the front, left and right - then, Morgan moves into a Martial Arts stance and holds. Carl and the others clap their hands in approval, and Eli yells out in a teasing manner, "Great moves Morgan! Can I join your class?" Morgan rejoins the circle and remarks, "Only if I can learn how to shoot arrows like you!" Eli grins at Morgan's reply. Barry looks at everyone and comments, "And that brings us to weapons, right?" All the guys nod and make their way to the side of the barn interior that has tall wooden cabinet doors. As the guys approach the wall of cabinets and each stands before a compartment, Eli remarks, "Everyone's weapon has been cleaned and ready." Eli opens the door of the first cabinet and brings out a large black bow and black leather quiver full of black arrows. Steve opens the second cabinet and removes two dark long curved metal Indian war clubs. Barry opens the next cabinet and takes out a long black chain with a sharp black metal dart. Morgan opens his cabinet and removes his two black metal batons, each with an eagle claw on the end. The four hold their weapons and look at Carl as he opens the last cabinet and brings out the short black Ninjato sword and the long black Katana sword. He claps the swords and looks at his friends and comments, "Time to shine!" The five buddies walk back to the middle of the arena and reposition in much wider circle. Eli asks, "Who's going first?" Barry chimes, "I'll go" and he steps into the open area and holds the chain taunt with extended arms - he rapidly spins and twirls the chain to fire the dart in front, back, and side to side. Barry moves around as he quickly manipulates the chain dart with amazing skill and speed - then he stops. He looks at his friends and they all nod. As Barry gets back into the circle, Morgan steps into the centre and lifts his metal batons high in the air - then, Morgan crouches and swings the batons to the left and right, flips forward to rapidly swing the batons low to the ground and then up at head level. Morgan quickly pivots and delivers defence and offence moves to the front and back, then quickly spins into a fighting stance and holds. His friends clap as Morgan leaves the middle. Steve steps into the centre and positions his war clubs. He looks at his friends, then launches out with a series of blows, blocks and swings, as he swiftly moves in different patterns. The black war clubs twirl and rotate with precision. Steve displays great control and skill for attack and defence positions. Finished, Steve walks back to rejoin his friends as his buddies clap. Next, Carl steps into the centre and raises the Ninjato and Katana swords in a fighting stance. Carl quickly launches out with swift chops, slices and blocks, the two steel blades spin and twirl with blistering speed. Carl swings the Ninjato in front and the Katana in back at the same time, then, switches the Katana to the front and the Ninjato to the back. Carl spins and crouches low with sword slices at knee level, then spins to bolt upright with powerful sword swings at chest level. Then, Carl back-flips to land in a crouch with both swords in a battle position. He straightens up and looks at his four companions who smile and nod. The last one is Eli and all eyes are on him. Eli turns to face the back wall of the barn that has a row of targets. He removes two arrows from the quiver, fixes them on the bow and draws back the string and shoots. The two black arrows fly through air and each arrow hits a bullseye. Next, Eli takes out three arrows and positions them on the bow. Eli pulls back the drawstring and fires - three arrows zip through the air and each strike a bullseye. The others clap their approval! Eli glances at his buddies and remarks, "Watch this!" The men look at the back wall and see three tires suspended from the back rafters - each tire hangs by its own cord. Eli draws back the bow and shoots, the black arrow sails straight and cuts through all three cords to drop the tires. Thud! The four guys clap and cheer! Eli smiles and remarks, "Now that our monthly practice is over - I got a big table of food set up in the house - that's if you're hungry?" The guys break out with big smiles and Carl remarks, "Lead on brother - we're famished!" Each man returns his weapon to his cabinet, then they make their way out of the barn toward the house, chatting as they walk.

CHAPTER FIFTY-FOUR

The Part Time Job

Carl and Tommy are seated at the dining table. Kathy sets out salad, bread and lasagna and sits down. The three pass the food around to fill their plates and begin to eat. Tommy looks at his grandpa and grandma and comments, "I'd like to get a part time job!" Carl and Kathy exchange glances and Carl remarks, "That's great Tommy! What kind of job you looking for?" The teen replies, Something that won't interfere with school or the Dojo. - Maybe some fast food places with flexible hours." Kathy gets up and goes into the kitchen and returns with an apple pie. She cuts and serves three portions. She glances at Tommy and mentions, "You should work weekends - that wouldn't affect your school or Martial Arts." Tommy digs into his apple pie ... and pauses, "You're right grandma! Lots of fast food places need part time help on weekends." Carl eyes Kathy and they both smile.

The next day, after school is over, Tommy stands at the town's road near the Highway that has all the fast food outlets. He takes a deep breath and starts to walk toward Flip Jack's Pancakes, opens the door to go inside and stands at the counter. He gets an attendant's attention to speak to the Manager. Tommy waits a few minutes, then a bald middle-aged man with shirt and tie approaches him. Tommy hands him a resume and asks about part time work. The man gives the resume a quick glance then shakes his head indicating - no! Tommy nods and thanks the Manager for his time and then he exits the store. Tommy lifts his eyes over to Primo Pizza. He walks on the sidewalk toward the store and goes inside. Tommy stands near the Host/Hostess podium and asks to speak with the Manager then waits. Soon, a lady approaches wearing a dark jacket and white shirt and introduces herself as the Manager. Tommy hands her his resume and enquires if there are any part time openings? The lady shakes her head and replies no! Tommy smiles, says thanks and leaves the food outlet. Outside on the sidewalk, He notices the Chop Stick Express with its red neon sign. He decides to venture there and enquire. Tommy enters the business and looks around at the oriental decor and staff attire. He asks for the owner and an older man comes up to him. Tommy gives his resume and asks about any work openings. The man puts up his hand and motions no - then leaves. Tommy exits Chop Stick Express and ambles over to lean against a street light. At this point he's frustrated and getting discouraged. He stares at the ground for a bit then looks around and spots the brightly lit Burger Barn. He shrugs his shoulders and mumbles, "Why not!?" Tommy goes over and opens the store's front door and approaches the counter. There are three staff cleaning equipment and doing prep work. A teen behind the counter looks at Tommy and asks, "Can I help you?" Tommy replies, "Is the Store Manager here?" The staffer remarks to his coworker, "Go in the back and get Sam!" The coworker quickly disappears - and in a few minutes returns with the Manager. The man in his business shirt and tie gives Tommy a look over and asks, "Hello! I'm the Manager. What can I do for you?" Tommy smiles and hands the man his resume and asks, "Thank you for seeing me Sir! My name is Tommy Long Grass - I'd like to ask about part time work?" The Manager scans the resume and looks at Tommy and replies, "Let's go to the office and talk." Tommy comes through the counter and follows the Manager to his office at the back. The office is small and neatly organized. The Manager sits in his chair behind the desk and Tommy gets a chair in front and glances at the bulletin board arrayed with corporate memos, staff schedules and letters. The man takes a closer look at the resume and grabs a pen from a desk caddy and asks, "So Tommy, tell me something about yourself?" Tommy looks him straight in the eye and politely replies, "I live on the Reservation with my grandparents, and I'm a Sophomore at the District High School." The Manager comments as he jots some scribbles, "I don't see it on your resume. Have you ever worked fast food before?" Tommy is candid, "No Sir! I haven't (Smiles) But I'm a quick learner and a good worker!" The man leans back in his chair to relax and ponder, then glances at Tommy and asks, "Tommy, I like your attitude! (Eyes wall schedule) Can you come in this Friday night 6pm for training?" Tommy's eyes light up and with a wide smile he replies, "Yes Sir! I'll be here 6 pm sharp!" The Store Manager extends his arm and shakes Tommy's hand and remarks, "Welcome to the Burger Barn family! We'll see you Friday." Tommy responds with gladness as he shakes the boss's hand, "Thank you Sir! Thank you very much!" The man jots some notes on the resume, opens the file cabinet and picks out a folder and slides Tommy's resume in it. Tommy rises from his chair and exits the office and retraces his steps to the front. He goes through the service counter and walks out the front door.

Friday night at the Burger Barn…

The town's fast food strip is packed with all kinds of people buying food at the various outlets. Everyone is hungry and energetic, pumped with weekend excitement. In the Burger Barn, there's lots of orders and kids pack the interior waiting for their food. Tommy is decked out in his new Burger Barn employee outfit as he flips burgers and puts together hamburger orders behind the counter. The other experienced staff take the orders and handle the cash register. The Manager comes to the front counter area and checks Tommy's progress - he smiles and returns to the back office. In the parking lot next door to the Burger Barn, there's a custom car show featuring tricked out cars with glossy paint jobs, gleaming chrome, and eye-popping details. The owners proudly stand beside their rides as the weekend crowd mill about scoping out the vehicles on display. Next door people jam the Burger Barn to get eats. Tommy and the staff are super busy. The customer line-up is non-stop. Tommy assembles an order and takes it to the coworker at the cash register and sets it down on the counter. Tommy lifts his eyes - Spike is standing in front of him at the counter. Both momentarily freeze! Spike sneers and remarks, "Look who we have here!" Tommy replies, "Your order is ready." Spike gets tiffed and snipes, "What's wrong Homes forgot your old crew!" Tommy turns about and returns to the grill loaded with sizzling hamburgers. Other customers want their orders and they press in on Spike. The coworker checks the order receipt and tells Spike, "That will be $16.50 please." Spike hands the guy $20 and gets his change. He abruptly turns and jostles his way through the crowd and exits the front door. Standing outside - Spike is fuming mad and kicks a garbage can over scattering its contents. Spike swags over to where his crew are hanging out near the car show. The rowdy crew greet Spike and quickly grab their food and start to chow down. Spike has a scowl and a gang member asks, "What's wrong man?" Spike gets angry and replies, "I saw Tommy! He works in there." The other crew members gather around as they munch their burgers. Another thug questions, "What you gonna do Homes?" Spike glances at his homies with a smirk and responds, "Only one thing to do - tell Bossman! Let him know! (heads for car) We gotta go!" The crew quickly jump into their rides and fire up the engines and peel out with squealing tires.

Somewhere out in the remote desert...

Spike and the crew pull their cars onto the grounds, and the armed lookouts let them pass into the sprawling auto yard. Spike and gang exit their rides and stride through the open large metal doors into the Northwest Gang hideout. The bright lit interior is filled with gangsters chopping vehicles and stacking auto parts. To the far right on an elevated platform is 'Command Central'. Bossman and key lieutenants with attractive babes, chill in a stylish tricked-out lounge, fitted with custom upholstered seats, crystal chandeliers, chrome and smoke glass coffee tables, overflowing liquor bar, and large screens for video games. Bossman sees Spike approach and stands to his feet. Spike feels nervous and stops a couple feet away. Bossman eyes the young thug who just disrupted his special time. Spike apologizes, "Sorry to interrupt you, Bossman!" The Top leader snarls, "What is it?" Spike takes a step closer, "Found out where that traitor kid works! - What do you want us to do about it?" Bossman stares at Spike and crew for a moment, then he gets a sinister grin and replies, "Wreck the place! Let 'em know that he's the reason! (Laughs) After that, no one will hire him!" Spike glances at his crew, then looks at Bossman and replies, "Done Boss! Just like you said!" Bossman turns around and gets back to relaxing and quickly has a babe attached on each arm. Spike and the crew hustle back through the warehouse interior and go directly to their cars, crank the engines and zoom off toward town.

CHAPTER FIFTY-FIVE

Carl's Younger Days

Carl sits beside a small secluded lake nestled in the sandy terrain of the desert region. This is one of his favourite spots to visit and enjoy the peace and tranquility. The quiet of the untouched wilderness is broken only by the occasional call of a hawk and the sound of the desert wind blowing across the rugged surroundings. Carl drives out here sometimes so he can be alone to reflect and think things through - this time, his mind is on Tommy. Carl realizes his grandson is dealing with the changes brought into his young life; he knows because he sees the lad struggling with school, trying his best at the Martial Arts class, and avoiding any of the bad guys from his former gang. As his grandfather, Carl deeply cares for Tommy and wants the young lad to find a better life, and Carl's determined to do whatever it takes to make that possible. After all, the kid really has no one else; his older brother travels from one construction job to another never being home, and there's no other relative available to help. Carl picks up a small stone and tosses it into the water nearby - Plunk! He watches the ripples spread out across the water's smooth glassy surface, the stone makes circular waves that fan out and eventually disappear, the lake's surface returns to its mirror-like state. As Carl shifts his eyes across the lake's glassy appearance, his gaze stops at the water's edge and he looks at his reflection in the water. Thoughts of being a young lad like Tommy fill his mind as he remembers his younger days.

Carl is an eight year old kid, tall and lanky like a string bean. Other kids make fun of him because he's either too skinny or too tall, and some physically push him around. One day as young Carl sits alone pouting about how the kids make fun and pick on him, his grandfather Kamatsu, one of the old Shoshone warriors sits down beside him. Young Carl looks over, and his grandpa asks, "What's wrong - why are you sad?" Carl remarks, "I don't like feeling different and being picked on all the time!" Kamatsu leans in and gently whispers, "Do you want to learn to be strong - so no one can push you around?" Carl nods his head, then Kamatsu remarks, "You are old enough to begin training?" Carl asks with a puzzled look, "What training?" Grandfather Kamatsu places his hand on the lad's shoulder and replies, "Martial Arts! You will learn to be strong (Points) Strong in your body, your mind, and in your heart!" Carl's eyes brighten and he smiles and responds, "Yes grandfather! I'd like that kind of training!" The grandfather stands up and looks at Carl, "Tomorrow, I will begin to teach you (Kamatsu grins) Make sure you eat all your breakfast, tomorrow will be a long day!" As his grandpa leaves, young Carl smiles at the idea of getting strong enough not to be pushed around anymore!

The next day, bright and early, Carl stands with his grandfather in a wide open area with short grass situated a short distance in the woods. Kamatsu looks at Carl and comments, "You will train here in secret so others will not see. You will need to focus and work hard! - Can you do that?" Young Carl smiles and nods. The grandfather asks, "Stand like you do when you're with the other kids." Carl gets into his stand - and the grandfather reaches out and pushes the lad and Carl lands on the ground. The young lad gets up bewildered, and Kamatsu grins and remarks, "Let's begin with knowing how to stand so others cannot push you over." Carl likes that and smiles wide. Kamatsu instructs, "Copy how I position my feet and hold my body." As Kamatsu gives the example, Carl is keen to copy his grandfather's stance in every way. When the lad is fixed in position, Kamatsu reaches out and pushes from the back, the front, and the sides - the lad holds strong and solid. Carl is surprise and delighted! Carl remarks, "I didn't fall! I didn't fall! (Looks at grandpa) But why?" Kamatsu leans in with a smile and relies, "I showed you how to place your feet and body to stand strong and not be pushed over!" Carl chimes with eagerness, "Teach me more grandfather! I want to learn more." The old Shoshone warrior chuckles, "There are many more things for you to learn (waves his arm) as many things as there are different trees, birds, plants and animals!" Carl replies in excitement, "I'm ready grandfather! I want to learn it all!" Kamatsu nods at his grandson and comments, "Standing is just the start - in days ahead, I will teach you how - push back, block a punch, throw a punch, hold someone, and also break someone's hold. That is just the beginning!" Young Carl exclaims, "Teach me everything grandfather! I never want to be pushed around again!"

Kamatsu looks into the lad's young eyes and replies, "This kind of training is very special to make you strong to help yourself and to help others. Never use it to do wrong. Do you understand?" Carl stares directly at his grandfather and replies with confidence, "Yes grandfather - I understand!" Kamatsu smiles and nods, "Good little one! Very good! - I believe you will be a fine student!" Over the coming days, months and years, as Carl grows into a strapping teenager and a muscular young man. The Ninjan Master, Kamatsu, teaches Carl to use weapons like the Sickle, throwing Stars, the Tomahawk and the War Club. However, the weapon that Carl displays tremendous skill and ability with is the sword. The young man handles the Ninjato and Katana sword with great ability as he chops, spins, twirls, and slices the steel blades with precision and prowess. Eventually, Carl and Kamatsu spar with steel swords - the Ninjan Master executes swift slices, rapid chops, and quick thrusts - and Carl blocks, deflects, and counter attacks. When they both stop, Kamatsu smiles at his grandson's progress and proven skill.

A hawk soaring above calls out over the dry rocky landscape, and Carl emerges from his inner reflection. He stands to his feet and leaves the smooth flat rock where he sat, and walks to the Malibu parked a distance away. Carl stops beside the car and looks up as the hawk circles overhead. He smiles and gets into the Malibu, starts the engine and drives toward home.

CHAPTER FIFTY-SIX
Trouble Follows Tommy

The weekend crowd are lined up to order and the Burger Barn is packed with kids. Spike and the crew enter the premises and muscle their way inside - the street thugs shove, push and menace others out of the way. A couple boyfriends try to protect their dates, but the crew punch them out giving the boyfriends bloody noses and busted lips. Customers start to flee and exit the store. Now, Spike and crew have the entire store to themselves. The Manager and bewildered staff watch as Spike and his crew break windows, cut the seats, table tops, and walls with knives, smash light fixtures, and pour condiments all over the floor. The interior of the Burger Barn is a disaster - one huge mess! The Manager shocked and angry calls out, "Why are you doing this?" Spike swags up to the counter and looks the man in the eye and coldly replies, "Because of that Tommy kid you hired! He use to be one of us - we'll just keep on following him around (sweeps arm) and do more like this!" Spike and the crew scram out of the store and jump into their cars and peel away. The Manager runs out the windowless front door and catches one of the licence plates - and quickly scribbles it down on a piece of paper from his pocket. The man turns and goes back inside the destroyed interior, the workers are stunned and afraid. A couple girls are crying and the Manager and others try to console them. The Manager glances around the store's interior and surveys the damage.

POLICE SIRENS AND FLASHING LIGHTS.

The Police cruisers pull up and Officers quickly exit the cars and come into the store. An Officer remarks, "What happened here?" The manager approaches the Policemen and hands the piece pf paper and replies, "Some street gang came in here and started to trash the place. Fortunately, no one was hurt. (Looks at store) But this place is ruined!"

A Policeman looks at the licence number and remarks, "Good work! We can run this plate in our system." The Manager calls over his employees and releases them to leave the mess and go home. As the kids exit across the floor, they try to avoid the broken glass, smashed furniture, fixtures, and small pools of condiments. Outside the Burger Barn, Police stretch out the yellow Police tape to seal off the store - now a crime scene. A few minutes later, Tommy drives his Mustang toward the Burger Barn and sees the Police cruisers with flashing lights. He cautiously steers into the parking lot and stops. Tommy is surprised! He glances at the entrance - the front door just an aluminum frame with no glass, the stores windows are broken and have sections where sharp jagged glass protrude. Tommy sits in his car and stares at the wreckage. The Store Manager comes over and Tommy asks through his open window, "Sam, what happened?" The Manager replies, "Some gang came in - wrecked everything!" Tommy looks at his boss with concern, "Anyone get hurt?" The man replies, "No! Thankfully no one got injured - But the staff got really shook up - I sent them home!" Tommy gazes up at his employer and comments, "The store - it's terrible!" The man gazes down at Tommy and takes a deep breath and remarks, "That's why I have to talk with you!" Tommy looks up puzzled, "About what?" The man bends down eye level and replies, "Tommy, I like you! - You're a good kid and a good worker - But (Pause) that gang mentioned you by name and said they'd follow you around! I can't have that kind of trouble! I'm sorry Tommy, but I have to let you go!" Tommy is stunned and acknowledges, "I understand Sir!" At that moment, a big pickup truck advertising GENERAL CONTRACTING pulls up in front of the store and a large man gets out, and the Manager leaves Tommy and goes over to talk with the contractor. Tommy glances at the ruined business outlet, starts his car and pulls out of the parking lot and drives down the street.

Carl relaxes in his armchair as he reads the newspaper, and Kathy sits on the sofa and knits her afghan throw. They hear the Mustang drive onto the property and the engine cut out. A minute later Tommy comes in through the front door and goes directly to his room and slams the door. Carl and Kathy exchange concerned expressions. A few minutes later after he's cooled down, Tommy comes out of his room and sits on the sofa with a downcast expression. Kathy reaches out her hand to touch Tommy's shoulder and asks, "What wrong Tommy?" The teen looks at his grandparents and replies, "The Burger Barn let me go! No more part time job!" Carl puts down the paper and blurts,

"What!?" Tommy turns to his grandpa, "The gang I ran with trashed the place - said they'll follow me around. The Manager got scared!" Kathy moves aside her knitting and scoots beside Tommy to console, "That's awful dear! - Don't let it get you down Tommy. We know you're trying - something else will turn up!" Tommy glances at his grandma with eyes full of worry, "If I get another job - the gang will just show up and make trouble! (Looks at grandparents) I don't know what to do?!" Tommy gets up and retreats to his room in brooding silence. Carl and Kathy sit quietly in deep concern.

CHAPTER FIFTY-SEVEN

Police Survelliance

The Police Precinct is busy! Officers at desks are working on files, and others are coming and and going as duty shifts change. An Officer at a computer screen uses the Police system to search the car licence number supplied by the Manager of the Burger Barn. He keys in the plate number and the system displays a photo ID, address, vehicle registration, and a criminal record. The Officer clicks the Print button and goes to the printer to retrieve copies. He takes the printouts to Chief Rogers's office. The Police Chief scans the information - looks at the subordinate and orders, "Get this information out to all our units - be on the lookout for this car!" The Officer nods affirmative and takes the info to the dispatch desk. A Police cruiser on patrol spots Spike's car and runs the plates - Confirmation! The two Officers tail Spike's vehicle from a distance and watch it pull into a residential property and four thugs exit the car and go inside the house. The Officer driving the squad car gets on the Police radio, "Unit 5 reporting. We followed the gang car to an address - 1816 Montgomery Drive. The suspects went inside the house. Over!" The Police Dispatcher responds, "The Chief will send an unmarked car for surveillance. Over-Out!" The Officer on the scene replies, "Ten Four!" The Police cruiser quietly pulls away from its location.

Soon, an unmarked car with two plain clothes Policemen pulls into a spot for the stakeout. Time lapses as the Officers watch and wait, and wait, and wait. Finally, the two undercover Officers see four gangsters leave the house and get into the vehicle, start the car and drive out onto the street and pull away. The unmarked cruiser starts up and follows. The gangster car travels through town streets unaware of the Police tail. The thugs drive onto the Highway and head toward the desert region. The undercover cops keep their distance. The suspect's car turns onto Pine Bluffs Road, the road sign is weathered and faded and barely readable. The stakeout team turn and follow with stealth keeping well back. After some considerable miles, out in the middle of nowhere, the gangsters pull into a large derelict property that's surrounded by a high galvanized fence and barbed wire. This was a thriving industrial auto yard that's no longer in business and sits abandoned and empty - or so it seems. The undercover unit stop their car in a hidden spot and watch through binoculars. Armed thugs appear and open the tall metal gate and let the suspect's car pass through, then they close the gate secure. An Officer in the stakeout vehicle picks up the Police radio, "Stakeout unit reporting in. The car entered an old abandoned auto yard located on Pine Bluffs Road. Armed gangsters are inside. Over!" The Police Dispatcher replies, "Come back to the Station. Chief Rogers wants a Precinct Briefing!" The Officer responds, "On our way! Ten Four!" The undercover Police car turns around and heads back to town.

CHAPTER FIFTY-EIGHT

The Making of Bossman

Bossman stands on the raised lounge platform and surveys the sprawling gang hideout. He watches groups of men chop and dismantle numerous cars - sparks from welding torches and metal grinders spray the air, expensive engines are suspended on hoists, industrial racks are full of auto parts. Bossman glances to an array of shiny new vehicles parked nearby waiting for attention. The big man stares off into space...

FLASHBACK!

Bossman is a young skinny kid just surviving on the rough streets of an inner city project. Many buildings are rundown and in decay and sit abandoned with broken windows and gutted interiors. Young Bossman, whom the local thugs call "Lil' Bones" because he's so young and thin, acts as a 'lookout' for local pushers dealing drugs and other illegals. The kid sleeps in an abandoned building with some other street kids. To help get by, the kid goes uptown to shoplift stores and pick pockets in crowded city buses. Anything he steals and brings back, he barters with the local hoods for cash - but because he's young and naive, they rip him off many times. Still, to a street kid, a little of something is better than plenty of nothing! As Lil' Bones gets bigger and older as a teenager, he joins a neighbourhood street gang. Now, Bossman gets involved with drugs, violence and turf wars, and has run-ins with the cops. In one battle with another gang - the teenager kills a rival. The Police get a tip and Police cars descend upon the empty city lot where the fight takes place. Gang members see the cops and try to split - every man for himself. In the pandemonium, with gangsters and Police running in all directions - Bossman gets apprehended and arrested. Soon, he's before a Judge and sent off for incarceration. As a skinny teenager in Prison, Bossman gets beat up a few times - but each time he gets smarter, tougher, becomes a survivor. The young inmate starts to lift weights and eats everything the Prison Cafeteria can dish out. With little else to do behind bars, Bossman lifts weights and learns Martial Arts and practices 24/7. Over time, he becomes bigger, stronger and more lethal. In one Prison fight, Bossman breaks both arms of an attacker, and soon, Bossman's rep in Prison grows and he becomes respected and feared by the others. When Bossman is released from Prison, he starts his own street gang. His gang quickly grows in numbers and controls whole neighbourhoods. On the streets, as it was in Prison, Bossman is known and feared as a big mean brute with the muscle, street smarts and Martial Arts, to eliminate his foes. One day, the gang leader looks at the USA map and envisions expansion. Bossman begins to move his gang into other cities and eventually dominates entire regions. At this time, Bossman names his gang the Northwest Gang, and loyal gang members get NWG tattoos. This was when Bossman and the Northwest Gang invade the area towns and the Indian Reservation! Bossman claims the entire area as NWG Turf!

FLASHBACK ENDS

A gang lieutenant approaches the lounge platform and remarks, "Cars for Europe are ready!" Bossman barks an order, "Ship 'em off - we're a day late!" The lieutenant nods, starts to walk away, then turns to Bossman and comments, "I miss the big city! This place has nothing - just two-bit towns!" Bossman 'schools' his lieutenant and replies, "Nothing is why we're here, Homes! Less heat than LA! These cops are not the LAPD - we're cool!" The veteran thug nods with a grin and heads onto the chop floor and over to a bunch gangsters standing by expensive cars. Bossman gets out his cell phone and pulls up Contacts - Spike, then Bossman sends off a text - "DUMPSTER KID" - and presses Send. He leans against the lounge's chrome railing and waits a bit, and his cell BUZZES. Bossman checks Spike's reply text - "KID 2 DIE!" The big man smirks and pockets the phone.

Somewhere in town, Spike puts away his cell phone. He and the crew sit in their three tricked out cars in a parking lot. Spike looks at the guy in the front bucket seat and remarks, "Let's roll! Boss wants us to dumpster that traitor!" Spike sticks his arm out the car window to wave and signal the other gang members to move out. The three gang cars exit the parking lot and turn onto the road and start to cruise streets looking for their former associate. Spike and crew drive slow trying to find Tommy. Going past a number of streets, Spike turns a corner and spots Tommy's Mustang parked on the street. Up ahead, he sees Tommy and Sarah walking together on the sidewalk, and then they turn to enter a Gift Shop. Spike and the other two cars go further up the street to find some empty spots, they park beside the curb and cut the engines. Spike and his crew exit the cars and begin to walk back toward the store.

Inside the Gift Shop, Tommy and Sarah stand in front of a display of beautiful high quality porcelain figurines. A sales lady approaches with a friendly smile and asks, "Looking for something special today? (Eyes Sarah) Perhaps something for the young lady?" Tommy looks at the lady and replies, "Oh no! Sarah and I - we're just good friends - only good friends!" The sales woman looks at Sarah and smiles and remarks, "My apology! I just thought you were boyfriend and girlfriend. You both look so good together!" Sarah blushes. Tommy points to the figurines on the display shelves in front of him and comments, "I want to get my grandma a nice gift! She likes these kinds of things." The store clerk picks up a pretty figurine that's close and remarks, "These are exquisite! People collect them - and we're the only store in town that carry this product line." Tommy turns to Sarah and asks, "What do you think of these?" Sarah picks one up to examine and responds, "Very pretty! - your grandma will love it!" Tommy lifts his hand to move a stand of hair off his face, scans the display shelves, then points to a pretty figurine with brunette hair in a red dress and remarks, "That one! - Grandma looked like that when she was younger!" The sales lady retrieves the figurine and comments, "That's a beautiful choice! I'll wrap it up nice for you." Tommy, Sarah and the sales lady walk over to the store's sales counter. The clerk steps behind the counter, checks the price tag, then sets the figurine on the counter. The lady bends down and brings out a gift box with white wrapping tissue inside. The sales lady carefully lays the figurine in the soft layers of paper, covers it snugly with wrapping tissue, then tapes the box secure. Next, she unrolls and cuts some gold ribbon and ties the box with a fancy bow. Tommy raises his eyes brows and asks, "How much is it?" The lady holds the box and replies with a smile, "That will be $50 dollars please!" Tommy digs into his jean pockets and pulls out some crumples bills - and sorts out three $10 bills and one $20 bill. He hands the cash to the lady and the store clerk passes over the gift. Tommy turns to Sarah and mentions, "We gotta hurry back before grandma gets home! She's out getting groceries. As the two leave, Tommy tosses the gift box up and down in his hand. The sales lady is alarmed and quickly calls out, "Please be careful! - That's fine china!"

Tommy and Sarah emerge from the store, Tommy has the gift box under his arm. Suddenly, Tommy and Sarah are confronted by Spike and his crew of thugs. Tommy and Sarah step off the store steps to stand on the sidewalk. Spike swags up and gets in Tommy's face and snarls, "You shouldn't have ditched us, Tommy! Now we got orders to tidy up business!" Sarah steps in between Tommy and Spike and remarks, "We're not bothering you - leave us alone!" Spike looks at his crew and they all laugh! Spike turns to Tommy as he eyes Sarah, "We don't need little girls to interfere with big boy stuff!" The gangster grabs Sarah by her shoulder and shoves her aside. Tommy gets a serious expression, shakes his head side to side and remarks, "You shouldn't have grabbed her!" Spike replies with a smirk, "And why not?!" Spike no sooner has his words out when Sarah grabs and twists Spike's arm and powerfully kicks him into a parked car nearby. Before the crew can realize - Sarah spins around with a roundhouse that flattens a thug beside her. Now, the thugs on each side pull out knives, chains and pipes. Tommy and Sarah exchange a quick glance and Sarah remarks, "Just like we practiced last week!" Tommy nods his head. Tommy and Sarah quickly stand back to back. The gangsters attack from both sides. One swipes his blade and Tommy knocks the knife out of the attacker's hand, then Tommy delivers a Dragon Fist that flattens the guy. A big thug swings his steel pipe to hit Sarah - she kicks him hard in the 'family jewels' and he collapses on the sidewalk withering in pain. Two holding knives attack at the same time - Sarah blocks and counter-attacks. She grabs one's guy's arm to dislocate his shoulder, then rakes her nails across the other thug's eyes - causing momentary blindness. Other gangsters swing a chain and pipe at Tommy. He jumps aside to dodge the chain, grabs the guy's arm to flip him onto the cement. Tommy knocks the pipe out of the thug's hand and kicks him in the groin - he buckles in agony. The two thugs still standing look at their fallen comrades and put up their arms not to fight! POLICE SIRENS! Police cruisers zoom in and screech to a stop in the street. Officers quickly jump out to grab and arrest Spike and his crew. Officer Stibbs comes over to Tommy and Sarah and remarks, "What happened Tommy?" The trio watch as the Policemen take Spike and thugs into custody. Tommy looks at his Police friend and replies, "They jumped us! We just came out of the Gift Shop." Stibbs turns his gaze to the store and the lady clerk standing in the window and comments, "The sales lady called the Police - good thing she did!"

Spike and two other gangsters sit handcuffed in the back of a cruiser. The Police put the remaining thugs into the other squad cars. Tommy looks at the scene and remarks, "That use to be me once - No more Now!" Stibbs steps close and pats the teen's back and encourages, "You'e on the right path, Tommy! - Better days are ahead!" Tommy glances around and picks up the gift box and brushes off some street dust. He looks at Sarah and Stibbs and remarks, "My grandma's gonna love this gift! It's pretty like she is. (To Stibbs) We gotta get going!" Officer Stibbs watches as Tommy and Sarah walk to the Mustang, get in, and drive off down the street.

CHAPTER FIFTY-NINE
Operation Desert Hawk

Police Chief Rogers holds a station wide Precinct Briefing, all Officers are in attendance. The meeting room is packed and everyone is buzzing about the reason for the important gathering. Chief Rogers stands at the front of the room and a senior Officer hands out information sheets to the assembled troops. When everyone gets the papers, the Chief speaks up, "Everyone pay attention! The Northwest Gang hideout is the old abandoned auto yard and warehouse out on Pine Bluffs Road. A Police raid named: Operation Desert Hawk, will be coordinated with SWAT and other Police jurisdictions. Okay everybody (Determined look) - Let's go arrest these gangbangers!" The Officers disband and exit to their cruisers. Cars trunks open up and the Police put on their bulletproof vests and get tactical weapons - semi-automatic submachine carbines, combat shotguns, riot guns, and ballistic shields. The Officers get fitted and stand battle ready. Police Chief Rogers exits the Station and goes to his cruiser and pops the trunk. He grabs his ballistic vest and straps it on, then reaches in and gets the 16mm assault rifle. The Police Officers assemble around the Chief and wait instructions. Chief Rogers looks at his men and remarks, "Listen up! SWAT, State Troopers, and Tyler Units are working with us. We drive to Miller Junction - there's a big gravel pit there - that's the rendezvous point!" The Policemen nod acknowledgement and Chief Rogers and the Officers get into their Police cars and pull out of the parking lot. People in town watch with curiosity and interest as the line of cruisers go through the town streets and head toward the highway.

Later on, Police Chief Rogers and the Officers drive into the large gravel pit. The steep sides provide excellent concealment for the rendezvous. Before them in the wide open area normally used for the big dozers and shovels, are State Trooper squad cars, the SWAT armoured vehicle, and Tyler Police cruisers. Armed Troopers and Officers and the SWAT team, are gathered in groups. Chief Rogers and his force drive up, park and get out of their cars and walk up to the other units. Chief Rogers approaches the SWAT Commander, then waves over the Trooper and Tyler leaders, When all four are together, the SWAT Commander pulls out an area map and they study it as the Commander remarks, "The access points are here and over there. We know from intel that they have heavy firepower at the gates - likely inside the warehouse too!" Chief Rogers injects, "We have the element of surprise!" The SWAT Commander faces Chief Rogers and remarks, "This is your jurisdiction - so you have the lead in this Operation! What do you want us to do?" Chief Rogers looks at the map and the outline of the gang headquarters and replies, "Attack from two access point simultaneously! Take out their guards. SWAT at the front door - Troopers at the back door! Once inside the property we storm the warehouse!" The State Trooper Captain remarks, "Sounds like a right good plan!" The Tyler Captain exclaims, "Been waiting to get this gang! - They totally ruined our town!" Police Chief Rogers looks at the three leaders, "Let's do it then! - Take 'em down!" The four Police leaders disperse, each one going to their own men. All the Officers double check their pistols, assault rifles, shotguns, and grenade launchers - all locked and loaded! Operation Desert Hawk is in full force, and the Police Units get into their vehicles and head out of the gravel pit.

CHAPTER SIXTY

Bossman Orders A Wicked Deed!

An area grocery store is busy with people getting groceries. The parking lot is full of vehicles coming and going. Kathy drives in and finds a spot midway in a row and parks her car. She exits and grabs a shopping cart and enters the store's sliding entrance doors to disappear from view. Tucked away, a few rows over, is the black sedan with dark tinted windows. Inside the car, a gangster is on his cell phone, "Bossman - she's here! - just went inside." The thug's phone speaker carries Bossman's reply, "You know what to do!" The gang lieutenant hesitates a bit then replies, "In broad daylight? With witnesses?" Bossman barks, "Just follow my orders!" The gangster replies, "Done Boss! Just like you want!", then he ends the call and pockets the phone. The Northwest Gang lieutenant and three big thugs sit in the sedan and wait…and wait. After a while, Kathy comes out of the store pushing the shopping cart loaded with groceries. She wheels the grocery cart near the back of her car, pops the trunk and begins to load in the bags of grocery. As Kathy leans in to place a bag, suddenly, the black sedan screeches to a stop and two big thugs quickly exit and grab Kathy! The woman screams and struggles trying to break free. One thug flings open the sedan's back door and the two brutes physically throw Kathy into the back seat and slam the door shut! The black sedan roars away. Meanwhile, customers had heard Kathy's screams and witnessed the abduction - one lady is on her cell phone calling 9-1-1.

The black sedan tears across remote desert roads and Kathy sits in the back seat between the two thugs. She glances at her abductors and quickly reaches to grab the handle to open the door. The thug stops her and she fights with him; in the tussle, top buttons on her blouse get ripped. The guy grabs her arm to hold her and she bites his hand - he yells and smacks his palm her across the face - Kathy's nose bleeds. She desperately pleads, "Let me go! Please! I won't say a thing to the Police - just let me go!" The gangsters are silent and stone-faced. After a brief lull, Kathy tries again to escape from the car and the thugs rough her up; now, Kathy sits captive with messy hair, torn blouse, bruises and a bloodied nose. She stares out at the desert as the car speeds toward the gang hideout.

The black sedan drives onto the property and slams on the brakes spraying stones and dust. The lieutenant and gangsters exit and standby. A big thug yanks Kathy out of the car manhandling her. She fights back and her blouse sleeve gets torn. The gangsters march Kathy into the cavernous warehouse, across the busy shop floor, and through a steel door into a dingy dim lit room with a rusted overhanging florescent light. Kathy struggles but to no avail. One thug forces her to sit in the tarnished metal chair while another thug ties her feet and arms secure to the heavy object. Kathy's face shows courage and defiance! She eyes her captors with distain. Tied to the cold steel chair, Kathy sits alone - vulnerable - exposed. Her blouse is ripped and the missing top buttons reveal her smooth skin and traces of her womanly form. All across the shop floor, curious gangsters stop work and walk toward the side room where they saw the woman was taken. The room starts to fill with rough looking men covered with sweat, grease and grime - each one jostling to get a better look at the attractive woman tied to the chair. The onlookers leer at her. Kathy looks into their eyes and finds no pity - no mercy - no help - just wanton desire! A loud voice bellows from the back of the crowd, Bossman barks, "Back off! I said back off!" The men quickly disperse to clear a path for Bossman. He saunters up and stands in front of Kathy and she lowers her eyes to the floor. Bossman steps closer and towers over her and remarks, "Hope you find the accommodations to your liking? Best I could do on short notice!" Kathy lifts her gaze and looks directly into the brute's eyes, "You did wrong coming onto our lands! These are Indian lands - Sacred!" Bossman squats down eye-level and replies in a pompous tone, "These are my lands! Northwest Gang lands! (Thugs cheer) This territory belongs to us now! (Looks at her) You belong to us now!" The men yell and cheer more! Kathy stares back and replies adamantly, "I belong to my husband! - and no one else!" Bossman brushes his rough hand down her cascading hair, his hand slides along the front of her torn blouse - and stops near her visible cleavage. Kathy grimaces and turns her face away. Bossman places his hand on Kathy's head and forcibly turns her face toward him and coldly remarks, "You belong to your husband! - That's exactly what I'm counting on pretty lady!" Kathy in anger spits on the hoodlum's face and yells, "You're nothing but sticking trash! - Pure filth!" Bossman stands up, wipes the spit off his cheek and tilts his head to crack his neck. He calls over a lieutenant and whispers in the man's ear and the underling looks at Kathy and nods. Bossman turns around and looks at the group of men and callously announces, "Boys! - She's all yours! Show her a good time!" The men part and Bossman walks out of the room laughing. The men begin to close in around the frightened lady as Bossman leaves the office - Kathy screams repeatedly!

Carl is in the living room when his cell phone BUZZES. He greets the caller, "Hello!" Bossman's voice replies, "I have your wife! - She's a fine looking woman!" Carl is shocked and alarmed and quickly replies, "Whatever you want, deal with me! Leave my wife out of it!" Bossman stands outside the former warehouse office and holds his cell phone in the air - Kathy is crying and screaming! The thug asks, "Do you recognize that voice? - The voice of your wife?" Carl is livid and retorts, "What do you want?" Bossman laughs and replies with a sinister chuckle, "What I want! What I want is for you and me to fight! Fight me! - If you win, you get your wife back!" Carl paces to and fro across the living room with the phone to his ear. He shutters at Kathy's cries and sobs in the background. Hearing his wife's distress, Carl boldly declares, "I'll fight you! Fight you man-to-man! (Pause) The old steel factory near Snake River!" Bossman revels at the reply he's waiting for and remarks, "Like I said - you beat me, you get your wife back - If not, well too bad! - Old man, get ready for the beating of your life!" The call ends.

At the warehouse, Bossman pockets his phone and circles his arm high in the air - the Boss's signal to move out. Thugs see the leader's sign and gangsters across the warehouse rally and run toward their vehicles parked in the big auto yard. Armed thugs jump into cars, SUVs, pickup trucks and cargo vans. The gangsters carry automatic rifles, semi-automatic pistols, machetes, chains, clubs and knives. Bossman strides over to a big black SUV with black tint windows, opens the driver door and stands on to the rocker panel for all to see. Bossman raises his arm and flags it forward - then gets inside, fires up the engine and peels out. Vehicles across the auto yard ignite their engines and tear out. From a bird's eye view, it's a long convoy of gang vehicles following Bossman's big black SUV.

CHAPTER SIXTY-ONE
The Ninjans Get Ready

Carl goes into the master bedroom - pushes on a false wall that opens to expose a jet black wooden cabinet. He dials Morgan's number and his friend answers, "Hello Carl!" Carl remarks in a serious tone, "That big city gang has Kathy! Their leader wants to fight me. If I win - Kathy goes free! (Pause) Call the others! We meet at the old steel mill." Morgan responds, "We'll be there!" Carl pockets his cell phone and swings open the cabinet's black doors to reveal an arsenal of weapons - swords, sickle, tomahawk, bow and arrows, knives, chain dart, blow pipe, metal stars, bombs, poisons, climbing rope and metal claw. A black Ninjan outfit hangs in the back. Carl quickly dons his Ninjan clothing and affixes weaponry - the long Katana sword and the shorter Ninjato sword, tomahawk, knives, stars, bombs, and rope. His dark form now bristles with instruments of death. Carl grabs some short containers and twists off the lids. He faces a wall mirror, then dips his fingers into the containers to smear on War Paint to create a fearsome look! Carl returns the false wall that hides the black cabinet, then he dashes out of the bedroom, across the living room and out of house - leaving the front door wide open.

An hour later Tommy and Sarah drive onto the property and park the Mustang. As they exit the vehicle they notice the front door is wide open. The duo walk to the house, Tommy holds the gift box in his hand. He remarks to Sarah, "That's odd! Grandpa doesn't like the front door left open! (Scans about) And I don't see grandma's or grandpa's car!?" Sarah responds, "Where are they? - out back?" Tommy and Sarah reach the front stoop and ascend the steps and go inside and look around. Tommy calls out, "Hello grandpa! - Grandma? - Anyone here?" Silence. Tommy goes to stand in the middle of the room and Sarah follows. As Sarah stands by, Tommy looks in the kitchen, the hallway, the master bedroom, the backyard - Nothing! He enters the living room and plops down in a dining chair with a dejected expression. Sarah tries to comfort and suggests, "Call their cell phones. Maybe there was a quick errand to run!" Tommy pulls out his cell phone and dials his grandpa's number. Ring! Ring! Ring! No answer! Then he dials his grandma's number. Ring! Ring! Ring! Again, no answer! Tommy looks at Sarah with worry, "Called both - Nothing!" Tommy sits at the table puzzled and perplexed. Sarah sits down beside him to console, "Let's just stay here and wait for them. - they shouldn't be too long!" Tommy nods and gives Sarah a faint smile and replies, "You're right! Grandpa and grandma will be back soon!" The two teenagers sit pensive and quiet - with the front door still open, they can see and hear the vehicles going by on Plains Road.

CHAPTER SIXTY-TWO

Shoot Out At The Auto Yard

Police Chief Rogers, Officers, and SWAT, reach the gang hideout and get into position. The Troopers and the Tyler Unit are prepped in the back location. Police Chief Rogers speaks into his handheld Police radio, "All units - GO!" The armed thugs guarding the metal gate are relaxed and distracted. Suddenly - CRASH! The SWAT armoured vehicle smashes through the gates leaving only crumpled twisted sheets of metal behind. Police cars directly follow the SWAT vehicle into the auto yard grounds. The armed thugs are taken by surprise, many scurry into the warehouse and shut the big steel doors. The armed gangsters still outside fire their automatic rifles and pistols at the Police. Officers quickly exit cruisers to take cover behind car doors and vehicles and return fire. At the same instant - gunfire erupts from the back gates of the auto yard. Automatic rifle fire. Pistol rounds. Shotgun blasts. The Police target the thugs shooting the automatic rifles - it's an intense firefight! Hot lead flies everywhere, automatic guns spray bullets that puncture cruisers with lots of bullet holes, some Officers get hit and wounded. SWAT and the Police set their sights on the automatic fire and take out the bad guys. Chief Rogers and the Policeman emerge from cover and rush the warehouse. The distant gunfire stops - then silence. Almost immediately, State Troopers and Tyler Police come around the far end of the long warehouse. They join up with Chief Rogers and the others. The Trooper Commander reports, "The back is clear! But we saw gangsters go inside." Chief Rogers looks at the SWAT Commander, and remarks, "SWAT will ring the door bell!" The Commander grins and replies, "That's what we do best!" The Policemen get into position and watch as the Armoured car rams the sealed entrance doors. BANG! The steel doors buckle and break wide open. The SWAT armour car zooms into the warehouse interior and skids to stop a couple feet from some expensive sports cars. The Officers race inside and spread out for cover. The cavernous interior is brightly lit by overhead florescent lights - the Police scan the interior and see cars, SUVs, trucks, that are chopped and dismantled. Chief Rogers gets the Tyler Commander's attention and orders, "Go to the back exit - make sure no one escapes!" The Commander replies, "No one will get past us!" The Tyler Commander with pistol in hand, waves to his men to follow as he exits the open warehouse entrance. Gang members are concealed throughout the vast warehouse, hiding behind vehicles, steel pillars, industrial equipment and racks of auto parts. The thugs open fire and the Police shoot their guns. An intense firefight! Bullets ricochet and bounce off the cement floor, steel columns and metal parts. One macho thug lieutenant steps out from behind a steel pillar and unloads his assault rifle at Police positions. As the thug exchanges ammo clips - SWAT blast him dead! Leaderless and scared, a couple gangsters raise their hands to surrender. Police Chief Rogers yells out, "You're trapped - surrounded! Give yourselves up!" He listens for a response - silence, then there's sounds of movement and weapons being thrown on the cement floor. Slowly, individual gang members rise to surrender with their hands in the air. Soon, all the remaining gangsters are in the open with both arms high in the air. From various positions - Officers, Troopers and SWAT approach with their weapons trained on the criminals. The SWAT Commander orders, "Lay face down with open hands extended in front of you! Stay that way - Don't move!" The Police rush in to put the criminals' arms behind their back and cuff them. Once secured, the Officers help them to their feet. The gang members look defeated and whipped. Chief Rogers approaches and asks, "Where's your leader? (Walks between them) Where's Bossman?" The thugs eye each other and remain tight-lipped - no one talks! Then, a young man in his early twenties starts to open his mouth, "He went…" An older thug eyes him and threatens, "Say nothing! Don't give them anything!" Chief Rogers steps up and looks the young man eye-to-eye and speaks in a fatherly tone, "Never mind him, son! Tell me what I need to know." The young man replies, "Bossman took most of the gang to a big fight! - that's what I heard." Chief Rogers questions, "Where's this big fight?" The young thug replies, "Something about an old steel mill - somewhere in the desert." Police Chief Rogers looks at the young man, "Thank you son! I'll remember your help when I fill out my report (turns to Officers) Some of you spread out, see if any are hiding!" The Policemen fan out and search the large warehouse interior. An Officer enters the defunct warehouse Office, and to his shock, he discovers Kathy on the cement floor badly beaten with signs of abuse! He calls out, "Chief. There's a civilian - a lady hurt bad and needs medical attention!" Chief Rogers and two Commanders enter the room and see Kathy with noticeable signs of trauma. Chief Rogers immediately uses his radio mic, "Dispatch. Send a Paramedic ASAP! We have an injured civilian in need of urgent medical care!" The Dispatch staff replies, "Ten Four. Ambulance on the way!"

Moments later…

The ambulance with lights flashing zooms into the auto yard and Officers guide them to the warehouse entrance. The back doors of the ambulance open and the paramedics spring out carrying a Jump Bag and a Trauma-Spine Board. They race inside and the Police direct them to the office. The paramedics see Kathy unconscious and rush to the victim, Chief Rogers and the SWAT Commander step aside to make room. The paramedic with the Jump Bag quickly inspects Kathy's vital signs. His partner positions the Trauma Board beside her body. As one paramedic turns Kathy on her side, his partner slides the Trauma Board underneath her body, then they ease Kathy onto the board and strap her secure. With a paramedic on each end, the two ambulance workers lift Kathy and quickly take her to the ambulance. Inside the Ambulance, one paramedic starts an I.V. drip in Kathy's arm, then he fastens leads from electronic medical equipment to her body. Beep! Beep! - Beep! The other paramedic preps a hypodermic needle and injects Kathy with antibiotics. He watches the heart monitor. The other paramedic closes the ambulance back doors, and gets behind the wheel, starts the vehicle and pulls out with the sound of the siren and emergency lights flashing. Police Chief Rogers, the Commanders and the Policemen watch the ambulance leave the auto yard and race off. Chief Rogers looks at the arrested gangsters huddled together in a group awaiting transport. He watches as Officers put them into the back seat of cruisers, then the Offices drive off. Chief Rogers radios the Station and remarks, "Dispatch. Requesting more ambulances and a helicopter to go to the old steel factory near Snake River. Over!" Police Dispatch replies, "Ten Four! Ambulances and helicopter notified. Over!" The Police Chief urges, "Tell them to hurry! Ten Four! Out!" He waves the Unit Commanders over and the leaders gather around. The State Trooper Commander asks, "What's the next move!" Chief Rogers looks at the Commanders and replies, "We head for an abandoned

Steel Mill in the desert at Snake River. Bossman took his Gang there to fight - Who we don't know?" But no one will be expecting us. Let's roll!" All the Police get into their vehicles and wait. Chief Rogers gets into his cruiser and flips on the flashing Police lights and peels out of the Auto yard. SWAT and the other Police follow Chief Roger's cruiser. The column of Police cars with flashing red and blue lights fade and become smaller as the Police Units travel farther into the desert.

CHAPTER SIXTY-THREE
The Big Battle

The old derelict Steel Mill sits in the rugged terrain out in the middle of nowhere. Abandoned broken buildings, rusted industrial machinery, neglected storage tanks, and large scrap heaps of discarded metal. The facility and site stand in eerie silence to its once busy productive past. Carl drives onto the property and takes his car across the large gravel lot and steers around a tall metal tank to park hidden away. He exits his car and scans around. Carl looks out to see four figures dressed in black rise from secluded positions. Morgan and the other Ninjans wear fierce War Paint - each brandishing their weapon specialty. Morgan holds up the two metal batons, each club with an eagle claw on the end. Barry swings the black chain dart to produce a whirling sound as the chain twirls through the air. Steve stands with a curved War Club in each hand. Eli stands layered with quivers of black arrows and raises up his large black bow. Carl pulls out his two gleaming swords and lifts his arms high in the air. - The Ninjans are ready for battle! Carl and the Ninjans set up tripwires linked to explosive charges. The Ninjans separate and take up ambush points - and wait. Morgan makes a bird call to get Carl's attention and points - the Ninjans look at the cloud of dust that rises in the distance. Carl prompts his fellow Ninjans, "Get ready - They're almost here!" The Ninjans keep out of sight and focus on the upcoming battle!

Bossman peers through the windshield and sees the dilapidated Steel Mill off in the distance. He presses the pedal to accelerate and zooms toward the factory, the long convoy of gang vehicles race to keep up. Excited and eager for a fight, the convoy of gangsters brandish their weapons out the vehicle windows - wildly yelling and displaying their submachine guns, 9mm pistols, shotguns, machetes, crowbars and knives! Bossman and his Northwest Gang drive past the chain link perimeter fence and roar onto the large gravel lot. Bossman and his thugs jump out and mass together - their numbers and firepower reveal a small army! Gang members are hyped up and edgy - Bossman puts up his hand in the air and everyone freezes, no one moves. The big man looks across the weathered industrial setting and squints his eyes to focus - no one - nothing there! Bossman brings his cupped hand beside his mouth and yells loud, "Old man! - Indian! - You here?" Only silence except for the crickets. A lieutenant leans in and comments, "Boss, maybe we got here first?" Bossman turns and pushes the guy aside and steps out a few more paces and bellows, "I know you're here! Come out and fight! - Like we agreed." Bossman turns to his crew and smirks. The eerie silence makes the gangsters nervous. Individual thugs point their weapon around at shadows, fidgety hands grip machetes and knives. Suddenly, Carl stands atop a steel tank some distance away and calls out, "The fight is between you and me! - not your entire gang!" The big thug glances at his soldiers and replies, "Where I go - my crew follow. Too bad you're outnumbered (looks at automatic weapon) and outgunned!" Carl boldly replies, "You don't have any honour!" Bossman spits on the ground, smirks and answers with bravado, "I have a gang - I don't need honour!" Carl quickly retorts, "That's what I figured!" Bossman taps a thug on his left to fire his automatic weapon at Carl. The thug unloads and bullets strike all around - Carl ducks for cover. Whoosh! A black arrow plunges deep into the shooter's leg bucking him to the gravel. Gang members blast away at Carl's location and bullets ricochet off metal surfaces. Suddenly, Carl pops up in another location visible to all. The gangsters shoot their guns at him, but Carl disappears. Bossman looks around at his men and sees the empty casings on the ground and yells, "Stop! Hold your fire! Don't waste your bullets - he's playing us. Just an old Indian scared and hiding. Everybody fan out. Let's get him!" The gangsters disperse into small groups and move forward to look behind bins and machinery, around corners, in containers, and under conveyor belts. One big thug steps between two steel drums and breaks a tripwire - BOOM! The blast breaks loose large metal pipes and supports that fall on top the big thug and crew members with him. The four thugs are injured and put out of action. Another set of gangsters go in the direction of the explosion to investigate - and run into Morgan. The Ninjan flails the metal batons with devastating effect. The three gangsters lay on the ground bruised, beaten and unconscious. The gang's numbers have just declined - eight thugs out of commission! Bossman eyes the fallen comrades, then looks at his remaining force and smirks - he feels his crew is still large - he still has forty armed thugs that can move and fight!

Carl stands at the open entrance of the first factory building, a long industrial shed that houses heavy machinery and equipment to make steel. Carl taunts and teases the criminals, "You're so many - and still can't get me!" Bossman grits his teeth in anger and waves his arm and the gangsters rush forward toward Carl. He watches and gages their approach - then disappears inside. The Northwest Gang descends on the building and spill into the cavernous room. Their eyes need to adjust to the dark interior. Shafts of sunlight pierce the interior here and there to illuminate the factory floor and equipment. Bossman and the gangsters fan out - weapons ready! The thugs are cautious as they creep deeper into the dusty old facility, They stop to listen - move ahead - stop to listen - then move ahead! TWIRLING SOUND! One gang member turns about - a metal dart is imbedded in his leg calf. Suddenly, the dart is yanked out to disappear into the shadows. The dart zips out from the shadows and sinks into his other leg - the gangster crumples to the floor unable to move. Gang companions fire their guns in a barrage of hot lead - bullets ricochet everywhere. As the gangsters continue to creep forward - going between the equipment and large machinery - Steve attacks with his War Clubs. Thugs are pummelled and knocked out - their guns and machetes drop to the cement floor. Clang!

MULTIPLE EXPLOSIONS! FIREBALLS!

A gang lieutenant sees the flickering shadow of flames outside. He and a bunch of others run out of the building to investigate. They're all stunned! Bossman and the rest join them at the shed's entrance. The glow of flames dance across their faces - gang vehicles are ablaze. As fire reaches the gas tanks, other gang vehicles EXPLODE! Not a single gang vehicle is spared - every car, van, SUV and truck are on fire! Carl's loud voice echoes from inside the building, "None of your gang can leave! You and your gang made a terrible mistake coming into this territory!" Bossman and the gangsters in crazed anger blast their guns everywhere at the empty shadows. Halfway down the building, Carl stands on top heavy machinery illuminated by a shaft of sunlight - it looks like he's under some kind of spotlight. Bossman barks to his crew, "There he is! - Get him!" The NWG members give chase and Carl turns and runs toward the building's large back exit doors. Bossman and the gangsters are in hot pursuit!

Carl runs into the second industrial building just ahead of the gangsters. The thugs stop and gather at the second building's doorway - cautious and wary. Bossman directs his troops, "We will corner him! One group go to the back exit and flush him toward us." The NWG force divide in two, and one group runs around the long industrial shed to its back exit doors, and move in with their guns ready. The late afternoon sunlight lessens and more effort is needed to see inside the shadowy confines of the structure. As a gangster steps forward into a shaft of sunlight - WHOOSH! A black arrow sinks into his right thigh and he topples to the concrete floor in pain. A gang member bends down to assist the fallen homie, and a black arrow goes through the young man's shoulder - he bellows in agony! Bossman motions the gang to keep watch above where the arrows came from. The gang leader and henchmen carefully inch along into the shed's interior. Four thugs scour the area to the left side of the interior - each welds a machete. Suddenly, Morgan springs out and the thugs swing wildly at him, the sharp machete blades slice dangerously close to his face and torso. Morgan swiftly ducks and blocks the machete attacks, and strikes the assailants with powerful blows to disarm and render them useless. Two thugs lay on the floor unconscious, the others wither on the ground in a world of hurt! The sounds of fighting brings more gang members over - but Morgan quickly vanishes into the dark recesses of the factory equipment and large machines. Bossman and his gang converge and see their fallen comrades. A gang lieutenant voices his concern, "We lost 6 more! - Now we're only 34 strong." Bossman looks at his underling and remarks, "So what! - The old Indian has a couple friends. It doesn't matter - soon, they'll be dead men! (Eyes gang) Spread out - let's get 'em!" In the middle of the long shed, Carl and his fellow Ninjans gather behind a giant foundry bucket - Carl, Morgan, Steve, Barry and Eli meet to update and plan. Carl comments, "Keep drawing them in!" Morgan replies, "They're running out of bullets - and courage too!" Barry remarks, "Their leader is a tough hombre! For him - it's do or die!" Carl glances at his friends and replies, "Leave their boss to me - we have unfinished business!" The four Ninjans nod agreement and they all disperse in separate directions toward different areas of the shed. By this time, the second group of thugs have entered through the back doors. The thugs spread out and check spaces as they work their way toward the front. Bossman and his group meet them in the middle. The leader questions his men, "See anything?" The lieutenant replies, "No Boss! It's like they disappeared." Bossman scans the interior, then waves his hand forward, and the assembled thugs move ahead with great caution. The criminals point their guns, machetes, clubs and knives in every direction. Suddenly, Steve throws smoke bombs in their path. POOF! POOF! POOF! Thick clouds of grey smoke fill the air. Swiftly, the Ninjans attack the confused and disoriented enemy with speed and ferocity - a barrage of black metal stars sail through the air to strike arms, legs, hands and torso. Carl and fellow Ninjans deliver strikes, blows, kicks and punches to bring down assailants left and right - the factory floor strewn with incapacitated thugs, unable to move or fight. When the smoke clears the Ninjans are gone - Scared and angry, the gangsters curse and fill the air with vulgar outbursts as they blast their automatic rifles, shotguns and pistols in all directions. Bullets ricochet across the shed. Bossman looks around - gang numbers are down to half - now only 17 thugs are with him. A lieutenant remarks with concern, "Boss, we should cut out! Half our guys are down!" Bossman chides him, "Shut up! (Waves his pistol) Only takes one bullet to end a man's life! And we've got slugs for each one of them. - Come on!" Bossman and his remaining thugs creep through the latter portion of the shed - Nothing! The gangsters see the open exit doors that lead to the back lot with heaps of scrap metal and rusted heavy equipment. Bossman and his crew walk out the back doors toward the piles of twisted metal and jagged steel.

The scrap yard is a jumble of rusted machine parts, steel plates, jagged metal cuttings, steel filings, twisted rebar, and large coils of industrial wire. The gangsters insert fresh ammo clips and Bossman directs them to fire their guns at the piles of scrap. Bullets fly and ricochet. Bossman and the gang stop shooting and wait - Nothing! The gang spread out and scale the large metal heaps to try and flush Carl and the others out. The gangsters step across the piles of discarded metal - their movement and body weight makes loud noises - CREAKS! SCRAPING! CLANGS! BANGS! On the far left, a thug spots Steve and fires his assault rifle. As bullets spray across the steel parts - one bullet tears into Steve's right side and he topples to the ground. The gangster exclaims proudly, "I got one! He's down!" The gangsters rush over to the fallen Ninjan, and a thug kicks away Steve's war clubs. A big thug kicks Steve in the face! Another thug swags over and points his pistol at Steve's forehead. The Ninjan is weak and gasps for breath. Bossman strides over and looks down with a sinister smile, and remarks, "Here's some gang justice for you!" As the gangster with the pistol chambers a round - ZIP! A black metal star strikes deep into the thug's hand and he drops the gun. Bossman and his crew spin around to see Carl, Morgan, Barry and Eli attack. The Ninjans attack from four sides - the Ninjans deliver strikes, blows and kicks that decimate the thug ranks, and the gangsters fall like dominoes! Only four NWG are left - Bossman and three of his henchmen. Barry, Morgan and Eli, keep their swords on the three underlings. Carl strides up to confront Bossman face to face - and stares at him, "Now, we can fight! No army of thugs - just you and me - man to man!" Bossman smirks, cracks his neck, takes a Martial Arts stance and replies with bravado, "Bring it on old man! You've never fought someone like me before!" Carl signals and the Ninjans take the thugs off to the side to leave room for Carl and Bossman to fight. Bossman scowls and rips off his top to reveal his muscular body with chiseled abs. The gang leader motions with his hands at Carl to come on! Carl circles to the right - then circles to the left - he releases a roundhouse which Bossman aptly deflects. Bossman laughs and taunts, "Not bad old man - but not quick enough!" Carl swiftly lunges in with a Tiger punch that hits Bossman directly in the face. POW! Bossman wipes his lip and spits out blood and smirks. Suddenly, Bossman flips and kicks Carl in the chest to knock him down into the dirt. Carl quickly gets to his feet. Bossman rushes in with a flurry of punches and strikes that Carl blocks and deflects, but one of Bossman's punches get through and strikes Carl and disorients him. Carl stumbles, temporarily stunned! Bossman sees his opportunity and quickly attacks with a powerful kick that sends Carl flying backwards into the dirt. Carl starts to get up and Bossman rushes in with a mighty kick to Carl's stomach. Bossman repeatedly kicks the downed Ninjan again and again. Barry stirs to help Carl but Morgan motions for him to hold off. On the ground, Carl lifts his eye to scan about, and Bossman kicks Carl in the side of the face. Bossman steps back and gloats to see Carl sprawled out on the ground - bloody, bruised, beaten and weak. Bossman mocks, "Lost your skills old man? (Eyes Carl) You're not so tough! … I'll kill you like I killed your old lady!" Carl is SHOCKED! He lays motionless for a couple seconds, the pain of the news strikes him to the core of his being. Morgan, Barry and Eli are horrified to hear of Kathy's death! Barry raises his sword to attack Bossman, Carl sees it and motions for Barry to stop - No! Carl stares at Bossman with righteous anger and rage. He lifts himself up and faces the arrogant thug. Carl points his finger and declares, "Today

- there will be justice for my wife - and justice for our Indian lands that you have defiled!" Bossman is livid and runs at Carl with series of swings and punches. Carl ducks and repeatedly strikes Bossman in the upper torso leaving the huge thug in severe excruciating pain! Bossman keeps flailing and punching away. Carl steps in and delvers a series of powerful blows to Bossman's groin, chest and back. Bossman steps back and briefly teeters, greatly weakened. He's dizzy and shakes his head. Blood seeps from the corner of his lip. Bossman wipes his mouth and looks at the blood on his hand. He coughs, grabs his chest and struggles to move but can't. The bewildered thug looks at Carl and yells, "What did you do old man? - What did you do to me?" Carl slowly walks up just out of arm's reach and replies, "Your body is going to lock up - and there's nothing you can do about it! You won't escape the Police anymore!" Bossman gasps as he stares at Carl, the big thug clutches his legs and chest as he strains and struggles. Carl, his fellow Ninjans, and the three remaining thugs, watch in silence as Bossman contorts and desperately fights to move but can't. Bossman's vision becomes blurred and he wipes his eyes, his power wanes and he wobbles on his feet - he loses strength and crumbles to his knees in the dirt. Bossman groans as he stares ahead and falls face-first into the dirt - locked stiff as a statue! Carl steps up to the fallen gangster, reaches into his tunic and brings out a small black feather and lets it fall onto the gangster's body. Carl looks over at the Ninjans. Morgan points and asks, "What about these three?" Carl replies, "Tie them up (eyes thugs) Can't tell who will find the first - the Cops or the coyotes!" The three thugs become scared and plead as the Ninjans bind their hands and feet. Once secured, The Ninjans put the three young men up high on a big metal drum well off the ground. Carl looks at the gangster trio and remarks, "The coyotes won't get you up here! We may live in the wilderness - but we're not savages!" Carl and the fellow Ninjans walk to their hidden vehicles. Barry and Eli help Steve to their truck. At their vehicles, the Ninjans exchange glances, and Carl remarks, "Thank you! I'm in your debt!" The others exchange looks and Morgan replies, "We're brothers! - Black Feathers!" Carl smiles and nods, and the five Ninjans get into their cars and drive away from the abandoned factory. As the Ninjans drive off into the desert, they can see the gangster's vehicles burning in the background, the flames light up the dusk.

Some time later, Police cars, SWAT and Paramedics arrive on scene. The Officers comb the area and find the factory grounds and buildings littered with injured and unconscious gangsters. Most of the thugs are beaten and wounded and need assistance from the Police and medical personnel. Officers rescue the three bound gangsters atop the high steel drum. As the Police help get them down, the trio speak about their ordeal and gesture wildly about samurai warriors. The Police Officers cuff the trio ignoring their story as wild imagination or a drug induced high. The gangsters are all handcuffed and rounded up in a group and guarded by armed Officers. Paramedics tend to those needing medical attention. A team of Officers find Bossman's locked body amid the grounds of the scrap yard. The brute is alive and totally immobilized. A Policeman bends down to examine the small black feather and picks it up. He remarks to his partner, "Huh! A little black feather. What do you make of this?" The other Officer looks at the feather and replies, "Likely a bird flew by - maybe a Starling." Four Officers lift and carry Bossman over to where all the other gangsters are corralled. The four Policemen lay Bossman's stiff rigid body on the ground - Bossman is alert and aware but he can't move or say a thing! Chief Rogers, the other Commanders walk around to inspect the crime scene. The leaders watch as Officers collect evidence, mark bullet casings, and inspect burnt out vehicles. As Chief Rogers and the other Commanders tour the crime site, a senior Officer with a clipboard approaches and shows them the collected data. Police Chief Rogers scans the details and remarks, "Whoever or whatever did this - gave us all the criminals! We have the entire Northwest Gang and its leader in custody!" Chief Rogers and the other Commanders smile broadly, then Chief Rogers and the Commanders continue their survey of the grounds. The old Steel Mill and property shimmer in an eerie glow as gang vehicles burn, and the flashing lights from Police cruisers and ambulances illuminate the night sky.

CHAPTER SIXTY-FOUR

A Sweet Tearful Good Bye

Carl and a Morgue Attendant walk to a stainless steel examination table, where a body lays underneath a white linen sheet. Carl's eyes sweep up and down the shrouded human form of a female. The Attendant pulls the sheet cover down to reveal the face and shoulders of the deceased. The man respectfully asks, "Is this your wife?" Carl swallows hard and fights back breaking down crying, and softly replies, "Yes! That's my wife Kathy!" The Morgue Attendant looks at Carl with sympathy, "I'm sorry Mr. Long Grass! (Pause) She died on route to the hospital. The Paramedics tried but couldn't revive her! - I'm sorry!" The Attendant covers Kathy's lifeless body - and Carl turns away and tears stream down his face, he sobs! Carl takes a deep breath and walks toward the Morgue entrance door, grabs the handle - then turns to look at the covered body of his deceased wife, Kathy. Carl stands motionless for a minute, then he clicks the door handle and exits the room.

At the funeral Service, Kathy's body lays serene in a polished rosewood open casket. Bouquets and wreaths of flowers from family and friends flank each side of the casket to honour and pay tribute to her memory. The Funeral Home's viewing room is filled with tearful people giving hugs of support, respectful handshakes, and gentle pats of condolence. Carl and Tommy are dressed in white shirt and black suit, and stand beside the casket. A large framed photograph of Kathy with her cascading hair and beautiful smile, sits in a picture stand a few feet from the coffin. The people that line up to pay their respects file past Kathy's lovely photo - many are brought to tears. She was well known and dearly loved as a fine lady that lived on the Indian Reserve. Her legacy of helping children read at the Library, volunteering with the local Food Bank, and visiting residents at the

Nursing Home, won her great respect and admiration throughout the community. Now, it was time for the community people to say their good bye to her. Kathy's siblings dressed in black and with swollen eyes from crying, sit in the front row of chairs in the viewing room, lending their presence and support to Carl and Tommy. As the individuals, couples and families file by the open casket to set their eyes upon Kathy one last time, Carl shakes their hand for showing their support, Tommy stands quiet and still on the other side of his grandfather. Carl glances at the front portion of the seating and sees his friends Morgan, Steve, Barry and Eli with their families. Carl nods to his old friends and they nod in quiet respect. Tommy glances around and spots Officer Stibbs dressed in a dark blue suit and tie, and the Officer gives a polite gentle wave to his young friend. The Officer takes a chair among those already seated. The Funeral Attendant quietly approaches and gently touches Carl's arm to indicate it is time to be seated. As Carl and Tommy sit with family in the front row, The Funeral Attendant respectfully closes the lid of the casket, and sets a beautiful bouquet of flowers on top the coffin. All eyes turn toward the Minister as he steps behind the podium that's set to one side of the closed casket and flowers. The Minister opens his Bible and looks out at the family and assembled friends and speaks, "Dear beloved, we are gathered here this day to honour and say our final good bye to Kathy Long Grass, - a loving wife, a caring grandmother, a dear sister, gracious aunt, helpful neighbour, and well-respected lady in the community. As the Funeral Home organist begins to play, the Minister encourages everyone in the room, "As the grieving family remain seated, let everyone rise and together we will sing the timeless hymn: Amazing Grace." Everyone stands, except Carl, Tommy and relatives; and the people raise their voices as the organist plays the well known melody.

Following the Funeral Home Service, at the Cemetery there is a long line of vehicles parked on the Cemetery's paved lane near the tombstones. The back door of the Hearst is open and the Minister and Funeral Attendants stand to one side as eight Pall Bearers lift and support the coffin. The Minister leads the Procession as the Pall Bearers carry the casket to the open gravesite; while Carl, Tommy and Kathy's relatives follow. The rest of the Funeral attendees walk behind the relatives. The burial Procession reaches the open grave and stop - the Pall Bearers position and carefully lower the casket onto the strapping that suspends the coffin above the open grave. Carl, Tommy and

Kathy's siblings sit down on a row of wooden folding chairs placed for the graveside ceremony. Morgan , Barry, Steve and Eli and their families stand close by. The friends and supporters gather around to fill in spots here and there. Tommy stares off into space. Morgan places his hand on Tommy's shoulder for assurance. Carl and Tommy look at each other - then turn their eyes toward Kathy's coffin before them. The framed photo of Kathy with her radiant smile sits atop the middle of the casket. The Minister opens his thin leather Bible and speaks in a comforting tone, "We enter this world with nothing and we leave this life the same - taking nothing with us. Kathy as a Christian, has gone to Heaven to live in Eternal Peace and Joy with her Heavenly Father. This is the Hope of all believers in Jesus!" The Minister steps beside the closed casket and brings out a small slender glass tube from his jacket, opens the top and pours white sand in the form of a Cross on top the coffin, and remarks, "Ashes to ashes, dust to dust, we commit our sister Kathy to the Lord, her spirit rests with God in Heaven, and her physical body will be raised to eternal life in the Resurrection!" The Minister steps away from the Casket and looks at the Funeral Attendants and nods. A Funeral Attendant retrieves Kathy's framed photo and brings it to Carl. The man steps back and looks out at the gathered friends and supporters and remarks, "We will be lowering the casket now. The Graveside Service concludes at this time and we wish to thank you for your attendance and support. As we escort the family to the Funeral cars, we kindly ask that you make your way back to your vehicles, and please join us for refreshments back at the Funeral Home Meeting Room. Thank You!" The Funeral Attendant gently motions with his hand and Carl and Tommy and Kathy's relatives stand and follow the Attendants to the waiting Funeral cars. The rest of the people disperse and make their way to their parked vehicles. Walking toward the Funeral Home's black limousine, Carl and Tommy exchange eye contact, the grandfather sees his grandson is very quiet and tight-lipped. Carl speaks softly, "I know you really loved your grandma - and you'll miss her very much!" Tommy looks at his grandpa with tears welling up in his eyes, "It's not fair! Grandma was a kind sweet lady. Why did she have to die?" Carl puts his arm around Tommy and draws him close and replies, "Evil people do evil things! It's our job as good people to stand against them - that's what your grandma did!" The Funeral Attendant opens the rear passenger door of the limousine and Carl and Tommy get seated inside - then the Attendant closes the car door.

Three months have passed since the funeral. Carl, Tommy and Sarah, stand before Kathy's grave, and Carl sets a container with a lovely bouquet of flowers in front Kathy's tombstone. Carl is silent and still as he stands at Kathy's grave. Tommy steps beside his grandpa with a serene smile and comments, "Grandma always loved those kind of flowers. She'd be happy!" Carl looks over at his grandson, smiles and pulls Tommy close. Sarah watches the tender scene with watery eyes.

CHAPTER SIXTY-FIVE

One Year Later

Tommy races in through the front door with his backpack and a large manila envelope. He puts his knapsack in an armchair and opens the large envelop and takes out the official paper with the High School logo - it reads REPORT CARD A+ …… Tommy smiles wide and sets the academic report in the middle of the table. He turns and grabs his backpack, goes into his room and tosses the backpack in a corner. With excitement in his eyes, he walks to a tall black cabinet and opens it.

Carl stands in the big backyard dressed in his black Ninjan outfit and holds two sheathed Katana swords. He hears the house back door open and turns to see Tommy standing in the back entrance dressed in a white Ninjan outfit. Tommy springs off the back steps and bounds toward his grandfather and stops a few feet away. Tommy bows and Carl bows in return. Carl smiles at Tommy's enthusiasm and tosses him one of the sheathed Kanata swords. Tommy catches the weapon and admires the white pearl inlay of the scabbard. With one hand holding the scabbard - Tommy uses his other hand to draw out the highly polished steel blade - slow and respectful. Tommy fully extends the sword blade and it gleams in the afternoon sun. Carl looks at his grandson and remarks, "Today, Tommy - you start your Ninjan training!" Tommy lowers the blade by his side and bows and replies, "Yes Sensi!" Carl gazes tenderly at Tommy, smiles and remarks, "Let's begin!" Tommy positions himself a few feet adjacent to his grandfather. The teenager keenly watches Carl's every step and move of the sword. The old Ninjan Master and the young apprentice flow in unison - the two swing and move their swords in a beautiful ballet of blades! As the afternoon sun casts sunlight on everything, Carl and Tommy are bathed in a golden glow.

Across the Indian Reservation, kids are returning from school, parents arrive home from their workday, moms and dads are preparing meals, and people get supplies at local stores. Morgan sits in his Dojo Office doing administration and clerical duties for a pile of new applications. Barry works in his busy auto shop to tighten a bolt on an engine. Steve just completes a welding job and lifts up his welder's mask to inspect the metal parts. On the outskirts of town, Eli stands in the corral as he breaks in a wild young colt. The Indian Reserve and surrounding desert region is full of life, of both human and creature. A rabbit runs through the sage brush, a ground hog raise its head from its burrow, and up on higher elevation, a black eagle with wings extended, swoops in to land on the branch of a tall pine tree and cries out - its call echoes across the rugged wilderness.

As Carl and Tommy train - Carl moves his sword with grace and power - swift and precise! Tommy does his best to keep up with the Ninjan Master. The two warriors move in tandem - grandfather and grandson smiling! Beyond the backyard, the tall grass sways and bends in the wind. As Carl and Tommy train with swords, at the house in the background, Carl's bedroom window is open, and a large black feather on a leather cord spins and twirls in the breeze.

THE END

ACKNOWLEDGEMENTS

The author wishes to acknowledge
and give credit to

Google.com
Wikipedia.org
History.com
Encyclopedia.com
Thoughtco.com

for the online sources
used for research in writing

Chapter Five:

A New Century And A Whirl Through Time

THE

GOLDEN

SEAL

NINJANS 3

This book is dedicated
to my three grown children.
Each of whom have their own
personality, skills and talents.
It's my wish to say in print,
I'm very proud of you!

CHAPTER SIXTY-SIX

The Bus To Venture

A Greyhound zooms along the ribbon of black tarmac in the hot desert. The Highway meanders around rugged hills and snakes between towering rock canyons, until it opens up to long empty stretches of pavement. Inside the air-conditioned bus, the passengers read novels, recline to snooze, or simply gaze out at the sage brush and cactus that dot the passing terrain. This is 'Big Sky' country with vast stretches of unoccupied land that has little sign of people or habitat. This sun-baked landscape belongs to the desert creatures of the region - the coyote, hawk, rattlesnake, cougar, and eagle. The only sign of human activity are the trucks, cars and buses that ply the highway, moving their way from town to town, and city to city. After considerable time, the Greyhound turns off the Highway onto a tarmac road, and motors past the large wood sign that reads American Indian Reservation of Venture. The bus goes past stores, homes, a Post Office, a Police Station, Community Hall, and a Baseball Diamond. The bus tires kick up a small trail of dust that covers the paved roadway. Inside the bus, passengers are a mixed bag of travellers - locals, visiting relatives, seniors, folks with city jobs, and High School and College kids. The students are either on their cell phones, slouch in their seats, or just stare out the window. The man driving the bus steers the vehicle toward the four-way stop with the flashing red light, slows the engine down and presses the brakes - this is the Venture's 'Town Centre'. The driver announces, "Last stop, Venture - everyone out!" The people get up to line the aisle to leave the bus. In the middle of the passengers is Jody Long Grass, a tall attractive athletic gal in her early 20's with long shiny black hair. As Jody reaches the steps to exit, she turns to the bus driver and comments, "I just finished College so I won't be riding with you anymore. Just wanted to say Thanks!" The driver lifts his cap visor for better eye contact, smiles and replies, "It's been a pleasure Jody! Wish more kids were like you - polite and respectful." Jody gives a parting smile, turns and descends the steps to the dusty ground outside. She hoists her backpack and looks around and spots the red pickup truck parked across the road and waves. Karen Long Grass, her good looking middle-aged Caucasian mom gives a wave and beckons from the open truck window, "Hurry Jody! - Or you'll be late." Jody quickly glances for traffic then scoots across the road. She tosses her backpack into the cargo box, climbs in the passenger seat to buckle up, then asks, "Is Grandpa at the house yet?" Her mom looks at her daughter and remarks, "He's so excited - he arrived two hours early. We don't want to keep your Grandpa waiting!" Karen starts the pickup and pulls onto the road as Jody puts down her window. As the truck moves along, Jody's hair dances in the breeze. Jody looks at her mom and grins, "I've been waiting for this all day!" Her mom glances at her and remarks, "All I know is he booked a fancy city restaurant — said he wants your Grad Dinner to be special! Just the two of you - A grandpa and his granddaughter!" The red pickup motors down the reservation road and Karen turns onto a Concession, the road sign reads - PLAINS ROAD. The truck goes over a couple hills, around some bends and down a straight stretch, until the pickup approaches a roadside mail box with large letters - LONG GRASS. Karen signals and turns into the driveway and cuts the engine. The mother and daughter quickly get out.

Inside the raised brick bungalow, Carl Long Grass, Jody's grandfather, is a tall fit elderly man with long braided white hair and a friendly face. He looks out the big front window and gets excited and yells out, "She's here! Brian - she's here!" Brian Long Grass, Karen's Native American husband and Jody's dad, comes out of the kitchen. Brian is handsome and muscular with salt and pepper hair that reaches his shoulders. Brian walks over to Carl, pats the old man's back and hands him the car keys and comments, "Your car's gassed up - all set!" At that moment the front door opens and Karen and Jody walk in. Carl breaks into a big smile as Jody rushes over with a hug. Carl gazes fondly at his granddaughter and remarks, "Are you ready for our fancy dinner?" Jody steps over to put her backpack in an armchair and replies, "Been excited all day, Grandpa! I've never been inside a high class restaurant before1" Karen slips alongside to playfully squeeze Jody's shoulder and comments, "I'm sure you'll be the first girl on the

Reserve to dine at a Three Star French restaurant!" Jody gives her mom a big grin. Brain speaks up, "We'd better let them go - it's a 90 minute drive to city, considering traffic - they should head out now." Carl walks to the front entry and takes his embroidered tan buckskin jacket off the coat rack, and turns to the trio and remarks, "As soon as she can change clothes and pretty up - we're outta here!" Jody beams a big smile and dashes to her bedroom and closes the door. There's the sound of rummaging with drawers opening and closing, Carl and Jody's parents exchange glances and grin. Suddenly, the handle clicks and the bedroom door opens to reveal Jody standing there in black dress slacks with a stylish red top and wearing a sparkling necklace with matching earrings. Karen, Brian and Carl are mesmerized. Brian with a faltering voice utters, "Is that my little girl all grown up?" Jody steps into the living room looking classy and chic. Karen comes over with a loving hug and remarks, "Honey, you look so pretty!" Jody smiles at her mom's words. As Brian and Karen step aside, Carl walks over and drapes an ivory shawl over Jody's shoulders, he smiles and comments, "This is what all the fashionable gals are wearing in Europe these days." Jody goes to stand in front of the full length mirror and twirls around and admires the new wardrobe addition, "Grandpa, it's beautiful! - I love it!" Carl looks at the parents, "We should be back by 10:00 pm." As the grandfather and granddaughter move toward the front door, Karen quickly blocks them and exclaims, "Almost forget - we need pictures! After all, this is an important occasion!" Brian and Karen hold ups their cell phones to snap photos. Jody is a little embarrassed and remarks, "Mom! Dad! Please!" The parents put away their phones. Carl turns and opens the front door and gestures to Jody with a polite line, "Ladies first!" Jody grins and replies, "Why such a gentleman!" As Jody steps through the doorway, Carl turns to Brain and Karen and remarks, "Only the best for my precious granddaughter!", then he shuts the door. Karen and Brian move to the large picture window and stare out as they watch Carl and Jody get into the car. Brian sighs and breaks the silence, "As soon as Jody got in her first year at College, he's been planning this big celebration. Now, he finally gets to show Jody off." The couple watch as the car pulls out of the driveway and heads down the road out of sight.

CHAPTER SIXTY-SEVEN
The College Grad Celebration

The Three Star gourmet establishment has richly upholstered wing chairs at tables with fine linen cloths, classy lamps, candles, and a lovely flower centrepiece. The restaurant interior is decorated with French paintings, sculptures, and large vases with beautiful flowers. The Maitre D has a jacket with tails and all the servers wear white gloves. In a small cove at the side, a string quartet sit on a raised platform and play classical music. On the sidewalk outside, Carl and Jody approach the restaurant entrance, and Carl opens the polished brass doors with bevelled glass, and they enter. As they stand inside the stately foyer, the Maitre D looks up from his podium with its tiny light and bids welcome, "Good evening! Do you have a reservation?" Carl steps toward the Maitre D and politely announces, "A booking for two - the name is Long Grass." The Maitre D scans the list, smiles and remarks, "Voila! I see your reservation. Please follow me to your table." The Maitre D promptly leads Carl and Jody to a table for two nestled along the decorative interior wall. Carl gets seated as the Maitre D pulls out a chair for the young lady. Once Jody is seated, the Maitre D smiles, turns and walks back to his podium in the reception area. Within seconds, two servers with white gloves attend, one gives Carl and Jody a Menu then stands ready with pen and order pad. The other server pours water into the two stylish crystal drinking glasses, then quickly leaves. Carl and Jody read over the Menu. Jody lifts her head to watch the string quartet play the lovely music of Mozart. She turns and looks at the Menu - then flips it over to see the back is blank! Jody leans forward and whispers, "Grandpa. There's no prices!" The grandfather smiles, looks at the server, who politely smiles, then resumes his order taking pose. Carl replies, "High class dining restaurants do not show prices." Jody's eyes widen as she responds,

"How will people know the cost?" Carl looks at Jody and explains, "When you dine at a place like this - you come prepared to spend a lot of money! Don't worry everything's okay! Remember, this is my Graduation treat!" At this moment, the server turns to look at the Maitre D who gives a puzzled look; the server tilts his head, shrugs his shoulders, then faces the table and asks, "Are you ready to order? - What will the Mademoiselle be having?" Carl gives Jody a reassuring look and smiles. Jody scans the Menu and remarks, "The Roast Chicken sounds nice." The server jots her order, then he casts a glance at Carl, who informs, "For starters - we will have the Steak Tartar, Salade de Maison and the Crispy Escargot." The server smiles widely as he writes, "And for your Main - Monsieur?" Carl replies, "I'll have the Duck Confit." The server gives an ever so slight nod and comments, "Excellent choice! The server asks, "And your choice of wine - Monsieur?" Carl lifts eyes and replies, "We will not be ordering wine tonight." The Server politely nods, smiles, takes both Menus and comments, "Please enjoy your meal." As the man promptly leaves to disappear into the far kitchen, another server approaches, lights the table candle, then quickly withdraws. Jody looks around at the restaurant's beautiful decor, and listens to the classical music as she basks in the glow of the candlelight, and exclaims, "This so wonderful, Grandpa! I feel special being here." Carl reaches out his arm to clasp his granddaughter's hand, and tenderly remarks, "You are special, Jody! Special from the first day you were born. You deserve a night out like this (Carl's eyes get moist) At my age, I might not get another opportunity to celebrate my granddaughter's accomplishments!" Jody looks at her grandpa and replies, "I've learned so much from you, Grandpa! It was you who trained me - taught me everything I know." As Jody fondly gazes at her grandpa, she remembers the time when being very young, she and Carl rehearsed Martial Arts Katas. She recalls how Carl taught her to punch, block, spin and kick. Jody reflects on how they practiced Sticky Hands, and how Carl taught her to throw the Shuriken, the sharp metal stars sinking deep into the wood targets. As the candlelight flickers, she thinks of the times when she and her grandfather sparred with wood Katana swords, and how they both sat in deep meditation. As other patrons get seated at tables nearby, Jody comes out of her inner reflection. Carl smiles at Jody and remarks, "I tried to teach you everything I know - hoping you'd go further and become even better." By now the server brings the Appetizers to their table. Jody gives the Tartar an odd look and pokes it with her fork and asks, "What's this?" Carl chuckles and replies, "Raw meat! It's delicious." As they dine, the restaurant gradually gets filled with patrons at tables. Jody and Grandpa Carl heartily enjoy their fine French cuisine. Jody savours the Roast Chicken and Carl feasts on the Duck Confit. When they finish their plates, a server pours them more water and politely removes their dishes. Jody dabs the linen napkin to her lips and remarks, "Grandpa, that was wonderful! - I've never tasted such nice food!" Carl replies with a twinkle in his eye, "I'm so happy you're enjoying this!" The attending server approaches the table and asks, "Monsieur, Mademoiselle - will you be having desert?" Carl looks at Jody and winks his eye and responds, "Are the deserts good?" The server lifts his eye brow in alarm and quickly replies, "Monsieur! The House of Andrea has the best deserts in the city!" Jody gives a slight giggle and Carl remarks, "In that case, please bring us the Opera Cake and the Poire Belle Helene." The server smiles and replies, "Your selection is superb! Merci!" As the server leaves the table, Jody playfully tilts her head at Carl and asks, "When did you know so much about French stuff?" The grandfather sits back in his upholstered dining chair and straightens his long white braids and comments, "When you've been around as long as I have - you pick up a thing or two - like French cuisine." Jody grins and can't resist asking, "What other stuff do you know?" Carl gazes at Jody and replies, "Over the years, I've learned some Spanish, French - and even some Japanese. (Pause) I've studied Japan for twenty years. The country has a fascinating culture. Actually, I'm planning a special trip there after the summer." Jody quips, "Special trip? - What makes it so special?" Carl looks pensively at his granddaughter and remarks, "There's unfinished business I must take care of. Something that's waited far too long!" At that second, the server brings the deserts and sets them down. Jody stares at the Opera Cake and the appealing Pear and Cream desert. Carl divides the two deserts and gives Jody a portion of each. Jody digs her fork into the Opera Cake and takes a bite, and her eyes open wide with culinary delight!

CHAPTER SIXTY-EIGHT

Trouble Downtown

Night is upon the city, and light from building windows and the glow of the street lamps create a warm atmosphere downtown. The restaurant's posh entrance doors open and Carl and Jody step out onto the sidewalk, exiting the fine dining establishment. Jody wraps the shawl over her shoulders to fend off the cool air of the evening. The grandfather and granddaughter hold hands and begin to leisurely stroll past trendy shops and interesting boutiques. Jody looks over and comments, "Thanks Grandpa! I'm so happy you took me here." Carl replies with an endearing smile, "I wanted you to taste gourmet food and enjoy a high class setting." They walk along and Jody stops to admire an outfit in the Boutique window. She remarks, "This place is so different from the Reserve. Everything is so new and shiny — so nice!" Carl bends his head slightly as he gazes at Jody and comments, "Life isn't always about what's on the outside. - What's on the inside is much more important!" Jody turns to chime, "The City seems to have it all - everything's here!" Carl replies in a voice schooled with wisdom and experience, "Our Reserve doesn't have all this fancy stuff! What we do have is very valuable! - Our people are linked to American History, and our Tribal roots go deep into the very earth." Jody reaches out to clasp her grandfather's hand, "That's why I love you so much, Grandpa! - You're so smart and so wise!" Carl playfully squeezes Jody's hand and replies in jest, "And really really old!" They both laugh as they walk the sidewalk and turn the corner. Carl and Jody stop as they see barricades with flashing amber lights across the street midway up their route. Maintenance crews are working to repair the sidewalk and repave the road surface. Jody exclaims, "What will we do?" Carl scans about and points to a side alley and comments, "I believe this alley will take us the next street over to the car." The grandfather and granddaughter turn from the sidewalk and proceed into the dark corridor.

The passageway has scattered lighting that only illuminates certain spots as the alley zigzags its way behind the large brick buildings. Carl holds Jody's hand as they go through the passageway. They turn a corner and enter one of the alley's open areas. Suddenly, they stumble upon a street gang with a drug deal gone wrong. A dead body lays on the ground in a pool of blood. The gangsters are shocked and rivet their attention. Carl braces and puts his arm out to protect Jody. The gang's big leader yells, "Witnesses! We don't want witnesses. Get 'em!" The street gang swiftly spread out to surround on all sides. Carl keeps his guard and swiftly eyes Jody and remarks, "Twin Tigers - like we practiced!" Jody nods and takes a battle stance and replies, "Back to back - Repeal attack!" Carl and Jody quickly position back to back. Grandfather and granddaughter get into battle stance for the pending assault. Jody's shawl falls to the ground. The gangsters pace back and forth and flash their knives and clubs to intimidate. A gangster threatens, "You're dead meat old man! (Leers) But that young thing with you (Laughs) We'll show her a real good time!" All the gangsters start to Trash Talk! Carl scans the circle of thugs and whispers a Ninjan adage, "Eagles fly above the storm!" The gang of thugs block escape as the gang leader stands in front of Carl. The hoodlums threaten from all sides, and the leader steps out to stare down Carl. Carl boldly holds his ground and doesn't flinch, Jody keeps her eyes on the gangsters confronting her. The gang leader sneers and remarks, "He's just an old mangy Indian. Home Boy - take Him out!" A big thug steps out from the pack to size up Carl, then the brute raises his big arm and strides forward. The thug swings his fist - Carl grabs and torques his wrist to buckle the brute to the pavement. Carl boots the him away. Carl looks at the gang and emphasizes, "We don't want trouble! Just let us go." Big Home Boy gets up in a rage and lunges. Carl spear-thrusts his fingers into the nap of the thug's neck. The gangster collapses to the pavement, contorts and gasps for breath. All the gangsters are stunned their big guy got dropped! Their leader yells, "Rip him to shreds! - Kill him!" Gangsters around Carl and Jody begin to flip and twirl butterfly knives. They attack! One thug wildly swipes his blade. Carl blocks and grabs his arm to snap and dislocate the guy's shoulder. The gangster drops in agony. One tough repeatedly jabs his knife at Jody's torso. She kicks the blade away and releases a roundhouse to knock him out! Two gangsters lunge at Jody and she spins to block and flip one hard to the ground. The other thug grabs and squeezes Jody tight. She gives him a forceful head butt and gets released, then she strikes his vulnerable areas to disable him. The thug falls over. From the side, one gangster swings mightily at Carl with a metal rebar. Carl dodges, then grabs and bends his wrist to buckle him down. Carl belts the guy unconscious. As Carl is turned sideways, three homies with clubs rush from the front. Jody calls out in alarm, "Grandpa! Look out!" The three thugs spread out and violently swing and swipe their clubs. Carl bobs and ducks to avoid hits. He blocks, grabs a club from one thug and knocks him out! Carl takes the club to block the other two attackers. One thug runs at him and Carl pummels the attacker in a flurry of blows. The thug caves. The other thug swings and Carl flips the third thug to land hard yards away. Carl quickly turns to check on Jody. She's worried! Carl is exhausted, sweaty, and catches his breath. The gang leader bellows, "He's done! Finish him off!" Jody cries out, "Leave him alone! He's 83 years old." A street thug exclaims, "What a tough old geezer!" The street gang break out laughing - then, they get dead serious. Carl leans his hand on Jody's shoulder to steady himself. Jody looks into his eyes - Carl shakes his head! The gangsters close in. Suddenly, Carl clutches his chest, his face in excruciating anguish - he collapses unconscious! Jody cries out, "Grandpa! Grandpa!" A gangster yells loudly, "Hey! The old man got a heart attack!" The gangsters start to edge forward as Jody is bent over her Grandpa. She lifts her head - there's fire in her eyes! Jody springs from her crouch, spins to kick two nearby thugs unconscious! She quickly pivots to drive her fist into a thug's throat, then, pokes her fingers into another's eyes. He screams! The street gang leaders yells, "She's just a girl! Show her who's boss!" Jody rivets her eyes to the leader and harshly remarks, "You beat up an old man - now try someone younger!" The remaining street thugs brandish their switchblades, knives and clubs to attack her. One thug stretches his arms to grab her, she zips between his legs and drives her foot into his 'family jewels'. The guy buckles over in pain! She flips upright to explode a roundhouse to knock out another thug. A homie to her side slashes his blade at her. She blocks his swing and wrenches his arm to dislocate his shoulder. Now, only the street gang leader and a lieutenant are still standing. As Jody strides toward them, the leader shoves the other guy forward. He forcefully swings his fist, Jody ducks each punch. She strikes him with a torrent of blows - it's light out! The leader stands there alone. He flips and twirls his butterfly knife with bravado and teases, "Just you and me, little girlie! Let's see how good you really are?" The gang leader swipes his blade at Jody's face. She ducks. He repeatedly jabs and Jody dodges each lunge. One blade thrust goes close by her face and cuts off some of her locks of hair. The thug boss swipes hard and cuts Jody's forearm, she grabs the wound - blood seeps down to her hand. Jody looks into the hoodlum's eyes with gritty resolve, "You picked the wrong Indians to mess with!" The thug lunges with all his might. Jody sidesteps, grabs his arm and wrenches the knife loose. She drives her knee into his face, then gives him a powerful double kick. The gangster drops to the pavement - knocked out! Around her, gangsters wither in pain, incapacitated, while others remain unconscious. Jody takes out her cell phone and quickly dials 911. The Emergency Operator announces, "Hello 911! What is your emergency?" Jody replies, "My Grandpa had a heart attack! Please hurry! Quick!" The Operator asks, "What is your location?" Jody swiftly scans about and replies, "Some crooked alley near a French Restaurant - workers are paving the street!" The Operator informs, "Please keep calm! Stay with your Grandfather. Help is on the way." Jody pockets her phone as she leans over Carl. She gently touches his face. Soon, the sound of Police and Ambulance sirens approach.

CHAPTER SIXTY-NINE

Hospital Emergency

Carl lays unconscious in an Intensive Care Unit bed. Hospital tubes and electronic leads connect his body to monitors and medical equipment. The steady electronic sounds of medical devices fill the room - Beep! Beep! Beep! Jody sits in a bedside chair and keeps vigil over her Grandpa. A nurse enters the room to check the leads, tubes - reads the monitors and medical equipment - then leaves. Seconds later, Brian and Karen appear in the doorway. They rush to Carl's side, their eyes trace the old man's motionless form. Brian looks at Jody with concern, "What happened?" Jody stands up, clasps her Grandpa's hand near the bed railing and replies, "We left the restaurant and walked to the car. The street was blocked so we took an alley - that's when we ran into the street gang." Karen utters in alarm, "Street Gang! Oh Jody!" Mom comes over to put an arm around her daughter. Jody looks at her parents and remarks, "Grandpa fought them real good - took down several until the heart attack. - I took out the rest (Pause) The Police arrested them all!" Brian scans the monitors and medical machines, and exchanges glances with Karen. He holds Carl's hand and comments, "He looks so weak and fragile - nothing like the Ninjan Master he is!" Brian has a Flashback to when as a teenager, Carl trained him with Ninjan swords. At that moment, the nurse enters the room, comes up to inspect the solution and check the IV needle in Carl's arm. She glances at the trio and gives an assuring smile. And comments, "The doctors will be in shortly to give an update." The nurse jots something on the bed chart and leaves the room. A few minutes later, two physicians wearing white coats, one young and the other older, walk into the room and approach the small family. The older doctor smiles and greets them, "Hello! I'm Dr. Churchill (points) and this is Dr. Swartz." Brian extends his hand to greet and comments, "Hi! I'm

Brian (gestures) this is my wife Karen and our daughter Jody." The two doctors go beside the bed to inspect Carl and to check the monitors and bed chart. Dr. Churchill looks at the family and remarks, "We want to run tests right away - lab work, X-rays, and a MRI. (Inspects Carl's chest) The surgery went well, but we just want to be sure everything is okay!" Karen looks at Brian and asks the seasoned doctor, "How long before you find out?" Dr. Swartz looks at the trio, smiles and replies, "The tests won't take long - we should know in a day or two." Brian pulls Karen to his side and nods acknowledgement. The two doctors bid bye and exit the room and turn the corner down the hall. Jody glances at her dad, "Is Grandpa going to be all right?" Brian gives her a reassuring squeeze, then glances at Carl and remarks, "Your Grandpa's a tough guy! I'm sure he'll be okay." Over the next couple of days, Radiology Technicians position Carl for X-rays, a nurse withdraws blood from Carl's forearm, Medical Technicians work on Lab samples, and Carl lays on a flat table nestled in an enormous MRI machine. Finally, a team of doctors examine the MRI, X-rays and Lab Reports.

Carl is awake and sits upright in his inclined hospital bed. He has an IV tube and a couple leads attached. A monitor stands on each side like two electronic sentinels. Brian and Karen sit in the upholstered visitor chairs, while Jody stands beside Carl hovering like a Guardian Angel. The sounds of the Hospital Intercom system echoes into the room - "Paging IV Nurse. Paging IV Nurse." At that moment, Doctors Churchill and Swartz and another doctor, all in white coats, walk into the room and approach the family. The physicians nod a greeting to everyone. Dr. Churchill holds a folder with X-rays, Lab Reports and Charts. The doctors exchange glances and Dr. Churchill clears his throat and speaks, "We've examined the X-rays, Lab results and the MRI. (Pause) I'm afraid we have bad news!" Brain, Karen and Jody perk up at Dr. Churchill's announcement. Carl lays in his bed quiet. Brian looks at the doctor with grey hair and asks, "What is it Doctor?" The senior physician casts his eyes on Carl, then looks at the other three, and replies, "The Stint Surgery went well and Carl's heart is stable and in recovery. - However, the MRI, X-rays and Lab Reports tell us that Carl has Cancer - Stage Four Lymphoma!" Brian's face turns white. Karen gasps aloud! Jody begins to cry and turns to hug her Grandpa. Carl is calm and serene. Jody looks into her Grandpa's eyes and remarks, "You'll be okay Grandpa? You're going to fight this!

Right?" Brian looks at the doctors, "Is there anything you can do? Radiation? Treatments? Chemo?" Dr. Churchill replies with tender diplomacy, "I'm sorry! There's little we can do when Lymphoma is this advanced." The elderly doctor steps up beside his patient, and Carl looks directly into the doctor's eyes and asks, "It's okay Doc! Just tell me how long I have?" The grey haired doctor looks at the family, then glances at Carl and replies, "Four months! You have four months before the Cancer takes over. (Pats Carl's arm) I'm sorry! (Pause) We've made arrangements for you to be moved to Palliative Care - that will make things easier for you." Carl looks at Dr. Churchill and remarks, "Doc. I've made peace with my Creator long time ago." Jody sobs, "Oh Grandpa!" Carl lifts his eyes toward Brian, Karen and Jody and comments, "I'm not afraid to die! - It's just hard to leave your loved ones behind!" The senior Doctor steps away from the bedside, and the three doctors tactfully withdraw to exit. Brain, Karen and Jody come beside Carl to comfort him with their support, hugs and tears.

Two weeks later...

The Palliative Care Wing has a residential touch. The furniture, vases of flowers, wall pictures and room decor, create an atmosphere similar to being at home. The Doctors, nurses and staff, do their best to help patients during their final days. Carl has lost muscle mass and looks thin and weak. His shoulder bones protrude, his once muscular arms are skinny, and his face is slightly drawn-in. When thirsty, he sips water through a straw and cup.

CHAPTER SEVENTY

Carl's Dying Request

Knock! Knock!

Carl lifts his eyes to the doorway to see Jody, Karen and Brian enter his room with loving smiles. Jody holds a fresh bouquet of flowers. She walks to the window ledge and places the arrangement near the Get Well cards and other flowers. Jody comments with a cheery smile, "Here Grandpa - these will help brighten your day!" Brian and Karen lean in to greet and hug Carl. Jody moves beside her Grandpa to reach out and hold his hand. Carl gazes at the trio and remarks, "Aren't you guys tired of visiting me? - Must interfere with other things you have to do!" Brian and Karen exchange eye contact and Brian replies, "What we need to do - is be with you! We love you!" Carl tears up and Jody leans in with an affectionate hug. Karen looks at Carl and comments, "We have things covered. Please don't worry about us." Jody looks into her Grandpa's eyes and speaks sweetly, "I don't want to be anywhere else but right here with you!"

Carl scans his eyes from Brian to Karen to Jody. He clears his throat and reaches for another sip of water. Jody grabs the cup and brings it near to make it easier for Carl to sip. Carl remarks, "Thanks Jody! - This medication dries out my throat. Ahem! (Pause) Brian, I need you to do something." Brian moves closer to stand beside Carl and responds, "Anything! Whatever you need!" Carl turns his face toward Jody, then looks at Brian and remarks, "Inside the black armoire, underneath my Ninjan robe - there's a black leather pouch that hangs on a hook. Please bring it to me." Brian nods and replies, "Don't worry! I'll get it for you." Carl gives a weak nod. Jody reaches to gently glide her fingers on the side of his white braid. Carl coughs and begins to close his eyes and quickly falls asleep. Karen watches Carl and comments with sadness, "He gets weaker each day!" Karen comes over to hug Brain for solace. Jody stands transfixed - she scans Carl's emancipated body and her eyes well up with tears.

Carl's house is a small white wood cottage with some green ivy that climbs one side. The cottage sits nestled amid lovely pine trees and faces a forest stream. Brian enters the home and goes into Carl's bedroom and stands before the big black armoire. He reaches out and opens the double doors. Brian's eyes glance at the interior filled with Ninjan weapons and clothing. He scans the black weapons - the Ninjato and Katana swords, war club, Tomahawk, battle Sickle, Knives, Shuriken metal stars, and black bow and quiver of black arrows. Brian stretches his arm inside and moves the black robe aside and sees the black pouch hanging on a hook. He grabs the black drawstring and lifts the leather pouch away. Brian closes the armoire, turns and leaves the bedroom and exits the small white cottage toward his car.

At the Palliative Care Unit, a nurse helps Carl with his meal as he reclines in bed at an upright angle. His arms are unable to manage the feeding task. The nurse spoon feeds him the last of the green peas and carrots. Carl slowly chews and swallows, then the nurse gives him a sip of water. Finished the meal, the nurse removes the food tray and heads toward the door. She greets Brian, Karen and Jody as they enter. Carl sees his family and manages a smile. He becomes energized at their presence and life comes into his eyes. Karen, Brian and Jody greet Carl with loving hugs, kisses, and hand touches of support. Brian raises the black leather pouch for Carl to see and remarks, "Brought the pouch as you requested!" Brian places the pouch in Carl's palm. The old man smiles deeply and looks at all three and comments, "Thank you very much! This pouch contains something very special!" He shifts his gaze to Jody and moves his finger to beckon her, and remarks, "Jody! Please open the pouch and take out what's inside." Jody nods, picks up the pouch and pulls the drawstring open. She reaches in her fingers with child-like wonder and remarks, "It feels heavy - maybe a stone?" Everyone's eyes are focused with intensity. She pulls out her hand and opens it. A shiny gold square pillar about 5 inches high lays in her palm, the object has strange engravings and peculiar indentations on all four sides. Jody holds it up for display to

Brain and Karen. Brian comes close and Jody deposits the square gold pillar into is hand. He closely examines it and feels its weight and turns it over a few times, and remarks, "Whatever it is - it's solid gold! Must be really expensive and worth lots of money!" Karen comes beside to see for herself. She handles the gold column, then gives it back to Jody. Jody lifts the pillar up for closer inspection and glides her fingers tips over the details. Her eyes zero in on the engravings, design, and indentations. Carl smiles at her and extends his arm with an open palm. Jody goes beside him and lays the gold object in his weathered hand, and comments,"Grandpa - what is it?" Carl gazes at the square gold column and remarks, "This is the Golden Seal! It's the key to a secret Ninja Treasure! (Pause) It's been passed down generation to generation." Brain, Karen and Jody exchange looks of surprise and awe. Carl lifts his eyes toward them and continues, "The Ninja Sword Master Katsu gave it to his son, Takeshi. The Ninja Master Takeshi passed the Golden Seal to his Shoshone Apprentice and adopted son, Yuji. Yuji granted it to his son, Kamatsu; who gave it to his son, George." At this point tears fall from Carl's eyes; and Brian, Karen and Jody try give comfort. Carl looks at them with watery eyes and keeps speaking, "My father, George, passed the Golden Seal to me!" Brian, Karen and Jody are spell-bound at Carl's words. Carl stretches out his frail arm holding the object and nods to Jody. She takes the gold piece and firmly clasps her fingers over it. The Grandfather looks tenderly at his granddaughter and comments, "Jody! This is for you!" Jody exchanges eye contact with her dad and mom and exclaims, "For me? - Why? - What about Dad and Mom?" The elderly man glances over at Brian and Karen, then looks at his bewildered granddaughter, and remarks, "Jody! I have a dying request that especially for you! This will help prepare you for Black Eagle." Jody injects, "But Black Eagle is only for the top Ninjans from different tribes!" Carl smiles at Jody and remarks, "You were too young and unskilled before - now, you're ready for the last and most important lesson." Jody asks with eagerness, "What lesson, Grandpa?" Carl responds in a firm gentle tone, "To release your warrior spirit!" Jody leans in close to her Grandfather and speaks lovingly, "Grandpa! You know I'll do anything you ask - What's your special request?" The old man shifts his gaze toward Brain and Karen who are listening intently, then Carl looks sweetly at Jody and comments, "I want you to travel to Japan and return the Golden Seal to the Ninja Clan! It belongs in Japan with its rightful owners - Will you do that for me, Jody? - I planned to return it this Fall (Coughs) Now, my time has run out!" Jody looks directly at her dad and mom, and Brian and Karen smile and nod their support. Jody crouches down eye-level with Carl and firmly clasps his hand, and promises, "Don't worry Grandpa! I'll return the Golden Seal to the Ninja Clan in Japan!" Carl's eyes twinkle with happiness and he gives a contented peaceful smile, and comments, "Each day, I slip away a little more - soon, I'll be gone! There's peace now, knowing the Golden Seal will be returned. (Falling tears) I promised my father to return it, but didn't! (Looks at Jody) Now Jody, you'll return it for me!" The conversation and old emotions have taken a toll on the old man, and Brian leans in with reassuring words, "Rest easy! Karen and I will do our best to help Jody honour your request!" Carl stares at them and softly replies, "I leave all my Ninjan belongings to you to share - The weapons must stay in our family!" Brain nods that he acknowledges and Carl smiles and shuts his eyes - he's very tired. Jody stands beside the bed and looks at her Grandpa laying still. She opens her hand and intently stares at the shiny Golden Seal.

CHAPTER SEVENTY-ONE
The Funeral

Bright sunshine covers the country Cemetery the day of Carl's Funeral. The old monuments and gravestones sit nestled amid the manicured grounds. Brian, Karen, Jody and friends gather to say their final farewell. A framed photo of Carl sits atop the lacquered mahogany casket that lays suspended on straps over a freshly dug open grave. Funeral Home attendants are next to flower arrangements and wreaths set up on both sides of the coffin. A Minister with a thin leather Bible in hand, stands near the top of the grave. People dressed in clothes with black and muted tones are clustered together in a semi-circle facing a black marble headstone that reads…

CARL LONG GRASS

Brian, Karen and Jody are in front, each hold a beautiful long stem red rose. Brian also holds a large black eagle feather. Jody quietly sobs and weeps. Karen wraps her arm around Jody to console. Around them, attending friends and supporters each hold a short stem red rose. A Funeral Home attendant nods to the Minister and the Clergyman lifts his thin leather Bible chest-level and begins to speak in a warm and comforting voice, "Dearly Beloved, we are gathered here to say our final good bye to Carl Long Grass - who has been preceded by his wife Kathy Long Grass. (Pause) Carl was a loving husband, a wonderful Father, and an exceptional Grandfather. Carl left this earth while we still remain." A few ladies in the group begin to sob. The Minister pauses slightly, then continues, "He expressed a faith in the Creator and in His Son, Jesus. The Scriptures tell us that God has made a home for Carl in Heaven - where he can dwell with God for all Eternity." The Minister reaches into his jacket and brings out a slender glass tube filled with white sand. He reaches out his arm over the top of the casket and pours the sand into the shape of a Cross and speaks, "Ashes to ashes, dust to dust. We commit our brother Carl's body to the ground. One day, Carl will arise - with no more cancer or pain - But with a Glorified body! That's the Blessed Resurrection!" The Clergyman closes the Bible and steps back. A Funeral Home attendant gently approaches Brian, Karen and Jody and speaks in a hushed tone, "You may say your final Good Bye now." Brian, Karen and Jody step toward the closed casket. A tear runs down Brian's face, Karen's eyes are watery, and Jody quietly weeps. Brian stands frozen for a moment, then he lays the rose and the black eagle feather next to Carl's framed picture. Karen gently places her rose beside Brian's. Jody quietly stares at her Grandpa's portrait - he's healthy, strong and handsome, with a big smile. Jody sniffles as she lays her red rose along side the other two. Brian and Karen put an arm around Jody and walk her back. Once there, they turn and face the grave again. The Funeral Home attendant motions and the rest of the mourners trickle forward to lay their roses on the coffin, then return to their positions. Soon, all the roses lay atop the casket. A Funeral Home attendant tactfully retrieves Carl's portrait. He walks up to the family and hands Brian the framed photo, and speaks softly, "We will be lowering the body at this time. (Pause) Please follow me to the limousine that will be taking you home." The man points the direction with a subtle arm gesture. Brain, Karen and Jody follow the man and leave the graveside. Once the family have departed, the other mourners quietly disperse. Across the Cemetery, the people make their way to parked cars, vans, pickup trucks and SUVs. The Funeral Home attendant escorts Brian, Karen and Jody to the shiny black Cadillac limousine. The man opens the rear passenger door and Karen, Jody and Brian get in. The attendant respectfully closes the door.

CHAPTER SEVENTY-TWO

A Country Far Away

The dining table is loaded with cooked food from caring neighbours, friends and community members of the Reservation - fried chicken, tuna casserole, cooked vegetables, mash potatoes, gravy, apple pie, pumpkin pie, a fruit tray, and fresh baked bread. Some family photos sit to one side of the large wood table. Karen, Brian and Jody are eating supper when Jody puts down her fork and picks up a photo of them with Grandpa Carl. She studies at the picture - then looks at her mom and dad and expresses her worry, "I promised Grandpa - but I don't know anything about Japan. And to make matters worse - I've never flown on a plane or even been outside of America before!" The parents exchange glances and Karen replies, "Honey, don't worry about that now - there'll be time to learn about Japan. Your dad and I will help!" Brian adds in, "Your mom's right! We can look at stuff online, find books and even get a Travel DVD about Japan." Her parent's words provide relief and Jody smiles. She picks up another photo of Carl and shows it to them - Carl is in a pink bunny costume. Jody giggles as she remarks, "Remember when Grandpa dressed up as a bunny for my 6th birthday?" Brain and Karen look at the photo and start to chuckle, Brian comments, "Your Grandpa sure went all out for your Birthdays. (Laughs) He ripped that bunny suit because it was too tight." Karen blurts out laughing and remarks, "And I had to sew up that big rip near the tail." Jody takes back the photo to re-examine the picture and asks, "What's so funny about the rip?" By now, Brian and Karen are in stitches laughing. Brian pipes up, "Because mom kept sticking your Grandpa with the sewing needle!" And Karen exclaims, "Afterwards, your Grandpa said - some Birthdays are a pain in the butt!" At this point, all three are sharing a good laugh and pass around more photos as they continue to eat and talk, while having a special family time.

* * *

The day is cloudy and overcast when Jody, Brian and Karen exit their parked car and go inside the Bookstore. They browse the store aisles and merchandise shelves filled with various books. Jody pulls out a large book on Japan. Brian and Karen find other books that feature the 'Land of the Rising Sun', and pick out a couple. The trio walk to another area of the store to search the DVD section. Jody finds an interesting DVD on Japan and grabs it. Jody carries the books and DVD, and they head toward the Cashier Counter. Jody sets the items on the counter and the Cashier scans and bags each purchase. The Cashier keys in the Cash Register and asks, "Will that be all?" Jody smiles and answers, "Yes!" The Sales Clerk asks, "And how will you be paying today?" Brian steps up to the counter and presents his bank card and replies, "I'll be paying with Debit!" The Cashier smiles, keys the Sales Terminal and hands it to Brian. He Taps his Debit Card and the electronic terminal hums and cranks out a sales receipt. The Cashier tears off the Merchant's portion, then she hands Brian the Customer receipt, hands over the bag of goods, and comments with a smile, "Thank you! Have a nice day!" Jody takes the purchase bag and the trio walk through the bookstore and exit to the sidewalk near their car by the curb. They get into the vehicle and Brian starts the engine and drives away from the curb and goes with the traffic, heading toward home.

At the house, Jody, Karen and Brian sit on the sofa and watch the DVD on Japan on a large flat screen TV. They see video of modern Tokyo with its sleek office buildings, neon covered streets, crowded subway cars, Buddhist temples, and Bullet trains. The DVD shows them neat uniform school students, traditional Geishas, Japanese cars, high-tech electronics, and Sushi Bars. Jody, Brian and Karen are fascinated at the terraced rice paddies, Oriental architecture, beautiful gardens, picturesque landscape, and magnificent Mount Fuji. Over the next few days and nights, they look through various books, and spend time visiting Japan websites online. As Jody collects information she jots down notes, and spends time flipping through the large travel book on Japan. Brian brings over Carl's extensive research notes, and the trio study the Grandfather's writings and illustrations. Eventually, with enough knowledge and information gathered; Brian and Karen and Jody work on Japan maps and travel plans.

* * *

Brian, Karen and Jody sit at the dining table one evening. Karen and Jody sip their mug of tea while Brian enjoys his cup of coffee. Jody remarks, "Sure wish you guys could join me overseas!" Karen and Brian exchange eye contact and Brian comments, "I'm sorry Jody! I'd love to go but can't - house construction has ramped up and my crew is on a tight deadline." Karen reaches out to clasp Jody's hand and explains, "Sorry honey! I don't have enough seniority with the Nurses' Union. I can't get time off until after January!" Jody cradles her mug of tea and looks at her parents with wistful eyes and sighs, "I know - guess I was just hoping." Brian taps his index finger on the table top to get Jody's attention and to reinforce the point he makes, "You can do it! Your Grandpa knew that better than anyone. - And your mom and I know it too!" Jody looks at her parents and a smile dawns across her face and she remarks, "Grandpa did say it will help me." Her dad nods as he comments, "Your Grandpa understood that somehow going to Japan would teach you - help prepare you for Black Eagle!" Jody's attitude and motivation becomes fortified and she declares, "You're right dad! I'm not going alone - I'm taking all the Ninjan training that Grandpa gave me!"

CHAPTER SEVENTY-THREE

Flying To Japan

Individuals and groups of people move to and fro through the Airport Terminal. The building interior is busy with Airport workers, Airline Flight crews, Ticket Counter attendants, passengers, family and friends. Travellers holding their luggage join various lineups, many with Boarding Pass in hand.

Jody in jeans and jacket with her stuffed backpack slung over the shoulder, stands beside her upright suitcase that sits on four stubby wheels. She holds a carry-on. Her parents stand nearby. Karen looks at Jody with a melancholy gaze while Brian scans the Departure Display. Her dad remarks, "Jody, it's almost time!" Jody looks at her folks and exclaims, "I miss you guys already!" Karen gives her a big mommy squeeze with comforting words, "As soon as you land - give us a call! Let us know you're all right!" Jody smiles and nods and hugs mom tight. Brian leans in to wrap his arms around both and gives a group hug. Jody gazes into her parents eyes and assures, "I'll call as soon as the plane lands and I clear Customs." Brian places his hand on Jody's shoulder and speaks in a fatherly tone, "Remember - stick to the plan we made! Follow each step. (Pause) If there's a problem - don't hesitate - call us!" Jody nods her head with a serious look to let her dad know she got the point.

TERMINAL ANNOUNCEMENT CHIMES
    "Boarding Call for United Airlines Flight 252 to Tokyo, Japan,
    at Gate 37 - Passengers can now board the aircraft."

Mom, dad and daughter have one last quick hug. Jody grabs her luggage trolly and steers it toward the Departure Zone. Airport Staff at the entrance check Jody's ticket and wave her through. Karen leans against Brian as they watch Jody go through the Departure Area sliding doors only to disappear behind the frosted glass. Karen looks into Brian's eyes and whispers, "She'll be okay, right?" Brian gives his wife a confident look and replies, "Jody can handle herself! I'm more afraid she might end up living in Japan - far away from us!"

Inside the Departure area, Jody stands at the Boarding zone for Gate 37, Flight 252 to Tokyo, Japan. She's in the lineup and moves forward when it's her turn. The Attendant checks Jody's Ticket and motions to go ahead. She joins passengers as they walk the Terminal Gangway to the parked aircraft. As Jody approaches the plane, a Flight Attendant inspects her Boarding Pass and points her down the aisle. Jody shuffles along with the other passengers in the congested cabin aisle as people find their seats and get settled. Jody scans the seat numbers and finds ROW 16 and SEAT A that's next to the window. She reaches up and places her backpack in the overhead storage compartment, shuts the door and gets into her window seat. Jody tucks her carry-on under the seat, buckles up and gets comfortable. As she lifts her eye to watch the other passengers move past her, she sees a middle-aged white couple come down the aisle checking seat numbers. The heavyset man looks at his Boarding Pass and remarks, "Our seats are here!" His wife, a lady with curly red hair that looks exhausted, comments, "Can't wait to sit down - my feet are killing me!" The man puts his hand on his belly, grimaces and remarks, "I think it's best if I take the aisle seat!" His wife nods and squeezes by to take the seat next to Jody. The man hoists their carry-on into the overhead compartment, closes the door and sits down.

CABIN CHIMES. SEAT BELT LIGHT BLINKS.

The couple grab their seat belts and buckle up. The lady turns to Jody with a friendly smile and makes an introduction, "Hello sweetie! I'm Agnes and this is my husband, Harold." Harold leans forward and gives Jody a polite wave and she waves back, and replies, "Hi! My name's Jody." Agnes studies Jody a bit, then she speaks, "Harold and I are taking an Oriental Tour that starts in Japan. (Pause) Are you Japanese?" Jody smiles and replies, "No. I'm not Japanese - I'm an American Indian - from Wyoming!" The lady gets apologetic and explains, "I'm sorry! I thought with your complexion and shiny black hair - you might be a Japanese girl." Jody smiles, shakes her head and responds back, "My Grandfather once told me that sometimes, American Indians can be mistaken for Asians. (Pause) He told me American Indians came across from Asian thousands of years ago." Agnes tilts her head and leans in close and whispers, "To be honest, honey, I wish I had your beautiful hair and tanned complexion!"

AIRCRAFT CABIN CHIMES

The big airplane engines fire up and the high pitched whirling sound can be heard inside the plane. The cabin interior slightly vibrates as the plane starts to taxi toward the runway. The Stewardesses stand in front of each seat section and begin to go through the Flight Instructions. The aircraft quickly finds its position on the runway and waits for departure clearance from the Airport Controllers. The engines begin to INCREASE THROTTLE. Jody peeks out her window to look across the flat Airport grounds with its many array of coloured lights and painted markings. Suddenly, the engines fire FULL BLAST and the plane begins Take Off. Jody is amazed at how quick the outside ground rushes by as the plane accelerates. Jody notices the cabin interior shakes and vibrates as the plane picks up more and more speed, she sits back in her seat and clutches the armrests with both hands. Agnes looks at Jody's semi-frozen state and remarks, "First time flying?" Jody turns her head and nods, "Yes! I've never been on a plane before." Agnes reaches to put her hand over Jody's hand and comments with a voice of experience, "Take off is the roughest part - soon, it will be smooth sailing." At MAX VELOCITY the entire plane shutters - Suddenly, the plane lifts off and climbs - the vibrations stop. The aircraft ascends at a steep angle and Jody looks out her window at the earth below to see a patchwork of farms, towns, wilderness terrain and sprawling forests. In a few minutes, the aircraft levels off and the SEAT BELT LIGHT goes out. Jody peers down at the snow covered mountains below. Throughout the cabin, many passengers unbuckle and prepare to relax. Jody lifts her head to see people read magazines and novels, parents entertain small children, and others lean back to snooze. Jody leans back in her seat and becomes more relaxed. Suddenly, Harold gets up, grimaces and looks at his wife and remarks, "I need the washroom!" Harold swiftly goes down the aisle toward the washrooms. Agnes turns her head toward Jody and asks, "Are you traveling with your family?" Jody turns toward her fellow passenger, smiles and replies, "No! I'm travelling by myself." The middle-aged woman comments, "Please don't think I'm nosey, but, why are you travelling to Japan by yourself?" Jody thinks for a few seconds and responds, "I'm going to Japan for research!" The woman's curiosity is peeked and she asks, "What are you studying that you have to fly to Japan?" Jody looks into the woman's eyes and replies, "Something to do with Martial Arts." The woman sits back in her seat and remarks, "Martial Arts!? Isn't that about fighting and hurting people?" Jody makes eye contact and responds, "I've studied Martial Arts since I was young, and I don't believe in hurting people. My Teacher taught me that." Agnes fixes her eyes on Jody, "What if some guys attack or assault you?" Jody leans forward with a determined expression and responds, "They'd wish they hadn't!" Harold ambles back down the aisle and sits down in his seat, looks at Agnes and asks, "Did I miss anything? What were you talking about?" Agnes places her hand on Jody's hand and replies, "Oh, just talking about girl stuff!" Harold shrugs and sits back in his seat. A Stewardess pushes a beverage trolly down the aisle and stops beside them, and politely asks, "Would anyone like a beverage?" Harold looks at the cart and remarks, "Got any beer?" The Stewardess smiles, brings out a bottle and Harold smiles wide.

CHAPTER SEVENTY-FOUR

Narita International Airport

Narita International Airport is a low modern building made of metal and glass with curved roofs. Two long separate sections jut out at one end, while the other end features two separate circular pods. From the view above, the Terminal layout resembles a stylized Japanese Kanji.

The United Flight 252 descends from its approach position and lands on the long tarmac runway of Narita International Airport, then taxis to the Terminal. The passengers gather their belongings and the Flight Crew oversee and guide them to disembark the aircraft. Jody walks with the other passengers in the enclosed gangway to the Terminal building. Japanese Staff greet them with the customary bow and direct the passengers to the area to clear Customs. The people get into lines and wait as Custom Officials process each traveller. One Customs Agent motions his hand to beckon Jody forward to his location. She reaches the counter and presents her American Passport and Airplane Ticket. The man scans her Passport and Ticket, then presses a Japanese Customs Stamp on a Passport Page and hands it to Jody. She secures the Passport and Flight Ticket in her travel pouch and moves away from the counter toward the revolving Baggage Carousels, to where other passengers await their luggage. After a bit of time watching others get their suitcases and belongings, Jody spots her luggage trolly, picks it off the Carousel and sets it down beside her. The young lady reaches into her jean pocket to bring out a small note card and reads the Travel Points that she and her parents prepared…

1. Clear Customs
   2. Get Japan Rail Pass
   3. Train to Tokyo Station

* * *

Jody pockets the card, adjusts her backpack and grips the carry-on, then she grabs the handle of the luggage trolly and heads toward the Airport Concourse. She scans the JAPANESE/ENGLISH signs placed throughout the Airport for the International travellers. Jody walks into the Terminal passageway and scans the interior and finds the sign pointing toward the Japan Rail Counter. Jody chooses to move through the outer pillars of the Main Lobby to avoid the milling crowds. She reaches the Counter and the lady smiles and bows. Jody takes out her travel pouch, unzips it and takes out 3,000 Yen, hands the money to the Japan Rail Agent and asks, "A ticket to Tokyo Station, please." The lady smiles, collects the bills, bows and hands Jody a One-Way Japan Rail Pass to Tokyo. Jody receives the Pass, nods to the Agent and turns toward the Concourse and follows the signage to the Japan Rail Platform. The glass doors of the Terminal slide open and Jody walks out onto the platform area fitted with scattered benches. She looks around at the others waiting and peers down the tracks and sees nothing but empty rails and arrays of track lights. Jody sits down on a bench and pulls out her phone and an International Calling Card, and dials home and waits - LONG DISTANCE DIAL SEQUENCE - the her mom answers with a sleepy voice, "Hello!" Jody announces with excitement, "Mom! It's me!"

Back on Plains Road, in the raised bungalow, Karen sits up in bed delighted to hear her daughter's voice all the way from Japan, thousands of miles away. She pushed her arm on Brian to rouse him. Brian rubs his eyes and wakes up - Karen puts the phone on Speaker mode, and asks, "Jody - Jody honey - so good to hear your voice! We put you on Speaker Phone. Was your flight okay?" Jody replies, "Bumpy at first but it was fine. I got the Japan Rail Pass, and I'm just waiting for the next train - it's an hour ride to Tokyo Station." Brian leans toward the home phone and remarks, "You all right? - Any problems?" Jody grins and responds, "Everything's fine dad! Following the Plan like we talked about." Her dad nods, smiles and looks at Karen and whispers, "That's our girl!" Karen comments in a motherly tone, "Call us when you get settled in your Hotel room. Let us know that you're safe!" Jody hears the sound of metal train wheels on steel rails and turns her head to see the train approaching. She replies to her mom, "The train is coming - gotta go now. I'll call from the Hotel." Brian calls out, "Remember Jody, stick to our Plan!" Karen adds in, "Stay safe honey. We love you!" Jody responds, "Love you guys! - Gotta run." Jody pockets her phone and grabs the trolly handle as she watches the train pull to a stop beside the platform landing. CHIMES sound as the train doors slide open. As other passengers enter the train to find seats, Jody steps into the passenger compartment and glides her luggage to a row of seats and sits down. She scans about at the Japanese travellers interspersed throughout the train car. CHIMES sound again and the compartment doors WHOOSH shut as the train pulls away and goes down the tracks. Jody watches railway lights and illuminated Japanese ads whiz by. She leans forward enough to glimpse the bright Tokyo City skyline up in the distance. Jody sits back in her seat and takes a deep breath. The train speeds through dense urban development - buildings, stylish condos, tall slender apartment towers, retail stores, and gleaming corporate office buildings. Jody watches in child-like wonder. She has a momentary flashback to Venture's four-way Stop and the spartan Indian Reservation. Jody looks out as the train approaches busy Tokyo Station with its network of train tracks, lights, switches, passenger trains and coloured platforms. She holds the trolly handle and pulls on her backpack as the train rolls to a smooth stop. CHIMES sound and the train doors open. Jody walks with the fellow passengers along the platform landing and takes the escalator and steers the trolly through the illuminated Concourse of Tokyo Station that is bustling with thousands of commuters, passengers and travellers. She follows the ENGLISH signs and enters the spacious Tokyo Station Lobby with its pillars and circular European style dome several floors high above the mezzanine ground level. Jody stares up at the molded details and decorative features reminiscent of architectural domes she's seen on TV travel shows about Europe. Jody lowers her eye and scans the busy interior and spots the GINZA navigation sign. She steps aside out of the way of the pedestrian flow to pull out the note card.

4. YOSAN BAJETTO HOTEL, GINZA

She tucks the note back in her jean pocket and moves in the direction of the passageway marked GINZA. The Concourse is lined with retail stores and Sushi Bars. Many Japanese travellers already carry the small customary gift package to honour the traditional custom of gift giving when visiting family and friends. Jody looks at the pedestrians around her - everyone has jet black hair and oriental complexion. Her eyes dart here and there, only to find one or two Caucasians in the mix. She continues along the marble tiled Concourse until reaching the CENTRAL EXIT doors. The glass doors slide open and Jody steps out to join bustling crowds of people, she has to maneuver and dodge passing people going to and fro on the busy sidewalk. Millions of citizens live in Tokyo City and to Jody it seems like there're all on the sidewalk before her. She glances about and sees to nook in a building exterior that's off the sidewalk and out of the way of the crush of people. Jody moves to the nook, reaching into her backpack and pulls out a folded city map of Tokyo. Her eyes sweep across the streets until she locates the Train Station and the nearby **GINZA DISTRICT**.

CHAPTER SEVENTY-FIVE

Yosan Bajetto Hotel

Jody traces the travel route from where she is to the Hotel. She folds the map up and returns it inside the backpack, then she strikes out to her destination. Jody walks until she spots the YAESU CHUO-GUCHI Street sign, turns right and continues along YAESHA-DORI AVENUE where she notices the various stores. She turns left and goes along KAJIBASHI-DORI AVENUE to where she sees the **YOSAN BAJETTO HOTEL** and breathes a sigh of relief.

Jody goes through the entrance doors and steers her luggage inside and walks up to the Lobby Desk. The female Hotel Receptionist gives Jody with a warm smile and respectful bow and greets her new guest in Japanese. Jody smiles and replies, "Sorry! I don't speak Japanese." The Receptionist smiles and responds in English, "Welcome to the Yosan Bajetto Hotel!", and gives a polite bow. Jody slides the trolly close and rests her elbow on the marble counter and remarks, "I'd like a non-smoking single room for three nights please." The young lady scans her monitor as her fingers move the mouse across the screen to highlight a rectangle, then she smiles, "Your room is 10-34. Room #34 on the 10th Floor." Jody takes out her zippered travel pouch and removes a Credit Card and passes it to the young lady. The Receptionist inserts the card into a small countertop terminal and enters keystrokes - ELECTRONIC PRINTING. A paper receipt emerges. The young lady hands Jody the Credit Card, the Receipt, and the Hotel Room Access Card. Jody smiles and comments, "Thank you! (Pause) Arigato!" The female staffer gives a big smile, bows and replies in English, "You are welcome! Enjoy your stay." Jody puts the Credit Card and Receipt into the travel pouch and tucks it into her backpack. She looks about the Lobby - the Receptionist lifts her arm, smiles and points to the Lobby Elevators. Jody sees the Elevators, turns to nod and smile at the young lady, then steers the Trolly and crosses the marble floor toward the Elevators to press the metal UP Button. CHIMES. The Elevator doors open. Jody enters, turns and pushes the button for the 10th Floor.

Jody pushes her luggage along the carpeted hallway and scans the room numbers. She passes 32 - 33 and comes to Room 34. She takes the Access Card from her jean pocket and inserts it into the door lock mechanism. Green Light. Click! Jody pushes down the lever handle and the room door opens, she moves the trolly through the doorway, shuts the door and locks the deadbolt. Jody turns about and views the clean modern room with its single bed with bedspread and pillow neatly tucked in, and a small desk with a convenient table lamp. Jody steps over to the bed, turns and flops onto the cover. She brushes her hand across the soft mattress and smiles delight. Jody is totally exhausted from travelling thousands of miles - she closes her eyes - and falls asleep.

Some time later…

Jody sits upright on the bed and YAWNS! She stretches her arms and rubs her eyes, then looks around the room. The luggage trolly is still by the door. Jody gets up, grabs the trolly and lays it flat onto the bed. She spins the combination, pops the latch to swing open the suitcase. Jody opens the dresser drawers and puts away her clothes. Then she shuts the suitcase and stands it next to the wall. The girl zips open her backpack to dig out a Tokyo City Map and spreads it out on the desktop. She eyes TOKYO STATION and the GINZA DISTRICT. Jody takes out her cell phone and notices the time is 7:00 PM. She brings out the International Calling Card and dials. ELECTRONIC TONES.

Across the Pacific Ocean, in Northwest America…

The cell phone BUZZES on the nightstand. Karen grabs it, presses Speaker Mode and gets Brian's attention. The mom asks with excitement, "Hello! Jody?" Jody voices comes across clear. "Hi mom! I've checked into the Hotel and got a nice room - but I'm feeling really tired!" Brian leans close to the phone, "That's just the jet-lag from your long flight. Rest up, you'll feel better tomorrow." Karen gets beside

Brian to caution her daughter, "Remember our talk! Always keep your travel pouch secure! Big cities have pickpockets, I'm sure it's no different over there." Jody replies, "Mom - don't worry! I'll be on my guard. (Pause) It's so exciting to be here! Tokyo is even better than those Travel Books. Everything is so lively and modern - Nothing like the Reservation!" Brian looks at Karen and remarks, "Why not do the Tourist thing for a couple days - see what Tokyo's like before you go to the Iga Mountains." Jody glances down and runs her fingers across the unfolded TOKYO CITY MAP and responds, "You think that will be okay?" Her mom advises with a motherly tone, "Jody honey - who knows when you'll ever be in Tokyo again? Head out and see the city (Pause) Take one of those Bus Tours." Jody smiles at the idea and replies, "Ok guys! If you think there's time - I'd love to see the sites here!" Jody stands up, walks to the window to part the curtain and look out at the bright city lights. Her eyes sweep across the city skyline filled with illuminated modern buildings. Brian encourages his daughter, "Jody, take a Daily Tour Bus - you can travel inland later on. Go ahead - enjoy yourself! (Pause) Your Grandpa would want you to!" Jody becomes still at her dad's words - then she replies with a wide smile, "You're right dad! Grandpa would be so proud I'm here in Japan doing what he asked! (Pause) Love you guys! Good night!" Her dad responds, "We love you, Jody! Take care. Karen squeezes in a quick good bye, "Love you Jody! Be safe." As the phone call ends, Jody draws shut the curtains and steps away from the window. She walks over to set her phone on the small desk, goes to the dresser, opens a drawer and brings out her pyjamas.

CHAPTER SEVENTY-SIX
Tokyo City

Bright and early the next day, Jody stands in the Lobby before the female Receptionist to ask, "Where can I get a Tokyo Day Tour Bus?" The young lady picks out a Tourist Brochure, hands it over and comments, "Day Tour Bus! You see Tokyo City on bus. Buy ticket - Tokyo building." Jody holds the Brochure and points to a Map detail to ask, "Is this the address? Can I get the Day Tour Bus there?" The Receptionist scans the Map detail, smiles and nods, "Yes! Day Bus not far. You walk 15 minute - Follow Map!" Jody replies with a smile, "Ok! Thank you! Arigato!" Jody clasps the Brochure, pivots around and walks out the Hotel Entrance to step onto the street outside. She checks the Brochure and heads up **KAJIBASHI-DOR AVENUE**. Jody turns right onto **MARUNOUCHI-DOR** and walks past buildings, stores and retail shops to arrive at the Tokyo Building.

Jody looks around and spots the sign and location for the DAY BUS TOUR. She moves toward the building, enters the Reception Area and approaches the Ticket Counter. She looks up at the overhead sign: DAY TOUR 1,000 YEN. A petite uniformed Ticket Agent at the counter, smiles and gives a bow, "Ohayougozaimasu!" Jody gets her travel pouch and removes 1,000 Yen and remarks, "I'd like a Daily Tour Pass please!" The young female clerk quickly smiles, prints out a **DAY PASS TICKET**, picks out a **BUS ROUTE BROCHURE**, and passes both over as Jody gives the money. The Ticket Agent smiles and politely speaks, "You follow Map - see Tokyo City. Very beautiful!" Jody opens the Map and notices the various Colour Coded Routes, and asks the young lady, "What Route will let me get on and get off to sightsee?" The gal behind the counter opens up a Map from the rack and points to a Route, "**Blue Line**. You stop, get off, get on. - Must use

Blue Line. Very important!" Jody examines her Map, nods and turns to look at the Coloured Bus Stops on the street outside. She looks at the female Ticket Agent, smiles and bows, "Arigato!" The young worker replies in Japanese, "Have a nice day!" Jody pushes open the exit door and steps onto the sidewalk outside. She navigates her way through the busy pedestrians to reach the **BLUE BUS STOP SIGN**, and stands with the DAY PASS in her right hand. She glances around the busy urban environment with gleaming office towers and contemporary buildings, stores and open spaces.

A DAY BUS approaches the Stop and slows to a halt. Jody steps back as all types of passengers exit onto the sidewalk to disperse into the pedestrian crowd. Jody climbs onto the Bus and presents her DAY PASS to the Driver. He looks at the Ticket, smiles and nods. She turns and goes down the Bus aisle and notices stairs that lead to the Upper Deck open-air viewing level. Jody makes her way up the steps to the Upper Deck and strolls the aisle to the middle section to get a seat at the Bus side. She sits down, dons her sunglasses and adjusts the strap to put the travel pouch to her front. Other people get on the Bus - Japanese and International Tourists. Some sit at street level, while others intersperse among the Upper Deck seats. ENGINE REV. The Bus pulls away to merge with traffic. Jody smiles - it's a bright sunny day - perfect weather for sightseeing. As the Bus moves through traffic, the wind blows Jody's long black hair around. After a few moments, the Bus passes **SHIBA PARK** where Jody looks at the red **TOKYO TOWER** for communication. The Driver stops the vehicle at a popular Tourist destination - Jody stands on the grounds near the ancient **IMPERIAL PALACE** with its stone walls. Back in her seat, Jody watches as the Bus goes through **UEDO PARK'S** wide boulevards and stunning flowers beds. The DAY BUS travels along the **SUMIDA RIVER** that flows through Tokyo City, and takes the passengers to the big bustling **TSUJIKI FISH MARKET** - the largest fish market in the world. Jody has never seen so many kinds of fish and is amazed at the variety and the sheer volume. Later, the Bus takes the sightseers to the **SHINJUKU-KU DISTRICT** with its colourful **TRENDY STORES** and noisy **PACHINKO PALORS**. Next, the driver takes the people to see the nearby **WEST SHINJUKU DISTRICT** dotted with prestigious **CORPORATE TOWERS.** Jody looks here and there with wonder. She has a big grin at seeing all the Japanese sites and attractions. Jody checks her Tour Brochure and the Street Map for the **SWORD**

MUSEUM near **YOYOGI PARK**. She looks at the upcoming **BLUE LINE STOP - YOYOGI PARK**.

344

CHAPTER SEVENTY-SEVEN
The Sword Museum

Jody stands up and goes downstairs to the rear exit doors of the Day Bus and waits. The Bus pulls up to the Blue Sign and stops. The Exit Doors open and Jody steps out onto the wide sidewalk. After a few seconds, the Bus pulls away and zooms down the road. Jody walks into Yoyogi Park and sees the sign for the **MEIJI JINJU SHRINE** and moves in that direction. She strolls past the Shrine, going further into the Park grounds. Jody is amazed at the colourful flower beds, manicured lawns, picturesque walkways, and the beautiful Japanese Maple, Pine, Oak, and Cherry trees. Yoyogi Park is a stunning natural parkland set within large modern Tokyo. In Jody's mind, she recalls images of the Indian Reservation of Venture set in the desert terrain; surrounded by cactus, sage brush, rock canyons, and rugged wildness. Back home, there's no train stations, malls, office towers, modern boulevards, or crowded city streets. On route through the grounds and cultivated ornamental gardens, Jody stops to admire a grand Cherry Blossom tree with its delicate pink flowers - so lovely - so breathtaking. She takes out the Tourist Map to check the location, turns and resumes her trek to the **Sword Museum**, a definite 'must see' while she's in Japan. Jody goes along the walkway, turns onto **SANGUBASHI**, then continues through a few streets until she spots her destination. Jody approaches the **SWORD MUSEUM**, reaches the front entrance, stops, takes a breath - then she enters inside.

The Sword Museum's First Floor presents the entire Sword Making Process for the education and benefit of the visiting tourists. The visitors can follow illustrated examples of the Stages involved - Raw Materials, Forging Techniques, Shaping, Grinding, Honing, and the finished polished Sword. Jody tours through each stage of the Sword

Making Process. She studies the illustrated displays and reads the descriptions. When she's seen enough, Jody climbs the stairs to the 2nd Floor. The Second Level displays the numerous Swords used through Japan's history. Each Sword is an outstanding masterpiece of traditional Japanese swordsmith artistry and exquisite design. Jody stands amazed as she's surrounded by all the fantastic Japanese Katana Swords. She moves throughout the floor. Every sword she sees, her eyes trace its unique features and design details, the rich colours, the highly polished lacquer, and the exquisite Japanese craftsmanship. Jody is transfixed as she stares at a stunning red Katana sword with an intricate handle and gleaming steel blade. As her eyes get lost on the red sword - for a few seconds, she imagines a Japanese Samurai welding the red sword as he protects defenceless peasants from armed bandits. Suddenly, the sounds of other tourists browsing displays makes Jody snap out back to the moment. She glances around to see the Lower Level staircase and heads downstairs. She exits the Sword Museum and pauses on the steps to gaze at the local neighbourhood. Jody spots some interesting stores up the street and goes to check things out.

Jody walks along browsing shops and casually explores side streets. She turns a corner and walks toward a five story building that features a neon sign - **KOI REN'AI CAPSULE HOTEL**. Five tough looking young men, Japanese HANZAI-SHU street thugs, stand on the sidewalk engaged in conversation and happen to be blocking the way. As Jody approaches and makes eye contact, she gets uncomfortable at the way they leer at her. One young man, the Hanzai-shu Leader, steps in front of her and remarks in Japanese, "What a pretty girl!" Jody stops and is reserved and polite as she replies, "I'm sorry! I don't speak Japanese." The Hanzai-shu leader grins as he looks at the others, then comments in broken English, "You tourist? - American?" Jody cordially responds, "Yes! I'm American." As Jody is focused on the man addressing her, one thug unbeknownst to her uses his cell phone to quickly take her photo. The gang leader eyes Jody and remarks to his companions in Japanese, "Gaijin! - She's very attractive!" The young man next to him comments, "We always need more pretty girls!" The Hanzai-shu leader replies, "Especially Gaijin girls - Worth lots of money!" At this point, Jody feels uncomfortable at the foreign banter and begins to step to the side to go around, "Sorry I don't understand what you are saying - I must go now!" The gang leader smiles, steps back and sweeps his arm with an inviting gesture, A gold bracelet with a tiny snake medallion hangs from his wrist, "Tokyo beautiful city! - You go see." Jody replies, "Thank you! Arigato!" She gives a polite quick smile and briskly walks away down the street, moving past buildings and stores. The five thugs watch her as she goes into the distance. The gang leader looks at his crew and orders, "Follow her. When you get a chance - grab her!" The four street thugs head out in Jody's direction.

Jody walks along admiring the quaint shops - stopping to browse and inspect knick-knacks, crafts, and curious retail items. She turns a corner and goes halfway up a narrow side street - SUDDENLY! - two guys step out from a street on her left, and two guys comes out from a street on her right. Jody is caught in the middle - she braces herself! As the street thugs close in - one guy reaches at Jody and she grabs and torques his arm buckling him to the pavement. The guy behind puts his arms out to snag Jody. She scratches his faces with her nails, spins about with a roundhouse that sends him flying backwards. The four thugs are surprised and one exclaims, "This Gaijin knows Martial Arts!" One gangster pulls out a knife and circles Jody and chimes, "She's just one - We are four!" He steps in to swipe the blade. Jody blocks, sidesteps to unleash a flurry of blows that stops him cold. He collapses! A thug yells out, "All attack now! Get her!" Jody dashes to her left and a thug pursues her. She quickly ducks behind a street lamp and he repeatedly tries to catch her - Jody grabs his arm and forcefully yanks the guy hard against the metal post - CLUNK! He's knocked out and crumples to the ground. The two thugs still standing attack her with knives - one on each side. Jody ducks the knife swipe and pivots to avoid a leg kick. She uses her both arms to grab and wrench the attacker's knife arm. He bellows in agony! Jody turns and kicks the last remaining thug in the crotch - THUD! The hoodlum drops like lead. She scans her foes - two are knocked out, two others wither in pain on the pavement.

LOUD VOICES!

Jody turns to see a group of Hanzai-shu at the far end of the street racing toward her. She dashes down the side-street with all her might - her legs eat up the asphalt. As the group of Hanzai-shu reach their fallen comrades, Jody has rounded the corner to disappear out of sight.

Some of the gangsters help the beaten thugs off the ground. The leader of the reinforcements yells, "You were told to catch the Gaijin!" The fallen thugs, now on their feet, nurse their injuries, one of them remarks, "That Gaijin fought like a demon! She must be a Martial Arts Master!" The Hanzai-shu lieutenant looks down the street where Jody vanished. The other gangsters assemble and stand ready. The lieutenant declares, "The Boss wants her! She can't get far - Remember (He smirks) - She's a Gaijin in Japan!" The leader waves his arm and all the gang give chase. Jody runs through a side street and looks over her shoulder - she sees the gangsters and they start YELLING and run toward her. Jody races past some streets and happens to spot **SANGUBASHI**, she quickly dashes down the road. She sees Yoyogi Park up ahead and runs fast onto the grounds. The Hanzai-shu are on her heels in hot pursuit and follow her into the Park. In the middle of the grounds, Jody stops near a cluster of trees to catch her breath. She lifts her eyes to see the thugs coming toward her. Jody sprints across some loose gravel and takes a tumble - her cell phone slips out of her jeans. Jody jumps to her feet and hightails it out of there, she's unaware the phone has fallen out and lays on the ground behind her. She runs across the parkland to exit Yoyogi Park and keeps on running street after street - until she finds herself in strange surroundings.

CHAPTER SEVENTY-EIGHT
The Harajuku District

Jody encounters crowds of Japanese young people that mill about the streets and sidewalks, dressed in colourful trendy clothes with exotic **Harajuku** flare. Everywhere she looks, the young people are dressed like **Fairy Princesses** and **Storybook Characters**, others dress in **Minimalism**, **Modern Chic**, and **Japanese Anime**, and some wear **black Goth** outfits. Jody turns to look for the gangsters and spots them entering the area. She scurries through the young people, who are either shopping, moving around, or just hanging out in small groups. The Hanzai-shu thugs run into the area and quickly spread out. Jody glances around and notices thick bushes in a concrete planter and ducks behind it, out of sight. Jody is bent down to catch her breath, she lifts her head and makes eye contact with a Japanese young man, **KEI**, sitting on a bench behind her. Kei is dressed as a Harajuku Hipster - black leather jacket, ripped designer jeans, belt with silver metal studs, a wallet chain, checkered shirt, and a French Tam. Kei observes Jody crouched down behind the concrete planter - his eyes convey that he's curious and somewhat puzzled?! Jody looks at him and desperately pleads, "Help me! Please! They're after me." Kei lifts his eyes to see the Hanzai-shu gangsters combing the area checking different groups. He gives Jody a quick glance, looks at the thugs, then extends his arm and motions, "Follow me - I will help hide you!" Jody smiles relief and quickly gets to her feet. Kei and Jody swiftly go to a side street to disappear. Kei takes Jody through some passageways and around corners until they enter a wide open pedestrian area filled with various groups of youth. Meanwhile,...the gangsters keep checking individuals and groups here and there. The thug leader barks, "Find her! She must be here!"

* * *

Over where Jody and Kei are…

Kei takes Jody up to a group of Japanese Goths dressed totally in black. They look at Kei and Jody. Kei scans their faces and explains, "We need your help! Some bad people are after this Gaijin girl. - Will you help hide her?" The Goth youths exchange glances with one another, then a guy steps out, "Bring her into the middle - we will make her look like one of us." Kei senses Jody is alarmed and doesn't understand, so he turns to Jody and remarks, "These kids are going to hide you." Jody gives a tight-lipped smile and nods. The Goths part to make a semi-circle and Kei brings Jody into the middle. The Goths close in around to conceal them. Jody scans their faces and appearance - heavy black lipstick, eye shadow, eye liner and mascara…all black pants, knitted tops, boots, hoodies, jackets, long coats, scarfs and hats. A trio of Goth girls begin to shed some clothes as items for cover. Jody puts on the black baggy pants, black boots, and slips on a long black knit sweater. One gal forms Jody's hair into a bun with a black ribbon, and fastens Black hoop earrings on her. Another puts on black polish on Jody's nails and black bracelets on her wrists. Two other girls apply black lipstick, mascara and eye liner. Jody stands still as they work on her. Finally, one girl put a black floppy hat on Jody's head. The Goth girls step back to admire their handiwork. Jody looks around and all the Goths are smiling at the transformation. Jody looks totally Goth! One of the Goth youth comments, "She's one of us! - GOSU!" Kei positions in front of Jody and remarks with a smile, "No one will know! You look completely different!" Jody looks at her black finger nails, and feels the hoop earrings, and glances at her black boots, pants and wrist bangles. Jody looks around at everyone, smiles and bows, "Arigato! Arigato!" Kei advises her, "You stay with the group - stay quiet, don't speak. I'll be nearby" Kei turns and walks away to mingle with a large group of young people. At this point, some Hanzai-shu thugs enter the pedestrian plaza and begin to check - thugs moving from group to group. The Goths stand in a loose circle. Two Hanzai-shu muscle in among them to check individuals. The thug with visible scratches on his face stands next to Jody. Jody stares straight ahead with a blank expression. The Thug raises his voice. "Have you seen a Gaijin girl?" All the Goths look stone-faced at the two thugs. A Goth youth responds, "As you can see - We are GOSU!" The gangsters give the Goth youth a mean stare. The thug beside Jody looks at her from head to foot (He pauses), then looks away and remarks, "Send word to us if you see the Gaijin girl! There's a reward." The two gangsters leave and hustle back to the other thugs. When they regroup, the Hanzai-shu hasten off and soon go out of sight. Kei walks back to the Goths and Jody utters her relief, "I was so scared they would find me!" Kei remarks, "I'll take you to a friend's house - it's not far - you can stay there." One of the Goth guys smiles and comments, "She can keep the clothes." As Jody and Kei leave the group, Kei turns to the Harajuku Goths, and bows, "Hontoniarigatozaimashita! All the Goths smile and the Goth leader replies, "Ochikara ni narete, Tanoshidesu!" Kei and Jody, who now looks like a Japanese Goth, briskly walk across the plaza toward a street corner and disappear.

The two travel through streets and past shops until they arrive at Kei's friend's place. It's a three story brick apartment building from the 1950's located on a Golden Gai narrow street, surrounded by small bars and noisy Pachinko parlours. Kei's friend's bachelor pad is on the top floor. They enter the building and climb the three flights of stairs. As Kei and Jody stand at the apartment door, Jody scans around at the 50's decor and colour scheme. Kei inserts a key, turns the doorknob and opens the door. He walks in a few paces, turns to Jody and beckons to enter. Jody glances left and right down the hallway, then steps inside. Kei closes the door and locks it and remarks, "This apartment belongs to my friend. He's away visiting his sick mother." Jody steps into the middle of the tiny apartment and sits down on a wooden chair. She turns her gaze to Kei and asks, "Where did you learn to speak English so well?" Kei smiles and replies, "My mother teaches English to Japanese Executives. I grew up with Japanese and English in our home." The young man walks over to the petite kitchenette and grabs a small plastic kettle. Jody comments, "How long will your friend be gone?" Kei replies, "Two weeks! That's how long his holiday time is." He runs the water, fills the kettle and plugs it in. He walks over to look out the window at the street below. Jody leans back in the chair with a sigh - she's perplexed, "Why did those guys chase me? I don't know them! - Never saw them before!" Kei gives Jody a serious look, "Those were Hanzai-shu - what Americans call Gangsters - Street Thugs!" Jody sits up alert and exclaims, "But why were they chasing me?" Kei notes Jody's bewildered expression and replies, "Because You are Gaijin and pretty! They wanted you for human trafficking!" Jody is stunned and shocked - a worried expression comes over her face and she remarks, "How am I going to finish what I'm here in Japan to do?" Kei steps near and sits in the opposite chair - with curiosity he asks, "Why are you in Japan?" Jody looks into his inquisitive eyes. She reaches into her travel pouch to bring out a small bundle and slowly unfolds the cloth to reveal the Golden Seal. Kei's eyes widen like saucers as he stares at the gold object with its engraved details and indentations. Jody comments, "I promised to honour my grandfather's dying request - to return the Golden Seal to its Ninja Clan!" She reaches out and places the Golden Seal into Kei's open hand. He closely examines the engravings and details, and runs his fingers over a Japanese Kanji. Kei looks at Jody and points, "This means Shinobi - the Japanese word for Ninja! These other words mean - Wealthy Puzzle! - it's like a riddle!" Jody becomes excited and responds, "My grandfather said the Golden Seal is a Key to a **secret Ninja Treasure**!" Kei's eye brows raise and his eyes widen, "Japanese folk stories tell of the Ninja hiding their gold and riches deep in a mountain cave, but no one knows its location! Over the years, many have tried and failed." Jody holds up the gold object and remarks, "My grandfather said this will help find the secret treasure and open the way!" Kei sits back, rubs his chin and ponders a few seconds, then declares, "I will help you keep your promise to your grandfather. What you seek to do is very important and special - Japanese call it - **BUSHIDO**! The way of the **SAMURI** - the **Way of HONOUR**!" Jody smiles and leans forward, "Thank you for your willingness to help me! My parents and I made plans - I must go to the **Iga Mountains**." Kei smiles widely and nods his head, "Many Japanese know the old legends - the Iga Mountains were the ancient home of the Ninja! - I will take you there." The kettle WHISTLES. Kei goes to the Kitchenette and collects two cups. He opens a canister and puts a scoop of tea leaves in each cup - then pours the hot water. As Jody stands up to stretch, Kei walks over and hands her a cup of tea. Jody cradles the cup, slowly sips and sits back down. She comments, "This tastes so good! Thank you!" Kei sits down in his chair and remarks, "Most tourists are in hotels. What hotel are you staying at?" Jody takes another sip and replies, "The Yosan Bajetto Hotel in the Ginza District." Kei stands to his feet and goes over to open a closet to rummage around inside - he steps back holding a medium size backpack in hand, "I packed some clothes for the trip - we can go to your hotel and get your things."

Jody stands up to check for her phone. She pats her jean pockets -

nothing - she gets alarmed! Kei sees her concern and asks, "What's wrong?" Jody checks her pockets again, then quickly sifts through her backpack, "My phone! It's missing! (Pause) I must have lost it when I fell running!" Kei brings over his phone - opens the screen, touches it a few times, then passes it to Jody, "I switched it to English so you can use it." Jody smiles her gratitude, "Thanks! I really appreciate it!" Jody takes the phone, retrieves the International Calling Card from the backpack - and dials home. A BUZZ from the overseas call lights up Karen's phone on the bedroom night stand, she picks it up. Jody's voice carries through, "Hello! Mom, Dad. - It's me!" Karen shakes Brian awake and he rubs his eyes. Karen presses Speaker Phone and responds, "Jody, honey! We were wondering when you'd call. How was the Bus Tour?" Jody replies, "It was nice - saw some really cool stuff. (Pause) Mom, dad, I lost my cell phone!" Her dad leans close and remarks, "That's okay Jody, don't worry about it! We can cancel your phone from this end - no problem!" Jody is glad at her dad's words, "That's a relief! (Pause) Mom. Dad. I met a friend - Kei. He speaks English and Japanese, and is helping me with Grandpa's request." Karen smiles and Brian comments, "Jody - be careful! Stick to our plan and stay safe, okay!" Jody responds, "I'm following the Plan, dad! (Pause) Being cautious and taking care of myself!" Her dad remarks, "Good Jody! Keep in touch - let us know what's happening. Remember - we believe in you! You can do it!" Jody feels encouraged and replies, "I know dad - Thanks! (Pause) I really love and miss you guys!" Karen leans in over the phone, "And we love and miss you too!" Jody closes off, "Bye for now - We'll talk later." Her parents call out in unison, "Bye honey! We'll wait for your call!" With her call ended, Jody hands the cell phone back to Kei and comments, "Thanks Kei! I appreciate that so very much!" Kei pockets the phone and moves to the apartment window to peek at the street below. Jody asks, "Is it safe to go? What about those gangsters?" Kei peeks out the window again and replies, "We can use the backstreets to the Hotel - get your things - then leave your stuff here!" Kei slings on his backpack and Jody puts on her knapsack, and they both exit the apartment. Kei and Jody descend the three flights of stairs, leave the building and take a nearby alleyway. Kei and Jody sneak through the backstreets to reach the Yosan Bajetto Hotel. Soon, they stand outside the door of room #1034. Jody inserts the Access Card to open the door and they both go in, close and lock the door. After quickly gathering her things, Jody with backpack and carry-on, and Kei with the luggage trolly, enter the Hotel elevator. Back on the side streets and back alleys, Kei and Jody peek around corners to see if the coast is clear. Tracing their way back through the backstreets and passageways, soon, Kei and Jody bring the items into the friend's small apartment. Jody gets certain things and re-supplies her backpack. Kei takes Jody's belongings and stores them out of sight in the closet.

CHAPTER SEVENTY-NINE
Journey To The Iga Mountains

At the Hanzai-shu Headquarters, the assembled thugs stand around with nervous expressions. Each hoodlum wears the gang's bracelet that has a small medallion featuring a snake. The Boss, the Hanzai-shu Leader, paces back and forth in anger. He abruptly pivots and points his finger at his henchmen and bellows, "You let a little girl - a Gaijin girl escape! You're not gangsters - You're school children!" One man timidly steps forward and bows low to remark, "The Gaijin girl defeated all our attacks - we were outmatched! She's a Martial Arts expert!" The Leader glances at his gang and all the thugs nod their heads in agreement. The Gang Leader forcefully stomps his foot and holds up his cell phone. He pans his arm to display - JODY'S PHOTO - and sternly orders, "Put the word out! Hunt down the Gaijin girl! Whoever finds her will get a large reward!" The group of thugs nod at each other with sneers and ghoulish grins. The Hanzai-shu Leader strides across the room to a set of Samurai swords mounted on the wall. He grabs the Katana, pulls out the blade and raises the long sword in his hand. The man turns and tilts the polished steel blade back and forth - admiring the shiny razor sharp lethal edge. A gang lieutenant steps out from the ranks and snaps a bow, "You will get the Gaijin! No one escapes you." The Boss looks at the thug, then fixates on the steel blade, and remarks, "This Gaijin needs someone special! - Someone who has never failed us! (Pause) Time for our KOROSHI-YA......our Professional Killer!" The gang members exchange glances and gloat with smug sneers.

Jody and Kei are at the Train Counter to purchase two Tickets to ride the SHINKANSEN - the famous Bullet Trains of Japan. As Kei passes over the money for the fare, the Attendant hands two Tickets to Koyoto

- then politely bows. Kei gives Jody her Ticket who securely stores it in her zippered travel pouch. They walk to the Departure Platform and wait with the other passengers. CHIMES. The sleek glossy Bullet Train approaches and quietly stops. Jody and Kei, each with backpack, enter the Compartment Car and get seated in the front right section. Soon, passengers fill all the available seats of the Train Car. CHIMES. The Shinkansen rapidly pulls away from the Platform and quickly zooms along the track. Jody looks out the window to watch Tokyo buildings, parks and suburbs zip by. She glances at Kei to ask, "How fast are we going?" Kei peers out the window as the cityscape flies by, and replies, "200 Kilometers per hour!" Jody has an alarmed expression and remarks, "Won't we fly off the tracks?" Kei grins, sits back to relax and reply, "Bullet trains do not run on rails like other trains. Shinkansen move by magnetic levitation! The train doesn't touch the ground. Very safe! Very fast!" Jody's eyes widen - she sits back in her seat and looks around the compartment. Fellow Japanese passengers sit back to relax, read magazines, watch video on cell phones, eat snacks - or just snooze. Jody seems to have just settled in when Kei announces their destination approaches. In a matter of minutes, the Bullet Train comes to a smooth stop at the Train Station Platform. Jody scans her eyes across the structure's interior and sees the sign: KOYOTO STATION. The train doors open and passengers flood out to stream along the Platform. Kei and Jody walk with the moving throng. Up ahead, a Kyoto young thug stands next to a building post on the Platform. The thug lifts his head and is stunned to see Jody walk by. He quickly brings out his cell phone to check Jody's Photo - then swiftly dials the Hanzai-shu Leader to inform, "She's here! The Gaijin girl is in Kyoto! Some hipster guy is with her." The Gang Leader orders, "Follow them! Tell me where they go. - We'll send someone!" The young man with cell phone to ear, gives a slight bow and replies, "Hai!"

Jody and Kei arrive at the Kyoto Bus Terminal amid the groups and individuals seeking travel to various points. The Buses are parked in marked-off coloured destination zones. Kei and Jody purchase Bus Fare and watch the passengers disembark as new passengers stand ready to board the vehicle. The Bus Drivers sit in command behind the steering wheels. Jody and Kei climb onto the Bus, show their Tickets, and find seats in the vehicle's middle - Jody gets the window seat and Kei gets the aisle. Off to the side, away from the passenger loading area, the young thug watches them as he lurks behind an

Advertisement board. The Kyoto gangster looks at the display above the Bus's large front window - the LED lights read - IGA MOUNTAINS. The Bus Terminal is busy and noisy. The young thug brings out his cell phone to dial and brings it close to his ear. At the Hanzai-shu Headquarters, the gangsters relax and chill out - some play cards, a few flip through magazines, and others stand to smoke cigarettes and talk. The Hanzai-shu Leader sits comfortably in a overstuffed leather Club Chair. His cell phone lays on a nearby table. It BUZZES - he answers and hears the Kyoto thug's voice, "The Gaijin and her hipster friend are on a Kyoto Bus to the Iga Mountains!" The Gang Leader sneers and remarks, "Good! Wait there until our Associate arrives on the Shinkansen. Show him the Bus Route they took!" The Kyoto thug replies, "Hai! I will be here." The Gang Leader ends the call and stands to his feet. All the gangsters rivet their attention to their leader. He points to a nearby lieutenant and gives an order, "Call the KOROSHI-YA! (Professional Killer) Tell him to go to the Kyoto Bus Terminal. He is to bring the Gaijin to us - if she refuses - then kill her!" The lieutenant snaps a bow, "Hai!"

Somewhere in Chino City......a modern upscale white stucco and black timber bungalow sits surrounded by traditional Japanese landscaping - sculpted shrubs, trimmed trees, pruned flower bushes with arrayed rocks and stones in raked gravel beds. The home is a western style bungalow blended with traditional Japanese gardens - this is the home of the professional killer! The Koroshi-ya is a fit middle-aged man of above average height with grey streaks in his black slicked-back hair, his face is hard and chiselled - befitting his deadly trade. He stands in the living room and walks to a back room where Katana swords of various colours hang on the wall. The man opens the back room's sliding door and steps out onto the polished wood deck that overlooks a picturesque oriental garden. His eyes glance at the beautiful flowers, manicured grass, red Japanese Maples, and water pond filled with Koi fish.

CELL PHONE BUZZ

The Koroshi-ya pulls out his phone to listen to the Hanzai-shu lieutenant at the other end, "There is a Gaijin girl you must bring to us! Go to the Kyoto Bus Terminal - our man will meet you at the Train Station." The killer's cell phone vibrates and he looks the screen -

JODY's PHOTO. The Contract Killer studies Jody's picture and facial features, then responds, "A Gaijin? I've always hunted rival gangsters - but never a Gaijin girl!" The Hanzai-shu lieutenant remarks, "This girl needs your special skills - She's a Martial Artist! If she will not cooperate - Kill her!" The Man's eye brows raise and his eyes widen, he demands, "Tell your Boss - I want triple my regular fee! You will have her soon!" The Koroshi-ya ends the call and goes into the back room, strides over to a glossy white Katana sword to snatch it off the wall. The Killer pulls out the sword blade to masterfully twirl and repeatedly slice the air. His eyes zero in on the highly polished steel and the razor sharp blade. The Assassin turns his gaze to the wall with three rows of white knotted Japanese funeral cloths, each knotted cloth hangs on a wooden peg. The Koroshi-ya has a flashback to when he killed someone - he would hang a white knotted funeral cloth as a Kill Trophy. The man stares at the last peg - it sits empty.

CHAPTER EIGHTY

Searching The Ancient Past

The Bus leaves Kyoto City behind and enters the countryside. Jody and Kei look out the bus window at the passing terrain. - small villages, rural dwellings, farms, crops, fields and trees. The vehicle travels winding roads as it ascends to higher elevation. Jody gets her backpack, reaches inside to bring out some folded papers. She turns to Kei and comments, "My Grandpa Carl studied Japan for many years. I have his research notes about Ninjas in the Iga Mountains. You can look at them." Jody hands the notes to her friend, and Kei sees the papers are a rich mix of research details, hand drawn illustrations, Japanese Kanji and personal notes. He slowly peruses the findings and notices a sketch of a cave sealed with a massive metal door and lock with the Japanese Kanji TAKARA (Treasure) written beside it. Kei comments, "I've never seen this information before. It's wonderful!" Jody leans to peer closer, "My parents and I tried to figure things out - but couldn't! What do these Japanese characters mean?" She points to a trio of Japanese Kanji. Kei's expression is intense as his eyes closely examine the script - then his eyes brighten as he breaks into a big smile, and remarks, "The first word is NAZO which means puzzle or riddle. The second character is GESENAI - meaning inscrutable or incomprehensible. (Pause) The last word is MAMOTTA which translates - protected." Jody is awe-struck and takes a few seconds for Kei's explanation to sink in, then she talks excitedly, "Puzzle. Incomprehensible. Protected. The Ninja treasure is in a secret cave that no one can find. That makes it incomprehensible. It's protected by a great metal door and lock - and my Grandpa always said - the key to the puzzle is the Golden Seal!" Kei leans back with a big smile in amazement. Then he looks at Jody with a serious expression, "You cannot tell anyone else about the Golden Seal! Your life would be in great danger - many would try to kill you to get hold of it!" Jody stares at Kei with a frozen look and remarks, "Would you try to take the Golden Seal?" Kei takes offence at the question, sits forward and sternly replies, "If I wanted to - I could have easily turned you over to the Hanzai-shu." He locks eyes with Jody and continues, "The gangsters saw me with you. My life is in danger too! (Pause) After you return the Seal and go back to America - I'm still here in Japan - still in danger from the gangsters." Jody's defensive expression changes to meekness and she sincerely apologizes to her friend, "Kei. I'm sorry for thinking that way about you! You've been more than good and helpful to me from the start. (Pause) Please accept my apology? - GOMEN'NASHI!" Jody bows low and hold that position. Kei looks tenderly at his companion and extends his arm to gently raise Jody's face and he smiles, "I accept your apology! Please know we are together in this quest you promised your grandfather. We are what Japanese call - NAKAMA - partners. Buddies!" Jody is greatly relieved at Kei's words and gives him a big hug. They both sit back in their seats with a renewed sense of friendship and shared purpose.

At the Kyoto City Train Station, the Shinkansen whooshes to a stop, the passenger doors open and out steps the Koroshi-ya dressed in a medium grey suit, carrying a long slender case. He stands on the platform and scans about - he's an imposing figure. The young thug hastens up to the man, stops within a few feet and bows waist-level. The older man eyes the younger and orders, "Show me to the Bus Terminal and the Route the Gaijin took!" The young man promptly replies, "Hai! It is not far - you will be there soon." The Koroshi-ya strides forward with confidence. The young thug follows subservient behind the man. In short time, they enter the interior of the Bus Terminal and the Kyoto thug bows and points his hand toward the boarding zone for MEI PREFECTURE - IGA MOUNTAINS. The Assassin looks at the parked bus ready for upcoming departure. He extends Japanese currency in his hand - the young thug bows and receives the money with both hands outstretched. The Koroshi-ya barks, "Buy me a round trip Ticket!" The young gangster bows again and quickly replies, "Hai!", then races off toward the inside Ticket Counter.

As the Bus climbs higher and higher in evaluation, Jody and Kei see a quaint village sprinkled amid the hilly mountain terrain. The traditional Japanese wood houses resemble a bygone era. Village residents quietly go about their daily chores and activities. The Bus stops on a flat stretch of the tarmac, and Kei and Jody disembark to stand on the dirt roadside. The Driver shuts the door and the Bus zooms off and the duo look around at the scattered wooden dwellings. Jody scans to her right and notices an elderly lady sitting on her porch in the shade. Jody taps Kei's shoulder and comments, "Let's try her?" Kei and Jody walk up to the house and respectfully bow before her. Kei politely asks, "Grandmother, do members of the old Shinobi Ninja Clan still live here?" A smile comes across the old lady's wrinkled friendly face and she replies, "I do not know any Shinobi. But you are welcome to ask the other villagers." Jody and Kei glance around at the small homes that dot the rolling hillside. Kei turns to the elderly woman and bows, "Arigatou gozaimasu!" The old lady smiles and nods. The two friends turn and begin to walk up a winding gravel path to a set of homes on a terraced level. Jody looks around the mountain setting, marvels and remarks, "Imagine! This is the very ground where the ancient Ninja lived! Wow!" Kei stops walking to observe the vista and nods, then he waves his arm for them to move on. They reach the first house. Jody looks expectantly at Kei, and he gives an encouraging grin - steps to the front door and lifts his hand - KNOCK! KNOCK! Inside the wooden home there's the shuffling of feet, then an elderly man opens the door and squints at the two young people standing before him. Kei steps forward, bows and respectfully asks, "Grandfather, are there any Shinobi living here?" The old man grins with a twinkle in his eye and replies, "Shinobi is a very old name! No one here has that name." Kei glances over to Jody with a disappointed look. Kei asks further, "Grandfather, can you think of anyone that might answer our question?" The old man rubs his fingers on his chin, shakes his head and responds, "I know of no one. (Pause) But you can still ask the others." Kei bows to the elderly man with expressed gratitude, "Arigatou gozaimasu!" The old man nods, smiles and closes the door. Jody moves beside Kei to enquire, "What did you find out? Any Clan members here?" Kei looks at his friend and replies with a sad expression, "These old people can't help us - they don't know anything!" Jody ponders a second, then remains undeterred, "Let's keep asking - we're right here in their ancient home!" Kei sighs - he points to a row of dwellings on the opposite hillside, and comments, "We can try there!" The two walk down the grade, across the road pavement, and up the winding gravel path that leads to the other buildings. The pebble trail leads them between large boulders on each side. Kei and Jody tread the stone pathway through the big rocks to the terrace area above. They walk to the first house of the tiny row. Kei steps onto the small veranda and KNOCKS! A few seconds later, a middle-aged man stands in the door's threshold and eyes them both. Kei bows and asks, "Uncle, do you know anyone here related to the Shinobi Clan?" The man thinks for a moment, steps forward to point toward the end of the homes and comments, "The last house! A lady from the city moved here three years ago - the house belonged to an old woman - the family name was Shinobi!" Kei bows to reply, "Arigatou gozaimasu!" Kei lifts upright, smiles at Jody, grabs her elbow and urges her to go along the row of homes. Jody is surprised and curious, "What did he say?" Kei replies with delight, "A Shinobi survivor lives in the last house!" Jody exclaims with excitement, "At last! A Ninja Clan member!" The man in the first house watches as they hasten toward the last house, he shakes his head, steps back inside and shuts the door. As Jody and Kei get closer, Kei remarks, "A woman is in the last house, someone with the name Shinobi." Jody looks at her friend and comments, "Let me knock. It might be better if the woman sees it's a young lady!" Kei nods agreement and steps to the side. Jody steps onto the small porch, stands in front of the door, lifts har hand - and KNOCKS! The muffled clatter of Japanese wooden slippers gets louder - then stops. A middle-aged woman dressed in a Kimono with pinned up hair, opens the door and looks at Jody with a surprised expression. She glances over at Kei and he bows and remarks, "This Gaijin girl is looking for any survivors of an old Ninja Clan. - Is your family name Shinobi?" The lady politely smiles then shakes her head, "My family name is Suzuki! I came here to help my grandmother but she died last year." Kei turns to Jody with a dejected look, then bows to the woman in the doorway, "Aunt. Arigatou gozaimasu!" Jody and Kei turn and start to walk away when the woman interjects, "My family name is Suzuki, but my elderly uncle is a Shinobi!" A big grin breaks out on Kei's face and he looks at Jody, "She has an uncle that's a Shinobi!" Jody quickly spins about to gaze at the lady in the kimono and remarks, "Ask about her uncle's house?" Kei moves his eyes to the lady and asks, "What house is your uncle's?" The woman's face becomes sad as she replies, "My uncle no longer stays here in the mountains. He lives in the SAGA REGION near the sea. He makes pottery!" Kei asks further, "What pottery town does your uncle work in?" The lady ponders a couple seconds, then responds, I cannot tell you because I do not know. (Pause) But I can give you a sample of his ceramic artwork. Each potter has their own style - you can look for his work." The woman suddenly disappears from view - Jody and Kei can hear the sounds of rummaging. The lady quickly returns to the doorway holding a small ceramic bowl that features surging blue waves and swirling white clouds. She passes the bowl to Kei. Jody and Kei examine the fine quality and beautiful pattern. Kei lifts his eyes to the woman and bows - Jody follows suit. Kei speaks their gratitude in Japanese, "Aunt. Thank you very much for your help!" The lady smiles, turns to go inside, and closes the door. Kei steps beside Jody with a big smile, Jody asks, "What did she say? What is it?" Kei replies with delight, "She said her uncle carries the name Shinobi. He lives in the Saga Region near the coast (shows bowl) and makes this kind of pottery." Jody inspects the bowl again with excitement, "Fantastic! All we have to do is go look for him." Kei looks into her eyes, "It might be difficult. The area has four towns famous for pottery. We might have to visit each town!" Jody clutches Kei's arm in her exuberance, "We're so close! Let's go and finish what we started!" Kei nods and safely stores the small bowl in his backpack. They begin to walk back down the pebble walkway that leads between the big boulders on either side.

CHAPTER EIGHTY-ONE
Menace In The Mountains

As the Jody and Kei retrace their steps and go between the large boulders - Suddenly, the Koroshi-ya steps out from seclusion and holds a drawn Katana sword. The man waves the shiny steel blade across their path, beckons with his free hand as he utters broken-English, "Gaijin! Young girl - go Tokyo! Now!" Kei automatically freezes with his mouth open. Jody stares at her foe and slips off her backpack - it falls on the stones with a THUD! Jody quickly warns her friend, "Kei. Quick! Turn around and run!" Kei looks at Jody, nods and bolts out of there as fast as his leg can carry him. Now, just the two of them are on the stone pathway in the middle of the boulders. Jody and the Koroshi-ya lock eyes - both stand ready!

The professional killer lowers the sword blade and holds it at his side pointed to the ground. The man extends his open hand as an invitation. Jody shakes her head and begins to back up to create space between her foe. She watches poised and alert, her arms positioned for battle. Jody stays focused on the man as she backs up against the rock wall. The Assassin's eye brows furrow and his face contorts in anger. He bellows loud in Japanese, "Insolent Gaijin girl! I will take you to Tokyo - alive or dead!" The Koroshi-ya lunges and swings the Katana blade at her. Jody leaps up and uses her leg to spring off the rock to summersault and land behind the surprised man. He swiftly pivots around and Jody kicks hard at the loose gravel on the ground. Pebbles and dirt forcefully spray the man's face. He instinctively raises his arm and closes his eyes. In the distraction, Jody bolts toward some tall slender trees at the end of the boulders. The man wipes debris from his face and gives chase. Jody grabs a sapling and uses her arms and knee to snap the young tree into a crude wooden staff. As the man rushes up, Jody spins and twirls the staff about her torso and locks into a Martial Arts defensive stance. The Koroshi-ya edges closer with caution. He sways the sword blade from side to side. Jody's eyes follow the sword's movement. She quickly scans around and yells, "My friend, I hope you listened and took off!" There's an echo in Kei's voice as he replies, "Still here! I cannot leave you alone." The killer lifts his head to look around at where the voice came from. He refocuses his energy at Jody and prowls back and forth in a semi-circle. The Assassin tilts his head upward and roars, "Tokyo hipster! After I kill your Gaijin friend - I'm going to slice you up in tiny pieces!" The man shifts his eyes onto Jody. He swiftly lifts the sword with both hands and slashes. Jody swings the staff against the sword blade. The man repeatedly slashes - Jody uses the pole to block and deflect the attacks. In seething anger, the Assassin swipes the sword at the young girl's face and head. Jody ducks and swings the pole to knock the blade sideways. She spins the staff and strikes the arm that holds the blade - the sword drops! The Koroshi-ya grabs his elbow which is in great pain. Jody swiftly plunges the staff into his stomach, then snaps the pole upward to hit his chin sending his head backwards. The man falls to the ground with a bloody mouth. Momentarily stunned, he lays on the ground - his grey suit dirty, ripped and torn. The man shakes his head alert and shifts to rise on one knee. Jody holds the staff in an overhead strike position. She looks at him and shifts her eyes to the ground, her foot is on top the Katana sword on the ground. The man raises his arm and waves his hand side to side to feign surrender! Jody watches him like a hawk. As the man slowly gets to his feet, he reaches behind his back to bring out a big knife. He lunges at Jody and the blade just grazes her right outer thigh. Jody powerfully slams the staff across the man's head that drives his skull hard into the rock surface. The tremendous blow stuns and drops him. He GROANS! Jody picks up the white Katana and points the blade at Koroshi-ya and shakes her head - No! She watches as the man props himself up against the rock. Jody remarks in an angry voice, "Stop! No more! - Leave me alone!" Jody holds the sword in one hand as she leans the staff against the rock surface, with her free hand she picks up her backpack, then she grabs the staff again. She carefully backs up as she keeps her eyes on the downed assailant. The man is wounded, worn down and winded. He watches as Jody holds the weapons and backs further and further away until she clears the stone pathway between the boulders.

Jody scans about the hillside and surroundings as she moves down toward the roadway. At the pavement, she moves her gaze around and spots Kei who is peeking around the corner of a house. Kei's eyes light up and he races out from his hiding place. He rushes up to Jody, looks at the katana and exclaims with excitement, "You beat him! You won!" Jody keeps the sword at a downward angle, and partially leans on the staff, and replies, "I remembered my Grandfather's teaching! How your weapons can be in nature - like gravel and trees." Kei glances at the killer's white Katana and grimaces, "I'm Japanese, but I don't like swords - so sharp and dangerous! (Grins) I prefer video games - much safer." Jody lifts the white Katana in the air - the blade gleams in the sunlight. She remarks, "My Grandfather said - swords are neither good or bad - it depends on the person holding the blade!" In the distance, there's the sound of a BUS ENGINE. Kei looks down the tarmac and comments, "Another bus approaches. We can wave down the driver and show our Return Tickets." Jody gives the staff a quick look and tosses it aside - then she eyes the exposed Katana blade, and remarks, "Will the driver let us on the bus with this?" Kei smiles and takes off his jacket to wrap and cover the blade. He replies, "It will be okay with the driver. This is Japan - everyone respects and values our history - especially Japanese swords!" They watch as the Kyoto Bus looms larger on approach. Kei steps onto the pavement and waves the driver to stop. The bus slows to a stop, the side door opens and the driver peers down at them. Kei and Jody ascend the steps and present their Return Tickets. Kei shows the wrapped Katana and the driver nods. Kei and Jody moves through the aisle to grab two seats near the back. The driver shuts the side door, presses the gas pedal and the vehicle motors forward. The bus continues its journey over the serpentine roadway of the Iga Mountains. Kei and Jody watch the rolling mountainside, vegetation and wooden homes.

Up the hill, off to the side, stands the Koroshi-ya in his torn dirty grey suit. He watches the bus motor further and further down the road. He brings his hand up to his face, and he glides his fingers over the large red welt on his forehead. The man turns about and makes determined strides up the pebble pathway toward the row of tiny wooden homes. Soon, the Assassin stands outside a wooden house and lifts his bruised scraped hand - KNOCK! KNOCK! KNOCK! There's the sound of approaching footsteps and the door latch CLICKS. The woman in the Kimono holds the door open with one arm as she stands in the doorway. She scrutinizes the stranger standing before her. The

Koroshi-ya steps forward with an intense stare, and declares, "Two young people visited you - what did you tell them?" The lady looks at the man's dirty ripped clothes, and the red welt on his forehead. She becomes anxious and replies, "They were just tourists - I told them nothing." The man rebuffs her with a stern voice, "I don't believe you! I know you said something - what was it?" The woman gets nervous and starts to shut the door. The Koroshi-ya swiftly barges in to push the door wide open - he looms in the doorway. The woman backs up into the home interior and remarks in a trembling voice, "I live in this tiny village - I know nothing!" The man steps through the doorway into the room and scowls. He yells at the terrified woman, "You say you know nothing - but I have ways to make you talk!" The Assassin gives the lady a menacing look, the lady SHRIEKS as he pulls out his large knife and slowly shuts the door.

Miles away, on the Bus ride back to Kyoto City, Jody turns her gaze to Kei and politely asks, "I'd like to use your phone again to call home. Is that okay?" Kei smiles and brings out his cell phone and hands it over. Jody smiles and pulls out the International Calling Card and dials home. Across the Pacific Ocean, Karen's cell phone BUZZES on the night stand next to the bed - still asleep she fumbles around to grab the phone. Karen blinks her sleepy eyes open and answers. Jody's voice fills her ear, "Mom. Dad. - It's me!" Karen's eyes open wide at hearing her daughter's voice and she stretches out her arm to shake and rouse Brian - he stirs awake. Karen replies, "Jody honey! How lovely to hear your voice. How are you sweetie?" Jody glances over at Kei and responds, "I'm okay! Wanted to call to tell you guys I got great news!" By now, Karen has put Jody on Speaker Phone so Brian and her can listen and speak. Brian echoes Karen's interest and asks, "What's the news Jody?" As the bus winds its way down the curves and straight stretches of the highway, Jody looks at Kei and replies, "Someone in the Iga Mountains gave us valuable information. Right now, we're following a lead to find a Shinobi survivor!" Brian and Karen share big smiles and Karen remarks to her daughter, "Jody, that's wonderful! We're so proud of you! (Pause) And your Grandpa would be so proud of you also!" A tear forms in Jody's eye as she hears her mom's reply. With emotion in her voice, Jody tenderly conveys, "I miss you guys very much! (Pause) And I miss Grandpa too!" Kei notices Jody's teary eyes and puts his arm on her shoulder as comfort. Jody looks at Kei and comments to her parents, "We're going to travel to the Saga area in

Southern Japan. The Ninja Clan survivor is in that region." In their bedroom, on Plains Road in the Indian Reservation of Venture, Brian and Karen send their love and support to Jody over the phone, her mom admonishes, "Please be careful Jody! Be wise and stay safe!" and Brian enquires, "Any problems? You're okay right?" Jody lowers her eyes to the white Katana wrapped in Kei leather jacket, and tactfully replies, "I'm okay, dad! Everything is under control." Her parents' faces show relief at Jody's words and breath easy. Jody eyes Kei and remarks, "Better go now. - I'll call again later. Love you guys! Bye." Karen and Brian lean over the cell phone and reply as loving parents, "We're looking forward to your next call. We love you too, Jody! Bye." Jody touches the phone screen to end the call, and hands the phone back to Kei. She gives a big smile and comments, "Arigato! I really appreciated using your phone so I could call home!" Kei leans back in his seat and replies, "It's good to call your parents - especially when you're thousands of miles away. (Pause) The Japanese believe it's very important to honour your parents!" Jody smiles and comments, "My Grandpa told me the Bible teaches the same thing!"

CHAPTER EIGHTY-TWO
Trouble Back Home

Brian and Karen are in the pickup truck stopped at the RED traffic light, waiting to turn onto the Regional Highway. Vehicles zoom by in both directions. The light goes GREEN. Brian signals right and pulls out - SUDDENLY - a big tractor trailer fails to stop at the RED light and SLAMS into the pickup truck on the driver's side. The tractor trailer brakes and the transport wheels lock up and smoke comes off the tires as the trailer jack-knifes. The collision and impact hurls the pickup through the air - the truck smashing, bouncing and rolling across the pavement. Cars, trucks and vans come to a SCREECHING HALT! People quickly exit vehicles and run to assist the crash victims. A tall man in a cowboy hat, a middle-aged lady, and an old couple gather at the mangled red pickup. White engine smoke seeps from the truck's crushed crumpled hood. The 'Good Samaritan' strangers peer in to the truck's passenger cabin - Karen and Brian are severely banged up. The injuries look bad. The two occupants look like contorted rag dolls. A young mother standing with her small child dials 9-1-1.

The Trauma Team at the Hospital's Emergency Department give Brian and Karen Priority 1 medical care. The Doctors and Nurses hover over the devastated couple, each one in their own Hospital gurney. Nurses and ER Technicians attach leads and medical cables. The Doctors examine head and limbs, give injections and check monitor readings. One veteran ER Doctor inspects Brian and quickly announces, "This man has two broken legs, four fractured ribs, and swelling of the brain - We need to induce a Coma!" The other Doctors scan the monitor readings and nod agreement. One Physician goes beside Karen to examine her and remarks, "This woman has a broken leg, a fractured collar bone and a punctured lung! - We'll move her to the O.R." The

Nurses and Orderlies rush to prep Brian and Karen according to the instructions. The team of Doctors set up the procedure to induce Brian into a Coma. Brian's body lays motionless in the Emergency Room. Meanwhile, a Nurse and an Orderly push Karen out of the Emergency Room through a set of double sliding glass doors toward the Operating Room.

Once inside the O.R., the Nurse, Orderly and O.R. Technician transfer Karen's body onto the stainless steel Operating Table that's been prepped and covered with green O.R. sheets. As Karen lays still and serene, O.R. Staff have covered her body with the green medical fabric, only exposing bare skin for the area to be operated on. Nearby, a Surgeon stands ready with O.R. gloves pulled up to his elbows, wearing a surgical cap and mask, an O.R. body suit and protective shoe covering. Medical Technicians attach monitor leads and O.R. Nurses set up the needles for the I.V. and the Anaesthetic. The Surgeon steps up beside the Operating Table and reaches his hand to grab a concave overhead lamp and lowers it for better lighting. He looks at the stainless steel trolly arrayed with surgical scalpels, clamps and plyers, that's been positioned beside him. Two O.R. Nurses dressed in protective medical attire, one beside the Surgeon and the other directly across the O.R. table, stand ready to assist in the Operation. The Surgeon selects a razor sharp scalpel, and extends his arm to hold the tip of the scalpel a couple inches above Karen's exposed skin. The Surgeon looks at Karen out under the Anaesthetic, then he closely focuses on where he will make the incision and calmly remarks, "Okay everybody! Let's help this woman get better!"

CHAPTER EIGHTY-THREE

Searching The Pottery Towns

It's mid-morning, as Jody and Kei ride the Regional Bus, as it enters the Saga Region that's located in the South West area of Japan. The Bus travels toward the pottery town of **ARITA**. Heading to the town's centre, the Bus passes over one of Arita's bridges decorated with ceramic designs. As the vehicle reaches the middle of town, Jody and Kei look out the window to notice the various SIGNS and BANNERS that advertise the different Pottery Shops located in the community. When the Bus stops, Jody and Kei exit their vehicle to stand beside the roadway. Jody holds up the Shinobi's uncle's ceramic bowl and remarks, "The Map says the Saga Region begins here. Let's start our search, then move to the other towns." Kei nods and comments, "We'll look for this bowl pattern and ask the Potters if they know the artist!" The duo begin to walk toward the Pottery Shops that pepper the street ahead. At the first Shop, Kei and Jody show the small bowl to the lady Potter and she shakes her head - No! In another Shop, Kei bows and talks with an elderly man who waves his hand indicating he doesn't know. Further up the road, a middle-aged Potter holds and examines the bowl, only to shake his head - No! Throughout the morning and into the afternoon, Kei and Jody visit Pottery Shops on various streets, searching for clues and answers. At one location, Kei shows the bowl to a husband and wife Pottery team - they both don't know anything!

On the Bus again, Jody and Kei travel to **IMARI**, a Pottery Town known for its artists producing a distinctive blue ceramic vase. Reaching the town's Pottery section, Jody and Kei look through Shop shelves displaying local ceramic wares. Kei talks with an old man, someone that exhibits years of craft experience - alas, the man shakes his head No! In one Shop, Jody finds a small bowl but it doesn't match the Shinobi Potter's unique style. Once again, as they experienced in ARITA, Jody and Kei go in and out of various Shops but find nothing! Calling it quits for the time being, Jody and Kei walk to a street bench and sit down. The two friends are exhausted and - somewhat dejected! Jody exchanges eye contact with Kei and remarks, "We have to keep looking!" Kei stretches out his legs and replies, "None of these towns have an artist with this style!" Jody turns to face her buddy and comments, "Someone has to recognize the bowl, somewhere! (Pause) What's left?" Kei leans back, takes a breath and replies, "YOBUKO. It's a fishing town - but many artists have shops there." Jody stands to her feet, adjusts her backpack and motions with her arm, "Come on! We have to keep going!" Kei gets to his feet and they walk over to the Regional Bus Zone.

On the Bus yet again, Jody and Kei sit in the front section of the seats and watch the lovely landscape as the vehicle motors along the Highway. After a while, the Bus brings its passengers into the quaint picturesque fishing town of YOBUKO. The Driver steers the Bus through the hamlet's tiny streets until it stops at the Passenger Zone near the fishing wharfs. The Yobuko Harbour is filled with various fishing boats. As Jody and Kei exit the vehicle and move off to the side, SEAGULL CRIES, catch their attention. The two look to see a flock of seagulls flutter above a fishing boat at the Dock as men manoeuvre a net full of fish to offload their catch. Jody and Kei scan the surroundings, and Kei points to a side street with various Banners that belong to Pottery Shops, he exclaims. "Look! A row of Pottery Shops!" Jody replies. "This is the last place - I sure hope he's here!" The duo walk up the pavers toward the first Banner and enter the shop. They are greeted with smiles and bows from a middle-aged husband and wife. The man remarks, "Welcome to our shop! Please look around at our work." The wife adds in, "Our pottery depicts the beautiful ocean." Jody touches Kei's arm and she brings out the small ceramic bowl. Jody comments, "Maybe they will recognize who makes this bowl?" Kei takes the bowl from Jody and presents it to the couple, and enquires, "We seek the artist who makes bowls like this one!" The man clasps the bowl and shows it to his wife. The couple study the bowl - turning it over in their hands to closely inspect the ceramic style. Then the man hands the bowl back to Kei, and remarks, "I've only seen this style once - an old artist used this pattern (Pause) But we've not seen him in a long time." The wife looks at Kei and shakes her head. Kei looks at Jody - who hangs in expectation. He gives her the bowl and comments, "They say an old man used this style - but it was a long time ago!" Jody lowers her gaze to the floor, ponders a second, then suggests, "Ask if they know where he might be?" Kei nods and turns to the couple, "Do you know where he is? - where is his shop?" The man puts his fingertips on his chin and thinks a bit, then his eyes light up and he responds, "There is an artist Co-operative at the town's big wharf. Many artists use it as they tour to sell their ceramic wares. Perhaps he's there!" The man bows after his remark and Kei bows in return, "Uncle. Thank you very much for your help!" Kei turns to Jody and motions her to leave. She eyes Kei and asks, "What did you find out? Is he here?"

As they step out of the shop onto the pavers, Kei looks over at the big wooden wharf at the end of the street. He points and comments, "The Shinobi artist may be at the Co-operative near the wharf. Potters come and go - travelling about selling their work." Jody gives a SIGH and puffs a strand of hair off her face, "Let's go check - I hope he's there. I'm getting tired of all this searching around!" Jody and Kei walk down the street toward the big wharf with its groups of men working their nets and fishing boats.

CHAPTER EIGHTY-FOUR
The Hidden Message

The Artist Cooperative occupies a large open-air timber shed that has a metal roof to protect from the rains, yet, lets the sea breeze freely flow throughout the vast structure. Underneath the galvanized roof, numerous artists have stalls that display their ceramic work for sale. The entire layout and design resembles a large open-air market, however, instead of vegetables, these artists and vendors sell pottery.

Kei and Jody enter the long wide structure and start to meander through the rows of stalls, checking the various pottery styles. They tread down one row and up another - they have no results! The two stop beside a thick timber post, and Kei comments, "I don't see anything! (Shakes head) All this pottery - and nothing!" Jody slings off her backpack to take out the small bowl. She brings it up eye-level to focus and study it - she looks intently at the blue waves and the swirling white clouds. Still holding the bowl eye-level, she gazes to the right and suddenly notices the very same bowl on a nearby shelf. Jody points and exclaims excitedly, "They're here! The bowls - are here!" Kei spins around and they both stare at the stall across from them. The stall shelves display the very same bowls in different sizes. An elderly man sits relaxed on a wooden stool. Jody and Kei step into the stall and bow before the old man. Kei presents the small bowl to the man, and his eyes light up! Kei politely enquires, "Grandfather, is this bowl your pottery style? Are you the elderly uncle of the village woman in the Iga Mountains?" The old man looks into Kei's eyes, smiles and nods. The aged artist clasps the bowl and gives a quick inspection, then returns it to Kei, and remarks, "The bowl is mine and bears my artist style! - It has my tiny Kanji! (Pause) Examine the clouds." Kei cradles the bowl and slowly turns it over and over as he examines the clouds - then, Kei smiles as his eyes spot the small hidden Kanji for the Japanese word - Mountains! He passes the bowl over to Jody and remarks, "Look carefully at the cloud pattern.(Points) You'll see a hidden Kanji for mountains!" Jody scrutinizes the bowl's design - turning it over in her hand, her eyes tracing the swirling cloud pattern - until - Jody's eyes get wide, "I see it! - a faint Kanji hidden in the clouds!" Kei and Jody look at the old man and he smiles and nods. Kei bends down eye-level and asks the elderly artist, "Grandfather - do you belong to the Shinobi Ninja Clan?" The old man is suddenly surprised. He glances around and uses his index finger for Kei to come closer. The old man leans forward and quietly remarks, "I am Shinobi but not a Ninja! - I took the Pottery path. (Pause) My older brother is Shinobi Ninja!" Kei responds with excitement, "Where can we find your brother? Is he here in the Saga Region?" The aged artist diverts his eyes to Jody - then back to Kei, and replies, "My brother is in the Tokyo area. I have not seen him for many years. You can look for him there (Pause) Ask for the Beautiful Artist!" Kei taps Jody and motions to stand up. Kei looks at the old man and bows low, Jody does the same. Kei remarks, "Grandfather, Thank you for answering our questions and helping with our search!? The old man's eyes twinkle and he nods with a smile. Jody and Kei turn to leave the stall.

SUDDENLY - the Koroshi-ya springs out from behind the wall holding a red Katana sword. The killer, dressed in a black suit - lifts the blade, points at Jody and demands in broken-English, "American girl - You go Tokyo!" The Koroshi-ya extends his other arm to beckon with an open hand. Kei and the old man instinctively back away toward the rear of the stall. Kei glances and notices there's a service door nearby. Jody scans the stall shelves packed with various bowls of the old man's style. She returns her focus to the professional killer, shakes her head and cries out, "No! NO! - Leave me alone!" The Assassin becomes red-faced in anger and he yells, "American girl - you die! YOU DIE!" The killer lunges forth and swings the sword at Jody. She swiftly tilts to avoid the blade - then quickly steps backward. Jody sees a wooden bucket on the floor close by - she grabs the handle and brings the bucket in front of her. The killer chops the blade downward from a high angle and Jody swings the bucket to block and deflect the sword. The man counters with a slice at her torso - Jody twirls the bucket to block the strike. She backs up again - now, she's halfway into the confines of the stall. Kei and the old man cower in fear. The Assassin creeps closer with the sharp sword blade pointed level at Jody. He thrusts the blade at Jody's midsection, and Jody pivots to deliver a powerful roundhouse that blasts the man into the wall of pottery shelves. BANG! CRASH! The stall shelves fall apart. The ceramic bowls fall to hit the floor and break into jagged pottery pieces. The Koroshi-ya regains his footing and swings wildly and Jody ducks each sword slice. The man spins the blade and it slices Jody's right shoulder. She grabs the wound - blood seeps down her arm. Jody locks eyes with her attacker. He YELLS and swings the Katana blade with all his might - WHOOSH! Jody tilts her head back and the sword narrowly misses her face - and embeds deeply into the thick timber post beside her. The man struggles to pry the sword free - it's stuck! Jody kicks the man in the groin and he buckles in pain. He reaches out his arm and grabs Jody. She quickly scoops up a large jagged piece of pottery and swipes hard across the man's face and leaves a deep gash. The killer grabs his face and SCREAMS in agony. Jody turns about and leaps high in the air and comes down on the embedded blade with all her weight - the force snaps the blade in half. Kei calls out to Jody - he has the Service Door open and waves to her, "Jody! Hurry! Escape!" Jody dashes for the open door and once she's through, Kei SLAMS the door shut and locks it! In the stall, the killer is bent over clutching his face. He stands upright and notices the Katana handle amid the broken pottery of the ground. He kicks the floor spraying shattered pieces of pottery across the stall. The Koroshi-ya stares at the broken blade embedded in the post - filled with rage and venom - the Koroshi-ya YELLS OUT, "Kisho Kiri Karasu Gaijin!" The Assassin makes a VOW - to kill off the Gaijin!

CHAPTER EIGHTY-FIVE
Mending A Wounded Warrior

Kei and the old potter stand by and watch as an aged fisherman applies the healing arts of Acupuncture and Cupping to Jody. She lays unconscious as numerous Acupuncture needles stick into her skin and cover her body. The old fisherman places and removes glass cups on Jody's back and shoulder. Not far away, a clay pot, a bundle of assorted herbs, and a cup of dark liquid, sit on the worn wooden table nearby. Kei looks at his friend and remarks, "When will she be better?" As he continues to help Jody, the aged fisherman replies, "In three days - the wound will heal and she will be strong enough to travel." Kei and the old potter exchange glances. Kei asks the aged potter, "How will we find your brother?" The old man responds, "I know only what's been told. People in the Tokyo Arts Community know of him as the Beautiful Artist!" Kei studies the old man for a second and comments, "Tokyo is a vast city! What Art Community is he with?" The elderly artist shakes his head with a sad expression and replies, "Young brother, I have no idea! (Pause) You may need to check them all - Fashion Designers, Musicians, Actors, Calligraphers, Tattoo Artists, Painters, - even Sculptors!" Kei looks at Jody laying motionless, he turns to the stone fireplace and stares at the dancing flames of the crackling fire.

THREE DAYS LATER.....

Kei and Jody are onboard the north bound Shinkansen as it speeds toward Tokyo. As the outlaying area and the outskirts of Tokyo come into view, Kei leans over to his friend and remarks, "Soon, we begin the final phase of our quest! Jody stares out the window as the buildings and cityscape zip by. She leans back in her seat and momentarily closes her eyes - She pictures the sparse semi-desert Indian Reservation of Venture. She imagines Her mom, dad and her around the family table. Lastly Jody recalls how Grandpa Carl passes the Golden Seal into her hands. Jody comes out of her daydream and remarks to Kei, "I'm glad you're with me - Tokyo is kinda your city! You're gonna have to take us to the various spots!" Kei smiles and nods, "I'm a Harakuju Hipster (Grins) You're right! Tokyo is my city!" He leans back in his seat and closes his eyes - and unexpectantly begins to SNORE - Jody grins and quietly giggles.

CHAPTER EIGHTY-SIX
Quest Through Tokyo City

Kei and Jody exit the Bullet Train and walk the Station Platform mixing with the busy crowd of passengers. The duo exit the doors of the Shinjuku Station onto the busy boulevard full of pedestrian traffic. Tokyo is a mega city with millions of inhabitants, the city streets and transit are always full because people are everywhere. Jody spots a street planter with a bench and motions Kei toward the quieter setting. As the two sit down, Jody asks, "Kei, I need to use your phone. (Pause) I better call to update my mom and dad on what's happening." Kei nods and hands his phone to Jody as she pulls out the International Calling Card and dials home. HOME NUMBER RINGS. Jody looks at Kei and dials again. HOME PHONE RINGS. A serious expression comes over Jody's face as she hands the phone back. Kei sees Jody's worried countenance and asks, "What's wrong?" Jody lifts her eyes to Kei and replies, "No answer! - It's not like my parents to not pick up. Now I'm worried!" Kei reassures his friend, "I'm sure there's a good explanation. Hey, you'll get through next time!" Jody gives a hopeful smile and the two get off the bench to resume their trek down the busy street. As they walk, Jody looks at Kei and remarks, "You said you have a friend in the Entertainment District. Will he be able to help?" Kei replies as he strides along, "Koji works at a popular Night Club. He's connected and knows lots of people." Jody quickens her pace and replies, "Well! - Let's get started!" They move along with the pedestrian traffic.

It is night time in Tokyo's Entertainment District. Inside the Night Club where Koji works, young people pack the dance floor as the animated DJ pumps the EDM to blast out the music. Coloured lights and lasers illuminate the Club's space. Groups of patrons party at tables with lounge chairs that surround the Club's neon-lit interior. Jody and Kei are at the front of a line inside the Club's front lobby. Kei talks with a Security Staff who's fitted with a communication headset. Kei tells the guy, "I want to talk with my friend Koji! He works here." The guy turns his head to look into the Club's interior - then waves to beckon with his hand. The Club's hallway soon fills with the massive body of a huge Security guy. The big brute strides toward Jody and Kei - then breaks out with a huge smile, and remarks, "Kei, old friend, so good to see you. (Pause) Do you want to get into the Club?" The big friend manhandles Kei in a friendly way, as Kei attempts to fend off the playful action. Kei looks at his childhood buddy and asks, "Koji, pal - I'm with this Gaijin girl. We need to ask you something important!" Koji glances at Jody, then scans the lobby and gestures to gather in a side cove and comments, "Let's go over there. I'm on duty so I can't talk long." The trio walk across the lobby and huddle in the room's cove, away from the line of patrons and Security Staff. Kei looks up at his big friend, "You've worked the Entertainment world for many years. My Gaijin friend, Jody, needs to find someone called the Beautiful Artist. - Have you ever heard that name before?" Koji ponders a few seconds, then puts his hand on Kei's shoulder and replies, "I've met lots of Celebrities, Performers and Artists, but I don't know this Beautiful Artist!" Kei exclaims, "Koji, if you don't know - how will we find out?" The large guy looks at Kei and Jody and replies, "Someone in Tokyo's art world is bound to know who you're looking for. - Keep searching!" The big guy turns and walks away to disappear into the Club's neon-lit hallway. Jody tugs on Kei's arm and asks, "What did you find out?" Kei responds, "My friend doesn't know - but he said we have to keep looking!" Jody gets a big frown. The two exit the Club's lobby doors.

Kei and Jody encounter Tokyo's night life as they continue to search venues and seek answers. At a Paint Studio, Jody and Kei talk with two artists that indicate no knowledge. In an alleyway at a Theatre Backstage door, Kei questions an Actress, and she doesn't know. Jody stands to the side and watches as Kei talks with some Fashion Models - they reply NO! Later on, Jody and Kei sit with an old Sculptor - he shakes his head NO! The duo enter a shop that sells lovely Japanese Dolls - they leave shortly with no success. At one point during the evening, Kei and Jody speak with a Lady Calligrapher, but she has never heard of such a person. As Jody and Kei walk along, they notice a street lined with Tattoo Parlours. They look up at an overhead Banner that features a Dragon amid Cherry Blossoms. Jody turns to Kei, "Let's try here!" Kei grabs the handle and pushes the front door open.

The Tattoo Parlour walls are covered with colourful vivid drawings of Koi Fish, Cherry Blossoms, Samurai Warriors, Galloping Horses, Bamboo Forests, and Fierce Dragons. The Studio interior features stone carvings, vases of beautiful flowers, and lovely Bonsai trees on display stands. Jody and Kei step into the golden glow of the Tattoo Parlour. They move to the middle of the shop and look about. Out from a beaded curtain, steps an elderly Tattoo Artist, who politely bows and greets them, "Welcome to my humble studio!" Kei and Jody bow respect, and Kei asks, "Grandfather, we look for someone that you might know." The old man moves to sit on a carved teak bench and replies, "Who is it that you seek?" Kei responds, "Do you know someone called the Beautiful Artist?" The old man's eyes twinkle as he smiles wide. He stands up and walks over to stand before a watercolour painting of a Samurai Warrior, and comments, "The one you seek is indeed a Beautiful Artist. I've known him for a long time!" Kei turns to Jody with excitement, "He knows who we're looking for!" Jody's eyes grow wide - she's thrilled at the news. Kei looks at the Tattoo Artist and remarks, "Kindly tell us where we can find this person?" The man moves to a large stunning Bonsai tree that sits on a table and he touches the branches with care and respect. The elderly artist gazes at Kei and Jody as he rests his fingers on the elegant time-sculpted trunk of the Bonsai tree and replies, "The man you seek - gave me this outstanding Bonsai tree many years ago! (Eyes Bonsai) Wonderful isn't it? (Pause) We call him the Beautiful Artist because he nurtures and shapes these beautiful bonsai." Kei turns to Jody, "The one we look (Points) gave him that Bonsai tree!" Jody looks at the Bonsai and old man with an exuberant gaze. Kei shifts his eyes to the aged tattoo artist and asks, "Where can we find him? It is very important!" The old man comes up to them and responds, "He owns a Bonsai Nursery on the outskirts of North Tokyo! - The Nursery Banner has a Bonsai over the Kanji for Sword. The Nursery borders a protected forest area." Kei bows very low to the elderly man - who bows in return, and Kei remarks, "Grandfather, our deepest gratitude for your help!" Kei looks at Jody and motions for them to leave. Jody bows to the elderly man and accompanies Kei toward the front door.

The old Tattoo Artist watches them as they leave the Tattoo Parlour. On the side walk outside, Jody tugs on Kei's arm, "Where do we go next?" Kei glances at Jody and remarks, "The outskirts of North Tokyo. We look for a Bonsai Nursery!" Jody and Kei walk down the street past a Noodle Bar.

A couple of Hanzai-shu thugs are inside and the two gangsters recognize Jody. One thug quickly pulls out his cell phone to call. At the Hanzai-shu Headquarters, gang members cluster in different groups, some smoke cigarettes and talk, others drink and play cards - while some peruse magazines, and others simply chill out. The Hanzai-shu Leader's cell phone BUZZES - and he picks up to hear the voice of one of his henchmen, "Boss. We saw that Gaijin girl - she's near the Tattoo Shops." The Gang Leader sneers and orders, "Good! Follow her - but stay out of sight. Let me know where they go." At the Noodle Bar, the thug bows as he holds his phone, "Hai!"

CHAPTER EIGHTY-SEVEN
Bonsai Over Sword

On the northern outskirts of Tokyo City, the rural countryside basks in the warmth of the morning sun. A gentle wind blows through the trees and the leaves rustle in the breeze. Birds on forest branches chirp their songs into the air. The sky above is a light clear blue.

A Transit Bus drives the country road and brakes at a rural Bus Stop. Jody and Kei step off the Bus into the roadside gravel. The Bus signals and proceeds down the road. A short distance down the road is a tall post with a Banner that flutters in the gentle breeze. Jody and Kei walk toward the weathered wood post, stop and look up at the white Banner that features a black Bonsai over a red Kanji for Sword. Kei and Jody begin to move over the tarmac toward the large wooden gate of the Nursery entrance. Jody remarks to Kei, "I'm feeling nervous to finally meet him - just think! - the last member of the Ninja Clan!" Kei watches his friend and comments, "You have flown from America - travelled Japan - fought Japanese gangsters and searched hard - Now! - You complete your quest!" They both turn and face the Nursery entrance and Kei pushes the heavy timber gate open. Before them is an oriental pathway that goes under a large red Japanese Tori Gate, then leads toward a wide open area of fields and trees. Passing beneath the Red Tori Gate, Jody and Kei tread along the manicured garden pathway until they come to an open area with rows of wooden tables. A potted Bonsai sits on each table. Jody and Kei look around and see wood buildings that line the ground's perimeter. The Bonsai Nursery is clean and tidy, simple and refined. Off to the side, a Bonsai worker dressed in plain tunic and trousers, exits a building close by. He approaches them and bows low, "Welcome strangers! How may we help you?" Kei glances at Jody, then he looks at the worker and remarks, "We seek the one called the Beautiful Artist! My Gaijin friend has something very important for him." The worker's eyes get wide and his eye brows raise. He quickly turns and hastens to the large central wood building and enters inside. Within seconds, an elderly man with white hair braided in a ponytail, accompanied by several workers, exits the structure and make their way toward Jody and Kei. The elderly man is dressed in a simple plain tunic and trousers. He stops a few feet from Jody and Kei - Kei and Jody bow low in respect to him. The man comments, "I am known as the Beautiful Artist! My worker tells me that you wish to speak with me?" Kei looks at the aged man and remarks, "Grandfather, my Gaijin friend, Jody, carries a special gift for you!" Kei lifts himself upright and extends his arm to Jody. The elderly man turns his gaze to Jody and smiles. Jody straightens up and reaches into her backpack to bring out the cloth wrapped item. She respectfully approaches the old man and puts out her arm. The old man takes the wrapped bundle and holds it in his open palm. He carefully unfolds the cloth to reveal the object. The Beautiful Artist's eyes grow wide, his eye brows arch, his mouth drops open - he's totally awestruck! **THE GOLDEN SEAL!** The old man turns the Golden Seal over and over in his hand - to closely examine the engravings and details. With jubilation, he holds it up for the gathered Nursery workers to see. The workers murmur with excitement! The old man stares at Jody for a few moments, then he asks, "Where did you find the long lost Golden Seal?" Kei steps forward and bows low to explain, "Grandfather, my Gaijin friend, Jody, carried the Golden Seal from her home in America, to deliver it to you - the last of the Shinobi Ninja Clan. (Pause) My friend has fought and defeated Hanzai-shu thugs to return this special gift to you!" The Beautiful Artist's eyes become moist - he is choked up with emotion. The old man steps softly to stand before Jody - Jody bows low and holds her position. The Beautiful Artist has a tender smile and he places his hand under Jody's chin to gently coax her upright. Jody straightens up. The elderly man looks at Kei and points to Jody and remarks, "Your Gaijin friend - Jody - is a true warrior! The Shinobi Ninja Clan is indebted to her for bringing us the **GORUDOSHIRU - our Golden Seal!**" The old leader turns and beckons to an aid close by and whispers into the his ear. The aid quickly bows and runs off to the large central wood building. Within a few minutes, the aid returns to hand a black velvet pouch to the elderly leader. The old man opens the pouch, turns to Jody and extends his hand - and looks at Kei, who remarks to Jody, "I think he wants to give you something!" Jody opens her hand and the Beautiful Artist lays an engraved thick gold medallion on Jody's palm. Jody's eyes zoom large. The old man remarks, "I give your Gaijin friend - the **SHOCHO TUKEN -** a special Ninja Token only given to the **IDAINA SENSHI** - a Great Warrior! It is our humble way to say Thank You for returning the Golden Seal!" Jody stares at the glistening gold object. Kei steps beside her to explain, "The Shinobi Ninja Master has given you a great honour! This Gold Token is only given to a Great Warrior! - He wants you to have it!" Jody looks at the elderly Ninja Master and bows low, and comments, "Okini Arigato!" The Beautiful Artist smiles deeply and nods acknowledgement.

SUDDENLY!

The Koroshi-ya and the Hanzai-shu Leader step out from around a building, each holding a Katana sword. The Gang Leader YELLS, "Attack! Wipe them out!" Thugs with swords, axes, knives and clubs, pour out from bushes, trees and buildings toward Jody, Kei, and the gathered Nursery workers. The Hanzai-shu Leader and the Koroshi-ya run directly at Jody and Kei. Jody steps in front of Kei to protect him. The Beautiful Artist, the Ninja Master, grabs a bamboo pole to defend. The old Ninja Master looks at his Nursery workers and instructs, "Defend - but do not kill any!" All the Bonsai workers, who are secretly skilled Ninjas, swiftly grab shovels, rakes, wood poles, and garden tools for weapons.

The Hanzai-shu thugs and the Ninja - CLASH!

Thugs swing swords, swipe knives and flail clubs at the Bonsai workers, who unleash their Ninja fighting skills! One thug swings his blade and the Ninja ducks, summersaults forward to kick the hoodlum unconscious. Another gangster repeatedly jabs his knife at a Nursery worker, who spins around to grab the thug's hand to disarm. The Nursery worker pummels the gangster to knock him out! The Hanzai-shu Leader raises his Katana, and with two henchmen with long knives - attack the old Ninja Master from three sides. The Gang Leader and the two thugs swing their weapons. The aged Ninja Master skillfully dodges the sharp blades, and twirls the bamboo pole to knock out both henchmen. Now, just the Hanzai-shu Leader and the old Ninja Master face each other! As the two men confront each other, all around them, the Ninja Bonsai workers decimate the street thugs with a barrage of kicks, powerful strikes and devastating blows. The hoodlums lay across the Nursery grounds - injured, defeated and unconscious. The Gang Leader and the Beautiful Artist circle each other, the Gang Leader boasts, "The Koroshi-ya told us about the Golden Seal - and the secret treasure!" The Beautiful Artist replies in a determined voice, "The treasure belongs to the Shinobi Ninja Clan! You will not get it!" The Gang Leader thrusts his sword blade repeatedly as he moves about - the old man moves the pole to flick the blade away each time.

Off to the side not far away...

The Koroshi-ya, who is extremely angry, twirls his sword before Jody who is unarmed. The professional killer boldly states, "You die American girl! - I kill - You die now!" Jody keenly watches as the killer paces back and forth in front of her. He sweeps the razor sharp blade from side to side. Jody crouches slightly with both arms extended for battle. She quickly glances at a nearby table with a large Bonsai. The Koroshi-ya lunges the sword to attack. Jody swiftly pivots and dashes toward the nearby table, the killer racing after her with the sword pointed at Jody's back. Jody runs and stretches out to grab the thick branches of the Bonsai tree. Her fingers hook the top branches and she spins about to kick away the oncoming sword. She powerfully swings the potted Bonsai tree at the killer's head. CRASH! The Bonsai's stone planter smashes into the killer's head - the stone basin cracks and splits apart and loose dirt falls - the Koroshi-ya's eyes roll as he's knocked out and drops to the ground! Jody stares at the fallen killer as she catches her breath. Now, all eyes are on the Hanzai-shu Leader and the old Ninja Master. The Gang Leader scans around to see thugs scattered about - unconscious, injured or surrendered. The Beautiful Artist remarks, "Your gang is defeated - Give up!" The Hanzai-shu Leader smirks - then raises his Katana sword and cries out, "Never! - I will kill you instead!" The Gang Leader wildly swings the Katana blade - the old man deftly ducks and dodges each attack. As the Gang Leader lunges to skewer the old man, the Ninja Master stops him with a mighty blow! The aged Ninja Master quickly strikes the gangster in several places all over his body - then the old man steps away. The hoodlum is locked - unable to move a muscle whatever - he's frozen like a statue! The Beautiful Artist remarks, "There! You will stay this way until I release you." The Hanzai-shu Leader bellows, "Old man, what did you do? (Straining. Grunting) I can't move! Can not move!" The Ninja Master replies, "I simply locked you up until the Police arrive to officially lock you up!" The Ninja Master glances at his Nursery workers and makes a quick gesture. The Bonsai Ninja gather all the gangsters together and tie them up for the Police. The Bonsai Ninja fashion intricate rope bonds to hold and secure all the Hanzai-shu. Jody approaches the Beautiful Artist, and Kei steps out from amid the Nursery workers to join Jody. She bows low before the old man and comments, "Thank you for saving me from those gangsters! Okini Arigato!" The elderly warrior gives Jody a tender smile. He reaches into his tunic and brings out his hand to display the Golden Seal. He speaks in broken-English, "Jody - you - Ninja! (Points) Ninja!" Jody's eyes light up - she grins wide. Kei is gobsmacked! Jody looks at the Beautiful Artist, scans the Nursery grounds and all the lovely Bonsai trees, then turns toward Kei, "I did it! - completed my Grandfather's dying request and returned the Golden Seal! (Pause) Now, I must return home." Her good friend remarks, "I'll go with you to the Airport. After all, your Japanese isn't that good - you need me!" Jody with a twinkle in her eye, replies, "That's right - you're a good translator - and a pretty good friend." Kei smiles. As the duo turn to leave the Nursery grounds and walk down the path, they turn and wave to the Beautiful Artist and the Bonsai workers, who wave back in return. With Kei and Jody well down the path toward the front gate, the Ninja Master grips the Golden Seal in his hand and raises it in Victory!. All the Bonsai Ninja rally around - and CELEBRATE!

CHAPTER EIGHTY-EIGHT

Flying Home

Kei is with Jody outside the International Departure lounge at the Narita Airport that's located on the outskirts of metropolitan Tokyo. Travellers and tourists mill about the busy interior of the Terminal. Individuals and families steer luggage trollies here and there toward various Airport Gates. Jody stands next to her luggage trolly and she shifts her backpack to be more comfortable. She holds her Boarding Pass and gives Kei a tender gaze, "I don't know how to thank you for all your help! - I couldn't have done it without you!" Kei smiles in a sheepish manner and replies, "I was honoured to assist you - not every Japanese guy gets to fulfill Bushido these days! (Grins) Very cool!" Jody gives Kei an offer, "If you ever get to the States - look me up! You got my address." Kei tilts his head with a smile, "America is a long way from Japan! (Laughs) Maybe, I'll visit when I'm old and have enough money." Jody looks wistfully at her friend and leans forward to give a quick kiss on Kei's cheek, "You're welcome to visit anytime! Call me - you have my number." Kei nods and Jody moves her trolly toward the Departure Zone entrance - the frosted glass doors slide open to give access. Jody looks at Kei one final time, gives a big wave and walks through into Departures - and the glass doors close. As she makes her way, Jody notices an Airport Pay Phone Kiosk.

Jody walks up to the Kiosk and grabs the phone handle, swipes the credit card and dials home. She listens to the ELECTRONIC TONES then her mom's voice on the Answering Machine, "We can't come to the phone right now. Please leave your message after the tone - BEEP!" Jody blurts out, "Mom. Dad. I've been trying to reach you! I heading home. See you guys soon, ok. Love Ya! Bye." Jody hangs up the phone receiver and moves her trolly toward the Boarding Zone. She joins some other passengers who are lined up in front of the United Airlines Boarding Desk, where Airline Staff check Boarding Passes. Just beyond the Boarding Desk is the enclosed Gangway that leads to the aircraft. After her Boarding Pass for United Airlines Flight 252 is checked and her trolly tagged for loading, Jody walks with other travellers on the Gangway toward the plane's open doors where the Stewardesses greet and direct them. Jody shuffles down the cabin aisle to her row, stores the backpack into the overhead compartment, sits down and tucks the carry-on under her seat. She sits in her window seat that's situated a few rows ahead of the plane's wing. The seat beside her stays empty as a middle-aged businessman settles into the aisle seat. Jody glances around as passengers clog the aisles as they find their seats and hoist their luggage into the overhead bins. **CHIMES. SEAT BELT LIGHT.** Passengers quickly get seated and start to buckle up. The Stewardesses position at the front of cabin sections and start to give Flight Instructions. **AIRCRAFT ENGINES HIGH PITCH WHIRL!** The plane begins to roll forward, taxis and positions on the Airport tarmac. The big engines **THROTTLE. VROOM!** and the plane quickly picks up speed on the runway and the velocity pushes Jody back in her seat. She glances around as the plane's interior vibrates. This time - Jody is relaxed and calm! The plane reaches Lift-Off and the shaking stops. The aircraft climbs at a steep angle - then it levels off. **SEAT BELT LIGHT OFF.** Jody looks out her window at the wonderful Japanese landscape below. Hours later, the aircraft flies the clear night sky where bright stars fill the heavens. Inside the Pilot's cockpit, the Altitude Gage reads - 30,000 feet. As the plane heads over the Pacific Ocean - Jody's seat is reclined as she sleeps peacefully curled up in a blanket.

Near dawn, the Aircraft lands safely on the runway flanked by coloured navigation lights on the grounds of Sweetwater County Airport. The plane taxis to the Terminal as an Airport worker waves lit batons to guide the pilots to dock with the extended Gangway. Jody exits the Passenger Gangway and walks through the Airport to retrieve her trolly, then she goes through the Terminal Exit Doors. Taxis are parked out front and she gets a cab. As the driver stores the trolly in the trunk, Jody gets into the back seat. The driver gets behind the steering wheel and looks at Jody, who remarks, "1580 Plains Road, Venture Indian Reservation." The driver nods, enters info on the GPS, starts the engine and the cab's meter - then, the cab drives away from the Terminal. As the Taxi Cab rolls along, Jody looks out at the city lights of Rock Springs, Wyoming. As the morning sun breaks the horizon, the taxi passes over the Highway until coming to the rural tarmac roads of the Indian Reservation. The Driver turns onto the Concession with the sign that reads - **PLAINS ROAD**. Jody stares out the back window at the semi-desert terrain The taxi approaches a raised ranch bungalow up on the right. The roadside mailbox - **LONG GRASS**. The taxi turns into the laneway and parks. The driver exits the car and gets the trolly out of the trunk and sets it on the grass. Jody gets out of the car and hands the driver the proper fare plus a generous tip. The Driver nods appreciation, gets into his car and drives off.

In the morning light, Jody stares at the the house - curtains drawn and no sign of life. She grabs her trolly and carries it to the front cement step, inserts and turns her house key and opens the door wide. Jody happily yells out, "Hello! Mom. Dad. I'm home!" **SILENCE**. Jody lifts the trolly inside and sets it near the front window - then closes the door. She quickly walks around the house - peers in the kitchen, looks in her parent's bedroom, the backroom - Nothing! Jody's greatly puzzled?! She sits bewildered at the dining table, and goes to the home phone beside the sofa - and dials the RESERVATION POLICE. ELECTRONIC DIAL TONES. An Officer picks up, "Hello. Venture Police Station." Jody remarks in a serious tone, "Hi. My name is Jody Long Grass - and my parents are missing! - I can't seem to contact them. It's not like them and I'm worried!" The Officer enquires, "What did you say your name was?" Jody replies, "Jody Long Grass. My parents are Brian and Karen Long Grass. I've been trying to phone them for days - and they're not home!" The Policeman comments, "I'm going to put you on hold as I check our system." Jody replies, "That's okay. I'll hold." TELEPHONE SILENCE. The Reservation Police Officer comes back on the phone and asks, "Hello Jody - do you live on the Indian Reservation at 1580 Plains Road?" Jody quickly responds, "Yes! That's our home address!" There's a few seconds of silence, then the Officer speaks, "Jody. (Pause) I'm afraid I have some bad news for you - Your dad and mom were in a terrible car accident with a tractor trailer. We arrested the truck driver on DUI and running a Red Light - We put him in jail!" (Pause) The reason you weren't able to reach your parents is because your dad and mom are at the Regional Hospital - listed in Critical Condition." Jody is stunned and shocked by the tragic news - she's speechless! The Police Officer voices concern, "Hello Jody!

- Jody you still there?" Jody quietly responds, "Thank you for letting me know! (Pause) I've gotta go now." Jody puts down the phone receiver and stares off for a moment. Suddenly, she dashes over to grab her backpack and rushes out the front door.

CHAPTER EIGHTY-NINE

Parents In Critical Condition

Jody walks through the sliding glass doors of the Regional Hospital and enters the modern lobby. She scans around and makes a beeline to the lady Volunteer wearing a smock behind the Information Desk. The kind faced lady looks up and Jody remarks, "Hello! I'm looking for Brian and Karen Long Grass?" The woman types in keystrokes and peers at the monitor screen, "Brian Long Grass is in the Intensive Care Unit. Karen Long Grass is in the Rehab Unit on the 2nd Floor." Jody smiles and comments, "Thank you very much!" Jody turns about and walks to the Lobby Elevators and stands beside a family of four who are waiting. ELEVATOR CHIMES. The elevator door opens and Jody and the family enter inside - and Jody pushes the 2nd Floor button. The elevator reaches the second level, the doors open and Jody steps out into the corridor. Jody moves to the Nursing Station to enquire about her mom's room. A Rehab Nurse guides Jody to the Hospital Room doorway and comments, "Your mother just finished her Rehab session an hour ago - she's pretty tired out." The Nurse turns and leaves. Jody looks at her mom laying in the Hospital bed with her eyes closed. The room has three other patients - their divider curtains are extended for privacy. Jody quietly comes up to her mom's bed. She glances at the blue marks of bruised skin and the tiny lacerations on her mom's face as a result of the accident. A Rehab sling suspends her mom's right leg. Jody bends down close to her mom's face and gently whispers, "Mom. Mom. - It's me, Jody! I'm back." Karen's eye lids flutter and she opens her eyes and looks up with a tired gaze - then smiles wide, "Jody honey, I'm so happy you're here! I was so worried about you." Jody leans in a tender gaze and lovingly stroke her mom's hair, then proudly remarks, "Mom. I did it! I finished what Grandpa asked me to do - returned the Golden Seal!" Karen's eyes widen and a motherly smile covers her face, "Your dad and I are so proud of you! - What you accomplished! (Pause) Did they tell you what happened?" Jody lowers to partially sit on the edge of the bed and replies, "A Reservation Officer gave me the details - that Transport Driver was arrested and charged for DUI and running a Red Light. He's behind bars now! (Pause) The Nurse told me you have six more weeks of Rehab (Pause) and Dad's in a coma!" Karen's eyes well up and tears roll down her face, "I don't know how long Brian will be in a Coma! The doctors are waiting for the brain swelling to do down. (Crying) Jody, I'm so scared we're going to lose him!" Jody leans in with a big hug and squeezes her mom's hand to reassure, "Dad's going to make it! Mom, don't worry, the Doctors will make him better - you'll see!" Karen turns her head toward the window with it's blinds pulled open, "I pray to God every day that Brian will get better. (Tears) I can't bear the thought of living without him!" Jody looks tenderly into her mom's moist eyes, "Soon, you both will be out of here and back home - just like before all this happened. - We'll fish at the Creek, and get ice cream at Emma May's." Karen smiles at her daughter's words, then looks at Jody and remarks, "I want you to call your Aunt Sally and ask her to come stay with you." Jody sits up straight and replies, "Mom, it's okay - I don't need help - you know I can handle myself." The mother replies with a faint smile, "I know you can handle yourself - But you still need company. It would make me feel better!" Jody rolls her eyes slightly then complies, "Alright mom, I'll call Aunt Sally!" Her mom comments, "That's good Jody! Do it for me - I'll feel better knowing someone is there with you." The talk has Karen tired out and her eyes get droopy, she remarks in a fading voice, "Sorry honey, this pain medication - makes me - so tired - I have to close - my eyes." Karen is out. Jody lets go of her mom's hand. She adjusts her mother's pillow and pulls up the bed cover - and leans over to kiss her mom's forehead. Jody leaves the Hospital's Rehab Department, enters the elevator and presses the button for the 5th Floor.

Jody reaches the floor level and enquires at the Nursing Desk about the patient, Brian Long Grass. An ICU Nurse lets Jody into the Intensive Care Unit and guides her to his location. As the Nurse returns to her station, Jody steps up close beside the bed and stares at her father. The rhythmic sounds of the Breathing Apparatus fills the room. Jody scans her dad's motionless form - and sniffles as tears roll down her cheeks. Jody has a momentary flashback to a better earlier time; to when she and her dad spent the afternoon fishing in a boat on a river. It was a warm lazy wonderful time outdoors together. Jody blinks her eyes and stares down at the IV tube, monitor leads, and the breathing apparatus over her dad's nose and mouth. She stands still for a couple moments, then turns to slowly walk away with watery eyes.

A few days later at home - KNOCKS on the front door! Jody gets off the sofa to open the front door to see who it is. Aunt Sally stands on the cement stoop wearing a big smile and holding a small suitcase. Jody greets her aunt with a smile, "Hi Aunt Sally! Come on in - I got your room ready." Aunt Sally, her mom's sister, is a happy plump lady with curly auburn hair and winsome eyes. The lady steps inside, gives a hug and looks Jody over from head to toe, and exclaims, "Jody - my how you've grown!" Jody grins as she replies, "Last time you saw me - I was in Grade 8." Aunt Sally sets her suitcase down, straightens her blouse and looks at her niece, and compliments, "You were a little girl then - But look at you now! Such a fine young lady!" Jody picks up Sally's suitcase and remarks as she motions to an armchair, "You must be tired from your long trip. I'll take your suitcase to the spare room - you can just relax!" The woman smiles wide, strolls over to the armchair, sits down and begins to preen her permed hairdo. Sally gives a SIGH and remarks, "Must admit - I'm a bit tuckered out from that long taxi ride." Jody smiles, turns and disappears down the hall.

Over the next few weeks, Aunt Sally preps and cooks food in the kitchen. She dusts, sweeps and mops floors and scrubs walls. The lady does the laundry, and Jody helps Sally fold the clean bed sheets. In the evening, Sally sits in the armchair sewing on buttons and crocheting doilies. Jody begins to see the wisdom of her mom's request to have Aunt Sally stay.

One late afternoon, Jody and Aunt Sally eat supper at the dining table - when there's **KNOCKS** at the front door. Aunt Sally opens the door to see who's calling - and looks out to see an elderly American Indian man dressed in a plain black tunic and pants standing before her. The man holds a black envelope. The man politely enquires, "Good Day! Is Jody Long Grass here?" Aunt Sally smiles and replies, "Just a minute please - I'll call her. (Turns her head) Jody. Jody dear - someone's here for you." Jody rises from the dining table and walks to the front door to stand beside her aunt. Jody looks at the man in simple plain attire and informs, "Hello! I'm Jody Long Grass!" The man smiles, bows and straightens up, then hands Jody the black envelope, and remarks, "You are invited to - **Black Eagle**!" Jody is surprised and shocked, her eyes get big like saucers. She looks down at the black envelope in her hand, and turns it over and touches the red wax seal that bears the Japanese Kanji for - Black Eagle. Jody's fingers slightly tremble as she opens the envelope - she takes out the parchment paper letter and slowly scans it.

FORMAL INVITATION TO BLACK EAGLE

Jody lifts her eyes to look at the elderly man and remarks with utter joy, "Thank You! Thank You so very much!" The elderly man steps back, bows low, returns upright and remarks, "The Competition starts in 3 weeks. Instructions and directions are included in the letter. (Smiles) Congratulations!" Jody and Aunt Sally watch from the open doorway as the man descends the front stoop, gets into a shiny black sedan with tinted glass, and the car drives away. Aunt Sally glances over at Jody standing still, and asks, "Is it something important?" Jody turns to her and holds up the letter and black envelope, and give an ecstatic reply, "Just the best news ever! (Pause) This is about Black Eagle!" Aunt Sally watches as Jody tears off to her bedroom with excitement and joy. The lady closes the front door and remarks in a whimsical mutter, "Imagine. All this fuss over a bird!"

CHAPTER NINETY

Black Eagle

The morning sun breaks across the rugged terrain. Somewhere in the rocky landscape, a cavernous stone amphitheatre with a wide flat centre and stepped elevations, lays secluded in the wilderness. This natural forum carved by wind and time, is this year's location for the authoritative and highly regarded, Ninjan **BLACK EAGLE** - a Tournament held every five years. Participants from various American Indian Tribes are selected and officially invited to the renowned Competition.

Jody stands with assembled guys and gals - each one is an official contestant for Black Eagle. They gather around a tall thick wood post deeply embedded in the centre of the arena's earthen floor. She looks around at her competitors - most are young people in their 20's and 30's. There a few males and females who are a little older. The contestants have mixed emotions, some stand alert and ready, others are chill and relaxed, some are talking, when unexpectedly, there's the high pitched **SHRILL** - a black whistle arrow strikes the top of the post several feet above the contestants' heads. All eyes rivet to the arrow. Next, the pounding sound of **Indian Drums** fill the air - followed by a loud **Indian War Cry**! Then - **SILENCE**.

Suddenly, The Grand Master and five Black Eagle Judges dressed as Ninjans quickly appear on an upper elevation. The Grand Master holds a golden staff. Jody and the other participants quickly look up. The Grand Master motions his arm and Ninjans appear on a lower level - each raise their weapon specialty high in the air - **Bow and Arrow - Open Hand - Tomahawk - War Club - Spear - Knife - Sword**.

The assembled young people look at the weapon specialists and the Judges. The Grand Master gazes down at the invited contestants and announces, "Welcome to Black Eagle!" Jody and the others swiftly focus on the Grand Master. The elderly Ninjan Master continues his address, "Today, you will be tested through the Fire of Combat! Each of you must prove your Ninjan skills with four weapons. Each one must defeat their opponent to advance to the next round. (Pause) The Winner will be awarded the Tournament Scroll and the Black Eagle Sword. A Judge on the Grand Master's left - lifts up his arm holding the Scroll, the Judge on the Grand Master's right - lifts his arm holding the Black Eagle Katana. The Judge holding the Sword announces, "The Ninjan who displays expert skills and defeats all foes - will received the Tournament Scroll, and be awarded the prized Black Eagle Sword!" The Grand Master steps forward and extends the golden staff out over the group of contestants, and remarks, "We have invited you here from many Indian Tribes. Each contestant will wear their Tribe's Ninjan outfit for the competition. - This is to honour your people and native culture. A Tribal Elder will accompany each of you. (Looks at the group) Now - Let Black Eagle begin!

The Judges and the Ninjans on the lower level disappear from sight. All the contestants look at each other - many are eager and pumped with excitement! Everyone turns their attention to the perimeter of the wide amphitheatre floor; various Tribal Elders dressed in their Tribe's attire beckon with their hands. Each contestant recognizes their Tribe's clothing and heads toward their respective Elder. Jody scans around, to her right is a middle-aged man dressed in traditional Shoshone garb. She walks toward him. As she gets near, the Shoshone Elder smiles and greets her, "Hi Jody! You don't know me - but I was a good friend of your Grandpa Carl. (Pause) Let's go and get you ready for the Competition!" The man escorts Jody to an area where there's an enclosure with opaque black canvass walls and roof covering. The man stops a couple feet before the enclosure entrance and points. Jody comments, "You want me to go inside?" The Tribal Elder responds, "Yes! You will find everything you need - Shoshone Ninjan clothing and various tribal decorations."

Jody glances at the man, nods and smiles, then walks to the entrance and disappears inside. Once inside the tent-like structure that's screened for privacy, Jody sees Shoshone Ninjan clothing on a long wood table. At one end are Tribal trinkets and decorations. At the other end, is a hand mirror, dark towel, and clay bowls filled with different coloured pigment. Jody steps close to the table and surveys her clothing options. After Jody has put together her outfit, she exits the dark canvass shelter and remarks, "Guess I'm ready as I'll ever be!" The Shoshone Elder turns around to face the enclosure entrance. Jody emerges dressed as a Shoshone Ninjan with a red feather in her long hair, and a hair braid on each side with coloured beads and silver disks. War Paint is on her face - red covers her forehead, black is streaked across her eyes from one temple to the other. Jody has applied the War Paint in the style of an experienced Shoshone Warrior! The Elder gives a big smile and comments. "You honour all our Shoshone people - and especially your Grandfather!" Jody smiles at his remark. The Elder motions that she join him. They both walk back to the arena's wide flat earthen floor. Some others contestants have already gathered and stand with their Tribal Elder. Jody and her Elder join them. A few others make their way onto the Tournament floor. Now, every contestant is in their Tribe's Ninjan outfit and war paint.

DRUMS BEAT

The Grand Master and the Judges assemble on an upper elevation that gives them a clear vantage point for the Competition. The Grand Master lifts his voice to instruct, "Contestants - step forward to form a single line and present yourselves to the Black Eagle Judges!" Each contestant steps out to help form a line across the Combat area. The Grand Master, the Black Eagle Judges, and the Ninjan Masters, fix their eyes on each contestant. All the young people look healthy and strong, fit and capable for Tournament Combat. The Black Eagle Judges gaze at the line of young warriors - they see - a young man standing tall and proud as a **SIOUX** Ninjan, beside him is an older man dressed in **CROW** Ninjan clothing, next in line is a young woman wearing a **CHEYENNE** Ninjan outfit, and to her right is a young man with an **IROQUOIS** Ninjan outfit and haircut. The Judges continue their visual sweep of the Competition entrees. They look at a woman fitted with **LAKOTA** Ninjan garb, next to her is a young man in **APACHE** Ninjan clothing, and beside him is Jody dressed as a **SHOSHONE** Ninjan. The Tournament Officials scan the line further to see an older man standing as a **NAVAJO** Ninjan, then a young lady in her **KIOWA** Ninjan outfit. The remaining contestants include - a young man in **ARAPAHO** Ninjan clothing, an older man dressed as a **BLACKFOOT** Ninjan, and lastly, a young man stands in his **UTE** Ninjan attire. The Grand Master and the Black Eagle Judges nod and bow to show their approval to all the assembled young Ninjans. The Grand Master waves his hand and all the Ninjan Weapon Masters appear - each hold a Tournament weapon high in the air - Bow and Arrow - Open Hand - Tomahawk - War Club - Spear - Knife - Sword. The Grand Master announces, "Each contestant must choose four weapons to display your Ninjan skill and combat ability! Each weapon will have three rounds. (Pause) Black Eagle Contestants - select your weapons and inform your Elder." The eyes of the contestants scan across the Ninjans holding aloft the combat weapons. Some candidates share a quick huddle with their Elder. Jody looks up at the weapon choices, then turns to her Shoshone Elder. The man remarks, "Have you made your selection?" Jody nods and confidently replies, "Yes! I pick the Bow and Arrow, Open Hand, Spear - and the Sword." All the Elders lead their fighters to pre-assigned Tribal spots on the arena's perimeter. As the young contestants stay in their respective locations, their Elders leave and later return with their candidate's selected weapons.

BEATING OF INDIAN DRUMS

The Black Eagle Judges assemble on their upper viewing level. A Tournament Referee walks to the middle of the arena to oversee each Combat Round. Jody and her fellow contenders stand at the perimeter and waited to be summoned. Jody glances about - some are cool and ready, while others are edgy and somewhat nervous. Jody inhales slow and steady - she lets out her breath and stands battle ready!

BOW AND ARROW COMPETITION

Jody and five others stand with their weapon facing targets. The Referee lifts up his arm and the contestants fix arrow to bow. The Referee drops his arm to shoot. Jody pulls the drawstring of her black bow and fires - her arrow hits the bullseye dead centre! Three contestants miss the mark, and two strike the target. In another Round, a Tournament Official tosses a squash high into the air - Jody shoots and her arrow pierces it through. The others shoot their arrows - and miss. For the last Round, three lit candles are lined up straight - one arrow must extinguish all three flames. The contestants aim and shoot their arrows - only Jody's arrow puts out all three candles. The Referee extends his arm to Jody as the Winner!

OPEN HAND COMBAT

In the first Battle Round, a young woman lunges and Jody grabs her and flips her over onto the arena floor. During the next Round, a big young guy throws punches at Jody, who ducks and blocks the attacks. She hits the attacker in a flurry of strikes and blows - that drops the guy to the ground. For the last Round, Jody fights an older man. He attacks with kicks and punches which Jody capably blocks and deflects, then Jody swiftly pivots with a powerful roundhouse that delivers a knockout! The Referee points to Jody - the Winner of Open Hand Combat.

SPEAR

The contestants in this Competition throw traditional Indian Spears at swinging targets. Only Jody and two other participants hit their mark. For the second Round, the contestants - jab, swing and thrust spears in combat. Jody deflects a spear jab, twirls her spear shaft and strikes hard to disarm her attacker - she holds the spear tip at his neck - her opponent surrenders. In the last Round, A young man stands yards away confronting Jody, the two contestants lock eyes. Suddenly the opponent throws his spear at Jody with all his might - the spear flies directly at her. Jody quickly leans her body and catches the spear shaft. She stands victorious as she points both spears at her surprised opponent. The Referee smiles and extends his arm to Jody - the clear Winner!

KATANA SWORD

There are six contestants with Katana Swords. The first Round has divided them into three pairs - each contestant must fight the other. Jody faces a young man who has apparent skill and quick moves. He and Jody spar with their Katanas. The young man swings and slices - his blade is fast. Jody blocks and counter-strikes. He swings hard and Jody ducks and unleashes a flurry of chops - her Katana blade moves swiftly. Jody strikes with blistering speed, her blade hits with ferocity, she out-manoeuvres and knocks her opponent's sword to the ground. From the other two pairs - a big guy and a young woman emerge as

Winners from their combat. The Referee points at Jody and the two other Winners. For the second Round, the Referee has the three Winners draw lots to determine battle order. Jody's lot is last, the big guy and the young woman must face each other. The big guy is strong and swings his Katana with power and might. The young woman is very fast and agile. Each contestant shows skill and experience. The two battle and their swordplay is fierce - the man releases a big chop and the young woman twirls her blade to disarm her attacker. The big guy nods and yields defeat.

At this stage, the young woman and Jody face each other. By now, everyone's eyes are glued as the young woman and Jody circle each other, each with their steel blade ready. The girl swiftly thrusts her blade and Jody blocks. Jody swings and her female opponent deflects the attack. Their swordplay is fast with advanced technical skill. The girl lets out a barrage of chops and slices, Jody backs up to block, deflect and counter-swing. The girl stops to catch her breath. Jody seizes the moment and attacks with speed and force to release a torrent of thrusts, jabs, slices, and chops - the young girl is barely able to defend! The girl dives to her side, rolls on the ground and springs to her feet - ready for battle with her sword pointed at Jody. The two female warriors circle each other - their sword tips touch again and again. Jody glances around and notices the Black Eagle Judges, Tournament Ninjans, Tribal Elders, and all the Contestants are keenly watching. Jody takes a quick breath, then runs full out at her opponent - Jody swiftly swings her Katana blade left and right in rapid attack - the girl repeatedly blocks. Jody leaps and summersaults over top the girl to attack from behind, her opponent turns to face Jody's flying blade - the young woman cannot keep up! Jody gives a powerful swing to knock the sword out of the young woman's hand. The female opponent stands empty-handed as Jody points the sword at her. The Referee walks to stand between the two and motions his hand to Jody as the **Champion**! Jody raises her eyes to the Grand Master and the Black Eagle Judges. The Officials smile their approval and bow - Jody bows respect in return.

POUNDNG INDIAN DRUMS. CHANTING

All the Tournament Contestants, Tribal Elders, Referees, Tournament Ninjans, are gathered on the arena floor before the Grand Master and the Black Eagle Judges. Only Jody stands alone in the space between the two groups. The Grand Master steps forward and proudly announces, "We honour you with this Tournament Scroll and the Black Eagle Sword. You are the Winner of this year's Black Eagle Tournament. - Congratulations Jody!" An Official awards the prized Trophies. Jody receives the Scroll and Black Eagle Sword with great humility and bows low in respect. (At this instant, she has a flashback to when Grandpa Carl taught her how to use the Katana sword). Jody looks at the Scroll and Black Eagle Sword with joyful tear-filled eyes. She turns about to the onlookers and lifts up the **Tournament Scroll** and **Black Eagle Sword** with a victorious smile. All the Contestants, Referees, Elders, and Tournament Ninjans show their support and CHEER!

CHAPTER NINETY-ONE

The Wilderness Sunset

A Flight Attendant pushes a well stocked beverage cart down the passenger aisle. A few rows up, a hand motions to her. The Stewardess stops the trolly and looks at the Japanese man in sun glasses and business suit with his head bowed. The Flight Attendant politely asks, "Would you like something to drink?" The man lifts his head and nods. The Stewardess is briefly startled at the big scar that runs down his right cheek. The Japanese man responds in broken-English, "U-isuki. (Pause) Whiskey." The Flight Attendant smiles and sets out a short glass tumbler, puts in two ice cubes and pours the Whiskey. She hands him the tumbler full of Whiskey. He reaches up to hold the glass - a gold bracelet dangles from his wrist that features a small medallion with a snake!

It's mid afternoon as Karen sits in a Rehab wheelchair. Jody gently pushes her mom down the hall to the lounge seating area. She positions her mom and then sits down in an upholstered chair. Her mom remarks, "The doctors said your father woke up yesterday for a few minutes. (Excited) I can't wait to see him!" Jody comments, "I miss talking with him - I want to hear his voice again!" Karen reaches out to clasp her daughter's hand and mentions, "When we both get out of here - we'll celebrate your victory at Black Eagle! - Your Grandpa would have been so proud of you!" Jody gives a reassuring smile and adds, "When the Hospital releases you and dad - we can go to our favourite spot. It's been a long time since we were there." Karen responds with a positive tone, "It'll be a real effort for your dad and I - but definitely worth it!" Jody smiles at her mom's comment.

A FEW WEEKS LATER

* * *

Karen, Brian and Jody stand on a smooth rock outcrop that juts out high above a beautiful wilderness valley. It's about to be a glorious sunset. Brian is still in recovery and weak, and Karen can only hobble with the aid of her aluminium crutch. Jody assists her dad and mom as the parents slowly shuffle forward a few paces for a better view. Brian feels inspired and remarks, "We've not been her since Jody was ten years old!" Jody chimes in a playful manner, "Tell me again - why this is your favourite place?" Karen puts her arm around Jody and Brian, and replies, "This was where your father asked me to marry him (Looks to Jody) And this was where we celebrated the news that I was pregnant with you!" Jody gives her parents a loving smile. The small family of three bask in the glowing sunset.

BUSHES CRACKLE NEARBY

Suddenly - the Koroshi-ya steps out with his Katana sword raised - the steel blade gleams in the sunlight. The killer vehemently yells in broken-English, "Gaijin - American girl - you die!" Jody steps toward her assailant with an angry tone, "Go away! - Just leave me alone!" The professional killer lifts his sword high, sneers and threatens, "Stupid girl - easy to follow - Now, I kill - regain honour!" The man bolts at Jody and swings his sword. Jody leans to one side - the Katana blade slices open her clothing. Jody grabs and swiftly swings the metal crutch just in time to block the descending sword blade. **CLANG!** She forcefully spins the crutch to knock the blade away. The killer inches forward flailing the sword wildly. Jody holds the aluminium crutch as a weapon and backs up toward the lookout's edge. She glances down at the wilderness below. Brian and Karen, both incapacitated and too weak to help, anxiously watch. The Koroshi-ya creeps ahead cautiously. He sways the sword side to side to tease and scare. Jody inches backward and stops - she's close to the drop off. Brian yells, "Jody. Stop! - No further!" The assassin turns toward the parents a few yards away, then focuses on Jody and gloats, "After you dead - I kill parents!" Jody's adrenaline surges, her body tightens - she dashes at the killer with the crutch raised. The Koroshi-ya solidly plants his legs apart and swings the Katana with all his might! The steel blade slices directly at Jody's head. Jody ducks to slide through the man's legs, the blade swing cuts off part of Jody's long hair - the locks fall to the ground. Jody springs up and wields the metal crutch in a flurry of blows - she strikes the man's head, sides, stomach, groin and face. Each blow sends the man backward - until the killer stands at the drop off. Bruised, beaten, bloody - the killer teeters back and forth at the edge. The man looses balance and starts to fall backwards with the Katana blade extended. Jody quickly grabs the sword blade to catch and hold the man from falling over. The sharp sword blade cuts into Jody's tight grip - blood oozes from her fingers. In pity, Jody looks into the man's desperate eyes - and pulls him to safety. Jody backs up. The man stands solid on the ledge, catches his breath and turns his head to look down at the valley floor far below. He looks at Jody, smiles sheepishly and bows. Jody slightly bows - still keeping her eyes on the man. The man's smile abruptly turns into a sneering scowl. He lifts his sword to attack - Jody quickly spins about with a powerful roundhouse that blasts the killer off the ledge - out into the air. The Koroshi-ya **SCREAMS** as he falls. Jody inches to the drop off and peers down at the killer's contorted dead body on the boulders and rocks below. She turns around and goes over to Brian and Karen and begins to help them up.

ONE WEEK LATER

Jody kneels at her Grandfather's gravesite. She looks at the polished granite tombstone.

KATHY LONG GRASS   CARL LONG GRASS

Jody reaches into her jeans and brings out the gold **SHOCHO TUKEN** - digs a small deep hole and places the Ninja Token into the ground, covers it with dirt, then pats it down. Jody quietly whispers, "I love you Grandpa! You taught me everything I know - You're the one that deserves this great honour." Jody rises to her feet, gives her grandparent's tombstone a loving pat, then turns and walks away with a big smile. She pulls out her cell phone and touches the screen - KEI's PHOTO. Jody exits the cemetery and looks at the open road before her. High above in the clear blue sky, a black eagle soars with its wings spread out.

CHAPTER NINETY-TWO
Somewhere In Japan

The Beautiful Artist and the Bonsai Ninja step carefully along a narrow tunnel hewn from the hard rock. Their modern LED lamps illuminate the path as they move through the dark, going further and further inside the mountain. The passageway was made long ago, when the Ninja Clan tunnelled deep into the mountain to create a secret chamber to store and hide their valuable treasure. Throughout their history, the Ninja Clan accumulated gold, diamonds, rare gems, silver, jade, and precious pearls. As the Beautiful Artist and the Ninjas shine their lamps - the light shows the large iron door and massive lock that guards and protects the chamber. The men move forward and gather beside the thick metal door.

The old Ninja Master remarks. "Shine more light." As more LEDS are focused where he stands, the elderly Ninja Master brings out the Golden Seal - and examines the base closely. He notices a Kanji that has a round dot - and presses. To the others' surprise, the bottom portion of the Golden Seal comes loose and sits in the Beautiful Artist's palm. The released item is a rectangular that is 2 inches in height. The indentations on each of the four sides are similar to the indentations of a key. The old man motions a nearby man to lower his lamp to cast more light on the massive lock. The old man looks at the unique piece in his hand - any one side could be the right key - the challenge and question is - which one? The legend passed down over time tells the danger of using the wrong key - the Chamber becomes destroyed forever! The Beautiful Artist studies the Kanji embellishments on the chamber door - one Kanji appears to stand out - that Kanji that can be written with three brush strokes. The aged Ninja Master examines the Key portion on all four sides - only one side has three indentations, the others sides have two, four and five indentations.

The men are both excited and nervous, everyone sensing the significance of the moment - standing at the very location of the Ninja legend and lore. The old man positions the Golden Key so the three indentations face the lock - he takes a breath and inserts the Key and turns. The lock over time has accumulated dust and debris and gives resistance. The Beautiful Artist exerts more pressure to turn the Key - the massive lock **CLINKS!** - the iron door cracks open. The old man steps back and motions for others to pry open the big door. As four men strain to pull the door open - dust and debris fall from the ceiling onto the group. As the dust settles - the iron door is wide open and the chamber inside is pitch black. The Beautiful Artist instructs, "Step inside and shine your lamps!" As everyone enters, the LED lamps reveal a vast chamber carved out of the mountain rock. The men shine their lights ahead - the old Ninja Master and all the Bonsai Ninja stare in awe - their mouths drop wide open. Light floods the interior making it sparkle, shine and glitter. Before them are piles full of gold, jewels, diamonds, jade, silver and pearls. The Beautiful Artist smiles with delight at finding the long lost **NINJA TREASURE!**

They all break out in CELEBRATION!

THE END